Diamond Pursuit

by

Patrick Shanahan

Published by New Generation Publishing in 2015

Copyright © Patrick Shanahan 2015
Cover design by Richard Taylor, BT Graphics

First Edition

ISBN 978-1-78507-273-4

www.newgeneration-publishing.com

 New Generation Publishing

This work is dedicated to my father,
Patrick Shanahan
- a real 'Man of Quilty'

Acknowledgements

The author would like to acknowledge those who helped with the research for this book. Thank you then to Sharon Shrubb, Steve Skarratt, Gaspar Weiss and Charles Barker for their assistance with general presentation, factual information and translations; to Alex Cooper for invaluable technical and practical aviation advice; to Andrew Farley for guidance on air crew processes; the Government Diamond Office for their industry specific help. In addition, I am grateful for the general guidance on police and border control matters from a number of sources who wish to remain anonymous.

My thanks once again to Richard Taylor of BT Graphics for his original cover design.

Finally, I would also like to acknowledge the many venues in Ibiza that appear in this book, none of which have any connection to the production of this work or indeed to any of the entirely fictitious events that appear in the story. Each of them made my research visits to the island most enjoyable.

Patrick Shanahan
February 2015

1

It was 4.15p.m. on Friday afternoon. The rain hammered on the windscreen of the car as I attempted to pull out of the Tesco superstore shopping centre. I say attempted because the rain was so heavy the windscreen wipers could hardly cope. Sheets of water slewed back and forth across the glass, turning the road ahead into a distorted blur as the wipers struggled to deal with the downpour even at maximum speed. It felt like it had been raining forever. We had battled through four months of the wettest winter on record with just a brief respite in March and April and now that May had arrived, it seemed to be starting all over again. Only this was not a shower. Deluge was the proper description.

My thoughts were drifting to balmy days on a sun kissed beach when my iPhone rang. Without looking at the caller ID, I hit the hands free button.

"*Hello mate. Where are ya?*"

"Oh hi Ces. I'm in the car. What're you doing?"

"*It's Friday mate. What d'you think I'm doing? Just finished work and I'm having a livener in Fad's. You coming down?*"

"I can't. Been shopping. Got all the stuff in the car."

"*Shopping? What for?*"

"Food. Louise is cooking tomorrow night for her mum and James ... her mum's bloke. Just left Tesco."

As the final word left my lips, I realised what was coming next. The thought flashed through my mind even before he said it.

"*Tesco! What did I tell you geezer?*"

"I was just helping out. Louise had to get it done before she started her shift and –"

"*I told ya mate, didn't I? Relationships only ever end up in one place. Tesco.*"

Cecil's jaundiced view was probably borne out of the bitterness of his own failed relationship. I knew he wasn't being critical of Louise and me. He liked Louise but he had to pass comment on relationships. I suspected that part of it was a fear of losing contact with a friend, lost to a relationship.

I laughed it off.

"It isn't that bad Ces. Shopping can be ... be, you know ... fun."

"*Fun?*" The derisory tone crackled across the line. "*Yeah. What bit was fun then mate? Pushing the trolley around? Was that fun? Yeah, I bet that's all you was doing. Trolley pushing. That's why birds take blokes food shopping mate. To push the frigging trolley about. They ain't got them there for any other reason.*"

I stayed silent as the memory of doing exactly what Cecil had said kicked in. My silence clicked with him.

"*Yeah, so that's what you was doing. See, I'm right mate about the Tesco thing. You are now the bloke with the trolley. Yeah, the bloke that's pushing a trolley with no fucking idea where he's going, following the bird about like he's some homeless puppy while she loads a pile of stuff in that he's got no idea he even needs. And if he says anything about it, he gets a look as if he's wandered into some NASA space laboratory and she's the frigging technician. Shut up and keep pushing sucker. Mate, it sets the tone, don't it. It's a control thing. Takes a geezer out of his comfort zone. Reminds him he's gotta toe the line in the relationship. So he ends up stuffed, don't he? He's hanging onto the trolley handle for all he's worth, a pissed off hopeless look on his face, knowing he'd sooner be anywhere other than going through a public display of having his cojones cut off and hung out to dry. But there's nothing he can do about it, is there? He's bought in. He can't stack the trolley right there in the aisle and wander off. His life wouldn't be worth living. Mate, I've seen it. Geezers with their souls cut out, a shell wandering about with no clue how they ended up that way, pushing that trolley on frigging autopilot.*"

My mind scrambled for a response. I felt uncomfortable. Some instinctive thing had prickled within me. Maybe it was the 'cojones' reference. I tried downplaying it.

"Ces, you have to get food, right, and you have to get it to the car and back home so somebody has to push the trolley. Which reminds me, I just told you, I got all the food in the boot and I have to get it back to Louise's place. All the frozen stuff's in the boot too."

"Can she not take it back? You gotta do that too, as well as trolley pushing?"

"She's gone in to work. She's working on some big case. Some big time racketeer thing."

"Not the bloke that was all over the papers, is it? Some Russian bloke or something ... foreign geezer anyway ... Carl or Kurt or something?"

"I don't know Ces. She can't say. All I know is that the NCA has been tracking this bloke for months and –"

"NCA?"

"The National Crime Agency. They're the people who target serious and organised crime on a national and international level, according to Louise. She's been dead busy since she got through the detective training programme. She doesn't finish until ten tonight so I'm helping out."

There was a pause whilst Cecil considered his response.

"So what about tomorrow then? We could do a little mumble on the town, yeah? Saturday night'll be banging."

"Sorry, Ces. I can't do that either. I'm doing the family thing tomorrow night. I've got to be at Louise's dinner party."

"Excuses, excuses mate." There was another pause on the line and I guessed that Cecil's mind was plotting something. *"So if Louise is at work geeze, you got time for a swift one tonight, ain'tcha? I mean, you done your stint around Tesco. Least you deserve is a cold one before you go home to put all that shopping away in your bird's fridge."*

The last few words were delivered with enough disdain to hit the spot.

"Okay ... just a quick one and I then have to get going."

The after work crowd were in MacFadden's and the place had a relaxed buzz. Carlos MacFadden, the bar owner, was behind the bar, a tea towel slung over his right shoulder and a frown screwing up his forehead.

"How's it going Carlos? Busy in here mate."

Carlos looked up from a Peroni pump where he was watching the flow of beer frothing to the top of a pint glass.

"Hola, Mateo. Aye, bastardin busy. Rushed a'ma feet an the wee lassies are nae due in 'til six o'clock. If a'd a known it was gannae be this busy I'd a got them in earlier."

Carlos's frown was not the only giveaway that he was stressed. The colourful mix of Scottish and South American ancestry that made up his personality usually reacted to any emotionally driven situation so that one or other of his tribal instincts came to the fore. Today it was the Scotsman in him, but it was never predictable. The 'wee lassies' were Hanka and Janka and they usually worked behind the bar at weekends.

"So you're in for a wee drink then?"

"Just a quick one. Meeting Cecil. You seen him?"

"Aye, he's away tae take a leak. He's left you a beer."

He reached across the shelf behind the bar and handed me a bottle. I took it and examined the label – '*Westmalle Trappist Tripel.*'

"Blimey, what's this then Carlos? Never heard of it."

"Och, you know Cecil and his beer. His latest thing. Made me get in a whole crate of the stuff. Anyway, here he comes now. He can tell you himself."

I turned away from the bar to see Cecil striding towards me. A firm handshake and a beaming grin told me he was pleased to see me. I knew Cecil didn't like drinking alone.

"You alright geeze?" he enquired, as he pulled up a stool at the bar.

"Yeah, I'm good Ces."

I raised the bottle and took a pull from the beer, savouring its fruity aroma and creamy, bittersweet aftertaste.

4

"Nice beer. What is it?" I asked, staring at the bottle.

"Mate, that's a proper beer ain't it. I can't do that corporate chain crap no more."

I took another sip.

"Quite strong. Tasty though."

"Oh yeah mate. Probably one of the best beers you're ever gonna drink. If they'd put that stuff in the space shuttle it would've definitely got into orbit a lot quicker, I'm telling ya. Drink enough of it and you'd best call the police and an ambulance for later, just to be on the safe side."

"Hang on Ces. I'm taking it easy. I need a clear head for tomorrow. I told you, I'm meeting Louise's mum and her bloke and, not sure exactly how to tell you this but ... well, I've got a bit of a surprise for Louise."

Cecil's eyes narrowed.

"So, what you gotta tell geeze?" he said, as he raised his beer to his mouth.

I came straight out with it.

"I'm getting engaged. I'm going to ask Louise to marry me."

The verbal reaction was probably what I had expected but the coughing, choking fit as Cecil gagged on a mouthful of beer first, was slightly alarming.

"Engaged? What the fuck, geezer," was what I gathered he was saying in between coughs.

At the sound of Cecil choking Carlos appeared from behind the bar.

"Hey, qué pasa Cecil? You okay? Let me get you some water."

Cecil seemed to make a quick recovery.

"Water? Frigging water? Get me another one of them beers Carlos. This geezer's trying to kill me here."

Carlos pulled two more Westmalles from behind the bar and flipped the tops. Despite the fact that we still had the first bottles to drink, Cecil took a slug from the fresh one. I waited until it had slipped down.

"You ok now mate?"

Cecil nodded.

5

"All I said was I'm getting engaged. Louise doesn't know yet but I'm going to pop the question tomorrow night. I've even been out and chosen a ring. I'm picking it up tomorrow." I felt the need to explain myself further. "You realise we've been together just over three years? The time's right … we get along great, no problems and –"

"Mate, there's no need to explain but you kept that quiet. No offence or nothing but you done that marriage thing before and it didn't work out."

My first marriage to Olivia had lasted just nine years. I'd had my fingers burnt but my time with Louise had made me see the good in relationships again and I'd gone from never contemplating the possibility of another marriage to knowing, that with the right person, it would work. I took a sip of beer and smiled at Cecil.

"I know, but that was then. Anyway, I was thinking that maybe we could all get together tomorrow after the dinner and celebrate. We could meet you down here or something. You know Sheryl is over from Canada for three weeks so the timing is all good."

"I know. She text me last week. Said we'd hook up." A concerned frown darkened Cecil's features. "Look, don't get me wrong mate. I got nothing against you getting married again and Louise is a great girl, just right for you in fact, but you gotta be sure. As you said, it's only been three years."

"I appreciate that and I know what you mean. But I *am* sure. I wouldn't have gone out and bought the ring if I wasn't would I?"

"I never know with you geezer. How much that set ya back then?"

"It wasn't cheap mate. Put it this way, no change out of two grand."

"Fucking hell mate, two bags of sand? Must be love."

"It's a platinum diamond solitaire. Louise likes diamonds."

Cecil stood up and grabbed my hand in a firm handshake. He followed it up with a Cecil style bear hug.

"Mate, congratulations. An engagement calls for a celebration." He turned to the bar. "Carlos, you heard this geezer's news? Crack open a bottle of your best Champagne and stick it on the tab."

It wasn't the chill from the breeze that blew through the open window that woke me up. Nor was it the raging thirst that clawed at the thick dry tongue that was sticking to the roof of my mouth. It wasn't even the fact that my suit jacket had wrapped itself tightly around my body in a semi-twisted position, after I had crashed on the bed without getting undressed. No, it was the loud, incessant jangling of my mobile that finally raised me to consciousness.

I grabbed it from my pocket and stared for a moment at the display.

Louise.

"Matthew, where are you?"

I glanced around the room. I wasn't sure at first. When you wake up you expect to see familiar surroundings like your own bedroom or perhaps even recognise the place you were in the night before if you were away from home. But for a moment I had no idea where I was and no recollection of how I'd got there.

"I'm ... err ... I'm ... still in bed honey. A lie in. Saturday and all that." I checked my watch - 10.35.

"Have you got a sore throat? You sound hoarse."

I cleared my throat in an effort to sound 'un-hoarse.'

"Err, no. Just need a drink ... of water, I mean ... thirsty. You ok?"

There was a moment's hesitation.

"I think so. I'm tired. I didn't get finished until gone one o'clock in the morning. Everything's coming to a head in this case I'm on, what with the court appearance in just under ten weeks, we're trying to pull together all the evidence so we have a watertight case."

Louise had told me very little about what she was working on but from what she had said, I knew it was a high profile operation. She had stumbled upon a much bigger fish following an arrest she had made for a house burglary, and that in turn had led to the arrest of a key player involved in an organised crime racket. Her view was that the less I knew about what she was involved in, the less likely I was to worry about her. She had been in the Metropolitan Police for several years so there was always an element of risk with her job and now that she had moved to detective rank, the

7

risks were greater. We had agreed that I shouldn't ask questions, which would also protect the confidential nature of her work, and she usually only ever gave me a very broad outline to the 'how was your day' question.

"Well, I'm glad you had a lie in too then," I said.

"Yes, I did. I got in last night and went straight to bed. But here's the thing. I went to the fridge just now to get some juice and there wasn't any. In fact the fridge was remarkably empty which I must say, Matthew, I found a little odd since we did all that shopping yesterday at Tesco and if I recall, you were going to put it all away for me. I checked the cupboards too and, well, the same thing. No sign of any of the stuff we bought. And you know we have this dinner party tonight –"

"Dinner party ..." I blurted out. I felt a hot flush rise from my midriff, spread upwards through my chest and hit my face like molten lava pouring from Krakatoa.

"Yes, the dinner party, for my mum who I haven't seen in three years. You remember that, right? Well, once I'd had my juice and perhaps some breakfast, I was going to start preparing the food, the food that doesn't appear to be in my house right now. So I assumed that you must still have it and for whatever reason, you've stashed it away in your own fridge and will be bringing it over later. Am I right Matthew?"

The frightening truth hit me even as Louise asked the question. The food. The food was still in the boot of my car. I didn't know how to respond. A rush of recollection began to flood my head. The Champagne in MacFadden's, the ultra-strong Belgian beer, a celebration, Cecil buying more drinks telling me he'd get me a taxi. And then it dawned on me where I was. Cecil's spare room.

"Matthew? Are you there?"

Louise sounded calm. Too calm.

"Err ... yes, sorry. Yes, I'm here."

"So where is here? I rang your house?"

"It's … I'm ... err ... I'm at Cecil's place." I had a feeling that conclusions would be drawn as soon as Cecil's name cropped up but she still sounded calm.

"*I see, so you're at Cecil's and all my food, all one hundred and fifteen pounds and thirty-nine pence of it, is in Cecil's place too then, all safely tucked up in his fridge and cupboards. Is that right?*"

"Well, no. Not exactly. I –"

And then she unloaded. I'd never really heard her that angry.

"*So, where the bloody hell is my food Matthew? What have you done with it? Don't tell me. Please don't tell me that you went out with Cecil, got yourself pissed up and left my food in the boot of your car. No, tell me that hasn't happened because if it has, you are dead meat.*"

It crossed my mind that Louise had summed up the situation rather succinctly.

"Uh ... well ... yes ... kind of," I said and stopped there, uncertain as to what I could add in mitigation.

Her calm seemed to return.

"*So what you're telling me, Matthew Malarkey, is that all the food I bought for tonight and for breakfast tomorrow is ruined and my dinner party is now right up the creek.*"

I tried to add an appeasing level of reassurance having admitted my guilt.

"Well, no, I'm not saying that ... I mean, I am ... but not that the food is ruined. I'm sure it'll be ... uh ... fine. It's been in the car boot overnight in a dark multi-storey car park and –"

"*Oh really? So is this car park in Northern Alaska? Or perhaps it's in Siberia where the temperatures are well below freezing. That would be ok then. I doubt it though Matthew. I suspect it's actually in Kingston where it's been sitting for over eighteen hours now. And in case you haven't noticed, after several weeks of rain, we have a blazing sunny morning. So it would be my guess that the two frozen chickens, the ice cream, the frozen peas, the yoghurt, the milk, the bag of ice cubes and all the other frozen items, are now one massive soggy mess trickling their way over the fresh veg and all the other expensive bits of shopping I bought.*"

"Err ... well, the tinned stuff should be fine and I could –"

I was unable to complete my sentence. The conversation was terminated, the line killed instantly.

2

I managed to rouse Cecil and persuade him to drive me back to my car. I flipped the boot lid and checked on the shopping. The tiny amount of optimism that I had tried to keep alive on the journey there was crushed out in an instant when I spotted the damp patch on the boot floor. I picked up one of the carrier bags. It was the one with the pack of ice cubes. Some of the pack was still firm but most of it had reached an advanced state of defrost. I checked on the other bags. The two chickens were so warm and soft to the touch, that in different circumstances, with a little encouragement and the help of a vet, they might possibly have flown away. I lifted the lid from the large tub of ice cream and found a creamy slush. The rest of the frozen food was in a similar state of thaw and the process had left other items that were in the same bag, wet, soggy and unusable. The only place for most of the shopping was the bin.

I pulled out of the car park and headed straight for home. I needed a shower, a change of clothes and time to think. On my way into the house, I lobbed the useless shopping straight into my rubbish bin. I kept the tinned food.

I stood in the shower, the warm water trickling through my hair and running freely down my back. It felt good and I had an idea. I turned off the tap, leapt out of the shower and grabbed a towel. I picked up my mobile and hit Louise's number. It rang several times and went to voicemail. I tried again. She wasn't picking up. Clearly, I was in the doghouse big time. I sat on the edge of my bed and tapped out a text.

'Honey, I know I screwed up. I'm really sorry. You were right. The food is ruined and it's too late to replace it all but I have an idea. I'm going to book a restaurant and take everyone out for a meal instead. I know it's not the same but the evening doesn't have to be a write off. And I'm looking forward to meeting your mum. Call me. Can we talk?'

It was ten minutes before I got a response.

'Ok.'

I sent back another text, *'Call me. We need to speak.'*

Five minutes later, my mobile rang. I jumped straight in with an apology.

"I'm really sorry honey. It was very stupid of me but I just forgot about the shopping. Cecil was on a roll with the beers and –"

"I hope you're not blaming Cecil, Matthew. It was your responsibility. I just asked you to do one simple thing and you managed to mess that up."

"I know. It was my fault and I'm not blaming him. I suppose I just got carried away. But what do you think of the restaurant idea?"

"It's fine. We don't have much choice now do we."

I could tell she was still annoyed with me.

"I know but let's make it a good night. I'll make it special. What about if I pick up a couple of bottles of Champagne and we have a nice pre dinner drink at yours first and then head out to the restaurant? I'll book a table for four and let's invite Sheryl to join us afterwards. What do you think?"

"Well you'd better include Cecil too then. According to Sheryl, she's seeing him tomorrow."

Cecil hadn't mentioned that fact. He had been having an 'on off' relationship with Sheryl ever since we had met her and Louise a few years earlier. The 'on off' bit was mostly to do with the fact that she lived in Toronto but they seemed to like each other and any time she came over to see Louise, Cecil would take her out.

"Okay," I said, "I'll let him know where we'll be once I book something. Is there anything your mum doesn't like, food wise?"

"*No, she's good with most things.*"

"What about, whatshisname ... her bloke?"

"*James. James Brogan. Try not to forget it later Matthew. I've never met him but I'm sure he eats most things. He's an Irishman.*"

"I'll book an Italian then. That's always a fairly safe bet. Let's say for about seven-thirty. I have a few things to do today but I'll come over about five-ish. That okay?"

"*That'll be fine. See you then.*"

I could still detect some irritation in Louise's voice.

"Louise, listen. Don't be mad at me. I'm sorry. I will make it up to you. We'll have a lovely evening."

"*Okay. See you at five then. Bye.*"

I hit the end call button and dropped the mobile onto my bed. I was determined to make sure the evening went well. If I was going to propose to Louise then it had to be a relaxed atmosphere, no tension between us especially with her mother there, someone I had never met before.

Louise's parents had split up when she was a child and her mother had eventually moved to Cape Town when Louise was at University. Her father now lived in Scotland where he worked for an oil company. Most of her relatives still lived in the UK, in Gloucestershire, but she didn't get to see her parents often. In fact, if I recalled, the last time she had seen them was at Christmas time, just after we had met and before we got together as a couple. Louise's mother had been in the property business, selling holiday homes and timeshare villas in the Simon's Town and Glencairn areas of the Western Cape. Ten years ago the property company relocated her to Ibiza where she had met the man she was now seeing, James Brogan. According to Louise, James Brogan owned a successful pleasure boat company that specialised in trips in and around Ibiza. He had a home in San Antonio and ran boats out of the harbour there. Louise had been to visit once when her mother first moved to the island but had never met James. Two years after arriving in San Antonio, her mother had resigned from the property company to help James run the boat business. They now lived together in his villa to the north of San Antonio.

I had a busy day ahead and needed to get cracking. I got dressed, downed two paracetamol to ease my fuzzy head and logged on to Google. I typed in *'Italian Restaurants Surrey'* and found several within the area. I settled for one called *Il Piatto Gustoso,* which was eight or nine miles from where I lived. It had some great reviews and when I visited their website, the menus looked delicious. I called and made a reservation for four people.

My relief at booking a restaurant and solving the meal issue didn't last long. I knew I could not sit back and chill. Next, I had to get to the Hatton Garden branch of Le Roux to collect the engagement ring I had bought. Le Roux was a high-end retailer of fine jewellery, part of an exclusive chain that had branches in a number of selected cities in Europe – London, Zurich, Milan, Paris, Amsterdam and Madrid. Given my limited knowledge of jewellery I had done some internet research, as I had wanted to find a retailer that might have something a little different. It was there that I had discovered the Le Roux website. The London store had impressed me with both its service and knowledgeable staff and I felt confident in my final purchase. Having found the ring I wanted, I had left it with the jeweller to get it sized properly so it would be the perfect fit when I gave it to Louise. I had borrowed a cheap ring from her jewellery box to get the exact size.

I drove to Wimbledon, took the train to Waterloo and two tube trains to Chancery Lane. From there it was a short five-minute walk to the jewellers. To my relief the ring was ready. I opened the box to take a look.

"A good choice, Sir. I am sure the lucky lady will be delighted," the salesman said, as I admired the gleaming diamond.

I placed the bag with the ring in it inside my jacket and headed back for the tube. By the time I had returned to my car in Wimbledon it was 2.40p.m. I had just over two hours to pick up the Champagne, get back home, get changed and get over to Louise. After the food fiasco, I needed the rest of the day to go smoothly and I certainly didn't want to be late.

As I sped down the A3, my phone rang. I hit the hands free button and heard the sound of Cecil's voice.

"Geezer, where are ya?"

"I'm in the car Ces. Just back from London. Got to get some Champagne for tonight and then get myself over to Louise's."

"Yeah, well that's what I'm ringing you about. What's the mumble later? I've been talking to Sheryl and she reckons Louise asked us to come out later and hook up at some restaurant with you lot. Thing is she don't know what restaurant it is so I said I'd give you a bell and find out."

"It's an Italian over in ..." Ahead I saw the pull in for the Tesco Superstore. I figured I might as well stop there for the Champagne, get in, grab it and get out again. "Hang on Ces, I'm just going to pull in to Tes ... err ... a shop to get the booze."

I turned into the slip road that led towards the superstore complex and drove straight into the maelstrom of Saturday afternoon shoppers. Some were pushing heavily laden trolleys across the car park, walking straight down the centre of the road, oblivious to the fact that they were holding up drivers looking to park; others were backing out of spaces into the mayhem whilst a queue of cars hovered, waiting for the space to be vacated. I did a complete lap of the car park perimeter but could see no empty space.

"You there mate?" Cecil's voice came over the speaker.

"Yeah, just looking for a parking space ... hang on."

"Mate, just tell me where the frigging restaurant is. I ain't got much time. Got to get sorted. I'm s'posed to be meeting Sheryl at half four."

"It's called Il Pia ... hang on, sorry mate. Just seen a space."

I assume it was the fact that I was in a hurry, trying to talk to Cecil and the hurly burly of the car park that caused me to be oblivious of anything else. All I saw was a solitary vacant space to my left. I swung the car in nose first without hesitation and killed the engine.

"Sorry Ces. It's bloody mayhem here trying to get parked."

"You back in Tesco again then are ya?" he chuckled.

I ignored it. "Right, the restaurant. It's called Il Pia –"

The frantic knocking on my window cut my sentence short and caused me to swivel to my right.

14

"Ces, there's some woman knocking on my window. Hang on. Sorry mate."

I pressed the window button and the glass slid to the half-open position. A middle-aged woman in a red coat was staring directly at me. As the window came to a stop, she started talking.

"What do you think you are doing? You've just taken my space."

"I'm sorry. I haven't taken anything. There was nobody in it."

"I was just reversing into it when you pulled in there like some bloody maniac. Did you not see me? No bloody manners."

"Hang on lady. I'm sorry but it *was* an empty space. I didn't see anyone. How am I supposed to know somebody else is trying to get in it? Have you not seen the place? It's everybody for himself?"

"That's as maybe but I was here first and this is my space."

"Tell her to piss off, stoopid bint." Cecil's voice came loudly across the hands free speaker.

The woman took a step back, a total look of shock on her face.

"What did you just say? How dare you talk to me like that. Not only have you no manners but you are a rude, foul-mouthed yob."

"Wait a minute. No ... look, that wasn't me. It was my friend Ces and he's talking to ... I never said anything ..." I turned away and spoke directly to the hands free. "Cecil, I'm going to have to call you back. I'll text you or something."

Without waiting for a response I hit the 'end call' button, swung the door open and got out of the car. Close up the woman was probably in her late fifties or early sixties, with tinted blonde highlights and blazing blue eyes. Behind her, a white Audi was positioned across the roadway, the driver's door wide open, and a plume of blue exhaust flowing from the rear.

I pushed a button on the key fob and locked my car door, a sure fire signal that I was not giving up my parking position. She had irked me by calling me a yob. I turned towards her.

"Look, lady, firstly I am not a yob. I'm just a bloke in a hurry who has to be somewhere. I'm going to be in that shop just five minutes and then I'm out of here. You can wait here and grab this precious space when I return or you can do the sensible thing and drive around until you get another one. If you hadn't called me a yob I might have been inclined to give it to you. But too late now. Secondly, it isn't anyone's space. It's called a space because it's empty and that means anyone can drive in to it. That's the definition of space – something that's free, available, or unoccupied. So it couldn't have been *your* space because it was precisely that ... unoccupied. Perhaps next time you should be quicker off the mark."

With that, I walked away but not before I had noticed the woman's face had turned the same colour as her coat. I heard her practically spit the word 'yob' again as I walked off, but I ignored it.

By the time I had returned to my car, carrying two bottles of Champagne and a bouquet of roses, the woman had gone and had, presumably, parked elsewhere.

Back at home, I had another quick shower, a shave and got ready. I chose a black Paul Smith suit and a pale pink shirt. I wanted to look my best when I popped the question. I took the ring out of the bag, opened the box to have one more look at it and then put it in my pocket. I fired off a quick text to Cecil.

'Sorry about all that palaver earlier mate. The restaurant is called Il Piatto Gustoso. It's up near Walton-on-the-Hill. Look it up online and you'll get the details. Come up about 10ish. C u l8r.'

I jumped in the car and made it round to Louise's place just before five. She looked pleased to see me, all the earlier tension now gone. She kissed me on the lips in greeting and pointed at the bouquet.

"Oh, lovely roses. You shouldn't have darling. I'm over the food thing. It's okay. You boys will be boys sometimes and, to be honest, your idea to book a restaurant has a lot more appeal now. It saves me cooking and I can relax."

I smiled, relieved that the earlier argument was sorted. Nobody likes rows. Louise and I rarely had words and, if ever we did, it made me feel totally put out.

"Yes, nice flowers, but not for you honey. I got them for your mum. I hope she likes roses."

"Oh, she'll love them. That's very thoughtful of you. Come through. They've just arrived."

Louise led the way to her sitting room. I followed, a tiny knot of apprehension in the pit of my stomach at the prospect of meeting people close to her. But I felt good, I was smartly dressed and I had chosen a great restaurant.

"Matthew, this is my mum, Eleanor."

My jaw dropped. The bouquet of roses suddenly went limp in my hand and followed my jaw to the floor. The red coat blazed in front of me like a psychedelic hallucinatory vision.

She said one word.

"You!"

3

There was nothing I could say. No words that could have adequately redressed the earlier meeting. The blood rushed to my face in the presence of the woman whose car park space I had taken. I caught sight of the bewildered look on Louise's face. I glanced back at Eleanor and noticed the same blue blaze in her eyes. I fumbled on the floor for the roses and picked them up. In a fuzz of confusion I half-heartedly held them out towards her while I fought to find something to say.

It was James Brogan who broke the silence.

"Looks like the two of you might have met before then? Don't tell me, you're the young fella that her ladyship here had the run in with today in the car park. She told me all about it." He stretched out a hand towards me. "Hello there. I'm James. James Brogan and you must be Matthew."

I went to take his hand and realised I was holding out the bunch of roses. He laughed and took them from me.

"Sure, isn't that grand. It's the first time a fella has ever bought me roses. Thanks a million Matthew. What d'you think of that Eleanor?"

James had a broad Irish lilt but with a gravelly resonance that said he may well have been a man of the country.

Eleanor did not seem too amused. I managed to gather my wits about me, helped by James's light hearted approach to the situation.

"Look Eleanor ... I mean, Missus Penny ... I'm really sorry about earlier. I'd just had a bad start to the day and I was worried about being late tonight and meeting you both. I wouldn't normally have ... and it wasn't me who was rude to you. It was Cecil –"

"What, Cecil was rude to my mum?" Louise had recovered from her bewilderment and seemed to be grasping some semblance of what had happened.

"No ... he was just talking about ... about somebody else ... and he was on hands free." I realised that the more I said the worse it could get so I tried to get to the point. "I know there's nothing I can say to make it better Missus Penny but it's not like me to be argumentative and ... well, I can only say I *am* really very sorry."

"Argumentative? Perhaps not. Opinionated then, shall we say?" Eleanor responded, her tone measured and crisp. "And thank you for the lecture on space. Most enlightening, I have to say."

I glanced quickly at Louise. A raised eyebrow told me that she was wondering what I had said to her mother.

"Yes, sorry about that. I just got carried away ... the, you know ... situation, stress of finding a ... a ... gap to park in ... but, look, Eleanor ... err, can I call you Eleanor?"

"It's my name."

"Of course. What I mean is, we've got off on the wrong foot and, well, I don't want that." I paused for a moment and noticed that her blue eyes had calmed a little. "Oh, and the roses are for you."

"Well, isn't that a thing now," James said. "There's me thinking you'd got me them flowers and sure don't you know you're taking them back again. C'mon son. Let's forget this and have a drink." He turned towards Eleanor. "C'mon now Eleanor. It sounds to me like there was some sort of misunderstanding here and we shouldn't be letting that spoil our night out. Louise, I see the boy brought in a couple of bottles. Why don't you fetch some glasses and we can all lighten up here."

James seemed to have a permanent twinkle in his eyes and when he smiled the smile lines creased across his tanned face. He looked as if he was in his early sixties, with rugged good looks that had been honed and weathered by the sea air. He still had a full head of hair which swept back off his forehead and rested in waves just above his ears. Although it was still predominantly dark it was streaked with white and it gave him a wild, earthy look. With his easy charm and in the way he had diffused an awkward situation, I had started to like him already.

Eleanor went with Louise to the kitchen to get the glasses. James winked at me.

"Relax Matthew. I would have done the same myself. Sure that woman shouldn't be driving that big Audi around at all. She only hired it on Friday when we got here. She can't park the thing at all. She's a blasted menace on the road, but there's no telling her."

The restaurant I had chosen lived up to all of its great reviews. The food was excellent, the wine easy on the palate and the whole place a buzz of excitement. There were two large parties on either side of us, one celebrating an anniversary and the other a birthday. As the evening wore on Eleanor began to relax with me. I hoped it was the fact that I seemed to be a nice polite person after all and not the yob she had originally taken me for. It could have been the wine that was playing its part too as she seemed very enthusiastic about the Chablis. But I didn't mind. The more light hearted the atmosphere the more relaxed I began to feel too. James was great company and I could tell he liked the good life.

We finished the pudding course and I decided to order Champagne. There would be good reason to celebrate but I felt very nervous about the marriage proposal. It wasn't because I thought that Louise might not accept. It was just that it was a big moment in my life and it would be a very public gesture. I poured a glass of water to relieve the dryness in my throat and patted the side of my jacket to ensure that the box that contained the engagement ring was still in my pocket. I decided that I would make my move once Cecil and Sheryl had arrived. The waiter brought an ice bucket to the table with four glasses and began to peel the foil from the Champagne cork. I asked him to wait, telling the others that we would open it when our friends arrived.

"Well in that case let's finish off with a liqueur while we're waiting," James said and nodded to the waiter. "We'll have four Sambucas, my man ... with the beans."

"Yes Sir, con la mosca."

"The beans?" I said.

"Sure Matt. Coffee beans. Have you not heard of it at all?" James replied.

"Well, yeah, I've heard of Sambuca but not with coffee beans."

"Well, you live and learn. That's how the Italians like it. Sure when I've been over there now to Salerno don't we have it all the time. Isn't that right Eleanor?"

Eleanor nodded.

"It is. The beans are said to be for health, happiness and prosperity."

Health, happiness and prosperity. That sounded very appropriate given my intended marriage proposal.

Four Sambucas were delivered to the table. The waiter struck a match and lit each one so that a bright blue dazzling flame danced on the surface of the liquid.

"Good health." James raised his glass, blew out the flame and downed the drink in one, then chewed on the coffee beans. The rest of us followed his lead.

"Geezer, looks like I turned up just in time." Cecil approached the table with Sheryl following behind.

I did the introductions and when I'd done Cecil pulled me to one side.

"You done the mumble yet mate?"

"The mumble?"

"Yeah, you know. The ring thing."

"Oh no, I was waiting until you two got here. I've got Champagne for a toast and a bit of a celebration. Which reminds me, I've only got four glasses. Pull a couple of chairs up and I'll go get two more from the bar. It's a bit cramped but it'll be fine."

Cecil turned towards Sheryl who was chatting to Louise and her mum.

"Might try one of them Sambucas myself. Fancy one Sheryl?"

"Okay. You order another round mate while I get two more Champagne glasses. And Ces, good to see you. Glad you came," I said, genuinely pleased that Cecil had made the effort.

"Wouldn't have missed it mate. Bit of a trek though. It's in the middle of bleedin nowhere."

I laughed and wandered off to the bar. My spirits had lifted, not least because of the impact of the Sambuca but also because I felt I had some moral support with Cecil there. I got two glasses from the bar and began to walk confidently back towards the table. Ahead of me I saw the waiter pouring out several more Sambucas and James lighting each one as the glass was filled.

Perhaps I should have been paying more attention to where I was going and perhaps I shouldn't have held the glasses by their stems with the flutes facing downwards, waiter style. As I strode forward, the leading glass caught the top of a customer's chair and shattered on impact causing the other one to shatter too. The surprised customer swung around, catching my left side with his elbow. The glancing blow caused me to step back in surprise straight into a waiter who was carrying a birthday cake to the accompaniment of a rousing chorus of happy birthday. Our paths met in a perfectly synchronised twirl. As the waiter stumbled, the cake flew from his hands, landing upside down onto an adjacent table. Gravity, coupled with the hard surface, ensured it squashed almost flat, cream and jam squirting out of the compacted sponge onto the table cloth. The single candle in the centre of the cake fell off mid-flight, straight into a glass of red wine where it was immediately extinguished. The commotion brought two more waiters scurrying across to help. I began to apologise profusely to staff and customers alike. The birthday party did not seem to think an apology was sufficient and one of the women started shouting at me. She must have been the birthday girl as she had a badge on that said '*Nifty at 50.*' To my relief a waiter came to my rescue, manhandling me away whilst he attempted to calm the irate woman down.

Back at my own table, I tried to ignore the five astonished faces staring at me. I particularly tried to avoid Eleanor's gaze. It was Cecil who spoke first.

"What's going on mate? What was all that about?"

I couldn't answer. I needed some water. In my heightened state of tension, I should have taken more care and as I reached over to pick up the water jug, my sleeve caught one of the Sambuca glasses. It tipped onto its side sending a pool of burning liquid across the table straight towards Eleanor. In the fuel-soaked flaming trail that followed, the tablecloth caught light, which in turn set fire to Eleanor's napkin. She screamed. Louise and Sheryl joined in. James and Cecil jumped to their feet but before they could do anything, I reacted by hurling half the contents of the water jug in the direction of the flames. Unfortunately, Eleanor was in the line of fire and caught the first large slop of water straight in the chest. She lurched back in her seat, a look of sheer bemusement on her face. In a panicky reaction to try to rescue the situation, I grabbed the flaming napkin and shoved it off the table. To my disbelief it landed straight in Eleanor's handbag, which was on the floor next to her seat. The whole bag immediately burst into a yellow ball of flame.

"My bloody bag. You imbecile," Eleanor screamed. "It's got my hairspray in there. Look at it. It's about to explode."

I didn't look. There's no time for looking with words like 'explode.' I jumped to my feet, scooped up the bag and threw it towards an area of tiled floor where it could do the least harm. As it flew through the air, the heat trail brushed across two of the ceiling sprinklers causing them to activate. Instantly a steady stream of rain-like water burst from the ceiling straight onto the tables immediately below. Within seconds, as the fire alarms kicked in, the place was in uproar. The hairspray canister hit the floor and rolled across the tiles coming to rest against a leg of the birthday girl's chair. For a split second she remained motionless and then, as if reacting to a stray grenade, screamed and dived off the chair. Nifty at fifty seemed about right.

"What the fuck you doing you nutter?" Cecil grabbed hold of my arm. "You're gonna burn the frigging place down."

The swirling wail of the fire alarm added to the commotion and sense of panic. The birthday party was now in total disarray.

The birthday girl stayed down, a whimpering heap on the floor. A waiter picked up the hairspray canister and placed it on the bar. I felt responsible for the birthday girl's predicament and went over to her and offered my outstretched hand. As I pulled her to her feet, my foot slipped on the wet tiles and I pitched back taking her with me. She landed on top of my prone body, her dress riding high over her waist as she fell. A member of her party came to her rescue and tried to pull her upright as he let go a volley of abuse in my direction. He should have focussed on one task at a time. As the woman made it to her feet, she staggered back snapping the heel of her shoe which sent her sprawling again onto the floor. James and Cecil were on the scene in an instant, James helping the woman to a seat and Cecil explaining to the irate customer that he ought to think twice about what he was calling me if he wanted to leave the building in one piece.

I got back on my feet and surveyed the area. The remainder of the restaurant was on the move as staff frantically tried to organise what was now a general stampede for the exit, into their fire evacuation procedure. They had no chance. Curses and threats rang out as people made their way through the steady sprinkler shower, their hair and clothes dripping wet, their evening of relaxed conviviality a wash out, literally.

I was suddenly aware of Louise tugging my jacket.

"Matthew, what hell were you doing? Look at the place. You've ruined the whole bloody evening."

At that point I remembered the ring in my jacket pocket and my proposal. It crossed my mind that this was not the best time to pop the question.

4

I woke up confused and upset. Louise had not been in the best of moods and had gone back to her mother's hotel to keep her company. I had taken a taxi home with Cecil and Sheryl but they had gone straight back to Cecil's. My mind raced through the night's events again. It was a stupid accident. The reality was that there was minimal damage as only two sprinklers had activated. The worst it got was our table getting soaked along with the birthday party group and several of the customers as they rushed for the exit. It was only water, although Louise's mum had a different view, which she lost no time in explaining to me once we had made it outside.

Other than Eleanor's handbag, there had been no fire. But that hadn't stopped the panic when the fire alarm activated. Having evacuated the building the staff had to wait until the fire brigade declared the area safe. It seemed to me that the staff's biggest concern at that point was to ensure that the customers' bills were all paid. I'd made my apologies to the restaurant manager and paid my bill. I also offered to pay the birthday party group's bill too, which they accepted. It kept the peace and after all, they had missed out on a perfectly good birthday cake. The restaurant manager was good about it. He put it down to experience once he had managed to get everyone out. I assumed that he was keen, for the sake of his business, to get customers to come back, even if there were clumsy ones amongst them. The real damage was to my relationship with Louise's mother.

I couldn't see how it could survive two disastrous encounters. My plans to pop the question to Louise had also come unstuck.

I was sitting on the sofa drinking a cup of coffee when my mobile buzzed. I picked it up and checked the screen. No caller ID. I answered it anyway. It was James Brogan.

"*Matt. It's me James. I slipped out for a cigarette and thought I'd give you a call. Louise gave me your number. So how are you doing this morning young fella?*"

"Not that great James. I'm in the doghouse with Louise and I'm hardly flavour of the month with her mum after last night."

"*There is that, I have to tell you. She isn't too happy about her bag or the dress you soaked. But the two of them'll get over it, don't you worry.*"

"Will they? Maybe Louise will come round but I can't see Eleanor ever speaking to me again. Not after the start I've made. I think that's a doomed relationship." I heard James take a deep breath on the other end of the line as if he was about to say something. I got in first. "Can I tell you something James? Just between you and me."

"*Go on, fire away Matt.*"

I stood up and started to pace the room.

"You know what. I've got an engagement ring here. I had it with me last night and I was going to propose marriage to Louise. That was what the Champagne was for. Last night's little incident put paid to my plans but to be honest, I can't see it happening at all now. Even if Louise accepted, I'm sure Eleanor wouldn't want me as part of the family after what's happened."

"*Bejasus Matt, did you say marriage? I'm sorry to hear that. Sure it's –*"

"Sorry?"

"*No, I mean I'm sorry that your plan went wrong. It would've been a grand end to the night and I'm sure Louise would have jumped at marrying a fine young fella like you.*"

James's encouragement gave me a momentary boost and I was flattered too by the fact that he had a habit of referring to me as 'young' even though I had now slipped into my forties.

26

"You think so?" I said, "But what about Eleanor?"

"Well that's what I was calling about to be straight with you Matt. Listen, you don't want to be worrying over all that shenanigans last night. It's done now and the sooner we build bridges the better. So, I had this idea and I mentioned it to Louise last night back at the hotel bar although I still need to put it to Eleanor." There was a brief pause, presumably whilst he took a drag from his cigarette. *"You know we have this place out there in Ibiza? Well I was thinking that the pair of you should come out to see us, spend a few days relaxing and we'll get to know each other properly. You could stay at the villa, come and go as you want. What d'you think?"*

I was taken aback. It was a fantastic offer but I was cautious. "What did Louise say about that?" I asked.

"She's all for it. She thinks it's a great idea. And after what you said about an engagement ring, sure wouldn't it be a fantastic place for you to make your marriage proposal?"

I took a deep breath and sat down. I felt a surge of optimism but I was concerned about Eleanor. James seemed to guess what I was thinking.

"And don't worry about Eleanor. I'll sort that out."

"It would," I said. "Sounds a great idea. I really appreciate it, James."

"So look, if you can get the time off make it soon. The boat business is just gearing up now for the tourist season and that'll keep us all busy. Oh, and one other thing. Why don't you invite that friend of yours over too? Cecil and his lass. Seemed like a nice couple."

"You sure? Might be a crowd if we're trying to build bridges?"

"It's no problem Matt. We'll get them booked in at the Blau Parc. It's a nice hotel and a good location for all the bars and not too far from my place. They could come out for a long weekend. That way you'll have time with me and Eleanor for a few days and then, once the two of them are over, you youngsters can go out on the town."

"You're on James. Leave it with me and I'll get back to you."

"Good on you, son. And listen. Wee bit of advice. You might want to think about investing in a handbag."

"A handbag?"

"Sure ... for Eleanor. You're building bridges, right?"

"Oh, yes. Right."

Buoyed with new found enthusiasm, I rang Louise. She didn't pick up. I left a message and it was an hour later before she called back.

"How's my one man disaster zone today?" was her opening line.

"I'm mortified Louise. The evening wasn't meant to go like that."

"Of course it wasn't meant to go like that, silly. I didn't think you'd deliberately arranged it that way just to piss my mum off. And let me tell you Matthew, she is mightily pissed off. And to be honest I can't be doing with it all. I wanted you two to get on and things to go smoothly. The last thing I need is more stress. What with work and that ..." There was a brief pause. *"Look, I know I haven't told you much about what's going on, but it's a worry. It'll be the first time I've had to give evidence in such a high profile trial and to be honest I'm worried sick about it."*

"Just do what you've always done. You've been in court before."

"Yes, but this is big time. This guy is a proper player. Part of a full on organised crime racket."

"Yeah, I mentioned that to Cecil."

"What? What did you say? I told you, you can't say anything about my work. What did you tell him?"

"Nothing. I don't know anything, do I? I only said that you were involved in a big case. He mentioned that it might be that foreign guy that was in the papers last year and that –"

Louise let out a long sigh.

"See, this is why I can't talk about anything. I'd love to talk to you about what I do at work just like other couples do, but I can't. You have to understand that."

"I do understand. That's why I don't ask questions." I paused for a moment, my curiosity getting the better of me. "But, was he right? About the guy in the papers I mean."

"Let's just say he could be." She hesitated. *"Okay, between you and me, and you mustn't say anything to anyone because if it gets out, I could be in trouble. Yes, it is him. But that's all I'm saying."*

Something clicked in my head.

"Wait … I remember the name that Cecil mentioned now. Kurt something. Didn't the Sunday Times do some big piece on him saying he was involved in organised crime and he threatened to sue?"

"No names. But, there was press coverage, yes. If we can bring him down we stand a good chance of breaking the syndicate."

"Syndicate? What syndicate?"

"It's a well organised group and there are some dangerous people associated with it. Stop asking questions."

"So that puts you in danger then? I don't want you involved Louise. Can't you get someone else to give evidence?"

"There are plenty of other detectives involved already but he kind of fell into my lap because his house was burgled, can you believe. I don't think he would've reported it but he wasn't there that night and his alarm alerted the neighbours. I did most of the investigation into the burglary but he seemed reluctant to get involved, which made me suspect that maybe something else was going on. We caught the guys that did it eventually but I found some papers that raised my suspicions about this guy even more. I followed some leads and I've been part of the investigation into his activities ever since. In the end we made an arrest and although he's out on bail, there's a court appearance due and I have to give evidence. So I need to get this right. We need to convict him. If we can, there's a chance he'll give us the others that are involved in return for some leniency. Now let's leave it there. I've said enough already. Too much in fact. No more, okay?"

Louise's job worried me sometimes. When she had been an ordinary police officer, I knew she could get into some sticky situations but at this level there was more risk.

"Okay, but you just need to be careful honey."

"I am careful. I was talking to my mum about it last night ... well the bits I can tell her. She said I needed a break, to step back a bit from it all. You know what she said? She asked if I was sure it was the right job for me. Can you believe that? After all the time I've been in the force. I'd know by now if it wasn't."

"Well she might be right ... about the break I mean. And talking of breaks, James called me. He told me about his idea, about going out to Ibiza. What d'you think?"

"It's a great idea, especially if you and mum can get yourselves sorted out. I think we should book something next week. I mentioned it to Sheryl this morning and if she's going to be able to come out, we'll need to do it soon. She goes back to Toronto in three weeks. I've got some leave due so I'm sure I can get the time off, especially after all the hours I've had to put in lately. What about you?"

"Oh, I can square it with the boss, no problem. We can do the full week, seven nights."

"Fab. Let's book it. Cecil and Sheryl can come out later and it'll give you and me some time to catch up too."

That was all I needed to hear. Louise was keen and it would give me an opportunity to repair things with Eleanor. In addition, a sun kissed island would be a very romantic setting for a marriage proposal.

Gatwick Airport was buzzing with eager travellers. We had passed through check-in and passport control and had a couple of hours to kill before boarding. Louise was eager to browse the shops but I was never keen on shopping in airports. I'm a bloke – we shop when we need to; we go to airports to catch flights. I did however have one purchase I had to make. I passed my credit card to Louise.

"Do me a favour honey. See if you can find a suitable handbag for your mum. I think it would be a good idea if I replaced the one I vaporised last weekend."

Louise smiled and took the card. She knew that I was not a shopper so she was happy to go by herself. I found a table in one of the food outlets and ordered coffee and a bacon sandwich and flicked through the newspaper I had bought on the way through. I was looking forward to a week in the sun and, with Cecil and Sheryl due out later in the week, I was sure it would be a fun trip. I had decided to wait until they arrived before I asked Louise the all-important marriage question. The engagement ring was tucked away safely in my suitcase, concealed amongst the contents of my wash bag. It was better there rather than having to pass it through the security scan where I would have had to place it in a tray and run the risk of Louise seeing it.

As I flicked through the pages of the newspaper, I had a quiet chuckle at the memory of discussing the trip with Cecil.

"Ibiza? Yeah mate. Yeah, I'm definitely up for that. It's all gearing up about now for the party season. There'll be some right tasty birds down there."

"But you'll be going with Sheryl, Ces," I had reminded him.

"Yeah I know, but mate, when you're in a sweetshop you can look in all the jars, can't ya? Loads of scannies down there as well."

"Scannies?"

"Yeah, Scandinavian birds. A total Smorgasbord of pussy, geeze."

I had tried to focus Cecil on the fact that this was not a lads' trip. The reason for going to Ibiza was to relax and enable me to get to know Louise's mum, particularly as I was about to propose to her daughter.

"Yeah, but mate you don't go to Ibiza and not party, do ya? That's like going to a restaurant and not eating. Anyway, that James geezer seems like he'd be up for few beers. He's Irish ain't he, from County Clare where your old man was from, right?"

"I don't know, Ces. I didn't get round to asking him. And anyway, he's in his sixties. Nobody in their sixties goes out partying in Ibiza."

"Mate, you're never too old to party, not if you got the rogue gene."

I ignored Cecil's remark and focused on James's origins.

"So where exactly in Clare?"

"Quilty, he reckons."

"Really? That's exactly where my dad was from. That *is* coincidence then."

"And mate, trust me. He's definitely got that rogue gene. More to him than meets the eye. Don't be fooled by that old Irish charm he gives ya. You don't get a boat business and a villa out in Ibiza without pulling a few strings and greasing a few palms. I know these things mate."

Typical Cecil. Life was all one big party sometimes. And he thought he could read people. But he always made me smile and I was glad he was on the trip.

I sipped my coffee and focussed on the news. *More rain forecast for the UK; Interest rates set to rise; Government hints at euro referendum.* Same old stuff. I was glad I would be out of it for a week. I took a bite of my sandwich and browsed the sports section.

"Matthew?"

I thought I'd heard my name but I wasn't certain at first. I half turned in the direction of the voice. Then I heard it again.

"Matthew?" This time it was clearer and delivered with a familiar, soft Irish lilt. "It *is* you. What a surprise."

Sometimes the mind takes time to comprehend things when they are not expected. And the person standing to my left was certainly not expected. For a split second, my brain scrambled through its database to co-ordinate the information. But the green eyes, the sparkling smile and the silky brunette curls suddenly merged into immediate recognition – Erin Farrell.

For a moment I sat and stared at her, unable to speak. That was partly due to the fact that I was still chewing a mouthful of bacon sandwich, but also because the surprise had rendered me lost for words.

"How on earth are you Matthew?"

I swallowed the mouthful and attempted to form a response.

"I'm ... I'm very ... what are *you* doing here Erin?"

She brushed her hair away from one side of her face and laughed.

I noticed the tiny laughter lines that had become so familiar when I had last encountered her in Las Vegas. The mischief was still there in those green eyes too.

"Well it is an airport Matthew and as you well know, I'm a flight attendant, so I'm working. Otherwise I wouldn't be dressed in this uniform would I?"

"Working? But I thought you might have given that up after, you know ... the Vegas thing?"

A tiny frown crossed Erin's forehead.

"Shhh Matthew. I don't talk about that. I'm still working but only part time, sort of freelance shall we say. It helps keep the focus away from anything else I do too."

My mind flashed back to the crazy trip to Las Vegas for my fortieth birthday. It was over a year since I had last seen Erin. She hadn't changed at all. She was in her mid-thirties but still had the fresh good looks that I had found so appealing. It seemed too that she hadn't lost her ability to scheme. I left it alone.

"So where are you off to?" I asked.

"I'm flying to Innsbruck this afternoon and then back here on the return. I only do the short stuff now, no more long haul. Most of the European capitals, the holiday islands, that sort of thing. Where are you going?"

"I'm on my way to Ibiza. Just a week's break."

"That's nice. I'm often there myself. Majorca too. All the tourist stuff. It can get a bit tedious. You going on your own?"

"No. I'm –"

Erin shot out a hand and placed it on my arm. I couldn't help but notice the perfect red of her finger nails.

"Don't tell me. Are you still with ... what was her name? Lottie?"

"Louise actually. Yes. It's a ... kind of family trip."

"Very domesticated. What about your mad friend that was in Vegas. Do you still see him?"

"You mean Cecil." It couldn't have been anyone else. "Yes, I do. In fact he's coming out later to see us."

She laughed and flicked her hair back with a toss of her head.

"Not that domesticated then. Anyway, Matthew, I have to run. I have to meet up with the rest of the crew. Do you still have my mobile number?"

"No ... I ... err ... I didn't think I should keep it after what happened."

I watched as she opened her handbag and fumbled through it.

"Here, take my card. Don't worry, just friends. It would be nice to have a coffee sometime."

I took the card and stared at the gold lettering on the front. *E Farrell, Costume Jewellery*.

"It's just a little side-line, a hobby really. I started it with a girlfriend. Keeps us both out of mischief," she said, a surreptitious wink flickering across her face. "Anyway, call me. Bye."

As she walked off across the terminal, I tried to figure out whether she *was* just being friendly or whether there was something else. She had made a play for me in Las Vegas and she knew I found her attractive. Perhaps she didn't accept no for an answer.

I put her card in my pocket and decided not to dwell on it.

5

The first three days in Ibiza were magical. Lots of May sunshine, mild balmy evenings and a relaxed, convivial atmosphere. Days spent by the pool and evenings in cosy, authentic restaurants that only local knowledge could unearth. Eleanor and I had begun to build bridges. The two hundred and fifty pounds Louise had spent on the new bag had obviously gone some way to repairing the rift and she seemed more at ease with me each day. We didn't see a lot of her in the mornings as she was always tied up with paperwork for James's business.

James spent less of his own time with the boats and was more of the type of businessman who preferred to delegate. He told us one morning that he felt he had done his fair share of the 'graft' when he had first started the business. As it built up over the years, he had taken a back seat. But things had hit a rough patch around ten years ago and he went back to being more hands on, just to keep the business 'afloat,' as he liked to say. He had ended up financially strapped so let go several of his crew and sold two of the boats. When business began to pick up again and he had replaced the boats, he allowed the crews to run the daily routine. He now had four boats running and clearly things had improved significantly. His villa, with its kidney-shaped swimming pool, was evidence of that.

Each morning James would get up early and walk his two dogs, Mofo and Panzer. I wasn't sure they were dogs at all, as their appearance was closer to wild animal than domestic pet. They were of similar size, both hefty great beasts with great black manes and from a distance, I could have placed money on it that they were the offspring of the world's first pairing of a wolf with a lion. James assured me they were German Shepherds, good-natured, friendly and fantastic as guard dogs. I wondered for a moment if good natured and friendly were the right qualities for guard dogs but their noisy barking and boisterous enthusiasm at the sight of visitors, made me realise that both that and sheer size would be intimidating enough for any intruder.

The villa was situated in a beautiful location high above Cala Gració beach, about three kilometres north of the town of San Antonio. On a single level, its white washed walls and sloping terracotta-tiled roof were typically Spanish. On both sides of the property, rows of almond trees and palms framed the view out across the ocean and, as I gazed through the gap, I thought that a more tranquil location would have been hard to find.

And then, on day four, Cecil arrived.

Louise and I both knew that, in a town like San Antonio, a party animal like Cecil would never be content with a round of local restaurants and romantic nights. Even with Sheryl. We knew that at some point over the four days he was due to spend with us, he would want to go out and experience the night life that Ibiza had to offer. We had discussed it to the extent that Louise had suggested that 'the boys' should at least have one night out together whilst she did some 'girlie time' with Sheryl. A good plan as far as I was concerned. It was about management. Managing Cecil's expectations.

I was sitting by the pool sipping a cold drink when my mobile rang. Louise was dozing in the warm mid morning sun. Eleanor had taken the car, a brand new Range Rover, to Ibiza Town on an errand and James had gone down to the harbour to sort out some sailing schedules.

"*Mate, just got in. What's the crack?*"

"Hi Ces. How was your flight?" I replied, not ready to reveal so soon that the crack was nothing more than chill out time by the pool following a leisurely evening meal at a restaurant the night before.

36

"Yeah, sound mate. Frigging early start but worth it. I'm feeling a cold one already by the pool, bit a sun on the back of my neck, you know?"

"You at the Blau Parc then? What's it like?"

"S'alright mate, yeah. Nice hotel. Few birds round the pool already and it's right next to the Golden Buddha Bar so I might be checking that out later. Where are ya anyway?"

I was a little concerned that Cecil might be angling for a session.

"I'm at the villa with Louise. You're not on the beers already are you mate? And where's Sheryl?"

"Nah, ... warm sun, nice pool, good looking totty, so I'm feeling it, you know. Sheryl's in the room doing all that hanging shit up in the wardrobe thing. Thought I'd leave her to it and check the place out."

I heard Louise stir and then sit up. She mouthed a question that I took to be asking if Sheryl and Cecil had arrived. I nodded back. She pointed in the direction of the town and then towards the pool signalling that I should invite them up.

"You there geeze?"

"Sorry Ces. I was just, err, talking to Louise. Look, when you're sorted out with the room and that why don't you both come up here? We've got a pool and there's plenty of beer in the fridge. Maybe this afternoon. We could chill, have a few beers and then all go out tonight. What d'you think?"

"Sounds good mate. Where is it?"

"It's on a road called ... Carretera ... Carretera something. I'll text it to you. It's only about three kilometres up from the town. You'd be here in about five or ten minutes in a cab. Or you could walk up. It's a nice walk."

"Mate, I ain't walking nowhere in this heat. Text it then and we'll call a sherbet to bring us up later."

It was three in the afternoon when Cecil and Sheryl arrived. After they had declared a truce with Mofo and Panzer, who had treated them to a full inspection, I lead them out to the pool. Louise went to the kitchen to organise some drinks. Cecil wasted no time in making himself at home. Still fully clothed in shorts and a tee shirt, he spread himself along one of the sun loungers and placed the straw hat he had been wearing over his face. His only concession to the warmth of the sun was to kick off his open toed beach sandals.

I turned to Sheryl and winked.

"Tiring all this travelling by the looks of things."

"You know Ces, Mathew. He doesn't stand on ceremony," Sheryl replied. "Anyway, nice to see him chill for a change. We've got four nights so hopefully he'll wind down a bit."

I laughed. "You sure? What, Cecil wind down. I'm not sure that'll happen once he gets acclimatised."

Sheryl smiled. "We'll see. As long as he gets himself back to the airport on the right day he can do what he likes, I suppose. We've managed to book the same flights back as you guys."

Louise emerged from the villa carrying a tray that had a jug of orange squash and two bottles of beer on it. She placed the tray on one of the poolside tables, picked up the beer bottles and handed one to me. She walked over to Cecil

"Cecil ... got you a beer."

He swung his legs over the edge of the sun lounger and sat upright. He took the bottle and began to examine it, turning it slowly in his hand.

"Alhambra Especial. Good beer darlin. Additive free, quite smooth. It's all about the water they use in the brewing process. Gives it that smoothness. The brewery's near the Sierra Nevada Mountains so you get good clear water." He raised the bottle to his lips and took a swig.

"Cecil, how do you know that stuff? You seem to know something about every beer in the world," Louise said.

"I'm a connoisseur, ain't I," Cecil replied, as he raised the bottle again.

"And he's got a photographic memory," I said.

"And it just so happens he was talking to a waiter at the hotel earlier about the different beers they had in the cooler," Sheryl added.

Cecil laughed. "Yeah, but it's about getting information ain't it. You never know when this stuff comes in handy. Never know when you're gonna need it. Don't matter what it is."

The two girls looked at one another and began to laugh, probably wondering when such a titbit of detail about beer would ever be useful. Louise stood up and beckoned to Sheryl.

"Fancy a quick dip and then we can do some serious sun bathing."

As the two girls splashed around the pool, Cecil and I did some catching up.

"What's with them two fucking dogs?" Cecil said. "Mate, I thought one of 'em was gonna eat my leg. Scary. You don't wanna rub them up the wrong way, do ya?"

"They're good as gold Ces, honest. Once they get to know you, they're fine. Anyway, chill. It'll be a good few days break."

"You're right." He scanned the pool area, swigged his beer and said, "S'alright here, ain't it? Cold beer. Warm sun on your neck. Yeah mate. Beats all that rushing around back home. Been looking forward to it. I was glad to get on the plane."

"Talking of planes Ces, you'll never guess who I ran into on the way out here?"

"Who?"

"Erin. Erin Farrell."

Cecil shuffled forward on the sun lounger, an eyebrow slightly raised as the name conjured up a picture in his head.

"What, you mean that Irish bird from Vegas? No way mate. You sure? Thought she'd moved abroad or something."

"Seems not. She's working for one of the airlines."

"Yeah?" Cecil took a pull on his beer and smiled. "Mate she was alright. Sharp bird. She'd got a bit of a thing for you didn't she? Mate, you shoulda nailed it when you had the chance."

"I don't know about that Ces. I liked her but she was a handful." I glanced towards the pool. The girls were swimming back towards the steps. "C'mon, I'll show you round the villa. We'll leave the women to catch up on the gossip."

We strolled into the house. Cool air circulating from an overhead ceiling fan in the hall created a pleasant change of temperature. Cecil was impressed with the luxurious, tastefully furnished rooms.

"Looks like the geezer's got a few bob."

"I think they do all right from the business. No reason why not with all the tourists who come to the island."

Cecil strolled back into the hallway and pointed to a heavy oak door that was closed.

"What's in there mate?"

"It's the study … the office where they run the business. I've not been in there to be honest. James mentioned it when he showed me round but we didn't go in. No reason to. An office is an office. See enough of them at work."

"All the same mate, might as well take a look. If you're doing a show round geeze, might as well do it properly." He reached for the door handle and turned it. A push against the heavy door and it opened. "It ain't locked mate so I guess he ain't got nothing to hide." He noticed my quizzical look. "Like I said earlier, it's about getting information, ain't it?"

The room was spacious and cool, the shutters on a single window on the far side of the room, closed against the sunshine. Narrow slats of light seeped through the shutter gaps and cast several thin bands of alternate light and shade across the surface of a solid timber desk that stood on a rug in the centre of the floor.

"Dark in here," I said.

"Well, take them shades off you nob. That might help."

I removed the sunglasses and ignored the 'nob' remark. Cecil crossed to the window and pulled the shutters open so that the room was instantly bathed in light. The sudden influx of bright sunlight revealed nothing remarkable other than it was indeed an office. The desk surface was clear except for an empty filing tray, a glass bowl filled with an assortment of sweets and a small metal tray that held several keys. A soft leather chair was tucked into the space between the two sides of the desk. A line of bookshelves covered one wall from floor to ceiling. Against the opposite wall, two filing cabinets were stationed either side of a painting of what looked like a Spanish village scene.

"Not much to see then Ces," I said. "Like James said, it's just an office."

"Yeah, s'pose so." As he spoke, he pulled the leather chair out, swung it round and eased into it. "I could see myself out here mate. Running an empire, plenty of birds, chilling, you know the mumble."

"Don't suppose it's that simple. Grass is always greener and all that."

Cecil swung the chair round again, stretched out, hands behind his head and thrust his feet forward under the desk. As he did so, he let out a curse. At precisely the same moment, a whirring, mechanical noise kicked in and, just as abruptly, stopped again.

"What's up? What's that noise?" I asked.

I watched as Cecil ducked down beneath the desk.

"He's got a fucking industrial sized shredder down here. Stubbed me toe on the fucking thing. It's solid."

"You should've worn your shoes then." I resisted a 'nob' reference. "C'mon, let's get out of here. Don't want James to think we've been snooping in his office. I've only just got it sorted with Eleanor. Don't want her getting the wrong idea either. " I turned towards the door. "C'mon, let's go Ces."

"Hang on geeze, it's got something stuck in it."

Cecil disappeared under the desk again and began to drag the shredder out. Sticking out of the top was a sheet of paper that appeared to have been in mid-shred but for some reason had not gone through.

"It's hardly an industrial shredder, Ces. It's just an office unit. Leave it. We ought to get back to the pool."

"Hang on. What's the rush? I wanna see what this is."

He began to tug at the sheet of paper. It didn't move. I reached out and grabbed his arm.

"Ces, you'll rip it. Press the reverse button. It might eject itself."

He pushed the reverse button and sure enough the sheet of paper began to move upwards until he was able to free it from the machine. The bottom end hung in a series of long strands where the shredder teeth had begun to chew it up. He sat back in the leather seat and began to examine the document.

"The bin must be full up." I said. "That's why it didn't go through. Probably why the thing's so heavy too."

Cecil didn't answer. He continued to stare at the piece of paper. Finally he looked up, a broad smile across his face.

"Mate, I think that James geezer is doing a bit of the old mumble swerve."

"How d'you mean?"

He handed me the sheet.

"Take a look at this. It's got a load of birds' names on it … and dates too."

I took the paper and began to read it.

Caroline - 16 January
Sue - 3 March
Al - 18 March
Polly - 28 March
Ann - 10 April
Jo - 25 April
Kay - 17 May
Val - 28 May
Polly - 10 June
Ann - 17 June
Kay - 30 June
Jo - 5 July
Sue - 20 July
Al - 4 August
Val - 11 August

Below the last legible entry, the document had been shredded. I put it down on the desk and looked at Cecil.

"What d'you think it is?"

"Obvious ain't it mate? The geezer's got some birds on the go ain't he?"

"Birds? What, d'you mean he's messing about with other

women?" I paused as the implications of what Cecil had said sank in. "He can't be Ces. He's in his sixties and … well, he's with Eleanor."

"So when did that stop anybody?" Cecil replied. "I knew there was something about him. Stands to reason, don't it? Geezer's got boats. He's all tanned up, still looking alright for an old boy. Bit of a rogue mate. Told you, didn't I?" He picked up the sheet of paper and looked at it again. "Yeah, simple ain't it. He takes the birds out for a little spin in one of his boats and ... you know the mumble mate … they love all that. Sun, sea, nice boat. Bottle of the old sparkly stuff on the programme too I bet, and before you know it, the old bikini bottoms are off along with the top and matey boy is doing the deal. Can't say I blame him either."

"Wait a minute Ces. That's jumping the gun." I pointed at the paper. "I mean, look at the names. They can't be holidaymakers. They're the same ones over six months. And, what about Al and Jo? They could be blokes couldn't they?"

"Could be, but look at the rest of the list. All bird's names, so I reckon it ain't no geezer called Alan and if it was blokes, Jo would be spelt with an 'e'... J-O-E. More like Alison and Joanna or something. And they could just be his regular ones. The birds that work out here in the bars and stuff. Got himself a little regular thing. He probably has the odd mumble with the tourists too. I mean if that list weren't all shredded up, there could be more. Gotta take your hat off to the fella though."

I stretched over the desk and looked at the document again. I pointed at one of the entries.

"That's today. See, seventeenth May ... Kay."

"Yeah mate. It is. So that's what he's up to today."

I paused while I tried to recall exactly what James had said as we had eaten breakfast earlier that morning.

"All I remember is that he said he'd see us later as he had to go do some stuff with the boats ... sort out schedules or something."

"Oh yeah, right mate. I reckon he's been scheduling Kay all morning. Nice day for a little sort out on the water."

Cecil stood up, picked up the document, folded it and put it in his pocket. He followed my eyes.

"Information, geeze. Never know when this stuff comes in handy. Never know when you're gonna need it. Tumble?"

"You should get rid of it. Shred it," I said.

"It won't shred, will it. Shredder's full. If we try and empty it, all that paper's likely to spill and it'll look like somebody's been messing about in his office."

I felt uneasy. Just going into the office had made me feel like a snooper but now that we had found something that seemed private, I felt even guiltier.

"Look Ces, I don't want to get involved in whatever James is doing. That's his business and if it gets back to –"

"Chill mate. As far as that James geezer is concerned, that bit of paper got shredded or he wouldn't have left it, would he? Don't worry, I ain't gonna mention it to your bird." He reached forward and rummaged amongst the keys in the container. "All the same though, might as well have a look through the drawers now we're here, see what other secrets he's got."

"Leave it Ces. None of our business what he's got," I said, as I crossed the room to close the shutters.

Cecil hesitated. He shot me a glance and moved his hand across to the sweet bowl. He pulled out two wrapped sweets and threw one towards me.

"Okay mate. Let's go get some sun then."

On the way out, he tugged at the top drawer of one of the filing cabinets.

"Ces. Leave it. C'mon."

Back outside Louise and Sheryl were in the pool throwing a beach ball back and forth. Cecil slipped off his shorts to reveal a pair of black swimming shorts underneath. He winked at me, raced to the poolside and in one mighty leap dive-bombed Sheryl. Her excited screams were followed by a series of half-hearted attempts to splash him as he swam back towards her. I jumped in next to Louise and the four of us spent the next half hour soaking up the late afternoon sunshine, lazing in the cool water and enjoying life.

We were interrupted by Eleanor. She walked onto the poolside carrying a tray of drinks and placed it on the main table near a sheltered barbecue area.

"Hi guys. Come and get it."

Cecil led the way, still dripping wet from the pool, and made a beeline for one of two bottles of beer on the tray.

"I've made us girls a jug of Pimms," Eleanor said, pouring the orange coloured drink into three glasses, each of them filled with fresh mint and ice.

I picked up the remaining beer bottle and clanked it against Cecil's.

"Cheers Ces, mate. Welcome to Ibiza."

"Oh, and I found these in the study," Eleanor said. She reached into the pocket of her shorts and pulled out a pair of sunglasses. My sunglasses. "Somebody lost them?" she asked.

I was sure she was directing her gaze at me as she asked the question. Or perhaps it was my guilt. I had no choice but to own up.

"Err … they're mine, Eleanor. I … err … wondered where they were."

"I found them in the study actually, Matthew." Eleanor's eyes narrowed, a frown creasing her brow. She held out the glasses towards me. Cecil stretched out a hand and took them from her.

"My fault Missus P. I borrowed them off Matt. Left mine at the hotel. Yeah, I squint a lot in the bright sunlight, know whatamean? He's let me use them."

Eleanor turned her gaze on Cecil.

"But they were on the desk in the study."

"Yeah, sorry about that. I've gone in the house to use the bog … the facilities like, and got the wrong door. It was dark in there so I must've put the glasses down while I got my bearings and then realised I'm in an office. My mistake. No harm done eh?"

Cecil put the glasses on, smiled at Eleanor and took a long slurp from the beer.

"Anyway, where's the other half? He coming out for a little libation later?"

Eleanor raised a glass and took a sip.

"James? Yes, he called earlier. He's on his way back. He's had a busy day bless him."

I caught Cecil's smirk but immediately looked away.

"Well ... erm ... cheers then everybody," I said.

6

It was day six when things began to take a turn. The previous two evenings had been relaxed, the six of us visiting the sunset bars of Café del Mar and Café Mambo to watch the sun go down before heading off to one of the local restaurants for dinner. But it was clear Cecil was itching to get out and about on a 'boys' night. His chance came that evening.

Louise, Sheryl and Eleanor had gone to Ibiza Town for a day's shopping. James had gone out with one of his crews on a tourist boat trip to Formentera. Cecil and I had spent the afternoon by the pool at his hotel, the Blau Parc.

"Beer o'clock mate," Cecil said, getting up from the white sun lounger that he had occupied most of the afternoon.

I sat up, my eyes blurred from the short nap I had just awoken from. I looked at my watch in some sort of reflex check action at hearing a reference to the time, even though it was just Cecil's way of alerting me to the fact that he fancied a beer. It was ten minutes to five.

"Go on then. A lager please. Oh, and a bottle of water too."

"Water? You sure mate."

"Got to keep hydrated, Ces."

Cecil wandered off in the direction of the poolside bar, weaving his way between the sun worshippers stretched out on their sunbeds, their bodies shining with lashings of sunscreen and glowing that ruddy-brown that says they have marginally crossed into burn territory.

I reached into the rucksack I had tucked under the sunbed, pulled out my mobile from the pocket of my shorts and called Louise. They were still in Ibiza Town, having a late lunch and were going on to a local wine bar afterwards that Eleanor knew. She told me to go and enjoy a night out with Cecil and that maybe we could all catch up later on. As I finished the call, Cecil returned with two beers.

"Cheers mate," I said as he handed me one of the bottles. I took a sip, enjoying the cool sensation of the liquid as it slid down.

Cecil sat down on the sunbed and stared across the poolside at two girls who were applying sunscreen to already golden tans.

"Mate, that's the standard. See whatamean. Look at that. Bet they're scannies."

"What makes you think that?" I said, curious as to how he arrived at his conclusion.

"Mate, obvious ain't it ... tall, blonde, good looking, fit bodies. Don't that give you a clue then geeze?"

"Well, they could be from ... I don't know ... Sunderland."

"Sunderland? You sure? I mean nothing wrong with birds from Sunderland – I went out with one once, right salt an' all she was – but trust me, birds from Sunderland don't get that perfect all over tan in five minutes the way the Scannie birds do. It's the olive oil."

"Olive oil? What, they get a better tan because they put olive oil on their food? I didn't know Scandinavians –"

"Not on their food you nobhead. They put it on their bodies. Gives 'em the colour," Cecil interrupted, looking at me as if I was from another planet. He slurped a mouthful of beer and stood up. "I'm going over there, mate. Give them the old chat."

"Hang on Ces. We're going out tonight aren't we? I got the green light from Louise. The girls won't be back until later."

He turned round towards me.

"Yeah, course we are mate. Tell you what. You go get yourself changed and I'll meet you in the Golden Buddha Bar next door." He glanced at his watch. "Hour and a half, yeah?"

I was down at the Golden Buddha right on time. There was no sign of Cecil. I ordered a couple of beers and sat outside on one of the large sofa beds that faced out across the bay. The sun had started to slip down through the blue of the sky, its fiery glow creating a rippling golden path across the expanse of water that lapped against the sands of a small beach area below the bar. Just above the beach, a paved walkway curved its way between rows of tall palms and followed the shoreline towards the distant outline of San Antonio's main town. Groups of people, holidaymakers and locals, ambled slowly past, enjoying the last of the early evening sun and the spectacular view across the bay.

"Alright mate."

I turned to see Cecil approaching, a big grin on his face. He was wearing a black t-shirt emblazoned with the words 'Hed Kandi' along one side with a series of light blue arrows rolling down through the middle and pair of grey, linen draw string trousers. When compared to my plain white cotton shirt and dark jeans, he looked a lot more 'Ibiza.'

"Hi Ces. You look pleased with yourself. How'd you get on then? Were they from Scandinavia?"

"Course mate. I told ya. Denmark in fact. And what's more geeze, they're up for meeting tonight. Said we'd see them down at Mambo about eight o'clock."

"We?"

Cecil sat down on the sofa bed, stared out across the bay and then turned to look at me.

"Yeah, we. Me and you. That a problem?"

I took a deep breath.

"Kind of Ces. I'm here with my girlfriend. I can't really be arranging to meet other women."

"You ain't arranging nothing geezer. You're just tagging along as a wingman. And anyway, you ain't with your bird tonight, are ya? It's a boys' night out, right." He lifted the beer bottle and guzzled down half the contents, wiped his mouth and looked at me for a response.

"Well it's hardly a boys' night out if we're meeting up with two

49

Scandinavian women, is it? I mean suppose I ran into Eleanor or James and I'm sitting with ... well, you know. And anyway Louise said she might hook up later on."

"Chill geezer. You ain't gonna run into Eleanor are you? She's out with Louise and Sheryl in Ibiza Town. And as for James, mate, he ain't got much room to be criticising if he's shagging half the birds on the island, has he?"

"Wait a minute Ces. We don't know that. You can't just jump to conclusions based on a bit of paper. I mean they could be customers ... for the boat trips ... or maybe a staff rota."

Cecil ran a hand through his thick head of hair, a gesture I had come to recognise as something he did when someone didn't seem to be getting his point.

"Customers? Customers you reckon. So he does female only boat trips, yeah? Get real mate. As for staff, you ain't gonna run a load of boats with just women as crew. Anyway, I don't give a fuck what the geezer's up to. That's his business. All I know is I'm in Ibiza, I'm on holiday and I done a loada legwork to set us up with two right hot chicks and now you're going all lame on me."

"Ces, we were supposed to be having a night out. I didn't ask you to set me up with anybody. I know Louise is not here but I'm planning to ask her to marry me before we go back home. You do understand that don't you, and what it means? I'm getting engaged. I've got the ring on me so I'm ready to seize the moment."

Knowing Cecil the way I did, I realised as soon as I'd asked the question the kind of response I might get.

"Geezer, fuck all that engaged shit tonight. You can do that tomorrow. It's the last night. Better time too when we're all about. Nobody's asking ya to marry these birds. It's a bit of fun. Remember that? Don't mean 'cos you're with a bird you can't have a laugh. Sometimes you gotta compartmentalise –"

"Compart what?"

"Compartmentalise. Put things in boxes mate and now and then you open the box that's got the legendary warrior in it. Get that fucking sword out geeze and get on the programme. Grease it up and let it glint in the sun. Yeah?"

I watched Cecil neck the rest of his beer and marvelled at his ability to dismiss my situation as some sort of inconvenience to his social life.

"C'mon then geezer. Drink up. It's gone seven. Might as well get down there early, have a couple in Café del Mar, watch the sunset and then meet the birds in Mambo." He stood up and started to walk away. Suddenly he turned round towards me. "And mate, get on the old dog and bone to your missus and tell her it ain't happening tonight. It's a boys' night right. Tomorrow we'll do the coupled up thing, yeah?"

We strolled down to Café del Mar and took a couple of seats at the round terrace bar in the centre of the venue. The position, under the floating sail-style roof, afforded fantastic views of the ocean and the gradually declining sun. A buzz of anticipation drifted through the crowd as they settled into seats or just stood around, wanting to be part of the atmosphere.

Cecil ordered two bottles of Isleña beer, an Ibiza brew served in white aluminium bottles covered in a pink psychedelic pattern. We sipped our drinks and watched the sun slowly glide beneath the horizon, like some molten coin slipping into a slot, leaving in its wake a glowing orange sky. A backdrop of ethereal, chill out tunes, both spooky and uplifting, created an almost spiritual and hypnotic experience, enhanced further by the reverential mood of the crowd as they watched the mighty 'sun-god' end another day.

With the sun now out of sight, the orange glow faded to a deep blue hue and gradually the sky darkened into another Mediterranean night. We moved across to Café Mambo, another of the iconic Sunset Strip venues with its pink back-lit, white, stone fronted bar that ran from the dance floor to the left and curved away to one side. A venue full of beautiful, trendy people and great tunes. Cecil headed straight for a table next to the centrepiece Café Mambo mosaic sign, a prime spot in his opinion as it gave him views in all directions and was slightly removed from the more frenetic atmosphere of the DJ booth. The chill out sounds that typified the Sunset Strip had given way to a rhythmic mix of dance and funky house tunes.

Cecil headed inside to order some drinks and I sat for a moment taking in the atmosphere. Along the shoreline, rows of tables, each of them bathed in a pink haze of light that emerged between the fluttering canopies above, were filling with early evening revellers. Further across the bay, the lights of the town flickered into life, in sharp contrast to the darkness of the intervening water.

As I sat waiting for Cecil, I took a moment to consider how to handle my proposal to Louise. Ibiza was not a place for formality it seemed and I decided that relaxed and simple was the best approach. I had to admit to myself that I was apprehensive. It wasn't doubt that Louise might decline my proposal. Just that it was a big step, but I knew it was one that I wanted.

"You alright geezer? You look like you've been hypnotized or something." Cecil appeared at the table carrying two glasses. "Got a couple of Jack 'n' cokes. Get that down ya." He pulled out the seat and sat down. "Yeah, s'alright here mate," he said, as he scanned his surroundings. "Good tunes too."

I sipped my drink and felt the impact of the super strength measures.

"So, tell me Ces, these two girls, you never said what they do or anything. They on holiday?"

"Nah, they're doing the season. Came out in March. The one with that short hair's been out here a couple of times. They're handing out flyers mostly ... at night for the bars down the West End strip and in the day, they do promo stuff for the tourist trips. Don't think they earn a lot but you don't need much out here and it gets 'em the gig for the season. They're a bit of alright too mate. I reckon you'd like the blonde one."

"They both looked blonde to me," I said, slightly confused.

"You know whatamean. The one with the long hair. I'll go for the one with the short hair. Quite fancied her."

I tried to ignore Cecil's scheming and focussed on the promotional work that he said they did.

"They do the tourist stuff as well as the clubs? What, like the boat trips?"

"Yeah, all that kinda thing."

"Well, maybe they know –"

I stopped in my tracks.

Heading for the table were the two girls I had seen on the far side of the pool. A bit of 'alright' was an understatement. Across the pool they had looked like a couple of ordinary attractive girls but up close and dressed for a night out they were stunning. The one with the long blonde hair wore a pair of jeans that were so tight you could reasonably expect there to be an instruction manual on how to get them on and off. A simple white top that accentuated her golden tan, completed the vision. Her companion was equally as striking, the light from the bar glinting off a tight pair of silver shorts that hugged her toned thighs as she glided towards us. Her black scoop necked vest showed enough of her cleavage to attract attention, as if the shorts needed some sort of competition.

As they approached, I elbowed Cecil.

"Don't tell me it's them?"

"Right on the money geezer."

"Hello guys. Sorry we're a bit late," the one with the long hair said.

Cecil was on his feet in an instance.

"Mate, meet Estrid and Al." He turned towards the two girls, a hand outstretched in my direction. "This is my friend, Matt."

"It's Alida actually. Nice to meet you Matt," the one with the short hair said.

"Oh ... uh ... it's Matthew but Matt is fine. Nice to meet you too."

Estrid held out her hand. "Nice to meet you Matthew. You on holiday too?"

"Yes, I am ... just a week with ... with Cecil ... and my ... err, friends."

Cecil winked at me as if I had played the wingman role perfectly by not mentioning my girlfriend but the truth was I didn't feel that two girls in their twenties would be very interested in the family arrangements of a guy of my age. It turned out that Estrid was the older of the two at twenty-nine. Alida was twenty-eight.

Cecil went off to order drinks. For a moment, left alone with two smiling confident young blondes, I was tongue-tied but I made an attempt at small talk.

"Erm, nice jeans," I said to Estrid.

"You like? Stone-washed skinny Paige jeans actually."

"Oh ... okay … nice. They go with your shoes," I said, in an effort to cover up my lack of fashion knowledge and to make it look like I had taste. It was an easy win. I was certain she wouldn't be wearing something that didn't go with such a jeans statement.

"Thank you. Aqua marine stilettos," Estrid replied, stretching out her right leg and staring at the shoe.

I was glad I hadn't described them as 'blue.'

Alida, not to be left out, leant forward, a deliberate attempt to ensure that her low top displayed her cleavage to full advantage. Her tanned skin glistened under the glow of the lights.

"Uh ... nice pair of ... of, you know ... shorts," I said, tearing my eyes away from the point at which they had involuntarily become fixed. "They are … very shiny. The shorts I mean."

Alida shot a look at Estrid, a playful smile on her lips and then looked me directly in the eyes.

"You like women's clothes do you, Matt?" she said.

"No ... no, not at all." I glanced towards the bar to see how Cecil was doing with the drinks. He was being served as we spoke. "I mean ... err, yes. I do ... but on a woman, of course. Not that they'd be, you know ... anywhere else." I needed to change the subject. "So where are you both from then?"

"I am from Esbjerg in Denmark and Alida is from Aarhus. You know it?"

"No, I ... I can't say I do, to be honest."

"You never heard of Denmark?" Estrid glanced at Alida and they both giggled.

"Oh ... yes ... of course. I thought you meant ... the, erm … the places."

"And you Matt. Where are you from?" Estrid asked.

"London. You know London?"

"I do. It's where I got these jeans."

"Oh, okay," I said, trying not to stare at her legs again. "Cecil tells me you do the flyers for the clubs and the tourist attractions."

"Yes, we do. We work six days each week but it isn't too hard," Estrid said. "Alida has been here two times before and said it would be fun to do the season. Just flyers to the people on holiday. We get commission if they go to the bars and on the boat trips."

"Boat trips? You don't happen to know a James Brogan do you?"

I caught a quick exchange of looks between the two of them before Alida answered.

"Why? You know him?"

"He's a friend ... of the family. We're staying at his place. Well, I am ... not Cecil."

"Oh okay. Yes, we know James. He's one of the people we do flyers for. Very nice man. Lots of fun."

Cecil returned with four drinks, two more Jack Daniel's and cokes and two gin and tonics for the girls. We spent another hour chatting. The girls had both trained to be chemists and had worked for a large pharmaceutical company but wanted to have some fun before they focussed on careers again. Eventually they had to leave to dish out flyers along the West End Strip but said that if we were around later we could catch up and have a drink.

"So what d'you think mate? They're both right tasty but I fancy that Al myself. Seen them silver shorts? She couldn't get 'em any tighter. And Estrid's more your type geezer, with that long blonde hair."

"Hang on Ces. I told you. I'm not pairing up here. It was just a friendly drink."

"Geezer, I saw the way you looked at her. You fancied her big time. Don't try bullshit me. And I don't blame ya mate. She's got a shape on her that's for sure."

I picked up my drink and paused for a moment. "She's attractive, I'll give you that Ces. They both are. But –"

"Attractive! Geezer, what is it with you? They're both top totty mate. Tell me, where you, a man of your age, are gonna get some hot looking twenty something chick coming on to you like that? And trust me, she *was* coming on to you. You see her eyes and all them little touches on your arm? And her right knee touching yours. Mate, I don't miss much. So, I'd get real if I was you. You gotta be able to read them signs."

I couldn't decide if Cecil was over egging it to get me onside to further his own ambitions with Alida or whether he was telling it like it was. Estrid had been attentive. There was no mistaking that. But it was summer in Ibiza. Everybody feels good in the sun. There is no tension. People are friendlier. But I was flattered nonetheless and I wanted to believe that Cecil's observations were correct. It made me feel good even if I had no intention of doing anything about it. Cecil shook me out of my daydream.

"So mate. You with me? What you gonna do?"

"How do you mean?"

"I mean, you heard. They wanna see us later down the Strip, yeah? So how about it?"

I took a sip of the Jack Daniel's, placed the glass on the table and turned to face Cecil.

"Look, let's be realistic. Yeah, I suppose I did fancy Estrid. Who wouldn't? And, sure, it's an ego boost if she likes me. But apart from the fact I'm going to ask Louise to marry me, they know James. When you were getting the drinks they told me. How's that going to look then? I'm chatting up two birds on a night out who happen to know the bloke who's living with my girlfriend's mother. Imagine that gets back."

Cecil waved a hand dismissively.

"Yeah but James ain't got no room to talk has he? He's on the dabble ain't he. Trust me. You saw that bit of paper, yeah? Nothin'll get back. Them two girls are just up for a good time and like I said, I fancy that Al. Mate, at worst, all you gotta do is play the wingman and –"

"Wait a minute ... Al. That was one of the names on that bit of paper, wasn't it? Al ... Alida. And they both know James. It could be her. And I saw the little look between them when I mentioned

James. So, if you're right and he *is* having a dabble on the side, and Alida is one of his women, that makes it even worse. I definitely can't be getting involved."

Cecil rubbed his chin and looked around the bar. He turned back to face me.

"Yeah, but maybe you was right the first time. Could just be me speculating too much, you know. Putting two and two together and coming up with five. I wouldn't worry geeze. Nothin'll get back to James."

I could tell what Cecil was doing. He wasn't averse to changing the angles to suit whatever outcome he had in mind.

"Look Ces, you need to make your mind up. One minute you reckon it's a dead cert James is up to something and the next you're changing your mind. Whatever's the case, whoever's right, either way the bottom line is a man that is about to propose to his girlfriend shouldn't be going out to meet two women, even if they are tanned up good-looking Scandinavian hotties." I downed the contents of my glass and stood up. I reached into my trousers pocket and pulled out the box that contained the engagement ring.

"See mate." I opened the box to reveal the glittering diamond. "Just in case you don't think I'm serious."

Cecil's eyes flashed.

"Geezer, put that away. What the fuck you doing walking around with two grand worth of ring in your pocket? You'll get it nicked."

"Like I said, Ces. I'm serious. There was always a chance I'd run into Louise tonight so I'm prepared."

"Didn't you call her then?"

"I did but I kept it open." I put the ring back in my pocket. "Listen mate, I know you wanted a boys' night out but you go meet the two girls. You'll have a laugh. I'll get a taxi back to the villa and wait for Louise. You know it makes sense."

It was probably the prospect of having the pick of two hot ladies that convinced Cecil.

"Yeah, ok mate. You go home to your bird ... and put that fucking ring somewhere safe."

He stood up, shook my hand and headed off in search of the bright lights.

I had only walked a short way along the street between Café del Mar and Café Mambo when a car pulled alongside.

"You want a taxi my friend."

I walked towards the car window and bent down to see the driver.

"Yes. Great. I need to get to Carretera Cap Negret, por favor? I can show you where."

"No problem. Jump in."

I opened the rear door and slipped into the back seat. As I did so, I felt something shove hard against my left arm so that I tumbled sideways across the seat. I turned to see a bald headed guy in a dark suit and a white open necked shirt, sliding in next to me. I pulled myself up into a sitting position.

"Excuse me. What're you doing? This cab is taken," I said.

The door locks clicked into place and I knew something was not right. The driver hit the accelerator. I reached across to the door and pulled at the handle. It wouldn't open. Child locks. I turned towards my unwanted passenger. It was then that the real unease kicked in. Even in his seated position, I could tell he must be at least six feet three inches tall. The long scar running from his jaw, just in front of his ear, all the way down below his shirt collar told me that this guy could be trouble.

"What's going on? What're you doing?" I said, trying to hold on to the hope that perhaps he did just want to share a taxi. There was no reply. I leant forward to the driver.

"Could you let me out, por favor. I think there's a mistake here. I don't mind sharing a taxi but I need to –"

"No, mistake Señor Malarkey," the driver replied.

At the mention of my name, a chill ran straight through me.

"How do you know my name? What's going on here?"

I caught the driver's eyes in the mirror as he replied.

"No need to worry about that my friend. But since we know *your* name let me introduce you to your travelling companion."

I turned to stare at the tall bald guy. He continued to look straight ahead, his face expressionless.

"The gentleman sitting next to you is called Johnny Scalapino," the driver said. "But he's better known to his friends as Scalp. And you want to know why?"

I didn't want to know why. I looked at Johnny Scalapino's bald head, which up close seemed abnormally shiny as if buffed with a soft cloth, and thought that perhaps his nickname had something to do with his lack of hair. I decided that it was the wrong time to get personal.

"I don't know. I suppose it's because of his ... because of his second name ... Scalpa ... Scala ... whatever you said."

"Scalapino, Señor Malarkey. Scalapino, is what I said. But that's not why he's called Scalp. No, it's because he likes to take a trophy. He's half Comanche Indian and half Italian, a very passionate mix. And people who don't cooperate with him ..."

His voice trailed off. If the horrendous thought that had crossed my mind about Johnny Scalapino's name needed some confirmation, it was quickly presented to me. I heard the sharp click.

I turned in the direction of the sound to see a long steel blade pointed at my neck. Scalapino had a grin on his face and he was looking directly at me. Instinctively, I backed away but with nowhere to go, I ended up with my back hard against the car door. I held both hands up in front of me.

"Wait a minute. There's definitely a mistake here. What do you want?"

Scalapino said nothing. He continued to stare. It was the driver who did the talking.

"There's no mistake Señor Malarkey. You just sit back and enjoy the ride."

7

We drove north for about fifteen minutes. I had no idea where we were. Outside it was pitch black, the lights of San Antonio left far behind. My heart thumped in my chest but I said nothing. I had to try and keep calm. Scalapino was polishing the blade of the knife on the lapel of his jacket. It seemed to me that this was to ensure that it remained visible as opposed to any real need to shine it.

Suddenly the driver pulled the car off the road onto a wide area of scrubland. He killed the engine and released the door locks.

"Get out of the car Señor Malarkey."

I did as I was told, my mind racing. I wanted to make a run for it but my legs didn't feel reliable enough, such was my fear. I pulled the door handle and got out. Scalapino got out at the same time and came round to where I stood. He grabbed me by the upper arm and led me away from the car further into the scrubland. As my eyes became accustomed to the shadows cast by the full moon, I was able to make out a line of short bushy trees ahead of us that fanned out across the scrub. When we reached the trees Scalapino stopped and pulled me round to face the road again. The only sound was the incessant, whistling chirp of crickets calling to one another in the darkness.

A bead of perspiration trickled down the side of my face. I wiped it away with a shaking hand and noticed the car headlights dim and then switch off completely. The door opened and the driver emerged. He left the car unlocked and walked towards us.

"You hear los grillos, Señor Malarkey?" he said as he approached.

"Los grillos? What ... the crickets?"

"Yes, the crickets. That's the only sound out here tonight. Nobody else here my friend. Just the three of us ... and los grillos."

His tone was ominous. I glanced around to see if Scalapino had the knife but he must have put it away as I couldn't see it.

"It's a beautiful night," the driver said, staring up at the sky.

I knew he hadn't taken me out there on a sightseeing trip and I had to find out what was going to happen.

"Look Mr ... Señor –"

"You can call me Felipe. You don't mind of I call you Matthew?" His tone had changed, a hint of friendliness appearing. It gave me hope.

"No, no, not at all ... err ... Señor ... I mean Felipe." I brushed my damp forehead and cleared my throat. "It's just that ... that I was wondering why we're here. I think there must be ... some, uh … mistaken identity or ..." My voice trailed off as I reflected on the fact that he had called me Matthew. In addition to knowing that my surname was Malarkey, he had also got my first name correct. A debate about mistaken identity in the circumstances seemed pointless.

Felipe smiled. He pointed at me and nodded towards Scalapino.

"Revisarle los bolsillos."

Scalapino stepped forward and began to rifle through my trouser pockets. He pulled out my wallet and iPhone from one and the ring box from the other. He handed everything over to Felipe. Felipe put the mobile in his trouser pocket, opened the wallet and gave it a cursory glance before throwing it in my direction. He seemed more interested in the ring box. I picked up my wallet from the ground and watched as he opened the box.

"What have we here?" he said.

There was no need for me to respond. He plucked the ring from the soft cushioned insert and held it up towards the moonlight.

"Aha, a diamond." He glanced towards me, a grin playing on his face. "Looks expensive. For your ... novia?"

"Novia?"

"Yes, in English it is a female friend ... girlfriend, you know?"

"Err, yes. We're going to get married."

Felipe placed the ring back in the box. I thought he was going to give it back to me as he had done the wallet but he didn't. He put it in his jacket pocket. Then he rubbed his hands together for a moment and glanced both right and left as if checking that we were definitely alone before he said any more. When he did speak, his tone had changed yet again, his words very deliberate, the pitch slightly deeper.

"Matthew. Mistaken identity you say. No, as I told you earlier there is no mistake. We know who you are. You *are* the man I need to speak to. Now you listen very carefully." He took a step closer. "We know that your girlfriend, is with the police. We know also that –"

The word 'police' clicked. A shock wave cut through my chest. "Wait, what has Lou –"

"Matthew ... Matthew, shut up and listen to me. Your girlfriend is police, yes? She is involved in something, with someone, very important to us. And now we need you to make her keep away. If you don't and she continues with her plan, she will be in some very big trouble. You understand?"

I didn't understand. In fact, none of it registered fully at all. The shock of hearing that he knew what Louise did was still reverberating through me. I took a deep breath to calm the jumble of thoughts that were beginning to race around my head.

"What plan? What plan are you talking about? I don't understand. I mean I ... I don't know about any plan?"

Felipe shook his head and stared at the ground for a moment. When he looked up again he turned towards Scalapino.

"Él piensa que somos estúpidos."

Scalapino laughed and pulled the knife from his pocket. A sharp click and the blade flashed in the moonlight. I took a step to my right but Scalapino moved with me intercepting whatever move he thought I might try to make.

Felipe waved a hand dismissively.

"Amigo, you think we are stupid? Don't play the fool with me. Your girlfriend, she is going to give evidence in your English courtroom against someone very important. Someone very important to our operation. She is the police that arrested him, okay. She is in this investigation. She has files, records, evidence. We know all this, so I don't care what you try and tell me about what *you* know." He leant towards me. "Now you make it your business to know. You make certain that whatever happens, she does not give evidence against our man. She must destroy these records and our man must walk free. Walk away from these charges. No evidence."

Charges. Evidence. The words flashed through my mind, meaningless for a moment in the stress of the situation. And then I remembered another word. Syndicate. *'And if we can bring him down we stand a good chance of breaking the syndicate.'* The sentence that Louise had used unfurled in my consciousness. As it did, the reality of what I was being asked to do crashed in on me. Felipe must have recognised some change in my expression or body language.

"You understand me now amigo?"

I took a deep breath and shot a glance at Scalapino. His fingers toyed with the flick knife, his expression telling me that he only needed the smallest excuse to use it. I realised I had to stay calm and try to reason with them.

"Look, Felipe, what you are asking me to do is impossible," I said. "It's messing with ... messing with the British justice system. Perverting the course of justice or something, they call it. Messing with the law and the police. I can't influence anything. You have to understand, I'm nobody. I've got no say in anything. I'm not police. And if my girlfriend destroys evidence, she will lose her job ... her career. It's not so easy."

I paused, hoping my point had made sense. It didn't take long to realise that sense wasn't what Felipe was looking for. He spat on the ground and nodded towards Scalapino who took two strides forward and wrapped a huge arm around my upper body. His other arm shot upwards and I felt the edge of the blade push hard against my Adam's apple. My body immediately went into a rigid spasm as fear and panic gripped me. My head tilted backwards, an impulsive attempt to retreat from the knife. But there was nowhere to go. Scalapino's grip tightened, his breath warm on the side of my face. Felipe took a step towards me.

"Señor Malarkey. I don't think you are understanding this situation. It is not our problem if your girlfriend loses her job in the police. You maybe prefer if she lost her life? I don't think so. This is not about what you can do or cannot do. This is about what you *must* do. If you want your girlfriend to stay safe, you have to do one simple thing for us. One thing so that she stops her silly game. There must be no case. No evidence means no case. You understand now what it is I am asking you to do?"

Asking didn't seem to be the right choice of word but it wasn't the time to be pedantic. I raised a hand to show acceptance, fearing that if I nodded I might actually slice my own throat, such was the pressure of the blade. Felipe stepped forward and eased Scalapino's hand away from my neck. I took a deep breath. I still wasn't sure how I could influence anything. What was I supposed to do? Go to Louise and tell her to stay away from a case she had been working on because there was a threat? As part of the NCA her job presented threats all the time. If I said anything, her first instinct would be to tell her colleagues and superiors. She would feel protected. But why had they come to me and not approached Louise directly? Felipe saw my confusion.

"You have a question Matthew?"

I swallowed hard and coughed to clear my throat.

"Err ... yes, I mean, why have you come straight to me? You must know that it isn't easy for me to change anything."

A smirk played on Felipe's face.

"You mean you want us to go straight to your girlfriend and threaten her?"

"No, I don't mean that. I mean, it's just ... well, if somebody wants something done they usually go to the person who can sort it out ... not that I want you to go anywhere near Lou ... my girlfriend. No, you have to stay away from her. I don't want –"

"Hey, relax Matthew. It's very simple. Your woman, she is police. We know the risk. We know if we go to her, she may act you know ... estúpido. She might talk ... especially women, you know what they are like, yes? They like to talk. They tell people things. Then this whole thing will go wrong for us. And if that happens, she will get hurt. So we need, what you call ... surance –"

"Insurance," I said, without thinking.

"Sí, insurance. We come to you because you don't want your woman to get hurt. So you will try to make sure it don't happen, no? And you know, if you won't, how you say it ... cooperate with us, you will be in trouble too. So I know you will find a way to stop this and make sure your lady does not say the wrong thing to the wrong people."

I was still confused. I had no idea how I could make Louise stay away from the case and not give evidence.

"So what have I got to do? What's this one, simple thing I have to do for you?" I wiped a trickle of sweat from my face. "I don't want anybody to get hurt here."

Felipe beckoned to Scalapino and then pointed in the direction of the car. Scalapino strode across to the vehicle, opened the boot and began to rummage inside. When he returned he was carrying a brown paper package that was sealed with parcel tape. He handed it to Felipe.

"A job for you Matthew," Felipe said, holding out the package towards me.

I didn't move.

He waved it in front of me.

"Here, you take it."

I took it from Felipe and examined it. It was heavier than I expected, irregular and lumpy as if the contents had been dumped in and the packaging simply wrapped tight around to pull it into shape. On the front side, it had what looked like initials scrawled in felt tip pen across the tape and the packaging.

"What is it?" I asked.

"Sugar. Brown sugar crystals," Felipe replied.

"Sugar? Why are you giving me sugar? I don't take sugar ... in tea ... or coffee." The situation I found myself in, the threats, the fear, now alone with two strangers in the darkness of a remote area of scrubland, had begun to throw my thoughts into chaos.

Felipe glanced at Scalapino and laughed.

"Él no toma azúcar en el café."

Scalapino let out a throaty guffaw.

"What's so funny?" I said.

"I told Johnny that you don't have sugar in your coffee," Felipe replied.

"Well I don't ... but what is this? What am I supposed to do with it?"

The amusement disappeared from Felipe's face and he stepped closer.

"This package, you take it back to London for us. Okay. When you go home, you take it with you and –"

"Hang on. What is it? Drugs? Drugs ... yeah, it's drugs isn't it? Coke. I've heard about this. I know how it works. Mules ... that's it. You think I will be a mule. Taking drugs to ... Columbia ... or ... or somewhere. It was in the newspaper. I remember now. Two girl mules in Ibiza. Yeah, San Antonio. That's it. No, I can't do that. I'll end up in a South American hell-hole jail and I won't ever get out 'cos I'm a bloke and I'll never see –"

A stinging slap across my jaw, a blow I never even saw coming, stopped me in mid flow.

"Shut up Matthew. You listen to me," Felipe shouted. "When I tell you it is sugar, then it is sugar. We don't meddle with drugs. Too many people here do that. Not for us. No. That's for los idiotas." He spat on the ground. "No, our business has got style. So you have one thing to do for me. You take this package to London. You take it and then you wait to be contacted. Once you are contacted, we will arrange to collect it and then we can talk about your girlfriend. You don't tell anybody that you have it. You don't open it. You don't do anything except you take it back to London and wait to hear from us."

"But, how ... how does that help you ... with the evidence thing? How does that stop Lou ... the police giving evidence?"

"Not your problem, amigo. You just do what we ask. Then you wait. We will be in touch. You understand?"

"And after that you leave us alone?"

Felipe didn't answer my question

"I asked you if you understand."

"Yes, but I need to know if –"

"You understand?"

Scalapino flashed the blade.

"Yes, yes ... I do. I just take the package back to London. No questions. Okay."

"Good. You put it in your case. You tell nobody. I mean nobody. If you get this wrong, your girlfriend gets hurt. Then we will come for you."

I nodded. There was not much else I could do. That seemed to be sufficient for Felipe. Then I remembered the engagement ring.

"I ... uh, I wondered if I could have the ring back please. The engagement ring?"

Felipe pulled the box from his jacket pocket, flipped the lid and examined the ring.

"You want this back, eh?"

"Yes I do. It's for ... you know, getting married. It cost me a lot of money and I ..."

He closed the box and stared at me.

"More insurance, amigo. You want the ring back, you will get it." He placed the box back into a pocket. "But only when you get the package to London. Then we will return it." He nodded towards Scalapino and threw him the car keys. Scalapino marched off towards the vehicle.

I had one more question.

"My mobile. Can I have that back? People might try to call and if I don't answer, it will look funny."

"Funny? What is funny?"

"I mean, strange, not normal. And I ... we, need things to be normal or my friends will get worried."

He shoved a hand into his trouser pocket and pulled out the mobile. He looked at the screen and then back at me.

"Okay. Here, you take it. But no calls to anybody about this. You say nothing. If you want your girlfriend to be safe you play by my rules."

I took the mobile and put it my pocket. Felipe beckoned towards the vehicle, which now had its lights on and engine running.

"Now get in the car. We will take you back to your villa."

8

They dropped me about half a mile from the villa. When I got out of the car, the shock hit me. My legs wouldn't hold me up at first and I dropped down in to a crouch by the side of the road. My heart thumped wildly beneath my shirt. I put the package down on the ground and gulped in a lungful of the warm night air. I began to knead my temples, deep, hard strokes to try to release the tension. It had little effect. A jumble of thoughts whirred through my head. How had I become involved in such a mess? I hadn't done anything. I knew that sometimes I made bad decisions and I ended up in difficulties but this time I had done nothing. Nothing, except to come out for a quiet week in the sun with my girlfriend. The thought of Louise brought me to my senses. I wanted to warn her. I raised myself up and began to walk towards the villa.

I reached the front entrance. There were no lights on. Nobody home it seemed. I walked to the front door activating a security light as I did so. I had no key. I banged the doorknocker. There was no response. No dogs. I couldn't sit outside waiting for someone to come back. I needed to be with people. James had to be out with Mofo and Panzer. Louise was either still in Ibiza Town or on her way home. I pulled out my mobile and hit her number. Four rings and it went to voicemail. I killed the call. I felt a strange sense of relief that she hadn't answered. If she had, I might have been tempted to blurt out a warning that she was in danger. I realised I couldn't do that. I had to think clearly. Next, I called Cecil's number.

He answered.

"*Geezer. Changed your mind then? Where are ya?*"

"I'm at the villa Ces. Nobody's home. Where are you?"

"*I'm down the West End Strip, ain't I. Fucking Sodom and Gomorrah. You ain't seen nothing like it. Geezers off their faces, birds can hardly speak. I reckon half of 'em are on the old Columbian talc mate. Place is kicking off. Bars doing two for one and then loading you up with shots. Half the frigging booze they sell looks like it's ending up on the deck. I'm sticking to the floor in this place out in the lanes. It's fucking mayhem. You coming down?*"

After the relatively civilised week I'd spent in restaurants and cool bars, Cecil's description of the West End didn't have a lot of appeal but I didn't feel like being on my own.

"Don't sound much like the Sunset bars," I said.

"*Mate, trust me it ain't. Funny how you can walk five minutes from some blinding boutique bar and end up in a place that stinks like a gladiatorial arena.*"

"Okay. Tell me where you are and I'll try and get a taxi somewhere. What happened to the two girls?"

"*They're still here geeze. Been showing me the ropes ain't they? Yeah, you may as well join the party. Hang on while I find out the name of this bar.*"

"Just text it Ces. I'm going to find a taxi. See you soon."

"*Mate, we're moving on. Al reckons we should go to Gallery Bar. Blinding music up there. Hang on geeze ...*"

The call went quiet but I could hear the dull thud of a speaker pumping out heavy bass in the background.

"*Yeah, mate it's straight up the main lane, near Capone's. See ya there.*"

I cut the call. To my right three wheelie bins stood in a covered alcove against a wall. A small ledge ran along its base. I walked over, placed the package on the ledge behind the bin nearest the villa, and then went back out to the road and began to walk. I had been walking for just a few minutes when I picked up a taxi. A short trip later and I got out near the harbour and just a few metres from the area Cecil had referred to as '*Sodom and Gomorrah.*'

I was hit by a mind boggling array of sights and sounds - stag parties, hen parties, guys in fancy dress, girls in various states of undress, kebab shops, fish and chips shops, British pubs and karaoke bars, a lurid wave of colours against a black night sky, all crammed into a narrow lane that ascended on a shallow uphill route away from the main harbour. I pushed my way through the crowds spilling out of bars, a dense mass of bodies, weaving in and out in some sort of uncoordinated waltz from venue to venue, past brightly lit signage that beckoned the unthinking to indulge in yet more mayhem. The whole area was a cacophony of noise, a hubbub of chatter, squeals and high pitched yells, none of it making any sense as gangs of young guys chanted incoherent war cries at nobody in particular. I tried to avoid the insistent African guys selling watches, sunglasses and rubber, penis-shaped noses. Why exactly someone would want to walk around with a rubber penis dangling from their face, was not immediately clear to me.

Halfway along the avenue I found the Gallery Bar and ducked inside. Cecil and the two Danish girls were positioned right at the back in a prime spot next to the bar.

"Alright mate? You made it then. Got a beer for ya."

Cecil handed me a bottle. Estrid and Alida raised their glasses in greeting.

"You come to join us," Estrid said, a broad smile lighting her face.

I ignored the remark, took a long slurp from the bottle and sat down next to Cecil.

"Ces, we need to talk."

"No prob geezer. What's on your mind?"

"No, I mean, talk … not here. I … uh … look … somewhere …" I glanced at the girls. "… somewhere quiet."

Cecil let out a loud snort.

"Fucking quiet? Here? You winding me up mate?"

"No, I'm not. It's important."

"Geezer, you're right in the middle of the West End Strip. You seen it? There ain't nowhere quiet. Just say what you gotta say.

71

Nobody's gonna hear you anyway. Half of them are off their faces and the rest are only interested in getting laid." He leant towards me, his voice dropping into a conspiratorial whisper. "And talking of getting laid, mate, it's game on here if you play it right. Wing man … remember?"

"Ces, I'm not interested. I just need five minutes. Something's happened and I –"

My mobile buzzed in my pocket. I pulled it out and glanced at the screen. A text from Louise.

'Hope ur having a good nite. Left a key on the ledge behind the first wheelie bin in case ur late. x'

Wheelie bin. For a moment I panicked as I remembered where I'd left the package. Behind the bin, the third one as you walk towards the door. The first one she'd said. She must mean the first as you come in from the street. Or did she mean the first one as you come out of the villa? That would be the third one as you come off the street. The one where I had left the package. But she hadn't mentioned a package. But then she wouldn't, not in a text. What if she'd found it?

I stood up abruptly.

"Ces, I have to go. Talk tomorrow." I nodded towards the girls. "Sorry ladies. Have a good … you know."

Cecil sat open mouthed, his drink poised in mid-air. I didn't wait for a response.

I got back to the villa within forty minutes. The first thing I did was check the bins. To my relief the package was still where I had left it. I checked the remaining bins and found the door key behind the first one leading in from the street. I stood for a moment and took a deep breath. I had overreacted. I realised that, but my whole trip had been thrown into turmoil. I had wanted to tell Cecil what had happened just so I could share the problem but now I realised that it was best kept to myself. With Cecil's impulsive nature, he was sure to react and I could see that leading to more problems. I resolved to keep the matter to myself. It was the best chance I had of keeping Louise safe.

9

James had arranged to take us out on one of his boats the following day. It was our last full day before we had to return home. A mini bus picked us up after breakfast. We stopped by the Blau Parc and collected Cecil and Sheryl. Cecil seemed unusually quiet.

"Did you have a good time last night?" Sheryl asked as she strapped her seat belt on.

I glanced at Cecil before answering.

"Err … yes, not bad. We did the strip. Pretty busy down there."

"Busy. Busy's not the word," James cut in. "They do more dope down there than they do booze. The streets are running on Charlie."

"Charlie?" Sheryl queried.

"Yeah, coke. It's all changed. Back in the day, it was booze. You knew where you stood then. Now it's all pills and powders."

"We didn't see any of that," I said, catching Eleanor's eye. "We just had a few beers."

It was mid-afternoon before I got the chance to talk to Cecil properly. James had anchored the boat, named in honour of his Clare roots, *Man of Quilty*, some way off Cala Conta beach. Louise, Sheryl and Eleanor were enjoying a swim in the clear water. Cecil and I were on deck sipping a beer each when James approached wearing a pair of garish, multi-coloured beach shorts.

"You two fellas coming in for a dip?"

Cecil waved his beer bottle dismissively.

"Nah mate. You're alright. Give it a miss for a minute. Bit of a heavy one last night."

"Sure, won't a good swim clear your head Cecil. It'll liven you up no fear," James replied.

Cecil put his beer down and picked up a bottle of sun lotion.

"Maybe later geezer. Gonna soak up a bit more of the old currant bun. Last day and all that."

James walked to the edge of the deck.

"Suit yourselves boys. I'll join you for a beer after."

In a perfectly executed dive, he went off the edge of the boat and hit the water. The resulting splash had barely disappeared before Cecil was on my case.

"So, tell me then geezer, what was the big rush last night? And what was you going on about? All that, we gotta talk somewhere quiet shit."

"Oh, nothing Ces. I wasn't thinking straight. Just the mayhem down that strip, you know."

"Too frigging right you wasn't thinking straight. Screwed it right up for me, didn't ya?"

"Screwed what up? What d'you mean?"

"With them two birds. Estrid and Al."

"How's that then Ces? I didn't do anything."

"That's just it geezer. You was supposed to be the wingman."

"No I wasn't. You went off on your own if you remember. You were quite happy meeting up with the two of them earlier on. I just came later. By then I thought you'd have sorted it out."

Cecil frowned and squirted a shot of sun lotion into his hand. He began to rub it vigorously over his chest.

"Yeah, but even numbers always work. That Estrid fancied you mate. I told you that earlier. Would've worked out I reckon but you had to go say you weren't interested. Out loud too. That killed it. Then you buggered off."

"I had to get back mate. Louise texted."

"Yeah? Go running when your bird texts do ya? You was on a lads' night and she knew that. Anyway, you're doing the old engaged mumble tonight aren't ya so what was all the rushing after your bird about?"

I gazed out across the ocean seeking some sort of coherent explanation that wouldn't encourage further curiosity. A string of wispy clouds threaded their way across the blueness of the sky, the dark silhouette of a paraglider the only blot across its expanse. The sea shimmered silver, the gentle water flow rolling the sunlight across its surface. A light breeze made the mid-afternoon temperature tolerable.

No creative explanation was forthcoming. I turned towards Cecil.

"Change of plan Ces. Not doing it tonight."

"No? Why not? Changed your mind?" Cecil saw my hesitation. He grabbed his beer, took a swig and then turned his full gaze on me. "Wait a minute. Don't tell me. You ain't got the ring have ya?"

I picked at the label on my own beer bottle.

"No … it's not that … it's just that –"

"Don't bullshit me mate. You been banging on about asking Louise to marry you all trip and now when it come to the crunch, you ain't doing it? I don't think so. You ain't got the ring have ya?"

My lack of response told Cecil more than I could have done by agreeing with him.

"I knew it. Didn't I tell you not to be running around with a fucking two grand ring in your pocket? You lost it, ain't ya?"

I scratched my head in frustration at being drawn in to the conversation.

"Not exactly. I … I got … I got mugged."

"Mugged?"

"Yeah, two blokes took the ring as I was going back to the villa."

"That's what you wanted to chat about?" Cecil hit full flow. "So who were these two geezers? They must've seen you flashing the ring in the bar you nob. Told ya, didn't I? What happened then? They jump you? Knives? How'd they get the ring off you?

They take any money or anything else? You still got your watch on. They must've known you had the ring."

I necked the reminder of my beer and tried to change the subject.

"You want another one mate?"

"Yeah, I do but then you'd better sit back down and give me the full story. No way I'm having a mate of mine fucking robbed and the geezers getting away with it."

As I went across the deck to the icebox that James had filled with beer and soft drinks, I realised that Cecil was not going to let me fob him off with a soft explanation about the missing ring. Perhaps I had to trust him and tell him the full story. He was my best friend. If I couldn't trust my best friend who could I trust? I reasoned that it was better to have someone on my side rather than shoulder my problem alone. I pulled a couple of bottles from the box and returned to Cecil.

"Okay. You ready for this?" I said and handed him a beer. "But whatever I tell you, you have to promise … swear, that you won't say anything to anybody. Right? It's our friendship Ces. You can't say a word."

"Alright mate. Cut the fucking drama and talk."

Over the next ten minutes or so, I told Cecil about my meeting with Felipe and Scalapino. I told him exactly what had happened to the ring and I told him about the parcel. He listened intently as I talked and didn't interrupt once. But I could tell from the glint in his brown eyes that his mind was working overtime. Finally, when I had finished, he spoke.

"Mate, there's some odd shit going down here. Who are these two geezers? Maybe James'll have a clue. He's a local ain't he? We gotta understand what we're dealing with."

"Ces, no. You can't talk to James. I told you. Nobody. I can't risk this going wrong. Look, like I said, all I know is there is some connection with this big investigation Louise has been involved in. It must be bigger than I thought for them to be keen enough to stop it. These blokes are not two-bit muggers out to take some poor tourist for a sucker. No, it's bigger than that and I can't take

76

risks. They asked me to deliver their package to London and then wait for contact."

"Yeah, but deliver it to who? And what's in it? You can't just carry a package back on a plane mate without knowing what's in it. Supposing it was explosives? You know, blow the fucking plane out the sky. You gotta find out what's in it."

Explosives. I hadn't thought of that. I stood up and began to pace the deck.

"But why would they want to blow up the plane?"

"Well it would take Louise out of the equation for a start. Might solve their problem."

I picked up my beer. "But what good would that do? The case, whatever it is, would still go ahead wouldn't it? No, they want to make the evidence go away. Even if they did blow up the plane Louise's evidence would still be on file. That don't make sense. No, they want her to pull the evidence, tamper with it. I don't know how the package fits in but I have no choice but to co-operate."

"So what's the case she's been working on then?"

"I don't know. She won't tell me. Listen, we need to just –"

A sound from behind stopped me in mid-sentence. I turned to see James climbing up the ladder at the back of the boat. I crouched down next to Cecil, my voice dropping to a whisper.

"Ces, we just need to go along with this. I've tucked the parcel away in my suitcase. I don't know anything about explosives but it feels too small, too compact. I mean there'd be wires, batteries or something, wouldn't there? I can't open it either. They've got some sort of signature on it. If I tear open the package, it'll cut the signature and they'll know it's been opened. We'll be back home tomorrow. We can check things out then." I stood up as James approached. "Good swim James?"

James grabbed a towel and ran it over his hair.

"Grand. Sure the water's great. Nice and warm. You should give it a try the pair of you."

"We will," I said. "Anyway, you must be ready for a beer now after all that exercise." I walked towards the icebox. James followed me. I pulled out a cold beer and handed it to him.

"There you go. Cheers."

"Cheers," he said as he screwed off the cap. He took a long swig, let out a low belch as the bubbles caught his throat and stared for a moment out across the ocean. When he turned back towards me, he spoke in a whisper.

"So tell me young fella, what's happening with this engagement thing you were on about before you came out? It's your last night and you're a bit slow on the uptake. If it's happening here then tonight's got to be the night doesn't it?"

I hadn't expected the question. James picked up on my hesitation.

"Something wrong Matt? You and Louise alright?"

"Yeah ... yeah. Fine James. It's just that ... I ... err ... well, I feel pretty stupid really. I haven't got the ring."

"What? Ah, no. You lost the feckin thing?"

For a moment, I thought about what Cecil had said about talking to James to see if he would have any idea about who might have hijacked me. But I thought better of it. The threat was too real.

"No, nothing like that. I forgot it. Left it at home in London."

James laughed.

"Ah, you eejit Matt. What's wrong with you anyway? The prospect of a holiday took your eye of the ball no doubt. I wouldn't worry about it son. Sure I won't say a word. Just make sure you get the deed done when you get back home. She's a good girl that Louise. You won't find many like her."

10

There was no reason for it now that we had arrived back at Gatwick. No reason to feel the unease with such intensity. The aircraft had not been blown out of the sky. The package was still safely tucked up in my luggage as far as I knew and I should have felt relieved to be home. But as I hoisted my suitcase from the conveyor belt, I felt the trepidation. I had been put in an impossible position, I feared for Louise and I couldn't tell her a thing. I just needed to get my bag, get out of the airport and get home. My thoughts were interrupted abruptly.

"Excuse me pal. That's my bag you got there."

I glanced in the direction of the voice. A tall bloke in a tight blue t-shirt, his cheeks burned red by the sun, stood to one side pointing at the trolley on which I had stacked the bag. I followed his outstretched finger towards the trolley.

"Sorry," I said. "Your bag? I think there may be a mistake."

The bag I had picked up was a large black canvas, two-wheeled trolley exactly like the one I had packed that morning.

"No mistake pal. That's my luggage and you look like you were about to walk off with it."

I caught the hint of menace in his eyes. The thought crossed my mind that perhaps his ruddy features were not entirely due to sun exposure. Just as I was about to respond he made a grab for the bag. I couldn't afford to lose my bag. Instinctively I reacted and jumped forward to prevent him taking it. As I lurched forward, my left foot came down hard against the base of the trolley. The sudden impetus caused it to swing wildly round on its wheels where it caught a very pregnant woman, who was standing behind the ruddy faced guy, just below the knees. She reeled back from the impact but, in an effort to counteract the sudden shift in her balance and to save herself from going over, she wheeled round on one leg. Her advanced state of pregnancy was clearly a drawback in maintaining her stability and her efforts were to no avail. With a high-pitched shriek, she toppled straight over onto the moving conveyor belt. As she fell, her shoulder bag flew high into the air spilling what appeared to be a shop load of Mars Bars across the floor. I watched helplessly as the conveyor belt moved on, carrying the woman, who was struggling to right herself, past astonished travellers. It was the quick thinking of two guys who had just retrieved their own luggage that saved the situation from getting any worse. One of them managed to grab her right leg and spin her round so that her feet were dangling over the floor, while the other grabbed her hand and pulled her into a seated position. From there they pulled her onto her feet just as the carousel came to a halt.

I stood rooted to the spot as the woman clasped her hands around her bulging stomach. She was clearly disorientated and seemed to have no idea what had caused her to topple over. I grabbed her bag from the floor and began to scoop up all the Mars Bars that were strewn around the base of the carousel. There must have been at least forty of them. And then I remembered my luggage. I turned to see the guy I had confronted, walking away with the trolley. I caught up with him and grabbed the trolley handle.

"Sorry mate. This is definitely my case. You've made a mistake."

He wasn't persuaded.

"I told you, didn't I? No mistake pal. Now get your hands off this trolley before I break your bleedin arm."

My instinct was to avoid further confrontation, an instinct that was kicking in strongly as I stared at the bloke's bulging eyes, but my whole being was focussed on the package and the fear of losing it. A confrontation in the airport seemed more favourable than losing the package and facing the threat of repercussions from the Spanish villains. I reached out for the case. At precisely the same moment, Louise appeared next to me.

"What's going on?" she said, staring past me at Mr Angry.

"Err … nothing … it's ok honey. Just a mix up with the bags. I was just –"

"No mix up love. Matey here's taken a shine to my bag. Reckons it's his and he's chasing me round the bleedin airport. He with you?"

Louise ignored the question and took a step forward, the palm of her right hand held up in a placatory gesture.

"Hang on." She bent forward, inspected the bag and then pointed to a label. "I'm sorry, I'm afraid this is our bag. It's got his details on it," she said, pointing at me. "It's a Mandarina Duck. What's yours?"

"Samsonite."

"Well they do look similar I suppose. Easy mistake to make."

I felt the blood rush to my cheeks.

"Yeah, told you mate. It's mine ... a Mandarin Duck"

Louise smiled. "No, Mandarina. It's a brand Matthew. Don't worry about it. You've got your case. It's just a mistake. Everybody's a little tired with the travelling. Now let's leave this gentleman to find his own luggage."

I pulled my case from the trolley.

"And I don't know why you've got that trolley. You're bag has wheels," Louise added.

Mr Angry's face broke into a sneer. "Wanker."

"C'mon Matthew, leave it," Louise said, tugging on my arm.

"Too much sun. Fried what little brain he's got," I muttered to nobody in particular but Mr Angry had obviously heard. He turned towards me.

"What'd you say pal?"

I didn't need any more confrontation. I was tired. I wanted to get home. I'd had enough stress.

"Sorry. I was talking to my girlfriend."

He didn't look convinced.

"I was just saying ... err ... too much son. Flying is a pain is it not." I waited for a reaction. He seemed confused that I might refer to my girlfriend as 'son.' I took advantage of his hesitation. "You know, long day and all that."

He seemed satisfied. With a dismissive grin, he turned and walked off.

When he was out of earshot, Louise turned to me, her face a mix of concern and curiosity.

"What's the matter with you Matthew? You've been acting weird all day. And whose handbag is that?" She reached out and grabbed the shoulder bag I had picked up off the floor and looked inside. "Whose is it? It's full of Mars Bars. What are you doing with –?"

"Oh shit ... it's that pregnant ..." I stared around me looking for the woman I had knocked over. I spotted her by the carousel with two police officers who had found her a chair. "It's ... it's that lady's over there," I said, pointing in her direction. "She dropped it and I ...wait there Louise."

At that point, we were interrupted by Cecil.

"You alright, geeze? You look a bit off colour. Mind you, it's mayhem round that carousel. You'd think they was never gonna get their bags back the way they're all pushing each other about to get to the front. Then some bird's fallen on the frigging belt."

"Where's Sheryl?" Louise asked.

"She's over there waiting for her case. I'm just going back to help her. You got your bag yet darlin?"

"No. I'll come with you. Matthew, you go and give that lady her handbag back before she gets those two cops to arrest you. We'll take your luggage."

I reunited the pregnant woman with her bag. She was very grateful. She explained that she had cravings for Mars Bar Couer, a brand she couldn't get in England so had brought a job lot back with her. The shock of her accident seemed to be wearing off and I was pleased that she had no idea that I had been the cause. I took my leave and went back to find the others.

As I walked around to the far side of the carousel Cecil, Sheryl and Louise approached with their luggage in tow. Cecil pulled me to one side.

"Mate, Louise was saying you're behaving strange, starting a row with some geezer. You got to keep a low profile. Don't be drawing attention to yourself. The place is full of frigging cameras."

"I know Ces. And it wasn't my fault. Some bloke was walking off with my case. I'm a bit on edge anyway. I can't help it. I'm just ... you know, worried ... anxious."

"Listen mate. Chill. Take your case, just follow me, nice and calm through the old nothing to declare channel, okay. No dramas. Cool as you like. Out the other side, we get a cab and we're home in an hour. You with me?"

"Okay. I'm on it Ces. Lead the way."

Cecil ran his fingers through his hair, nodded to the girls and began to walk purposefully towards the customs channel.

11

It was as I walked beneath the '*Nothing to Declare*' signage that my composure began to unravel. I had entered a space where even the calmest of people experience a moment's paranoia. But at that point I was not the calmest of people. The channel was really just a short corridor framed on one side by a wall and on the other by a row of free standing partitions beyond which were several metal counter tops. The area contained by the partitions was completely deserted. Ahead of me there was a blank wall, and a turn to the left that was the exit out into the airport arrivals area.

My head throbbed with anxiety. A stream of random thoughts fought for coherence. My instinct was to race through the channel and get to arrivals as fast as I could. But that would definitely look suspect. If I ambled through slowly it would look too nonchalant and that would attract attention too. Yet there were no officials around. No sign of CCTV even. Was I being watched? Of course I wasn't. I had walked through the '*Nothing to Declare*' channel. I had done so many times and there was never anyone there. Why would anyone be bothered by some tourists from Ibiza?

I tried to focus on Cecil's steady gait. He didn't appear too concerned. His pace seemed about right but then again he wasn't carrying a package whose contents were totally unknown to him. I concentrated on his back, my eyes fixed, the suitcase a dead weight as I dragged it after me. The package hidden inside had taken on the proportions of a massive boulder. I felt like a wildebeest crossing a crocodile infested river, taking the risk to make it to the lush grasslands ahead.

We were only a few paces from the turn towards the arrivals hall when I heard the voice.

"Excuse me Sir. Could you step over here please."

I turned instinctively. A tall man in a pale blue shirt and dark tie stood slightly behind me and to my left. I swallowed hard as I took in the sight. The shirt had dark blue epaulettes with some sort of insignia embroidered on them. A uniform. A uniform meant official. Official meant a problem.

"Could you just step over here Sir," he repeated.

"Me?" I asked, although there was no mistaking who he meant.

To my right I caught sight of Cecil, hands waving animatedly, in conversation with another uniformed officer. A fog of indecision and insecurity alighted upon me. I stood rooted to the spot for a moment. 'Me,' I repeated in my head. I heard the officer's voice again, this time more distant as if he had turned down the volume.

"This way, Sir."

I turned towards him again only to see Louise and Sheryl approach.

"What's the problem, officer?" Louise said.

"There's no problem madam. Just a routine spot check. Now move along please."

Louise shrugged and turned towards me.

"I'll wait for you in arrivals Matthew. I'm sure you won't be long."

Panic stricken, my thoughts went haywire. Won't be long? How about fifteen years? That long enough? If he searched my bag, he would find the package. It had to be illegal. Villains don't give you legal stuff to take to another country. If it were legal, they would take it themselves or send it by post.

I watched for a moment as Louise and Sheryl headed for the turn at the end the customs channel and then disappeared from sight. Around me a steady stream of travellers were walking through, a mix of suntanned smiling faces, relaxed in the knowledge they had done nothing wrong, the occasional glance cast in my direction in that 'rather you than me' way that drivers eyeball an accident on the motorway. Why had they picked on me? It must have been the commotion in the baggage hall. Cecil was right. I had drawn attention to myself. Odd behaviour by passengers. Perhaps that's what they looked for.

"Sir. Please, this way," the customs officer said again, an arm extended in command, rather than invitation, towards the partitioned area. I looked around to see Cecil being led in the same direction by the other officer.

Once inside the partitioned area, both customs officers positioned themselves behind the metal surfaced counter tops and pulled on light blue surgical gloves. I was asked to place my bag on one of the counters.

"Where are you travelling from Sir?"

My mind went blank.

"Where? Erm ..."

To my right I heard Cecil's voice as he answered the same question.

"Ibiza, mate."

I caught his eye. A surreptitious wink played fleetingly in my direction, intended to reassure me, keep me calm. He looked cool. But then he wasn't carrying an illegal package in his suitcase that was about to be uncovered. I took a deep breath and licked my dry lips.

"Yes, me too. Ibiza. Just got off the ... err ... flight."

"Business or pleasure?"

"Pleasure. Holiday ... with my girlfriend. I was getting engaged ... to be married. We've been together for a while."

For a split second, I hoped that it was just a question and answer session. A routine spot check he had told Louise. Perhaps that's exactly what it was. They had to do something, the occasional check on 'nothing to declare' travellers just to ensure that it wasn't abused. Let the public know they were watching.

"And is this your bag, Sir?"

"Err ... yes ... yes it is?"

"Did you pack it yourself?"

"Yes, yes I did." There was no other answer.

"Has anyone asked you to carry anything for them?"

I gulped hard as I considered the question. I clung on to the hope that this might still be routine questioning.

"Carry anything? No ... not that I'm ..." I thought of Louise, and Felipe's threat. "No."

And then I heard the rasp of the zip on Cecil's suitcase. I knew exactly what it was even before I looked over. Even then I hoped that they would be satisfied with a search of just one suitcase.

Those hopes were shattered immediately.

"Sir, I have been authorised to search your bag. I will record the examination and anything found. Could you open the bag for me please."

I nearly asked why but something told me not to. I tried to buy some time.

"Is that necessary? It was just a holiday with my girlfriend. We were getting engaged as I said. Only we didn't ... not because we didn't want to or anything. Just that I lost the ring ... somewhere. I'm right in the doghouse now, you know." I hoped he would feel sorry for me. "Women eh? Trying to make it up to her. Supposed to be going for a big meal later ... right now in fact ... take her mind off it. She's looking forward to it. I expect she's hungry, waiting out there for –"

"The case Sir. Open it."

I struggled to find one more sentence that would distract him and get him on my side but his direct, hard gaze throttled whatever words were racing around in my head before they had time to organise themselves into anything resembling coherence. I gulped in a mouthful of air, my chest pounding beneath my shirt as I realised he meant business. There was no option but to co-operate.

"I ... yes, just getting the keys," I said and fumbled in my pockets. My hand found the suitcase key in my right trouser pocket but I ignored it. A last gasp attempt to delay the inevitable.

"Err ... sorry ... I think my girlfriend might have the key. What with me losing the ring and all that, I don't think she trusts me with anything." An accompanying half-hearted chuckle didn't seem to be making any inroads with the serious faced customs officer. "I could ... erm ... go outside and get her to open it. She's waiting for me. Probably starving too." I grabbed the handle and dragged the case off the counter." It hit the floor with a thump.

"Hold it right there Sir. You're going nowhere. You attempt to leave and you'll be arrested. Put the case back. If you don't have the keys, I can cut it open." He reached down below the counter and brought out a pair of scissors.

I glanced around at Cecil who took a step towards me. Behind him his case lay fully open, two stacks of clothes neatly piled to one side. His brown eyes focussed directly on my face, as if he was attempting some sort of mystic thought transference.

"Easy geezer. I think you *have* got the keys. You know, when Louise had to open it at Ibiza airport to get your passport out. She called you a dickhead, yeah, for holding the place up at the check in. Remember? Yeah, she gave 'em to you then. That's right, I remember now 'cos the case was lying open on the floor when you was both handing over the tickets and passports. Mate, easy to forget with all that commotion round the desk." Cecil turned to face the customs officer. "I mean people got no patience nowadays. Geezer makes a mistake and leaves his passport in his case, don't mean you gotta crowd him out, frigging pushing and shoving, does it? I mean everybody's gonna get on the plane. What's with all the rush?"

I was gobsmacked. Cecil was dropping me in it. Why would he do that? I stared hard at him seeking an explanation or at least a retraction of what he had just said. His eyes narrowed into an intense, focused stare. He bit his bottom lip and then bared his teeth slightly. In that moment, it dawned on me what he was up to.

"Blimey, you're right Ces. I have got them." I fumbled through my pockets again and this time pulled out the suitcase keys. I nodded towards the customs officer. "I'm sorry. I thought these were my ... err ... briefcase keys ... for work. Been a long day. Sorry about that."

"Just open the case, Sir. We've wasted enough time. I am sure you want to be on your way to your starving girlfriend," the customs officer said, nodding towards his colleague.

I gripped the key and slid it into the small padlock that held the two sides of the zip mechanism together. The package would be uncovered, no question of that but Cecil had created the possibility that the case had not been totally in my possession all of the time, giving me a possible explanation even if it was barely believable. I had to go with it. Feign surprise, shock at the inevitable discovery. Stay cool and act the part.

I pulled the two zips apart and flipped the lid in the most nonchalant manner I could despite the fact that inside I was a shaking wreck. With the case fully open the customs officer began to lift out the items of clothing one by one and place them alongside the case. He jotted some notes onto a form as he took the items out. At the adjacent counter, his colleague had given the nod to Cecil to repack his case having found nothing of interest. As he slowly repacked his belongings, Cecil kept his gaze fixed on what was happening just a few yards away at my counter.

I turned my attention back to my case. I knew it would be only moments before the package was discovered. But I was ready. The customs officer continued his slow, meticulous search. A pair of jeans was unwrapped, shaken out and then folded back up and placed on the pile. Two t-shirts similarly treated. My washbag was rummaged through and placed to one side. Three shirts that I had folded and placed in a neat line across the length of the case that very morning were removed. And there it was.

I reacted first.

"What the bloody hell is that? That's not mine."

In an overly exaggerated lunge, I shot out a hand and snatched the parcel. At the same time, I grabbed the scissors that had been left lying on the counter top and began to stab and cut frantically at the brown paper. The two officers failed to react to my sudden frenzied action and stayed rooted to the spot in surprise. By the time they had recovered some composure I had created a massive split down the middle and through the triple-wrapped paper, wide enough for me to tear it apart. I had no time to see what it contained. In an instant the officer who had been searching my case, vaulted across the counter to prevent me causing any further damage but, in his enthusiasm, he misjudged his leap and his momentum caused him to slide off the shiny surface directly into me. We hit the floor in a heap. The parcel flew from my hands showering a pile of brown, shiny lumps that resembled soiled stones, into the air and across the floor.

Cecil cut the gap between us in two paces. He grabbed the customs officer by the shoulders and pulled him off me. I rolled onto my side and got to my knees. Alongside me, Cecil had started to scoop up the parcel contents but was stopped by the other customs officer.

"Drop it. Leave it there and move away."

Cecil stood up, ran a hand through his hair a couple of times and then gestured to the officer.

"Sorry mate. Just trying to help. No problem."

In the following few minutes the area was filled with five more officers. Somebody must have been watching but I still could not see any cameras. Order was restored within seconds. Cecil and I were separated and taken into private rooms where a further search was carried out. Two hours later, I was informed that I was being arrested in connection with a smuggling offence and taken to see the designated Custody Officer.

From there it all went horribly wrong.

12

The designated Custody Officer was called Travis. Thin build with a goatee beard, his pale face suggested that he spent most of the working day in his office. It crossed my mind that he must be fed up of looking at sun burnt holidaymakers, such was the stern frown that caused his dark eyebrows to gravitate towards one another. He was sitting at a small desk and he indicated that I should take the seat opposite him. As I sat down, he shuffled several sheets of paper into a neat pile and placed them to one side.

"Mr Malarkey, as you now know our detection officers have conducted a thorough investigation into the contents of the package you were carrying and have established that it contained, predominantly, unrefined brown sugar cane crystals."

Sugar? That was what Felipe had said was in it. The customs officers had told me something else. So maybe they were wrong. Perhaps I was in the clear after all. But why would Felipe give me a pack of sugar to carry to the UK? I stared expectantly at Travis, a sense of relief and reprieve washing over me. It didn't last long. The word 'predominantly' suddenly skewered its way into my skull.

"Err ... but your detection officers have arrested me for ..." I hesitated, hoping to see a softening in Travis's features. He leant forward, his hands clasped together, his elbows resting on the edge of the table.

"Yes, diamond smuggling, Mister Malarkey. For the most part

your package did contain sugar. However, as explained to you by the detection officers, mixed in with the sugar was a quantity of diamonds. Conflict diamonds to be precise. In other words, illegal diamonds."

I sat back in my chair and stared at the ceiling. I had no immediate response, my mind focussed on 'illegal.'

"Mister Malarkey?"

Travis's tone caused me to focus.

"It's ... it's not my package. I mean ... it's just not mine. I don't know anything about diamonds."

"That *was* your suitcase that we searched was it not, Mister Malarkey? You did have the keys after all."

"Well, yes, it was, but the package ... I mean, the package wasn't mine." And then I blurted out the words that would incriminate me. "I thought it was just sugar."

Travis sat upright, his eyes firmly fixed on mine, his expression sombre and unchanging.

"So you *were* aware of the package then?"

"What?" I realised my error. "Yes ... but ... no. Not aware. I mean, not *aware* aware. I didn't know that ... I just thought –"

"Just thought what?"

My head began to pound. I could feel my temperature rising as my face reddened. Cecil had given me a possible get out that I had failed to take. Leaving the suitcase open at the airport after I had retrieved my passport, may not have been the most original idea but it could have cast some doubt about how the package had ended up in my case. My mind struggled through a gamut of thoughts, seeking a reasonable explanation now that I had dug myself a hole. There was no way I could risk telling Travis about the threat to Louise. I knew that the package had some connection with evidence that Louise had discovered but now that I knew what the contents were, it made even less sense than when I had questioned Felipe. How was that supposed to stop Louise's evidence? It seemed I was just a courier for diamonds, but why? My mind jumped back to the night I had been picked up.

Insurance.

Felipe had used the word insurance. Maybe that was it. Some sort of test to see if I was reliable. If I delivered the package as instructed, they would know that I was intimidated and that I would not risk going to the police, and nor would I take a risk with Louise's safety. But if the package was not delivered, what then? Maybe that was okay too as long as I kept my mouth shut and waited for contact.

"Mister Malarkey. You just thought what?"

The question hung there for a second. I had made my mind up. I could not say anything that would put Louise in danger.

"Err, sorry. Yes, I *was* aware of the package. I mean, aware that it was sugar. It was a ... a present." As I said it, I panicked. Who gives sugar as a present? "I just thought that it was sugar crystals so left it in my case and walked through the nothing to declare channel. I was just as surprised as you to hear there were diamonds inside."

Travis scratched his head and looked down at the sheaf of papers on the table, his face barely hiding his scepticism.

"A present? So where did you get it?"

"I ... err ... bought it. A market stall, in Ibiza Town. There's loads of stalls there. Can't remember which one to be honest. I'd never seen raw sugar crystals before so I ..." I knew that I was just spouting words and digging myself a hole. I tried the naive card. "Look, how would diamonds get mixed up with sugar crystals anyway?"

Travis pursued his lips and then let out a deep sigh, as if boredom had kicked in.

"You tell me Mister Malarkey. As I say, your so called present contained a quantity of uncut rough diamonds mixed within the sugar crystals, estimated value around seven thousand US dollars. You do not have a valid Kimberley Process Certificate for these diamonds and therefore they do not comply with the Kimberley Process Certification Scheme. In addition, the diamonds are not in the regulation tamper resistant sealed container as required under the scheme. In these circumstances, by walking through the 'Nothing to Declare' channel you have attempted to conceal banned or restricted material being brought into the UK and therefore you may have committed a criminal offence, which is why you have been arrested."

A criminal offence. The words seemed to prevent me from making any rational response as they sunk in. It was probably just as well as the only response that I could have given, that I could have carried off with conviction, was the truth. And that was not an option.

Travis gathered his papers and pushed back his chair.

"Thank you for now, Mister Malarkey. We have some further enquiries to make so I have to inform you that you will be detained until they have been completed. My colleagues will look after you in the meantime." He stood up and turned towards the door.

"Wait," I said. "The certificate thing. Could I get one now? You know, to cover the diamonds?"

Travis smiled and gave a slight shrug.

"I'm afraid not Mister Malarkey. There are several procedures to go through when you import rough diamonds and a number of documents to be checked *before* a certificate can be issued. In any case a certificate must be obtained in the country from which you are importing the merchandise."

"But I'm not importing diamonds," I said, exasperated that my one hope of avoiding a criminal offence had been stymied.

"It appears not. At this juncture smuggling seems to be the more appropriate term," Travis replied, as he opened the door to leave.

I was detained for another six hours whilst Travis and his team carried out further enquiries. Finally, the full extent of my predicament became apparent when Travis returned to question me further.

"Mister Malarkey, I have checked the manifest for your flight from Ibiza and I wonder if you might confirm the name of your travelling companion." He placed a green file on the table and opened it to reveal several pages of hand written notes.

"Travelling companion?" I immediately focussed on Cecil. He

had been part of the search. "You mean Cecil? Cecil Delaney. He hasn't done anything. Have you released him?"

"Yes we have but I didn't mean him. I was referring to the lady."

"Oh, yes, Cecil was with Sheryl. They travelled back with –"

"That's the Canadian national. I'm not interested in her. I was referring to the lady that travelled out with you and returned on today's flight."

"You mean Louise? Louise Penny. She's my girlfriend. Why?" I detected the brief smile that flitted across Travis's face.

"Thank you Mister Malarkey. I just wanted the name confirmed. She's a police officer, detective rank, I understand?"

A wave of unease began to work its way up from the pit of my stomach.

"Well, yes, she is but ... but what's that got to do with this? She's not involved."

"Involved?"

"You know what I mean. She didn't even know I was carrying ... I'd bought the ... err, sugar."

Travis sat back in his chair and folded his arms. He glanced down at the notes before speaking.

"We have two problems here Mister Malarkey. First of all, as we've discussed, we're not just talking about sugar. We're talking about illegal conflict diamonds that you've brought in to the country. The second problem is, it appears that your girlfriend is currently involved in a significant criminal investigation that coincidentally may be linked to similar illegal activity."

The unease erupted into full-blown shock.

Travis knew about Louise's investigation. But it wouldn't have taken long to put it together. He was in law enforcement. Similar illegal activity? What illegal activity? And he had said *coincidentally* but it could be no coincidence that Felipe had mentioned Louise and her investigation. So what was Felipe up to? A network of couriers taking diamonds through customs? If that was the case why give me diamonds to take through when what he really wanted was one of his associates off the hook? I had a direct link to Louise. He knew that, so why take a risk of giving me illegal goods?

I contemplated the gamble in front of me. If I came clean and told Travis the truth about the package, he could link it to whatever criminal investigation he had discovered. If he did, there was the possibility of the police catching the criminals, putting them away and in the process eliminating the threat to Louise. On the other hand, if Felipe was masterminding criminal activity from Spanish territory, it could take a long time to resolve and if Felipe got wind of my involvement in any investigation against him or anyone he was connected with, he may carry out reprisals against Louise and me. I could not take that risk.

"Hang on. I don't know anything about any criminal investigation. My girlfriend doesn't talk about her work. Look, I told you, I bought the sugar crystals as a present. I have no idea how diamonds got mixed in."

"Who for?"

"Sorry?"

"I asked who for? Who did you buy the sugar cane crystals for? You know, as a present."

My mind went into overdrive. I knew I could not afford too much thinking time if my story was to have any plausibility.

"A ... a work colleague. Err ... Jasper. Jasper Kane. It was an impulse buy. He ... he's a bit of a ladies' man. Always sweet-talking them so when I saw the sign on the stall that said sugar cane, it ... it made me think of him. So I thought it would be a bit of a wheeze to buy him some, you know. Bit of a joke ... on his, you know … name."

Travis pushed his chair back and stood up.

"Mister Malarkey," he said, his eyebrows now almost meeting in the middle of his forehead, "I must inform you that unless you have anything further to add, I will now refer this case to Her Majesty's Revenue & Customs office." He picked up the green folder and tucked it under one arm. "They will handle any further investigation and any subsequent prosecution."

13

The morning after my detainment by the UK Border Force my relationship with Louise came off the rails.

It had been two o'clock in the morning by the time I got out of Gatwick. During my detainment, I had missed three calls from Louise and two from Cecil. Louise's first two calls had simply been to enquire what was happening. Her third had been to say that Cecil was taking her and Sheryl home and that I should call her when I could. Cecil's calls were much the same, the first to say that the Border Force officers had released him with no further action and that he would wait for me with the girls in one of the restaurants in the arrivals hall. The second call, some two hours later, informed me that he had organised a taxi to get them all home and to give him a call when I got out of customs. I'd picked up the messages as soon as I got into the arrivals hall and called both Louise and Cecil straight away. In both cases, I got voicemail. As it was so late, I took a taxi home, got straight into bed and fell into a deep sleep.

Louise's call woke me at eight-thirty the following morning.

"*Matthew, I've been suspended from my job,*" was her opening remark.

"What? Suspended? What for?" I said, as I tried to rub the sleep from my eyes.

"*Matthew, don't play the fool with me. You know what for –*"

"Louise, hang on. No, I don't. What are you talking about?" I sat bolt upright in my bed.

"What I'm talking about is your run in with customs last night. I waited at the airport for ages. I couldn't get hold of you. Then Cecil suggested we went home and waited. I got back here to find two colleagues waiting for me. They took me back to the station at midnight where I was questioned about your illegal diamond smuggling."

The blood drained from my face as the memory of the previous evening's detainment came right back in to focus.

"Louise, look there's an explanation. I can –"

"Oh there's always an explanation with you isn't there. Well I don't want an explanation. You listen to me. I've been suspended from my job indefinitely because you've tried to smuggle in illegal rough diamonds, and it just so happens that I'm part of a massive criminal investigation into an international diamond smuggling syndicate. And now you, because of what you've done, have placed me under suspicion. You know what it looks like? It looks like I've fabricated evidence against a suspect we've got in custody, so that I can cover up the fact that you're involved in the very same smuggling operation. In fact, it looks like I'm using inside information to help you. Last night UK Border Force officers contacted my boss because, when they checked the passenger list, they discovered that I was travelling with you and that I was a police officer. Once they spoke to him, it was game over. They're running the rake over every piece of evidence I've gathered. Now I'm being investigated and my career is going down the pan."

My head spun with information but through the maelstrom of thoughts, one clear fact began to emerge. I had been set up. The package that Felipe had given me was not meant to be delivered at all. It was meant to be discovered. Somehow, Border Force officers had been tipped off. Why else would they have stopped me? It had to be a tip off. Felipe had wanted me to get stopped. That was his insurance. He knew there was nothing I could do to persuade Louise to conceal evidence but if he could get her off the case and undermine whatever evidence she had, that gave him the best chance of preventing a conviction against his associate. He seemed to have succeeded on both counts.

"*Matthew. Are you there?*"

I jumped out of bed.

"Yes, yes ... I'm here. Listen Louise. I can explain. The diamonds were –"

"*I told you Matthew, I don't want your pathetic explanations. To be honest, I've had enough of them. I don't know what you were doing with diamonds and right now, I don't care. All I know is that my relationship with you has affected my career this time.*" Her voiced cracked as she tried to stifle the sob. "*And ... and I've worked bloody hard to get where I am. I'm sorry, but it's over.*"

"What's over? Your career?"

"*No. This bloody relationship. I'm going to fight to save my career and it won't help having to worry about you.*"

I tried to keep a grip, to stay calm.

"Louise, please ... please just listen for a minute. I understand how you feel. I understand if you want to end things with me but please just listen before you hang up. I know you don't want an explanation but just let me tell you what happ –"

I stared at my mobile for a moment in disbelief. Was that it? Our relationship over for real. Terminated by the press of a button. Louise was normally so rational. I dialled her number. Voicemail. I waited ten minutes and tried again. Same result. Perhaps she had blocked my number. I needed to go round and see her. First I called Cecil.

"*Mate, how you doing? What happened? You get sorted?*"

"No, I didn't. Far from sorted. You sitting down Ces? You need to listen to this."

"*Yeah, fire away geeze.*"

In the next ten minutes, I explained to Cecil what had happened.

"*Mate, that's a bummer with your bird, what with you getting engaged and all that.*"

"Ces, it's not just that. Her job is at stake and for all I know the threat against me and her is still in place. If I go to the police and tell them the truth, how do I know that Felipe won't come after us? It sounds like a big organisation he's connected with, if what Louise is saying is right."

"*Yeah and you got another problem mate.*"

"Another problem? What's that then?"

"*Well if you go to the police with the story you just told me, they ain't gonna believe ya. At best they're gonna think you've made it up in the cold light of day, 'cos otherwise you'd have told 'em the mumble last night. And at worst mate, it's gonna sound like you and your bird's got together today and come up with a story to get the both of you off the hook, now she's in the shit. Mate, it's a no win situation. You're gonna need some proof.*"

I slumped down into an armchair.

"Thanks Ces. That's cheered me right up. Where am I going to get proof that some bloke in Ibiza has stitched me up?"

"*I dunno yet mate but what I do know, if the Revenue and Customs outfit prosecutes you, and they will, trust me, you're gonna need a good lawyer.*"

"Bloody hell, I don't need any of this. Look I have to go. I'm going round to Louise's to try and sort things out. If she loses her job over this, she'll blame me and I'll stand no chance of getting her back let alone marrying her. I need to sort it out today. I'm back at work tomorrow."

"*Alright mate but play it by ear. You go mouthing off too much she'll have to report it to her superiors and then that starts a whole new palaver. Once the old bill get on it, word'll get out there. Sounds like this geezer they're holding is big time, mate. He'll be connected. I don't reckon this ... whasisname in Ibiza?*"

"Felipe."

"*Yeah, this Felipe ... nah, I don't reckon he's the man. He's just one of the players mate, one of the fixers. His job right now is to keep the main man outta jail. If it leaks that you're talking, that's gonna make it look to them that their little scheme to discredit evidence ain't working. So the only way to fix that is remove the problem. And that's you.*"

"Ces, you're scaring me now. I mean, who is this bloke? What am I supposed to do then?"

100

"Mate, keep it cool. First thing you need to do is go see a lawyer. What about that bird you was trying to blag that time? Some blonde bint, weren't she? She was a lawyer –"

"You mean Diana Twist?"

"Yeah, that's the one. You went skiing with her when you was doing all that trying to impress shit. Good looking bird, if I remember rightly. Tap her up mate. She'll give you some advice. You're gonna need some when the old Customs people get on your case. And you'd have client confidentiality so you could tell her the whole mumble and she might have the swerve on this geezer the old bill's trying to take down."

Diana. Diana Twist. I had neither seen her nor spoken to her in ages. I recalled how infatuated I had been with her. Her intellect, sophisticated good looks and overall worldly aura had mesmerised me for a while. We had met when I was on a dating site but even though no romantic relationship had come out of it, we had become friends. She had helped me out at that time with a legal matter and I knew I could rely on her.

"Good idea Ces. I'll give her a call after I've been to see Louise. And listen, if you think of any way I can make my story stand up let me know."

I hung up and got dressed. Within half an hour, I was outside Louise's house. I rang the doorbell and waited. No response. I did the same again with the same outcome. It was only then that I noticed her car was not in the driveway. I ran back to my car, grabbed a pen and paper and scribbled out a note.

'Hi Louise. Called round to see you but obviously you are not in. I am so sorry that your job is affected. There is a proper explanation to this honestly. Don't mean to be cryptic but with the way things have gone now, I just need to sort out some stuff. I won't bother you anymore but please don't give up on us this easily. I love you. M.'

I pushed the note through Louise's door and went back to my car. Once inside I checked my mobile for Diana Twist's number and hit the button to call it.

"Twist, Swivell and Spinn," the receptionist answered.

I asked to speak to Diana. She was in court and not available.

"Would you like to speak with one of the other partners, Sir? Martin Swivell and Jacob Spinn are both available today."

I said that I needed to speak to Diana and asked if she could call me. As soon as I had finished the call, my mobile rang. Cecil.

"Mate, you round your bird's gaff?"

"Yeah, but she's not in. What's up?"

"Well, I've been thinking ain't I? What you said about making your story stand up."

A wave of optimism coursed through me. "And?"

"Well, like I said, you're gonna need some proof that you knew nothing about what the package had in it and that you was forced to take it to London under threat. I'm telling ya geeze, they ain't gonna believe your story now 'cos you said nothing when you was caught at the airport. In fact mate, all that fucking song and dance act you put on when they opened your case and you clocked the package, like you didn't know about it, then admitting that you did know about it, ain't helping your story one bit. Makes you unreliable."

"So how do I get proof then? How am I going to get anyone to believe me? I mean, I can just say I was scared, can't I? I'd been threatened after all."

"You can say what you like mate but it's just your word. Odds on that geezer out there in Ibiza ain't even called Felipe. Same for his buddy, Scalp." There was a pause before Cecil continued. *"So here's an idea. How about we put a crew together, get back out there and start looking for proof?"*

I couldn't help the sigh of exasperation that slipped out as Cecil's idea hit me.

"That's an idea? How do we go about that then? Looking for proof? And who's a crew anyway?"

"Keep your wig on geezer. What big ideas you got then? You ain't got none. The only place the proof is gonna be is where it started. We go out and ask questions, low profile maybe, until things begin to fit. Then, when you get some names, places, that sort of thing, you can put together a proper story."

"Simple then Ces! So who's going to be part of your big International Investigatory Cross Border Task Force then? Who's the crew that's going to be doing all this detective work?"

"Mate, don't gimme all that sarky shit. I'm trying to help you out here. We ... you, me and Jas take a trip out there, looking like lads on tour, and start feeling around."

Despite the anxiety that was slowly overwhelming me, I began to laugh.

"You, me and Jasper? Jasper Kane? Why do I get the feeling that that crew, as you put it, would *exactly* be a lads on tour trip? For God's sake Ces, I'm in the shit here. My relationship is over by all accounts and Louise is on the verge of losing her job and your idea is that the three of us go out and party in Ibiza on the pretence that we're some private detective agency."

I killed the call and started the car.

14

Diana was pleased to see me. She had returned my call that afternoon and had squeezed me in as her last appointment at the end of the day.

"Matthew, how on earth are you? You look great. Love the suit."

She kissed me on both cheeks. Instantly the heady scent of her perfume brought back memories of the night we had met. I remembered it clearly. I had been running late for our first date due to a taxi driver who had failed to grasp the simple concept that the second most desirable attribute in a professional driver, after mastering the skill of actually being able to drive, was the need to know where you are going. I had arrived flustered and anxious. My composure had not been helped by Diana's cool elegant demeanour and, even though today she was in work mode, she still exuded that mesmerising sex appeal that had bewitched me in the past.

Her PA brought tea and Diana and I chatted about old times for a few minutes before the point of my visit was broached.

"So, Matthew, what have you done this time?" Diana said.

I had to smile. She made it sound like I was a serial offender.

"It's complicated Diana."

She flicked a strand of blonde hair away from her face and reached for the teapot.

"It always is with you darling but there's nothing so complex that it can't be unravelled. Try me," she said, as she began to pour the tea.

Over the following fifteen minutes I told Diana the full story, leaving nothing out. I knew I could trust her and I knew that she would look at the whole scenario in a rational manner. It was her job after all. When I had finished, she sat back in her leather chair and fiddled with the pen with which she had jotted down a number of notes on a legal pad.

"Okay, so we have a few things going on here Matthew. First of all, you have effectively admitted the offence by saying that you were aware of the package. Secondly, it looks like it's being linked to a much bigger operation, the one that your young lady is involved in. That link makes it more high profile. So you can guarantee they'll have you in court in double quick time. They'll want to establish the connection before the other case goes to court. So prepare yourself."

"We'll that's why I've come to you," I said. "Oh, and I'm happy to pay for your time, before you say anything." I remembered the last time Diana had represented me. She had refused any payment.

"Matthew. You know my rule. I don't charge my friends."

"You have to charge. You'll end up broke."

She smiled broadly, revealing her perfect white teeth.

"Excuse me. I choose my friends carefully. They're not all villains like you Mister Matthew Malarkey. Now, you go and wait in reception. I have a few calls to make. I'm aware of the case involving this chap your girlfriend investigated and I have some contacts who might know the lawyers who are working on it. Leave it with me."

I sat in the reception area for thirty minutes or so before Diana called me back in. As I sat down, I noticed that the open page of her legal pad was almost completely covered in notes. She picked it up and rested it on her lap.

"Okay, so here's what we are dealing with. The National Crime Agency has been investigating the activities of one Kurt Kovalevski – apparently he's known by a number of other aliases ... let's see ..." She glanced down at the legal pad. "... including Claremont, Le Roux, Koetzer –"

"Sorry? What did you say?"

Diana looked up from the pad.

"Koetzer."

"No, before that."

She glanced back at the pad. "Le Roux."

I swallowed hard.

"Le Roux? Le Roux. That's the name of the jewellers that I bought the engagement ring from. I don't believe it. Is there any connection?"

"I don't know Matthew. There could be. He's known to have a number of business interests including the import and export of diamonds. Often those who are involved in criminal activity have a legitimate business through which they launder the proceeds of their illegal activities. "

I stood up and began to pace the office. Diana's gaze followed me around the room.

"So I was right. It *is* a set up." I turned to Diana. "What's he being prosecuted for?"

"Matthew, sit down and calm down. You didn't let me finish. I managed to speak with a contact at the CPS, who are putting together the prosecution case, and –"

"The CPS?"

"Crown Prosecution Service. They prosecute criminal trials and work with people like the NCA and the UK Border Agency. Anyway, the police believe that Kurt Kovalevski is importing diamonds illegally. They found forged Kimberley Process Certificates that related to diamond shipments from the Central African Republic, although these shipments have never seen the light of day. It appears that Kovalevski's defence team is alleging that the police have conspired with the gang who burgled his house, to say that these papers were stolen from his property in return for some leniency on the burglary crime. He denies ownership and says the police are fitting him up – his words, not mine."

"Wait a minute. Louise told me that she'd investigated a burglary at Kova ... Kovalevski's house and discovered papers that led to further enquiries into his activities. They have to be the forgeries then ... the Kimberley things ... certificates."

"There's more. Kovalevski was already on the police radar and had been arrested five years earlier for handling stolen goods. Once the forged certificates were found, police enquiries connected him to the diamond trade. A number of warehouses were raided around South London and in Surrey and the proceeds of a number of robberies were found. But the interesting thing was, that conflict diamonds to the value of over a hundred thousand pounds were found hidden in cases of unrefined brown sugar cane crystals."

"Sugar? Exactly like they did to me. Used sugar to hide the stones."

"Absolutely. Anyway, it appears that the police couldn't link Kovalevski to the robberies or the import of the diamonds directly. The warehouses were rented to a known criminal but the owner of the warehouses turns out to be none other than Kurt Kovalevski. So for the past few months the police have been trying to break the smuggling racket. They are charging Kovalevski with handling stolen goods and allowing his premises to be used to handle the proceeds of crime, but they would really like to find evidence that links him directly to the actual diamond smuggling. At the moment, all they have is the forged Kimberley certificates and the diamonds found on premises that belong to him."

"Sounds like plenty to me."

"Yes, but it's about tying up loose ends, making things fit. The forged certificates were never used."

"So what are these Kimberly Certificates anyway? Why go to the bother of forging them."

Diana leant back in her chair.

"I'm no expert on that area of business, but essentially the certificates certify that rough diamond imports and exports come from legitimate sources and that they aren't conflict diamonds –"

"Did you say conflict?" My mind flashed back to my arrest. "That's what the Customs bloke said. Conflict ... what, as in arguments?"

"Yes, but a bit more than that. Conflict diamonds are diamonds mined in countries that are using them to fund military activity and civil wars. Rebel leaders use the profits to buy arms. To try and stop that trade, the Kimberley Process Certification Scheme was created to certify that rough diamond shipments were conflict free. So now rough diamonds can only be imported or exported between countries who are members of that scheme. If you don't have a valid certificate and you attempt to bring in rough diamonds, you're breaking the law."

She paused for a moment, checking that I was following her. I nodded for her to continue.

"Anyway, the process imposes many stringent requirements and there are numerous checks and inspections. As for forging a certificate, they are extremely difficult to forge, not least of all because they need to be Government validated in the country the diamonds originated from and each certificate is uniquely numbered. So it isn't easy. My contact tells me that the certificates that were found appeared to be test prints. They'd never been used and were not in circulation. Apparently the numbering on each one was identical which suggests that they weren't intended for use and the forgers were using them to perfect their technique. It was this that made the officer suspicious."

"Louise?"

"Yes."

I stood up again, restless, as a swarm of thoughts collected in my head.

"Okay, so what have we got? These people in Ibiza know about the investigation into Kova ... whatever his name is."

"Kovalevski."

"Yeah, Kovalevski. And they also know that Louise will give evidence against him, based on these certificates and anything else she's uncovered. So they had to take her right out of the picture, which they did by giving me a package that had illegal diamonds in it. Then if there is a prosecution after that, Kovalevski's defence team will try to discredit the police evidence completely by saying it was a stitch up by Louise. You already said that he's claiming that the police fitted him up. That plays right into his hands. If he can pull that off it casts doubt on any direct connection to the diamonds found in his warehouse. At best then, the police will just be left with trying to get him for allowing his premises to be used to handle stolen and illegal goods."

"But they'll still have to prove that. It's likely he will argue that he rented out the warehouses in good faith as storage space and had no knowledge of what they were being used for. And the guys who were running the warehouse operation won't talk either. He'll have seen to that. None of this helps you though Matthew. We have no proof that they used intimidation to set you up and discredit Louise."

Proof. The same word Cecil had used ...'*start looking for proof.*'

"I know and I'm not sure how I can get proof. What sort of proof do I need anyway?"

Diana smiled and placed the legal pad on her desk.

"The problem is, we only have your word that you were forced to take the package back. If we go to the police –"

"No police. I told you, I can't risk the threat."

Diana threw her hands up and gave a resigned shrug.

"Then you've hit a dead end. Your claim that you've been set up can't be investigated. Haven't you got any photographs with any of these people in? They may have been watching you and perhaps ended up in pictures you took on the holiday."

I thought for a moment before answering.

"I don't know but ..."

"But what Matthew?"

"Oh nothing. Look, you said my court appearance might be notified soon. Is there any way we can put it off?"

"We can't put it off but I can apply for an adjournment on the basis that we need more time to prepare our case. You still have to appear but it might be accepted if the timescale is short between the arrest and the actual court date. Why?"

My mind was a whir of thoughts. A dead end. Proof. I needed proof. Perhaps Cecil had been right after all. I had no alternative. I had to get back out to Ibiza.

"Oh, no reason. Let's see when the date comes up and just go from there." I glanced at my watch. "How do you fancy a quick drink? The least I can do is treat you to a drink."

"Super idea. Where?"

"I don't know ... what about ... I spotted a little pub on my way here that looked –"

Diana stood up abruptly.

"Oh, I know. How about that bar you took me to before. Fad's or something?"

"My friend's bar, MacFadden's? Great idea. I'm sure Carlos would be delighted to see you. Okay. We'll need a taxi."

15

The letter arrived in the post two days later. A court date just one week away. I knew what I had to do. Show up, hope that Diana could swing the adjournment and then get back out to Ibiza as soon as possible. I could see no other way.

I sent Cecil a text.

'Ces, sorry about putting the phone down mate. I need to talk. Can we meet in Fad's tonight - sixish?'

Cecil was never one for grudges or dramas. It was all straight talking with him. In fact, I always suspected that he preferred harmony to confrontation although, if it came up, he would meet any challenge head on. My phone buzzed.

'No worries geeze. I'll be there.'

Cecil was already at the bar when I arrived. He was chatting to Carlos's back as Carlos loaded one of the refrigerators with bottles of beer. His greeting was the usual Cecil-style effusive welcome. No hint that he was in any way upset with me for cutting him off on the telephone. Carlos stood up, wiped down the bar with a tea towel, topped two beers and placed the overflowing bottles on the bar. Cecil tapped his bottle against mine and I got down to business. I told him about my court date, my appointment with Diana and then I got to the point.

"Ces, look, I think you were right." I ignored the half smile and ploughed on. "I've got no choice have I? I've got to present some sort of believable story."

"That's what I'm trying to tell you geezer. You got fuck all credibility. I mean from what you're saying, even your lawyer tart's got nothing to work with so what chance you got?"

"I know."

I studied Cecil's face. His expression stayed neutral even though I had a feeling he knew what I was going to say next.

"Okay, so let's say we do go out there, it has to be for one thing only and that's to find something that'll get me out of this hole. It's not a lads' trip so I think it should just be me and you."

"Hey, Mateo, I'd be handy out there. I speak the language after all," Carlos interjected.

Cecil smiled at Carlos.

"Mate, this is a Viking trip. I mean you're half this and half that ... what, Spanish, Scottish? I mean I never get it myself 'cos you never know what you are, do ya?"

"Peru Cecil, not Spain," Carlos said.

"Yeah, but that ain't Viking is it? See, we can't have anybody on the trip what can't do the rounds. You need an Irish background, 'cos let's face it, we got them Scandinavian bloodlines in Ireland. Yeah, so it's gotta be a two man operation. Blokes that can steam birds..." Cecil paused and glanced directly at me. "Not that we'd be doing any of that, but you know whatamean. Geezers that can self-operate in any environment. Self-sufficient, self-starters. Blokes that can drink beer, chat women and bring some Barolo to the party." He raised the beer bottle to his mouth, paused for effect and smiled at Carlos. "Kinda rules you out then Carlos, mate."

"That's not happening Cecil," I said, trying to bring some authority to the moment. "There's no steaming birds and –"

"That's what I said, didn't I? We wouldn't be doing that," Cecil replied.

"I mean it. I've got a relationship I need to fix and I want to clear Louise's name." I picked at the corner of the label on my beer bottle. "You know what though? Maybe Carlos has a point. It could be handy having someone with us who could speak Spanish. You know, to help make enquiries." I nodded at Carlos. "You up for that mate?"

Carlos flung the tea towel to one side and leant over the bar.

"Aye laddie. Count me in. I can get the wee lassies, Hanka and Janka to keep an eye on the bar. You take no notice of Cecil here. When you going?"

"Well, I have to wait for the court appearance first then we'll know what we're dealing with. Diana's going to try and get it adjourned. After that, I suppose it's as soon as I can get a flight. Just got to square it with work and that's it."

"Your lawyer'll get you the adjournment alright, Mateo. Aye, with them good looks she'd get whatever she wants," Carlos said.

I smiled at the thought.

"I wish it was that simple, mate."

Cecil put his beer onto the bar and pulled out his mobile.

"You know what boys? You know what I'm thinking? If it ain't just me and Matt going we might as well get Jas on the trip too."

"Hang on Ces. I told you. I don't want this turning into a lads' trip," I said

"Mate, it ain't turning into a lads' trip but you may as well make it look like one. You have a few beers, do a few bars and behave like four geezers in Ibiza on holiday. That ain't gonna look outta place, is it? But you go round doing nothing but asking a load of questions, it's gonna raise suspicions ain't it? So you gotta have some cover. Blend in, you know. Anyway, I already told you, I mentioned it to Jas and he's up for it." Cecil grinned, grabbed the beer and chinked his bottle on mine. "And the geezer was sound on the Vegas trip weren't he? Stop worrying. It'll be a right little tickle."

He began to tap out a text to Jasper. I glanced across at Carlos whose only response was a shrug of the shoulders. I had a feeling I had been duped but I wasn't sure.

The court hearing was a disaster. Diana got the adjournment just as she had planned but none of us had reckoned with the stringent bail conditions. On the grounds that I may be a flight risk, the court confiscated my passport. The decision was devastating. All my plans to return to Ibiza were shattered in an instant.

"I don't understand, Diana," I said afterwards as we sat in a coffee shop discussing the case. "Why did they have to take my passport?"

"It could have been worse. You heard what they said Matthew. They wanted to remand you. If I hadn't argued your case, you would've been spending tonight in jail. Count yourself lucky that at least you're able to move about freely, even if it is only in the UK. The court is taking this case very seriously. Let me put it bluntly. They think there's a risk that you might abscond. You have an association with a police officer who was involved in a significant criminal investigation. The diamonds found in your possession were concealed in an identical manner to those found to be part of that same investigation and, although you've not been found guilty of anything, they believe there's a considerable risk that you may not come back to face the charges. In short they have reason to think you are part of an organised crime gang."

I had no response. The confiscated passport blow was still sinking in.

"Anyway, you weren't planning on going anywhere were you?" Diana added.

I sipped my coffee and wiped the froth from my top lip. There was no chance of me leaving the country now.

"No, I'm going nowhere."

"That's okay then. I wouldn't worry about it. We have to be back in court in four weeks so it won't be too long. We'll need to use that time to make a case." She picked up her handbag from the vacant seat next to her and stood up. "Now, I'm really sorry Matthew, I need to get back to the office. I'm meeting a client in an hour and I have some prep to do." She leant forward and kissed me on the cheek. "Give me a call tomorrow afternoon. I'm going to contact the Border Force staff who stopped you and make some enquiries. I need to find out exactly why they selected you."

Left alone the desperation of my situation hit me. Unless Diana could come up with something, trying to provide proof that I had been set up now looked impossible. I called Louise. Her mobile went to voicemail. She was definitely ignoring me. So much for the magistrates '*association with a police officer*' statement. An ex-association and probably an ex-police officer if I could not prove my story.

I called Cecil.

"*How'd it go geezer?*"

"They took my passport Ces. The trip's off."

"*What? They took your passport? What for?*"

"Long story mate. Just something to do with thinking that I might not come back to court. Listen, I can't really talk now. I need to get my head round this. I just wanted to let you know that the trip can't happen. I have to go."

"*Hang on mate. Wait a minute. Me and the other two lads can still go. Try and find out some stuff. No need to blow the whole thing out. And Sheryl goes back to Toronto on Thursday so I'm good to go.*"

I felt the blood drain from my face. There was no way I could risk a Cecil led trip to Ibiza on my behalf without me. There were too many distractions out there for him to be able to stay focused. And an unfocused Cecil could possibly make things worse.

"No Ces. That's not going to work. You need me out there, not least of all because I could identify the two blokes who accosted me ... if I can find them. If you want to go there and party that's your call but it won't work without me there. You've got nothing to go on."

"*Well then mate, you're just gonna have to get yourself out there if you're gonna sort it.*"

"You like more coffee, Sir."

I looked up to see a young waiter clearing the adjacent tables.

"Err ... yeah. Please. I'll have a cappuccino, no chocolate."

"*What's that geezer?*"

"Nothing, Ces. I'm in a coffee shop. Anyway, look, how am I supposed to get to Ibiza without a passport? I'm screwed."

"*Don't you know anybody with a private plane or nothing?*"

I tried to stifle an involuntary giggle.

"Oh yeah, sure. I hang around with people with private planes

115

all the time, don't I? You have to come up with something better than that for crying out loud. Even if I did, it's still illegal to travel without a passport. You don't seem to understand Ces. My situation here is desperate. We have to think straight."

"Well mate, desperate men have to come up with desperate solutions, yeah. What about that bird you was telling me you ran into again, you know, from Vegas. She's got a plane ain't she?"

"What Erin?" I waved my left hand in a dismissive gesture just as the waiter was about to place the cappuccino on the table. The sudden movement caught the cup and saucer in a sweeping upward blow sending the coffee contents in a milky brown wave, directly over his green apron. I leapt to my feet in an instant, apologising profusely as the waiter stood mesmerised by the liquid dripping onto his shoes. He recovered his composure fairly quickly, probably because my attempts to wipe down his apron had begun to unnerve him.

He picked up the cup that had landed on the floor and simply said, "I'll get another Sir."

I wasn't sure if he was referring to another apron or another coffee. I sat back down again and picked up my mobile.

"Ces?"

He was still there.

"What the fuck's going on mate?"

"Nothing ... just a ... a clumsy waiter. Anyway, I need some better ideas than Erin."

"Yeah, but like I said mate, she's got a plane."

"But it's not *her* plane, is it Ces. They belong to the frigging airline. What am I supposed to do? Ask if she can borrow a jet to fly me out to Ibiza? It's not like a company car."

"I don't mean like that you nobhead. I mean, you know what she's like. Game girl, clued up. She's in the flight business. She might know the old swerves, sort out your problem."

"Sort my problem? Like how?"

"I dunno, do I? She's the one you should be asking, not me. Anyway, geeze I gotta go. Bell me later."

I sat for a moment and stared at the phone. Cecil had no ideas.

I had no ideas. There seemed to be no solutions and my mind was a fog of indecision. I stood up to leave.

"Your coffee Sir."

"Err ... it's okay. No thanks. And ... uh, sorry about your apron ... and shoes and the, you know ... the spillage."

16

With the rest of the day off, following the morning court appearance, I headed home. As soon as I got in, I tried Louise's number again. It went straight to voicemail. I killed the call before the message had finished. There seemed little point in leaving a message. She obviously had meant what she said. She wanted no contact. As I put the mobile down, I resolved not to call her again until I had cleared my name and sorted out the mess I was in. My mind was in turmoil, no clear thought patterns whatsoever except one - I needed a drink. I poured a large gin and tonic and slumped into an armchair. I was in a crazy situation, a desperate one. Cecil's words danced in my head, 'desperate men have to come up with desperate solutions.' But Cecil's desperate solution was to hire an aircraft from Erin or something similarly stupid it seemed.

I gulped a mouthful of gin and stood up. I remembered that I had Erin's card in the pocket of a jacket that was hanging in my bedroom wardrobe. Maybe there was no harm in a chat. I went to the bedroom and found the card just where I had left it. A nervous flutter ran through my stomach as I stared at the gold lettering.

E Farrell, Costume Jewellery.

How ironic, I thought, that Erin's sideline was jewellery and I was trying to get out of a diamond set up. I hurried back into the front room, took another large gulp of gin and tonic and picked up my mobile. With shaking hands, I tapped out the number that was on the card. Erin answered immediately.

"Erin? It's Matthew."

"*I know.*"

"Err ... well, I'm not totally sure why I called you but –"

"*Because you like me Matthew. I knew you'd call sooner or later.*"

"Well, no I don't ... I mean, yes I do. I do like ... but that wasn't ... it wasn't why ... I mean, I like you of course but, to be honest I'm not sure why I called. It's just that I thought you might be able to help with a ... with a problem, although I'm not sure how you –"

"*Well if you don't spit it out you won't find out will you? What's wrong?*"

"Well, with you in the airline industry, I thought you might be able to help me to ..." I took a deep breath. "I need to get back out to Ibiza to be honest."

Erin giggled.

"*Well book a flight then Matthew. They go there every day. There's no need to call cabin crew directly. Go on line. Everybody's doing it.*"

"Uh ..." And then I blurted it out. "It's not that simple. I haven't got a passport."

For the next ten minutes I explained my predicament to Erin. When I had finished she asked a question.

"*So, am I right in what I'm thinking? You think I can smuggle you out or something? Like you're hand luggage or perhaps get you loaded into the hold?*"

I could hear the laughter in her voice.

"I don't know Erin. Look, this is serious and I'm not thinking too straight to be honest. I can't travel in the normal way and ... well, you just popped into my head because you travel all the time. I thought that you might just know a way. Maybe cabin crew don't have to have passports as they sometimes fly out and return exactly the same day. I've no idea how you can help to be honest but I can't think of a way to get out there and I don't know who else to ask."

Erin paused for a moment.

119

"You there?" I asked.

"*Yes, I'm still here. We do need passports I'm afraid. But listen, I might have an idea. What're you doing right now?*"

"Nothing. I was just ... nothing."

"*Ok. Can you meet me in an hour? If what I'm thinking works, I don't want to be discussing it on the phone.*"

I felt a surge of optimism. I had no idea what Erin might be thinking and I was not even going to try and guess, mainly because each time I had tried to find a logical solution I had hit a brick wall.

"Sure. Where?"

"*I'm in Windsor but it would probably be best if I came to you. Do you know anywhere discreet?*"

"There's always MacFadden's. It's a pub, wine bar place here in Kingston. I know the owner. He could tuck us away in a corner, if you're ok with that?"

"*I don't mind being in a corner with you Matthew. You know that. Remember Vegas? We very nearly –*"

"Err, yes ... anyway, Erin it's two o'clock. I can do three-ish?"

"*Great. I'll be there. I guess it's on the internet. I'll look it up. See you in an hour or so.*"

I made sure I got to MacFadden's early. Carlos had just finished the lunchtime rush and was sipping a coffee behind the bar. He poured me a half a lager and made idle chit chat, aware of my nervousness. I had been there fifteen minutes when Erin walked in.

"Hi Matthew. Nice to see you again." She kissed me on both cheeks, one hand lightly placed on my shoulder.

"Good to see you too. Glad you could make it. Oh, and love the dress." The dress was way too distinct and stylish not to warrant comment.

"You do? Fantastic. You do have taste then. It's a Roksanda."

"A what?"

"Roksanda Ilincic. She's a ... oh, never mind. You guys, you –"

"No, really. I like it. Love the blue and black pattern." I had begun to ramble, the dress a distraction from dealing with the apprehension I had about meeting with Erin.

"Turquoise, actually. Not blue."

My mind flashed back to the conversation with Estrid and her aqua marine stilettos. I should have known not to simplify colours with women. I dismissed the thought.

"Oh ... uh ... yes. Anyway, what will you have to drink?"

"Just a coke will be fine."

Carlos busied himself behind the bar. Erin leant forward.

"I know him, don't I? The guy behind the bar?"

"Yes, you met in Vegas, briefly if I remember." I called to Carlos. "Hey Carlos, you remember Erin don't you?"

Carlos held out a hand towards Erin.

"Aye, I do indeed remember you señora. I never forgot those beautiful green eyes."

Erin smiled, the corners of her eyes displaying the hint of laughter lines.

"Yes, I remember. The casino in the Paris. You were with Matthew. Nice to see you. Now, we need a quiet table in a discreet corner somewhere, Carlos. Matthew and I have a bit of catching up to do."

Carlos stepped from behind the bar, led us across the room and indicated a table that was indeed in a discreet corner. As Erin and I sat down, I felt the apprehension begin to return. My fingers tapped out an involuntary beat on the wooden table. I had no clue what Erin's idea might be but I had a feeling that it would not be straightforward. And that made me nervous. I had to get to the point.

"So what's the idea then?"

She swirled the straw around the glass, poked the piece of lemon a couple of times and then took a drink.

"Okay. So, you have no passport and you need to leave the country. There aren't many options unless you pay for somebody to smuggle you out –"

"I don't know anybody who could do that, do I?"

She shot out a hand and placed it on mine.

121

"I know you don't. Even if you did it would cost you a fortune and then you'd have to get back into the UK again."

"So, what's the plan?"

"Hang on Matthew. I'm getting to it." She raised the glass again, sipped through the straw, and fixed her gaze directly on me. "You have to think like a con artist and –"

"A con artist? *This* is a plan?"

"Matthew! Stop interrupting. You asked me to help and I'm trying to do just that so shut up and listen until I finish. If you don't like what I say then go do something else. Okay?"

The green eyes flashed annoyance. There was no need to respond.

"By con artist I mean you have to make out you're something you're not. That's what they do to pull off a con. They rely on people seeing only what they see in front of them, never looking beyond the surface. And a good con artist plays on that. They build confidence in others in order to get whatever it is they set out to achieve. They create an image so that it is believable, believable enough for others to accept that what they see is the real deal."

She must have noticed the self-doubt in my eyes. She raised a red nailed index finger to halt any further interruption.

"The trick then is for us to create a situation where *you* are part of an environment that everybody accepts to be normal and routine."

I had to ask.

"So how do we do that and how does that get me out to Ibiza again?"

"Simple. We get you on board a flight as part of the cabin crew."

Simple. I heard the word echo in my head and felt a tightening sensation across my forehead.

"Cabin crew? But I ... how can I do that? I don't know anything about cabin ... stuff."

"You don't need to Matthew. You just need to look like you do. That's what I'm saying. Create an image that's believable. We get you into uniform and you simply blend in with the environment. Passengers, airline staff, they all expect to see cabin crew boarding an aircraft. It's normal at airports so you just become part of what they expect to see. Play the con in other words. Do it properly and nobody bats an eyelid."

As I absorbed Erin's words my instinct told me that her idea was madness. I took a gulp of the lager, swallowed hard and sat back. But what other solution was there? I couldn't travel to Ibiza legitimately so any solution had to be covert. Erin was right. It was a kind of con trick but nobody would get hurt. There would be no victims. I gulped at the lager again. Despite the tension in my head the idea suddenly seemed feasible. Feasible for someone else, but it was me that would have to go through with it.

"But how do I get to be a member of the flight crew? I'm sure you don't mean that I need to apply for a job?"

Erin raised her eyes to the ceiling and laughed.

"You are funny. No, nothing that drastic. That's where I come in. I can get you on as a dead head – it's like a spare crew member – on the pretence that you're flying out to hook up with a flight back to UK. It happens all the time. Crew fly out as backup for other flights. Once on board you just travel much like an ordinary passenger. The only difference here is that you don't actually hook up with anybody once you arrive. You just disappear. Leave it to me. I can sort out the paperwork. I have contacts."

After my experience with Erin in Las Vegas I had no doubt in her ability to plan but I was still apprehensive. Apprehensive but desperate.

"Supposing I decided to go for it. When could it happen?"

"Well, let's see. I'm doing the tourist runs right now and I'm on an Ibiza trip next week. It's better if you're on the same flight as me but if you want to go earlier I can get you over to Palma, Majorca and you can get a boat over from there."

"No, I'll wait Erin. I wouldn't want to add any complications." I rubbed my temples to ease the discomfort as another thought shot through my head.

"But, hold on, I'd still need a passport to travel wouldn't I?"

"Yes of course but –"

"Then we're back to square one."

"I can get you one."

"Get me one? A fake?"

"No Matthew, not a fake. A genuine passport, except it belongs to somebody else."

Erin's plan was coming at me too fast. Each aspect caused me more confusion. It had appeal but it was way out of my comfort zone. She noticed my bewilderment.

"Listen, I have a colleague who's off sick for several weeks. He broke his arm playing rugby. He keeps a lot of stuff in his personal locker at work, including his passport. I have his key. He was in a rush for the match and left his mobile in the locker. He asked me to get it for him so I still have the key. He won't be travelling anywhere with a broken arm so he won't need a passport. I can just borrow it for a little while."

"Borrow it? Steal it you mean? Isn't that illegal?"

"Of course it is but so is trying to leave the country when you've had your passport confiscated. Which bit of *illegal* are you more comfortable with Matthew?"

I had no response. Instead I focussed on the colleague she had mentioned.

"A rugby player you said? You want me to pretend to be him?"

"I don't want you to pretend to be him. I want you to be a member of cabin crew using another ID. That's all."

"But, a rugby player? He'll be a big guy ... muscles and stuff."

"The point is, he looks a bit like you."

"A bit?"

Erin leant forward, both hands flat on the table.

"Matthew, a passport is only a head and shoulders shot. It doesn't make any difference if he has muscles or plays rugby or whatever. He's got dark hair like you, similar features. Okay, perhaps he has more eyebrows –"

"More eyebrows? What ... three, four? How many more?" I was beginning to panic at the thought of the deception that was evolving.

"I don't mean more. I mean thicker. Nothing a bit of theatrical make up can't fix."

"Make up?"

Her eyes twinkled in that playful way that I had become familiar with and which I found so disconcerting.

"Yes, a bit of makeup. And perhaps you should have a touch of five o'clock shadow too."

"Are you trying to turn me into a drag queen? It'll never work Erin."

She giggled and sat back in her chair.

"Your call Matthew. What other ideas have you got?"

"I don't ... I haven't any ... the police maybe ... but ..."

"So go to the police."

"I can't, can I? Louise *is* police. They're already investigating her. You're right. I don't seem to have many choices. I have to get back out there and do some digging. I need to come back with something to clear my name and help Louise."

"So I can get you back out there. Use the passport. Just be cool. Like I said, you have to think like a con artist. Blend in. Make it seem like it's what you do. That's how they operate. Calm and cool. Just don't do anything stupid."

I sat back, trying to get my head around being *'cool'* and not doing anything stupid when something Erin had just said clicked in fully.

"Hang on. You said you can get me back out there. What about getting me back home again? How do we do that? Same thing?"

I noticed the slight wrinkling in the corners of Erin's eyes again as she replied.

"I'm afraid not Matthew. You're on your own on the return trip?"

A shock wave hit the pit of my stomach.

"On my own. How do you mean?"

"It can't be done. You'll need time out there to do whatever it is you need to. I don't know when you'll be coming back ... unless you do?"

I shook my head.

"Then it could be two days, maybe four, even a week. So I can't plan ahead. You'll just have to book a return flight yourself and come back through as a normal passenger. Remember, the point is that you need to get out there."

"In that case why don't I just fly out as a normal passenger using the passport? Why all the cabin crew thing?"

Erin shrugged.

"You could try but just supposing you get stopped on the way out at passport control. You won't get out of the UK. You have a better chance going through my way. Numbers, disguise. They're used to cabin crew. Sure they'll check your passport but it's routine. Travelling on your own, you only have to make one small mistake and your whole trip is down the pan. As I said, it's about creating an image, a cover even. On your own, you have no cover. You're ... on your own."

I thought it through for a moment. I wasn't happy about the return journey but my main focus was on getting back to Ibiza, a trip I had to make.

"It's a massive risk. If I get caught I'll be in even more trouble than I am now." I glanced towards the bar. "I need another drink."

"Here, let me get it," Erin said and waved in the direction of the bar. She caught Carlos's attention and in a flurry of hand signals indicated that she wanted the same again. Then she turned back to me.

"Look, of course it's a risk Matthew. But it's a gamble you have to take. You play the cards you've been dealt. You make the best connections with the hand you have and then bluff like Doc Holiday after three shots of firewater."

"Pardon," I said, unconvinced by Erin's analogy.

"Like in Vegas. You make your own luck with what you have in front of you. So, do it my way and there's more chance of pulling it off in a crowd than by yourself. The risk is still there but you stack the odds more in your favour."

I nodded.

"Okay. Okay. I suppose that makes sense. But I have to ask. Why are you doing this? Why are you taking such a risk? You could lose your job if you were found to be helping someone fly illegally?"

Carlos approached with the drinks. Erin took a sip through the straw and placed the glass back on the table. She sat back, a broad grin lighting up her face.

"Why am I doing it? You know me Matthew. I like the excitement. As I told you once before, it's more fun being naughty than being a goody two shoes all the time. Sometimes you have to live on the edge, let your hair down. And besides, I don't need the job, so if I lost it I wouldn't worry about it."

I smiled, the first time that afternoon that I had felt any sense of relief.

"I appreciate your help Erin."

She touched my hand, a light reassuring contact.

"Oh, and I kind of owe you. I remember how you were in Vegas. You didn't let me down ... so ... you know ... what are friends for?" She smiled, a thoughtful look on her face. "Now let's run through airport procedures."

17

Against my better judgement but in the knowledge that I was desperate, I steeled myself for the flight. The week had dragged and the delay only added to the tension I felt about what I had to do. I told no one about my plan other than a brief mention to Cecil that Erin had sorted something out for me. It wasn't that I didn't trust Cecil. Just that it was in my own interest to be as cautious as possible. In any case, Erin had sworn me to secrecy. Once Cecil knew I was able to go, he had organised the trip for himself and the other lads and they had flown out to Ibiza two days earlier. On their arrival, I had received a text to say they were checked in at the Blau Parc.

The night before the trip, I stayed at Erin's. She said that it would be an opportunity to go through the details of the flight and then we could travel down to Gatwick together. With a 6.10a.m. flight to Ibiza, we needed to be at the airport by 3.30a.m. The enormity of what I was doing hit home hard when she produced the passport.

"Okay, now this is your passport. Just familiarise yourself with the name. We call him JJ at work but the chances are we won't know any of tomorrow's crew and in any case, the crew don't look at your passport. I'm agency and it's only my second month with this airline. Most of them won't even know me. They won't give a strange face a second glance. Once on board we'll get you into a quiet seat and you can keep a low profile."

I took the passport and stared at the photograph. JJ was officially known as Jason Jefferies. The anxiety began to well up.

"It won't work Erin. I don't look anything like him."

"Of course you do. Same dark hair, similar style even. We have to do something about your eyebrows, sure, but I told you that. It'll be fine. And who looks *exactly* like their passport picture anyway?"

I tried not to dwell on Erin's last remark. I didn't mind not looking exactly like my own passport picture but not looking like someone else's was a different matter.

Erin saw my concern.

"Look, remember what I said. It's a con. You play the part and everybody goes with it. Act in any way suspicious or nervous or out of the ordinary and you'll blow it. Oh and you'll need this too." She handed me a card. "It's JJ's airside ID card. That needs to be on display. From now on, you *are* Jason, okay. It's all about confidence."

Confidence was the last thing I had. I didn't feel like Jason. I was in danger of going into panic meltdown.

"If by some miracle we get on the plane can I just sit somewhere at the back out of the way?"

Erin's frown at the question unnerved me.

"We'll see, Matthew. We have to put you where there's a spare seat. I've checked already and it's a busy flight. There are only a couple of unoccupied seats." She paused for a moment, before continuing. "There's always a chance the remaining seats could be taken up by stand-bys."

"Then what happens?"

She turned away and picked up a whiskey decanter from one of two matching cabinets that lined the wall to one side of the room.

"Fancy a shot?" she asked. "It'll help you sleep. We have to be up early."

"Wait a minute Erin. What happens if the seats are taken?" I asked again.

She poured two measures of whiskey into small glass tumblers and held one out towards me.

"Well let's just say you won't be in the passenger cabin."

I took the glass from her outstretched hand.

"Not in the cabin? Where then?"

"The cockpit." Erin's eyes twinkled.

I almost dropped the tumbler.

"The cockpit?" I raised the glass and downed the whiskey in one. Immediately I felt the hit to my throat and chest. "Bloody hell, Erin, how low profile is that supposed to be? Sitting in the cockpit with the pilot?"

"Two pilots."

"Two?"

"Yes, there's the co-pilot."

"Oh great. I'm travelling illegally, impersonating another bloke whose passport I've nicked and now I'll be sitting right up front, large as life, with the Captain of the frigging plane and his sidekick. What if I'm taken for a hijacker or something? I'll do time for this."

Erin laughed.

"I'm teasing you Matthew. Calm down. Back in the day they sometimes sat up front in what was known as the jump seat. Not anymore. We'll get you a passenger seat. Oh, and you'll do time anyway. Remember you're on a smuggling charge. It's a rock and a hard place as they say."

I held my glass out for another whiskey shot.

"Make it a large one."

She laughed and shook her head.

"Fraid not Matthew. Don't want you random breath tested and failing do we? That would cock things up completely." She must have noticed my quizzical expression. "Once you board in uniform, technically you're working. But, hey, chill. I'm just following the rules. Better to get the detail right than to slip up on something silly. Anyway, we need to get some sleep. I'll make up a bed for you on the sofa. Unless ..."

"Unless what?" I said, her pause throwing me for a moment.

She took a pace towards me and ran a finger down the buttons of my shirt.

"Unless ... you'd feel more comfortable in my room. It may be some time before you get such an offer if you do end up in jail."

I took a deep breath and stared at Erin. Her brunette hair settled loosely on her shoulders, a slight wave where she had brushed it away from her face. The green eyes danced mischievously, her lips slightly parted to reveal a hint of perfect white teeth. My mind flashed back to the moment in Vegas where I had almost succumbed to her charms. My resistance that night had been heightened by the knowledge that I was in a relationship with Louise. But now it seemed that Louise had given up on me. I felt a warm surge in my stomach. Whisky or desire for Erin, it didn't matter. I made a move to put the empty tumbler down just as Erin turned away.

"I thought so. I can see it in your eyes Matthew. You're still fighting for your woman. Of course. Why else would you be here?"

In that split second, the moment was shattered. Reality surged back through my thoughts.

"I ... err ... it's not that ..." I hesitated, collecting my thoughts. "Yes, I am. I have to sort this." I stared at the empty whisky glass, my need for a refill nagging strongly. "And, I'm not sure that I'd be any good for any ... you know ... err, with all this on my mind." I was embarrassed all of a sudden. I fancied Erin, there was no question of that and I found her hard to resist.

"Hey, I was only teasing Matthew. I know how you think. Now come on, it's an early start and you have to be on the ball."

My alarm shattered what sleep I had finally managed to slip into. I had lain awake for most of the first hour after I had settled on the sofa, worry combating the sleep inducing properties of the whisky. The remaining four hours had seen just fitful bursts of slumber and when the incessant computerised clang of my phone alarm broke the early morning silence, I sat bolt upright, disorientated and exhausted. As I swung my legs off the sofa, the door opened and Erin appeared, a pink towel, turban-style around her head, a similar larger towel wrapped tightly around her body. She sat down next to me, the towel riding high above mid-thigh as she did so. I turned my head away trying to focus my thoughts on the day ahead. The movement was clearly too exaggerated and Erin noticed.

"Relax. We haven't got time." She laughed and placed a hand on my shoulder. "You ready for this?"

I shrugged, aware that my face had coloured a dark shade of pink.

"Yes. I suppose so. Bit nervous but it has to be done." I would never be ready for what I had to do but there was no going back.

"I can tell. You look a little flushed." The glint of mischief that was a tell-tale trait in Erin's eyes when she was in tease mode, was full on.

I stood up.

"I'll be fine once we get going."

"That's the spirit Matthew ... actually, I should say Jason. JJ in fact. Starting right now, that's who you are okay. And speaking of which, there's one more thing you need to do."

I turned towards her, concerned about another task. I already had enough to think about.

"What's that?"

"Empty your wallet."

"My wallet? Why?"

"Yes. You need to take out anything that might identify you as Matthew Malarkey. We need to avoid slip-ups. You'll need to keep a credit card though in case of emergencies."

Emergencies. The whole thing was one big emergency.

"But what about cash? I'll need money."

"Of course. Take your debit card and we'll pick up cash on the way. You can leave the card in my car and I'll change the sterling into euros at the airport for you. No duty free shopping either I'm afraid. You need to avoid unnecessary checks. Okay?"

"Okay." As if I was even contemplating a quiet browse around the shops dressed in an unfamiliar uniform with somebody else's passport.

"Right, the shower's that way. Make it snappy JJ. Then we'll get you into uniform and sort those eyebrows. Oh, and don't shave."

I managed to keep it together until we reached Gatwick's North Terminal. At that point, my legs took on the qualities of a fresh blancmange and my stomach seemed to contain razor blades. We stepped through the departures entrance and I fell into step behind Erin. All I wanted to do was follow. Thinking was out of the question. We strode across the open expanse of the departures area, both of us pulling small cabin luggage bags behind us. All around, the airport was a bustle of early morning travellers, crew heading for their work stations and general airport staff. With so many people in uniform around me, I suddenly became very self-conscious of my own uniform. But nobody seemed to be taking any notice of me. Erin strode purposefully ahead.

"Where are we going Erin?" I asked, a desire to know what lay in store rather than where we would actually end up.

"The office. Need to sort your seat. The ground agents should've passed it with the captain and the cabin supervisor. Once we've done that we head through security. There's a special security channel for crew so just stick with me."

Erin handled the whole thing. I marvelled at her cool professionalism. No hint of the deception she had engineered. She introduced me to a number of staff, including the Cabin Manager, Sophie, a tall woman, with an efficient, no nonsense aura. I said as little as possible. There was a short crew briefing and a check though the manifest. Four crew, including Erin, were assigned to the flight. Within ten minutes, the standby ticket was produced and I had cleared the first hurdle.

"Great. Got you in the cabin. Now let's get through security. Have your airside pass ready. You'll need to swipe it."

I was focussed. I listened intently, my senses heightened by a nagging feeling that my cover would surely be blown any minute. The security channel was separate from the passenger channel. I swiped my ID and had to empty my pockets into a tray for the scanner. I placed my bag on the conveyor and walked through the

133

scan unit. No problems except the focus on me as an individual only served to heighten my paranoia. Once through, I walked to the end of the conveyor and waited to collect my bag. Erin caught up with me as I picked it up.

"There you go. Piece of cake," she whispered. "Okay, now just follow me. We're heading for gate forty-seven. They'll do a passport check there but it's a formality. Remember, you are crew. You look like crew, you have a ticket and you are supposed to be there."

Erin's voice was calm, her voice reassuring but my collar felt ridiculously tight.

"Okay. I'm on it."

"Good."

She began to head across the airport lounge in the direction of a walkway that had a sign overhead with the gate numbers. I followed closely behind. Ahead of us, the three other cabin crew members. With each step, my apprehension increased. I needed distraction. I tried to take in the sights around me. Through a long expanse of glass to my left, the sun was just beginning to turn the dark blue hue of night into the early morning light of a new day, a day I wanted to get through as fast as possible.

We stepped on to a travelator that flowed silently along the walkway, past several lounges, many filled with passengers awaiting the call to board their flights. As we reached the end of the first section of travelator, one of the crew stumbled and began to clutch her tummy. Instinctively, I reached out and grabbed her arm to stop her from falling.

"You okay?" I asked.

"Fine. Sorry, just feel a little queasy."

Queasy. That was all I needed. A queasy crew member. I almost told her that I felt the same way myself but resisted it.

"I'll be fine. Thank you," she said, although her expression suggested otherwise.

We reached Gate 47, turned right and walked to the passport desk. A young looking staff member with a smiley face gave my passport a cursory check and waved me through. At the end of the small lounge area, we sat and waited to be called on board by the Captain.

Five minutes later, we made our way through the jet bridge to the aircraft doorway. I stepped through and was on board the flight to Ibiza.

18

With no passengers in the aircraft the cabin was unusually silent save for a low hum from what I assumed was the aircraft's generator system. The Captain and his first officer stood to one side of the entrance and welcomed the crew on board. Once inside Erin indicated a seat, 7C near the front. I sat down immediately, anxious to hide away as the crew busied themselves with tasks.

Half an hour later, the passengers began to board. I sat back and tried to shut out the reality of what was going on around me. But it was impossible.

"Welcome on board this morning's flight to Ibiza ... please ensure your bags are placed securely ..."

I tried to loosen my tie as the heat increased around my collar and then realised I shouldn't. I had to present a smart image if I was to pull off the crew member impersonation. I glanced at Erin. She was all professionalism. A relaxed expression, the hint of a smile on her face as passengers filed by in that slightly chaotic way that people have when they are lugging hand luggage and looking for their seat numbers. She caught my glance and approached my seat.

"You ok?"

My gulp by way of response and the beads of sweat on my brow were probably good indicators of how I was feeling but I tried to speak.

"I just wish they'd get on with it. I'll be happier when we're off the ground."

Erin smiled and patted me on the shoulder.

"Relax. We can't go without the passengers. Won't be long now. It'll be fine. Just don't do anything to attract attention and nobody will even notice you."

She was right. I had to get a grip. None of the passengers were focussed on me. I tried to reassure myself that I was just part of the backdrop. Blend in. Relax. I took three deep breaths. Take your cue from Erin I told myself.

They were just about to close the cabin doors when it happened.

I had noticed her walking from the galley area and wondered why she was clutching her stomach. Then I remembered. It was the flight attendant whom I had spoken to earlier when she had tripped on the travelator, only this time her face was greyer than the seat covers on the back of the seats. Her eyes seemed to roll upwards and, without warning, she pitched forward, collapsing in a heap between the rows of seats in the centre aisle. The screams of shock from passengers immediately next to her alerted the crew. Instinctively I jumped up to help her back on her feet but the Cabin Manager, Sophie, barked out an order.

"Leave her. She's better on the floor if she's fainted." She beckoned to one of her colleagues. "Get the Captain."

The Captain emerged, knelt down and took one look at the stricken stewardess.

"Get the paramedics here right now. We need her off the aircraft right away. That's the third crew member that's gone down in the last two weeks."

"If it's any help she was holding her stomach earlier, before we boarded," I chipped in, concerned for the crew member.

"Thanks ...erm ..."

"Matth ... err ... Jason. JJ ... Sir."

"Stomach, eh? Bloody bug, it's taking out half the airline." The Captain stood up and addressed the passengers that were seated either side of the incident. "It's okay. She'll be fine. We'll be delayed a moment while we get her off." He turned to Sophie. "We got anybody on standby?"

"Sorry Sir. They're down to the bare bones. Two of the standby crew were needed for Heraklion earlier. There are three more due on shift in a couple of hours once they have done their rest period."

The Captain furrowed his brow, the response clearly not to his liking.

"A couple of hours? Hell, I can't miss the slot. The Spanish are talking about strike action anytime soon. We can't afford to miss this departure."

At that precise moment, I wished that I had remained seated and kept the low profile I had been trying to adopt thus far. The Captain's gaze settled on me.

"JJ, we're going to need you. We've got a hundred and seventy passengers and we're down to three crew. Sophie, take care of things here. I'll get on to ATC."

For a moment I stood mesmerised, wondering who JJ was. And then I thought I was going to pass out. My head suddenly became disconnected from reality. The buzz of the cabin a distant blur. The Captain's face took on the appearance of a distorted mask, his features swimming in a smudge of merging colours. I felt the beads of sweat forming on my brow.

"JJ? You okay?" Sophie's voice brought me back to reality. "You look very pale."

I rapidly considered my options. There were few. In fact, only one sprang to mind. Pass out like the other staff member. That way I could get carted off the flight by the paramedics too. But that wouldn't get me to Ibiza. I wiped the back of my hand across my forehead to mop up the sweat, swallowed hard and formed a response.

"Yes, err ... sorry, I'm not good with fainting. Just need some water and I'll be fine."

"No problem. Wait there and I'll brief you when I get back," Sophie said. She paused for a moment, a quizzical look in her eyes. "You've got a dark smudge on your face. Just ... just there." She pointed at the right side of my head.

Instinctively I raised my hand to the side of my head. As I did so, I noticed a black stain on the back of my hand. The eyebrow pencil that Erin had used to give me 'more eyebrows.'

"Erm ... yeah ... it's just ... just newsprint from the ... err ... you know, the paper. I'll go and clean up."

Sophie nodded and headed towards the galley. I looked around for Erin. She was half way down the aisle reassuring passengers that things were under control. I went towards her.

"Erin. Erin ... listen. I'm stuffed. They're asking me to –"

"You've got eyebrow pencil on your face you silly sod. Come here." She pulled a tissue from a pocket, dampened it on her tongue and began to wipe my face. I pulled away.

"Erin, leave it. I wouldn't worry about that. The whole thing's about to go tits up. They've asked me to step in for the sick crew member," I whispered, fearful that passengers would hear."

"I know. I heard," Erin said and continued to dab at my head.

"What? You heard and you didn't say anything." My whisper had turned into a shrill screech.

"Keep your voice down." She stuffed the tissue into a pocket, grabbed my arm and pulled me towards the rear of the plane.

"I didn't say anything because there's nothing I can do. You're on duty."

"On duty? What?"

"Look, I didn't go on about it because you have enough to worry about and I didn't think it would be an issue, but like I said last night, technically you're working. Once you fly as a crew member it counts as positioning."

"Positioning?"

"Yes. Duty. Part of your hours."

"My hours? I've got no frigging hours. I'm ... I can't believe this." I threw my hands up, the despair flowing through my body. Erin tugged hard on my jacket.

"Get a bloody grip. Sophie's coming. Just go with it. Find out what she has to say and I'll come and see you. Screw up now and both of us are in the shit."

Sophie handed me a beaker of water and led me back up to the front of the aircraft. She told me that she would need me to do the safety briefing and then check the cabin. If the flight was quiet they may not need much else.

With the sick crew member off-loaded, the aircraft began to push back from the terminal. The Captain's voice came over the intercom, a flurry of detail about the flight, '... *cabin crew, please prepare for departure ... cross-check and report ...*' but with my mind racing I only heard snippets.

Erin approached.

"She's asked me to do the bloody safety stuff," I said. "I can't do that, Erin."

"Yes, you can." Erin's voice was a low hiss, but the urgency still apparent. "You have to. Just follow what I do. She's got you at the front, so you'll be able to see down the cabin. I'm in the middle. Just watch me and listen to the PA."

I swallowed hard, trying to lose the lump that was forming in my throat.

"But you said don't draw attention ... I'm not trained for this. In fact I'm not trained for anything on here."

"I can't pull you off it. It'll look bad. Think about it. Why would a crew member not do it? It'll blow your cover if you don't."

"It'll blow my cover if I do you mean."

"You're making a bloody scene. You'll be fine. Follow what you hear. You've been on flights before as a passenger. You've seen it done."

"Yes, but I don't watch ... nobody watches the safety thing, do they?"

Erin's voiced dropped an octave and took on a stern, reproachful tone.

"Listen to me Matthew Malarkey." She paused and stared around the cabin as soon as she realised she had used my proper name. Fortunately, nobody had heard. Her voice dropped to a whisper. "Look, we've got no choice. Remember the con. Now grow a pair and stop whining. The Captain knows you're on board. He's told you you're on duty. There's no going back. Okay?"

There was nothing I could say. Erin continued.

"I've stuck my neck out here to get you on this bloody flight. I'm doing you a favour so consider this payback." She turned and walked away.

I was in a corner. No other options. If I was going to pull off the impersonation, I had to go the full way. The PA came to life and Sophie's voice cut through my indecision.

'*Good morning ladies and gentleman. My name is Sophie Carter and I am your cabin manager for today's flight. On behalf of Captain Reynolds and the crew I would like to welcome you on board ...*'

I stood at the front, in the centre of the aisle, aware that numerous faces were now staring in my direction. The bones and muscles that normally operated my legs appeared to have turned to some sort of glutinous substance and I wasn't convinced that they would hold me up for very long. As Sophie eased her way through her announcements, I tried to reassure myself. Most passengers don't watch the briefing I had said to Erin. No reason why they should all take a particular interest today. At least I hoped they wouldn't.

'*I would like to ask for everyone's attention, even if you are a frequent flyer, while we take you through the safety features of our Airbus ...*' Sophie continued.

I felt the hairs rise on the back of my neck. Ahead of me, I noticed Erin glance around, a slight nod of her head signalling encouragement. Then she reached down to her right and picked up a card. I glanced to my right and saw a safety card along with other bits of safety equipment. I picked up the card just as Erin had done.

'*In your seat pocket is a safety card indicating the exit routes, oxygen masks ...*'

I watched Erin hold her card out in front of her and did likewise. I couldn't help noticing that one of the passengers on my right had begun to tilt over into the aisle so that his shoulders were almost at right angles to his waist, his head angled down towards the floor. For a moment, I thought he was going over with the cabin crew bug until I saw that his eyes were wide open and he was staring at the safety card. I glanced quickly at the card and to my horror realised it was upside down. In my hurry to right it, I dropped it on the floor. I went to grab it but Sophie had eased smoothly into her next instruction and I noticed that Erin had put her card down.

'*There are eight emergency exits. Two doors at the rear of the cabin, four window exits in the ...*'

Erin's hands were outstretched in front of her. I followed her lead. Then she span around to indicate the doors behind her. I did the same.

'*Low level lighting will guide you to an exit ...*'

Erin pointed to the floor with both hands. Again I followed her lead. I began to feel an air of confidence. Maybe it was simple.

'*Please take time to locate your nearest exit. Don't forget that the nearest usable exit ...*'

I watched Erin reach forward again but I didn't see what she picked up this time. I began to feel the perspiration trickle under my collar. On the floor next to me was a seat belt, an oxygen mask and a yellow life jacket.

Sophie continued. '*...in the unlikely event of having to use an escape slide ...*'

Escape. Must be the life jacket. I grabbed it from the floor and quickly unwrapped the black tape that kept it neatly folded up. I stared straight ahead to see what Erin did next, the jacket dangling from my hand.

'*Your seat belt is fastened ...*'

Erin held both hands in front of her, just above eye level, a black demo seatbelt clearly visible. I couldn't afford to play catch up. I made a grab for the seatbelt that was down by my feet and slung the life jacket to one side. It struck a woman straight in the face in the centre seat to my right. She let out a yelp of surprise and then began to shout at me. I ignored her and stared ahead trying to see what Erin was doing. She buckled the seat belt and then pulled the loose end to demonstrate how to adjust it.

'*Whenever the seat belt signs are illuminated you must return to your seat and fasten your seat belt.*'

I held the belt out in front of me. My hands began to shake as I tried to insert the clip into the buckle. I couldn't line it up and it didn't go in.

'*We recommend that you keep your seat belt fastened at all times ...*'

Ahead of me, Erin reached forward again. I dropped the belt on the floor. I needed to be in tune with the audio.

'*If there's a failure in the air supply oxygen will be provided ...*'

Oxygen. I picked up the oxygen mask just as Erin had done. I watched as she held it up for the passengers, stretching it between both hands so it was fully in view. I did the same but made one mistake. Whereas she had held the yellow mouthpiece in one hand and the clear plastic bag section in the other, I held onto the mouthpiece but grabbed the elasticated strap instead of the bag. In attempting to replicate what Erin had done, I overstretched the elastic to such an extent that the whole unit shot completely out of my hand in a catapult action, and flew across the passenger seats. Its progress was halted when the plastic mouthpiece collided with the head of the woman holding the life jacket that I had lobbed away earlier. In shock driven fury she attempted to jump up but was restrained by her seat belt, which seemed to add to her indignation.

"What the bloody hell are you doing you imbecile?" she shouted, her face a boiling rage. "It's supposed to be a safety demonstration."

I had no time to debate with her. I had to keep up. I reached over and snatched both the life jacket and the oxygen mask.

"Sorry. Sorry madam. I'm just ... err ... showing what can happen if you ... if you get it wrong."

'*... place the mask over your nose and mouth and breathe normally.*'

A simple instruction. I placed the mask on my face, stretched the elastic over my head and let it slip into place.

'*Use the elastic strap ...*'

I'd already done that. I was ahead of the game.

'*To adjust pull the elastic straps on both sides ...*'

I pulled both straps, in line with the announcement. The mask tightened on my face. It felt a little uncomfortable but at least I knew it was on correctly.

'Remember to put on your own mask before helping others with theirs.'

Erin reached forward again. It had to be the life jacket. I was right.

'A life jacket is stored under your seat. In the event of landing on water ...'

I waited as Erin unwrapped her lifejacket, pleased that I was back in sync with the audio.

'... remove it and place it over your head.'

As Erin put the lifejacket on, I raised mine and eased it over my head.

'Pass the tapes around your waist ...'

Tapes? What tapes? In front, Erin was holding out a black strap that seemed to be connected to the front of the lifejacket. Mine didn't have one. I stared down at the jacket, its rounded edges dangling loosely at the top of my chest. There was no strap. I had a duff one. That had to be the reason. I tried to suppress the panic that began to rise from within, my breathing coming in short gasps.

'... to adjust, pull the strap like this.'

I flapped at the front of the jacket just as Erin seemed to be tightening hers. In my anxiety, I cursed out loud.

"What bloody strap?"

I heard a chuckle to my left.

"You got it on back to front mate."

I stared in the direction of the chuckle. A bald bloke was pointing at me. Ignoring the hot flush that swept up across my face, I swivelled the jacket around and the strap flapped loosely in front of me. I had to style it out.

"Well spotted Sir," I said. "That can be the difference between life and ... and ..." I hesitated, suddenly concerned about using the word on a flight that was about to take off. But I had nowhere to go with the sentence. "... and ... err ... death." It didn't matter. No one seemed to have grasped what I'd said. There was no point in trying to clip the strap together. I was losing ground on the demo. I wiped the sweat from my brow and tried to focus on the audio.

'... inflate it by pulling the toggle.'

I fumbled for the red cord but the audio was moving on.

'If the lifejacket fails to inflate or needs topping up, blow into this tube.'

Erin had turned slightly to her right and was holding up the red mouthpiece tube attached to the right shoulder of the jacket. She then held the tube close to her chin. I followed her action, first displaying the tube and then attempting to place it next to my own chin. As I did so, it hit the plastic oxygen mask, slid against the side and poked me straight in the eye.

"Ow, shit!" I couldn't help the reaction as I recoiled from the impact.

A ripple of laughter echoed between several rows of seats. I gulped hard, acutely aware that now everyone was watching the demo. What had happened to the indifferent frequent flyers?

'... a light and a whistle for attracting attention.'

"You won't need them mate. You've attracted plenty of attention already." The bald bloke raised a further ripple of amusement. I glared at him for a moment but I knew I had to ignore him and get on with it.

'... not to inflate your lifejacket until you are outside the aircraft. We also carry life cots for babies and ...'

Erin had begun to move along the cabin.

'Please now ensure that your seatback is upright, your tray table is stowed, your armrests are down and your seat belt is correctly fastened.'

I stood completely still, rooted to the spot, uncertain as to what I was supposed to do next.

'... cabin crew will now pass through the cabin ...'

Sophie had said that I would need to check the cabin. I had seen crew walk down the cabin pre-flight before, checking seat belts and overhead lockers. That was exactly what Erin was doing. I moved down the aisle hoping that I looked the part.

"Hey dad. It's Darth Vader."

A young boy was pointing directly at me and giggling. His dad joined in the merriment. I ignored them. And then Erin turned. I saw the moment's hesitation as she looked at me and then she began to point frantically at her face. I was about to rush forward thinking that she was suffering the stomach bug and was feeling sick when I felt a tap on my shoulder.

"I've had a complaint –"

I turned and came face to face with Sophie. The professional composure that had been on display all morning suddenly seemed to desert her.

"What ... what *are* you doing?"

"Mmmph ermmph phhmmmp mmermmmph –"

"I can't hear you. Take the bloody mask off. And that life jacket. What are you playing at?"

I had totally forgotten about the oxygen mask. My concentration had been so focussed on the audio and safety briefing, I had become unaware of it. I hadn't even noticed that Erin didn't have one on. And I assumed my difficulty in breathing was simply through nerves. I hurriedly grabbed the mouthpiece and pulled it up and away from my face.

"Sorry ... I ... err ... a complaint?"

"Yes, a passenger at the front has complained about your lack of professionalism at the safety briefing. She said you even hit her in the face with the oxygen mask and threw the lifejacket at her. What do you have to say?"

I had to think on my feet. Even though the plane was now taxiing, I felt sure they could still throw me off.

"Err ... I was just ... just, you know, adding a bit of fun to the demo. It ... uh ... worries me that people don't take it seriously and don't watch it so I thought I would lighten it up a bit to keep their attention."

"Well they are not going to take it seriously if you start throwing equipment at them are they? And what makes you think you can come on my aircraft and start playing by your own rules?"

There was no answer. I glanced around the cabin. The young boy who had pointed at me was smiling and clapping his hands. I winked at him and watched his grin grow wider.

"I'm sorry Miss Carter ... err ... Sophie. It was an error of judgement." I pointed at the young boy. "But at least there's one

146

happy customer. He paid attention and it's important for children to be safe. That's all I was trying to do. Make it more interesting ... not that it's dull ... I mean ... make it more memorable."

Sophie turned around to look at the boy and then back at me.

"Well just you make sure you follow procedures in future." She marched off along the cabin, her head held in a snooty, superior manner. I breathed a sigh of relief. At that moment Erin appeared by my side.

"What were you doing with the bloody oxygen mask? You're not supposed to put it on and then strut round the cabin wearing it. It's just a demo."

"I wasn't strutting. I didn't know, did I? And then I forgot about it. Look, it doesn't matter now. I got away with it and right now I need a drink."

She patted my arm. "I'll get you one when we're airborne."

'Cabin crew, seats for take-off.' The Captain's voice came over the PA system.

"Take your seat … JJ. I'll try to keep you out of the way on the rest of the flight. We might need help with the cabin service but I'll just get you to push the trolley at worst."

I returned to my seat and strapped myself in, relieved to be out of the spotlight. The aircraft rumbled over the concrete, the wheels bouncing lightly as it turned onto the runway in a perfectly executed arc, like a skater curving across the ice. It slowed and then came to a standstill. My heart thumped wildly in anticipation. The engine sound dropped into a deep throaty rumble. Tension gripped my whole body. The moment I had taken a huge risk for had begun. There was no turning back. An intense growl flared through the engines as the aircraft revved up to full throttle. In a sudden powerful thrust of acceleration, it shot forward, propelling itself along the runway until it began to soar against the pull of gravity. As it left the ground, I heard a sharp thump below the undercarriage. At first I thought it was my heart. Then I realised it was the wheels.

There was still a long day ahead.

19

We arrived in Ibiza right on schedule. My only other duties, thanks to Erin, had been helping with the in-flight drink service. I did nothing more than push the trolley and hand over a few of the orders that Erin had taken. The bonus was that it gave me access to the drinks and by the time I got off the flight, I had sunk three gin miniatures. I needed something to calm my nerves and to help me deal with the next stage of my journey – leaving the flight.

Erin took me to one side after the passengers had disembarked.

"Okay Matthew. Now you're on your own. Just head for the staff channel. Wave your ID pass at them and you'll be fine. If they want to examine it they will, but as long as you look the part, there'll be no problem. Just act calm and nonchalant. They're expecting to see flight crew. They're used to it. It's not unusual in an airport."

Calm and nonchalant. Easier said than done.

"Then what?"

"Your call. Once you clear the airport, get yourself a taxi and do whatever you have to do. I've sorted all the paperwork so nobody is expecting JJ on a return flight."

"But what if they stop me?"

"Don't even think about it. Remember the con. Now off you go ... and good luck."

Erin had been right again. Fuelled by the three gins, I breezed through the staff channel at customs and in no time at all I was outside the airport in the morning sun. I hopped in a taxi and went straight to the Blau Parc where I was booked in with Cecil. I handed over JJ's passport, signed a booking in form and took a room key. Inside the room, the curtains were still drawn and the mound in the bed told me that Cecil was fast asleep. He didn't stir, even when I approached and called out his name. A night on the tiles I assumed, enjoying the late night delights of San Antonio. I slipped into the bathroom and washed my face and hands. Next, I pulled out my swimming shorts from my case, hung the airline uniform in the wardrobe and headed downstairs for the pool.

Along one side of the pool area, rows of sunbathers were already in position for a day's sun worship, spread out on white sun loungers, drinks at the ready and sunscreen within easy reach. On the opposite side, the hotel bar opened out onto a terrace that was lined with tables and chairs. I walked around the pool, its green Astroturf surround an interesting contrast to the blue of the water, and headed for the bar area. I pulled out a chair at one of the tables, ordered a coffee and slipped into deep concentration. It had all seemed like a good idea to get back to Ibiza and sort out my problems but although I knew exactly what they were, now that I had arrived, I had no idea what to do next. Where would I start looking? What would I do if I did find Felipe or Scalapino?

My concentration was interrupted as Cecil approached in a pair of black swimming shorts, a towel slung over one shoulder and a bottle of sunscreen in his hand.

"Mate, you made it. So how d'you do that then with no passport?"

"Shush Ces. Keep your voice down. I have got a passport except it isn't mine." I then explained my trip to Cecil, swearing him to secrecy.

"So that's what the pilot's uniform is doing in the wardrobe. I was beginning to wonder. Thought I'd got so pissed last night I'd ended up in the wrong room. Bit worrying when I saw it was a geezer's uniform."

"It's not a pilot's uniform. It's cabin crew."

"Well they look the same don't they?"

"And another thing Ces, I'm JJ from now on, okay?"

"Whatever you want JJ." Cecil laughed and pointed at my face. "What you done to your eye geezer? Looks a bit bloodshot."

"Oh, just, uh ... I poked it with the ... my finger or something. Anyway, mate sorry I woke you."

"Nah, you didn't. I was getting up anyway."

"Yeah right. Looked like it too. You were snoring."

"Well you know how it is. Bit of a late one with the lads down in Sodom. You seen them?"

"No, I've not long been here. I expect you've taken them out of the equation as usual and they're still asleep."

"Yeah, lightweights." Cecil turned towards the bar area. "Where's the waiter anyway? I fancy a Bloody Mary and some breakfast."

I caught the waiter's attention and Cecil placed his order.

"So, what's the plan then geeze?" he asked.

"Not sure. I was just thinking about it. Now I'm here I don't know where to start."

Cecil ran a hand through his hair.

"Well, you got contacts here ain't ya? James for a start. And he's got all them birds who must know people. We can ask around, get them all on the case."

I looked up in alarm.

"No, no, Ces. I don't want James involved. If he's involved it'll get back to Eleanor and then it's certain to get back to Louise. Louise doesn't even know I'm here. If she finds that out she'll think one of two things. Either I am meddling in the case, which won't help her career, or that I don't give a toss about what's happened between me and her and I've just gone partying with the boys in Ibiza."

"But you *are* meddling in the case."

"I'm not meddling. I'm just trying to sort it."

The waiter delivered the Bloody Mary. Cecil took a long slurp and sat back in his chair.

150

"Mate, okay. The way I see it, if you don't wanna use your contacts we gotta go asking around ourselves. Get down the bars and see what we can find out."

"Ces, it's not a lads' trip trawling bars. I told you that. I'm here illegally for a start and the sooner I can get out of here the better. It's get the job done and get out."

"I know mate. But we gotta go where people go," Cecil said. He sat forward in his chair and stared at me intently. "Mate what about them two Scanny birds. What were they called?"

"Estrid and Alida," I said.

"Yeah, that's them. Estrid and Al. We could try and find them. They must know the swerve round here by now."

"I suppose so but they know James too so that's no good."

"Mate, you got start somewhere otherwise you're just wandering about hoping something'll turn up and that ain't gonna happen. If we find them, we just give them some bull about a surprise party for James or something and tell them they can't say anything to him about us being here. Sweeten them up a bit with a few drinks and tell them they'll be invited too."

He had a point. I couldn't just sit on my hands and wait for a break.

"Maybe." I beckoned to the waiter and ordered a coffee refill. "I suppose that makes some sense. You guys are only here a week, right?"

"Ten days, mate."

"Okay. And I've got less than a month before I have to go back to court."

"Yeah mate, so we gotta move on it. Take control. And them geezers who picked you up must've seen you down the sunset bars. We gotta start asking down that area. Plenty of other bars down there too. We'll get Carlos on the case. He knows the lingo. Not much else you can do?"

I scratched my head. I had no other ideas. Cecil's view was the only practical one there was.

"Sounds like a plan Ces. May as well soak up a bit of sun today and then take a stroll down there later and sniff around a bit."

"Good man. Now where'd that geezer go with breakfast?"

The four of us met up at six o'clock in the Golden Buddha. We had spent the afternoon by the pool discussing options for the evening. To me it sounded like Cecil and Jasper were intent on another night of mayhem in San Antonio. Carlos was happy to go with the flow but, since my arrival, he had become more aware of the need for me to fulfil my mission. We had finally agreed that there was no big plan other than to spend the evening keeping our eyes open and making like tourists. If I could find Estrid and Alida that would be a bonus. For the other three, doing the tourist thing didn't seem too difficult a task but for me it would be impossible to relax.

"Where'd you get that bracelet?" I said to Jasper as he returned from the bar with a tray of lagers.

He set the beers down one by one in front of us and then held out his right arm.

"You like it? There's a bloke down by the harbour with a stall selling them. You pick one out and he engraves your name on it."

The bracelet was nothing more than a cheap imitation silver chain with a nameplate attached. Typical tourist junk but a holiday memento nonetheless. I took a closer look at the nameplate. It had the words '*Keeper of the Treasure*' engraved across it.

"It's not got your name on it, Jas. It's got –"

"Keeper of the Treasure. Yeah, that's what my name means."

"What? Who told you that?" I asked.

"The bloke who sells them did. It comes from the Persian name Kasper he reckons, which means treasure. And jasper's a gemstone anyway so it all ties up."

A gemstone. My mind focussed sharply on the diamond problem again. Cecil interrupted my thought pattern.

"Mate, the geezer'd tell you any old bollocks to get ten euros off ya."

Jasper laughed. "Well better than the bollocks he told you then Ces. Listen to this lads. He reckons Cecil translates as blind."

"Blind?" I said.

152

Cecil waved a dismissive hand. "I told ya. The geezer's a con artist, ripping mug tourists off, selling them crap bracelets and making up meanings to make them think it's some sort of mystic hippy shit."

"He reckons it's from some Latin word that meant blind," Jasper added.

Carlos raised his beer and pointed at Cecil.

"Maybe you should've had *drunk* engraved on there too Ces. Would've been about right last night."

"Maybe you should've got one with the word nobhead on it Carlos, in big fucking capitals," Cecil shot back.

"Hey, boys. Cool it. It's only a bit of fun," Jasper said. "Bit of jewellery looks alright once the old tan develops. Anyway, yours was okay Carlos. You should've got one." Jasper turned to me. "According to the bloke, Carlos means manly."

"Och, I didnae need a bracelet to tell me what I already ken," Carlos said.

"I wonder what my name means then," I said. "Probably unlucky or something the way things pan out for me."

Jasper patted me on the shoulder.

"We'll go down there some time Matt. Check it out, yeah?"

I sipped my beer and thought for a moment.

"Maybe, but like I've said all along, I'm here to sort things out and we're wasting time sitting here right now. We need to get down the sunset bars. And remember what I said. It's JJ while I'm out here so lose the Matt thing Jas."

"Okay, no problem ... JJ."

Cecil stood up, drained his glass and ran both hands through his hair.

"Sunset bars sound good to me lads. I'm on it."

We made our way down onto the palm lined pathway that wound its way between the rocky outcrops of the shoreline and the rows of hotel restaurants filled with early evening drinkers. The descending sun had cast a yellow haze across the shimmering ocean surface and everything in its gaze took on a bright yellow glow. Where the path reached its high point, veering off to the left in a gentle slope,

153

the landscape opened up on one side to reveal a wide expanse of wasteland. Rows of people had gathered along the path to sit and wait for the sunset, happily chatting and drinking, their sun burnt faces a tell-tale sign of how they had spent their day. Occasionally a whiff of marijuana smoke would drift high into the air from the rocky beach. Portable music players vied for airtime as their varying sounds merged to create a party atmosphere. In the distance the tall white apartment blocks that overlooked the sunset bar strip, had taken on a pink hue as the sun settled lower in the sky. As we neared the bar area the crowd grew more dense, spilling out onto the rocks beneath the canopied walkway.

"Looks busy tonight lads," Cecil said, a smile of anticipation playing on his face.

We spent an hour in Café del Mar and then moved over to Café Mambo. The lads chatted happily, drank several beers and then switched to Jack Daniels and Coke, feet tapping to the beat of the music and one eye on the array of sun tanned ladies that flowed in a steady stream past the bar. I tried to relax and join in but my senses had gone into alert mode, my attention caught by every movement immediately behind me. At ten-thirty, we moved down the Sunset Strip to Savannah, its whitewashed arches overlooking the darkening ocean. It was there that we came across Estrid and Alida. Alida had a hand outstretched offering a flyer before she recognised us.

"Oh, hello boys. We thought you had gone home."

Cecil was on the case immediately.

"Yeah we did, but we had to come back once we knew there was two hot ladies like you two still on the island. Has to be done. I knew you'd miss us so we jumped on a fast jet and got right back out here. How you doing?"

Estrid glanced at Alida.

"We're fine. Busy, but we like it here. It's so much fun."

Jasper stepped forward, eager not to be left out.

"Hello ladies. I'm Jasper, a good friend of these two bad boys." He flashed the Jasper smile, the full switched on radiance that usually gave him a head start in the chat up stakes.

"Bad boys? Away wi'ya. These wee whippersnappers havenae gottae clue. Hola señoras. Mi nombre es Carlos. Carlos MacFadden, entrepreneur, bon viveur and master of the dance." Carlos edged between Cecil and Jasper and dropped in to a sweeping bow of greeting.

Both the girls began to giggle. Cecil turned to Jasper and me.

"The geezer's on one. He don't handle them JDs does he?"

The question didn't need an answer. The fact that Carlos had slipped into a mix of his Spanish and Scottish personas was always a sign that the booze had kicked in.

"I heard that Cecil. I'm a Scotsman. I can handle ma drink. In fact I can handle –"

"So what's with the lingo then Carlos?" Cecil cut in. "These birds ain't Spanish. They're from Denmark."

Carlos waved a dismissive hand. "Well I dinnae know any ... any Danish, do I?"

"You don't need to geeze. They speak English and what's more, they speak it a lot better than that fucked up mix of Scotspan you're trying to blag 'em with."

"Ah, away wi'ya Cecil. Women like a man with a brain, a man that's bi."

Jasper and Cecil burst into a fit of laughter.

"Always wondered about you Carlos. Now you're coming clean eh? Swing both ways, yeah?" Cecil said.

"Bi lingual, ya bastards," Carlos shot back.

"And what's all that bollocks about master of dancing? From what I've seen you dance like you got two wooden legs," Cecil goaded.

"Lads, never mind all that banter," I said. "I've got a lot of things to sort out here and this isn't helping." I gestured to the two girls to get their attention. "I hope you don't mind me asking but I wondered if either of you know or have seen a tall guy, bald head, very tanned face, about thirty-five or so in the area?"

There was a quick exchange of looks between the two girls but no immediate hint of recognition that I could detect.

"He goes by the name of Scalapino. Johnny Scalapino."

155

The name seemed to complete the picture.

"Scalp," Estrid said to Alida. "He must mean Scalp."

"Yeah, I do. You know him then?"

"Not very well. He works on the doors at some of the clubs and bars. He doesn't have much to do with us. I didn't know he was called Johnny," Alida said. "Everybody calls him Scalp."

"Which bars?"

"Different ones. We never know where he is going to be," Alida said. "He's like a ... a free person."

"Freelance."

"Maybe. But how do you know him? Why are you looking?"

I hesitated, a moment's apprehension. The fact that the girls knew him made the possibility of finding him very real. And that scared me. I hadn't thought through at all what I would do if I ran across either of the two guys that had waylaid me and then set me up.

"Err, well ... it's a party, err ... a ... a surprise for ..."

Cecil came to my aid.

"We got a job for him. You know we told you we know James, yeah? Well, we're throwing a party for his birthday."

"His birthday?" Alida said. "But that was in January."

Cecil hesitated but recovered quickly. "Yeah, I know, but we weren't here then were we. So it's a late one. A surprise. He don't know nothing about it. And we want Johnny ... Scalp, to run the guest list. There's gonna be some well famous celebs coming so we gotta get it properly organised. Mate of mine back in London told me to look up Scalp. Said he was the right guy for the job. We're hiring out one of the clubs. Maybe Es Paradis or Pacha."

The girls stared at one another for a moment. Estrid spoke first.

"Wow, that's so cool."

"Ces and JJ are well connected," Jasper said, winking at the girls. They both looked confused.

"Who is JJ?" Estrid asked.

"It's Matt here, isn't it," Jasper replied.

Cecil and I exchanged glances. Jasper was often a bit quick off the mark when women were around. Cecil flicked a hand through his hair and smiled.

"JJ? That's Matt's nickname from when he was kid. So we still call him that." He turned to me and said, "You don't mind the girls calling you JJ, do you geezer?"

"Err ... no, not at all," I said.

"Anyway," Cecil continued, "the party's all top secret. You say nothing to nobody, yeah?"

Both girls nodded.

"Okay, good. So, look, d'you know where Scalp is tonight then?"

"No," Alida said. "We don't always know but sometimes he's down some of the bars further along the harbour, like Ibiza Rocks and Itaca. He goes down there for a drink before he comes back up to Bar Street if he's working."

"We was down that way last night, weren't we Jas. Had a couple in Itaca," Cecil replied.

"If we see him tonight we can say you are looking for him," Estrid said.

Cecil held up a hand. "Whoa. Don't do that. It's a surprise, like I said. I don't want the word getting out before we've had a chance to see if he can do it. We get too many party crashers then there ain't gonna be any room for you two lovely ladies. And you wanna come don't ya?"

The look on their faces said it all. Cecil swore them to secrecy and we headed into Savannah for a few more beers.

Our trawl round the bar area that the girls had mentioned proved fruitless. In a way, I was glad. I was a mix of emotions. I wanted a break, something that would give me a clue to solving my predicament, but the apprehension I felt about confrontation made me want to put it off as long as I could. By one o'clock in the morning, I had had enough. In any case, Cecil and Jasper were ready to party the rest of the night, Carlos was drunk and I was exhausted after the long day.

I waited until Cecil and Jasper had left for their night on the tiles and then tried to rouse Carlos who had slumped in his seat, remaining upright only because his back was against the wall of the bar. He was not cooperating with my attempts to wake him, his only response being a few incoherent words in Spanish. In fact they could have been in Scottish. I sipped my beer and let my gaze wander around the bar. It was still lively, many of the late revellers having a last few pre club drinks at acceptable prices before the main event of their night.

It was then that I noticed him.

He stood alone, leaning against the bar at first, and then pacing up and down in short steps, almost a shuffle, furtive glances to left and right, the occasional surreptitious glance in my direction. I raised my glass and averted my gaze. I tried to wake Carlos again but he simply snorted and made himself more comfortable against the wall. I leaned towards him.

"Carlos. Wake up mate. We have to go."

No response.

I glanced towards the bar. He was still there, playing with the collar of his jacket and staring in the direction of the door. Tall and tanned, dark hair slicked back, he stood out from the crowd. It was the shuffling, a restless body language that spoke of unease when all around him were chilled and partying, that held my attention. Instinct told me there was something not right about him. No drink in his hand in a busy bar and he didn't look like he was queuing to get one. Tension began to take a hold as a mass of wild thoughts fizzed through my head. Another surreptitious glance towards me.

I tried rousing Carlos again.

"Carlos, wake up. You can't stay here mate." I shook him vigorously by the shoulders.

"Wassamadder ... estoy bien ... s'okay Mateo ..."

"Carlos, I told you. It's JJ."

"Que?"

"Never mind. I'll be back in a minute. Don't go anywhere."

I needed the toilet. There seemed to be no danger of Carlos going anywhere right at that moment. I had to get him back to the hotel. I looked towards the bar again. The tall stranger was checking his watch. At that moment, a sense of relief washed over me. Perhaps I was being paranoid. Nobody even knew I was in Ibiza. Maybe he was just waiting for somebody - a date or something. I stood up and headed towards the lavatories, trying not to look at him as I walked past.

If it hadn't been for the toilet attendant, perhaps I would have been more alert. He was standing by a sink area that was adorned by an array of toiletries. As I walked in, he greeted me.

"Welcome to my toilet. No spray, no lay."

"Err ... hi," I said and made my way to the urinal. When I had done, I walked towards the sink.

"No soap, no hope," the toilet attendant said and turned on a tap for me.

"Thank you," I said and focussed on washing my hands, aware that he was hovering next to me with a paper towel at the ready. Behind me, I heard the door open. I glanced up at the mirror above the sink, an instinctive action when your back is to a door, to see who had entered. But again I was distracted by the toilet attendant.

"You wash da finga for da minga, my friend." He handed me a towel.

"Sorry?" I said as I took the towel.

"You want spray?" He held out a Lynx aerosol canister.

"Err ... no, it's okay. Thanks."

I turned to leave and came face to face with the stranger from the bar.

20

White streaks of moonlight shimmered through patches of wispy cloud and cast a silvery haze onto the ocean below as it sprayed onto the beach. An assortment of colours, from the lights of the many bars and restaurants that ran along the adjacent walkway, drifted skyward until they were overcome by the blackness of the night sky. It was the last thing I saw.

I was pushed up against the side of a car and within seconds had a dark hood placed over my head. It happened so quickly that there was no time to take anything in. I heard a door open and I was shoved across the back seat. I became aware that there were two men already in the car, one in the driver's seat and another in the rear passenger seat. The stranger from the bar jumped in behind me so that I was in the middle.

Fear and panic hit stellar levels the minute the hood went on. The only reasons for a hood is either to ensure the victim has no idea where they are going or as a preliminary to execution. I prayed that it was not the latter.

Two of the men exchanged some words in Spanish and I heard the car engine start. I decided to stay quiet. There didn't seem to be any point in asking where we were going. You don't stick a hood on someone if you want them to have that information. My mind raced through the evening. I hadn't seen anyone familiar. I hadn't run into Scalapino or Felipe. So who were these guys? They had to be connected with Felipe. There could be nobody else on my case. But how did they know I was on the island? The two girls had been told to keep quiet. The boys had no idea who had originally waylaid me so it couldn't have anything to do with them. I thought back to the stranger. He hadn't said much when he confronted me in the toilets. He had simply grabbed me by the upper arm and manhandled me through a side door out onto the street. I had caught a brief glimpse of Carlos as we left, head on the table, clearly fast asleep. He hadn't seen a thing. Jasper and Cecil were out on the town and knowing their party habits, would be unlikely to surface much before midday. Cecil probably wouldn't even notice if I was not in the room. I was on my own.

And then a thought hit me. It had to be Cecil. Cecil was the reason they knew I was back on the island. It had to be him. He was the common denominator with my previous trip. He'd told Estrid and Alida that he had been down to Ibiza Rocks and Itaca the night before I had arrived. Johnny Scalapino's watering holes. Scalapino must have been there. He had to have seen Cecil. If he had reported that information back to Felipe then it would stand to reason they would tail Cecil to see what he was up to. As soon as I showed up it must have aroused their suspicions that I was up to something. And now I was in trouble.

The car cruised through the night for what seemed to be about an hour or so. With the number of twists and turns it made, I quickly became disorientated. I had no idea whether we had driven up to an hour away from where we had started or had just driven around in a circuitous route for an hour. To add to my sense of disorientation, nobody said word for the whole of the trip.

After a while the car stopped. The driver killed the engine and I heard doors opening. My hands began to shake and my stomach churned with apprehension. The lack of sight heightened my anxiety further. I felt a tug on my arm and I was pulled across the seat.

"Salir del coche ... out!"

I swung my legs out of the car and stood up. I could hear the sea in the distance. Again I was pulled by the arm and led forward. After a short walk across what seemed to be loose stone and gravel we stopped. I heard two of the men speaking again in Spanish.

161

One of them stepped close to me. He pulled the hood from my head. I blinked to clear my eyes in what little light there was. We were standing on a narrow cliff path, a ramshackle wooden rail separating us from a steep drop down the rock face to the water below. A silver ripple of moonlight bridged the expanse of water from horizon to shore. The man who had removed the hood was the dark haired stranger from the bar. In his right hand he held a gun. He stared at me for a moment and then nodded to one of his accomplices. The man pulled a torch from his pocket, flicked the switch and began to follow the beam of light down the path. A sharp push in the back sent me forward.

"Go."

A wave of panic shot through me. My instinct was to run but I knew I would not get far. I was outnumbered, three gangsters and a gun that swayed the odds in their favour. I did as I was told and began to follow the guy who had walked on ahead.

The path wound round the cliff face down towards a small sandy cove. Large clumps of rock, eerie grey shapes in the shadows of the night, overhung the route so that at times it was necessary to duck down in order to progress. At its steepest, roughly laid concrete steps broke the slope so that it was easier to negotiate. The place was deserted. Across the open expanse of water below I could see distant lights flickering, perhaps the lights of San Antonio. I had no idea. As we approached the beach area the only sound was the water lapping gently against the rocks. It was a good place to dispose of somebody. But if that was the plan why not just do it when we got out of the car? Unless they were going to shoot me on the beach and dispose of my body at sea. My thoughts were interrupted by my mobile, a loud jangling ring emphasised by the stillness of the night. Instinctively I pulled it from my pocket. I managed to catch the name '*Carlos*' on the screen before it was snatched from my hand.

"You no need this," the guy with the gun said. He stared at the screen for a moment but it appeared to hold no interest for him. In a sudden movement, he swung his arm over his head and launched the phone high into the air. I could just make out the dark image as it arced over his shoulder and fell into the scrub that protruded in random clumps from the rock face below us. I stood for a second in shock. My last connection with the outside world. I had no idea where I was being taken to nor what was to become of me and now nobody else would either. A prod in my back told me it was time to walk on.

When we reached the beach below, the guy with the torch focussed its beam on two pairs of battered wooden doors built into roughly hewn timber frames in the face of the rock. Rust covered chains, strung through metal eyebolts, held the doors closed and two heavy-duty padlocks secured the chains in place. Years of weathering had corroded the door hinges a deep, dark brown. In front of both sets of doors I could just make out a pair of metal rails that ran down to the water's edge, like train lines. I guessed that they must have been for launching boats.

The guy ahead of me stopped in front of the first set of doors, pulled a key from his pocket and released the padlock. As he dragged the chain away, the gunman pulled one of the doors open. He beckoned to me.

"Inside."

My hesitancy made him grab my arm and tug me forward towards the door.

In the dim light, I couldn't see much at all but I could just make out that the doors enclosed nothing more than a shallow, natural cave that looked to have been used as a makeshift store. The entrance had been built up with breezeblocks to support the doorframe and make a join with the rock. A musty, damp smell mingled with the odour of seaweed and decaying timber. I walked in and turned round to face my kidnappers. The guy with the gun stood framed in the doorway. The other two had taken up sentry like duty on either side of the cave entrance.

"Manos," he said, pointing at me.

My lack of action caused him to translate.

"Hands. Give me hands." He pulled a rope from his pocket.

I held out both hands.

"Behind," he barked.

163

I had no idea what difference it might make to him whether I had my hands tied behind me or in front of me but to me it made a big difference.

"Err ... if I want to go to the ... the ... err ... toilet. Los servicios?"

He stared at me for a moment and then glanced over his shoulder at one of his comrades.

"Los servicios. The toilet."

The three burst into raucous laughter.

"Señor, your hotel for tonight, it has no toilets."

Another burst of laughter.

"But if I want to ... to ... pee ... take a ... you know ... a leak?"

He waved the gun towards the back of the cave.

"You go in corner."

His amusement at my predicament seemed to make him relax and he beckoned to me to hold my hands out in front. With several wraps of the rope he encircled my wrists and then he brought the loose end down between my outstretched hands, looped it round a couple of times and pulled hard. It had the effect of tightening the rope so that it felt like I was handcuffed on both wrists. He finished off with an elaborate knot and stood back to admire his handy work. His two accomplices moved towards the doors.

"Okay, you see Scalp, mañana." He slipped the gun into his pocket and backed towards the cave entrance. As he turned to leave he hesitated, raised both hands in a prayer like pose and rested his face momentarily on the back of his left hand.

"Buenas noches. Espero que duermas bien." And then he was gone.

Immediately the two doors were swung into position, blotting out the light from outside. I heard the rasp of the chain being pulled through the metal eyebolt and then the metallic click of the padlock. Footsteps faded on the stony pathway and then a silence that was broken only by the distant sound of waves breaking on the rocks.

I sat for a moment trying to adjust to the darkness. As my eyes became accustomed to the gloom, I began to make out the contours of the cave. Its roof curved just a few feet over my head, a dark expanse of natural rock. I crouched down to feel the floor. Again just natural rock, bits of loose grit and stone, a cold hard surface. I edged my way slowly towards one wall and felt my way along it as best I could with my hands tied in front of me. Its cold clamminess was no surprise. I eased my way further back, uncertain about each movement, feeling my way with my feet in short tapping steps, concerned that there may be some crevice or hole in the floor that I might disappear into, but hoping there might be some escape option. I had moved about fifteen to twenty feet along the wall when my foot hit something metallic. I stopped. I kicked out again with the same result, a tinny, rattling sound. I eased my hands round and felt in front of me. A smooth metal surface, with a hard-edged corner. I ran my hands further upwards and hit what seemed to be a handle. In the darkness, with just my senses to guide me, it felt like some sort of tall box. And then I understood. A filing cabinet.

I slid my hands back towards the handle and pulled. A drawer pulled out, uneven in its action. An old filing cabinet it seemed, perhaps rusting, one that had stood there for years. But what was a filing cabinet doing in a cave? I raised myself onto my toes and lowered my hands into the drawer to see if there was anything in it. There was nothing. I pushed it shut. I crouched down looking for a second or third drawer. There were two more, both empty. Perhaps it had been dumped in there. I eased around the cabinet and found the rear wall of the cave. There was nothing else there, just hard, cold, clammy rock. I edged across the back wall and found myself on the opposite side in a few shorts steps. The rear of the cave seemed much narrower than the entrance. I peered back to the front and could see narrow bands of light seeping through the uneven join between the doors and the frame. In that moment I realised there was only one way out and that was the way I had come in. With a chain and padlock securing the doors, I was going nowhere.

I slumped down onto the floor and the reality of my situation hit me. I had been kidnapped by gangsters and I had no idea what my fate would be. Scalapino was coming for me in the morning.

The gangster with the gun had made that clear. My mind began to hurtle through a series of conflicting thoughts. I had been warned the last time to do what they had asked or suffer the consequences. But I had done what they had asked. And I hadn't gone to the police. So what was their problem? On the other hand, the fact that I had returned must make me a threat. And if I was a threat, I had to be removed. Perhaps they would just warn me. Threaten me with violence if I didn't get off the island. What if they found out I had travelled illegally? They could use that. Get me locked up. That would take me out of the picture and discredit me even further. My only hope was that the boys would eventually wonder where I was and report me missing to the police. And if that happened I would be locked up in any case for illegal entry. I was in a no win situation either way. But it could take all day before the lads realised I was not at the hotel and by that time Scalapino would have come to get me.

I sat on the damp rock floor, despair creeping over me. I began to shiver. Cold or fear? I wasn't sure which. Both perhaps. My fate was out of my hands. I realised that I had no hope.

And I had no choice but to wait for Scalapino.

21

I could just make out the time on my watch by standing close to the door. A couple of hours had passed. A couple of hours in which I had continuously mulled over my options and every time came to the same conclusion. There were no options. But I knew I had to dismiss such thoughts. They were not helping my state of mind. I began to think about Louise and the reasons I had come back to Ibiza - to save our relationship and to save her career. And now I may never see her again. I needed to speak to her.

I dragged my hands over to my pocket to get to my mobile. As I did so, I realised the bulge in my pocket was my wallet and that my mobile was somewhere out there on the rocks, probably smashed to pieces. The wallet contained twenty euros and the credit card that Erin had suggested I keep for emergencies. This was, without doubt, an emergency but twenty euros and a credit card were of no use in a deserted cave at the bottom of a cliff face.

And then an idea occurred to me.

I got to my feet. With both wrists tied together it was difficult to get a hand into my pocket, but somehow I managed to slide my little finger and my ring finger in far enough to grip the top of the wallet. I held on to it and tugged. My grip didn't feel tight enough but the wallet began to ease upwards as I pulled. Just as it was almost fully clear of the pocket, it slipped from my grip and fell onto the ground. I dropped to my knees and began to scrabble around trying to find it. Luckily, it hadn't gone far. I rolled into a seated position and, holding the wallet in both hands, managed to get it open. The rope rubbed painfully against my wrists as I manoeuvred my hands and eased out the credit card. Once I had it out, I let go of the wallet.

I folded the card in half, right down the middle. It didn't give easily at first. Next, I bent it back the other way. In the light that cracked through the doorway I could just make out two small white streaks along the top and bottom edges as the stress bit into the plastic. I carried on folding the card back and forth until the streaks merged and became a distinct crease right through the centre. I continued bending it until the crease became completely flexible. As I did so, I could feel that a small split had developed right in the centre of the plastic. Encouraged by this, I twisted the two sides so that a tear started at the top. It was then a simple matter of splitting the plastic along the crease so that the card separated into two pieces, each piece having a sharp serrated edge where the split had occurred.

I placed the two sections together so that they were doubled up with the serrated edges aligned. I gripped the makeshift tool between my fingers and the heel of my hand and began to saw at the rope around my wrists. With limited hand movement, it was an awkward action and difficult to get any significant pressure. The rope chafed with each movement. In the darkness it was hard to tell whether it was having any effect, but I persevered. There was nothing else I could do.

After ten minutes or so, I realised that I had managed to cut through a few strands but the pressure of the rope rubbing on my wrists was making them sore. I stopped for a moment, but the minor success of getting through a few strands spurred me on. If I could get the rope off then maybe I could find a way to tackle the door. I continued the sawing action, back and forth in one spot until finally I felt the edge of the card rasp across my wrist. The rope had been cut through. I threw the credit card aside, raised my wrists towards my face and caught the loose section of rope between my teeth. I tugged at it so that it slid under the knot at the centre. I did this three times until the rope felt loose enough to wriggle my left hand free of its grasp. Once I had one hand out it was simple enough to pull the rope free of the other hand.

I got to my feet, the adrenaline coursing through me as I contemplated what I needed to do next. With the doors the only way out, I decided to focus my attention there. As I had been dragged inside I had noticed the rusty hinges and the weathered timber. There had to be some weakness there.

I edged towards the back of the cave to where the filing cabinet was and removed one of the drawers. Then using it as an improvised battering ram, I smashed it hard against the corner of one of the doors where the topmost hinge joined it to the frame. Nothing much seemed to happen except that the door wobbled a bit as it absorbed the impact. I swung the drawer again with the same result. A third blow and this time I thought I heard a crack. Unable to see properly in the dark, I felt around the door edge to see if I had managed to shift it. A section of planking appeared to have splintered where it joined the hinge. I pushed at it and found that it moved outwards. I pushed harder until it started to creak and break away. A final push and it split completely and dropped outside onto the ground. The gap it left was big enough for me to get my arm through but that was all. A cool draft of air wafted in, chilling the sweat that was pouring down my face. I sensed freedom and it renewed my enthusiasm.

I stood back, the cabinet drawer held at shoulder height, and this time took a run at the door. The sudden impact of metal against wood caused me to be thrown back off my feet and I heard the drawer clatter on the rocky ground. I jumped up immediately and examined the door. Another fragment of timber, this time a thinner, longer section had splintered outward pushing the hinge away from the concrete frame. I wrenched the broken timber off and checked it with my fingers. There was a distinct gap between the hinge and the frame. I could feel the bolts had moved almost free of the concrete. The gap was no more than an inch or so but enough to tell me the door was under pressure. Something clicked in my brain and I became a man possessed. Several more running leaps at the door ended with the drawer bent and buckled but the door had moved enough to tear one of the bolts completely out of the frame. Ignoring the pain in my shoulders and arms that my excess of force had brought on, I threw the drawer to one side and attacked the door. I grabbed the edge and began to shake it violently back and forth so that it wrenched on the hinge. With each forward thrust I leant my whole body weight into it. Finally the rusty hinge gave way, pulling the remaining bolt clear out of the concrete frame in a splintering, cracking surge of timber fragments. With the force applied, the bottom hinge, although still in place, twisted across its length so that base of the door was pulled inwards and the top leant outward at an angle.

I wasted no time. I pulled myself up into the gap between door and frame and then lowered myself, head first, onto the ground outside. For a moment I sat there, exhausted by my efforts, letting the cool pre-dawn sea breeze wash over me. But I knew there was no time to waste. I had to get out of the area. I had no idea when Scalapino would come for me. I got to my feet, brushed down my shirt and started to climb up the path that I had been marched down earlier that night.

And then something occurred to me.

I had left my wallet and my torn credit card on the cave floor.

"Bollocks." I stamped hard on the ground in frustration. The card was of no use but it had my real name on it. I couldn't risk it being handed in to the authorities. It was proof that I was back in Ibiza. I had only brought it on Erin's say so and for my return flight. If the gangsters found it, they could use it to support any story they might concoct. And the wallet had twenty euros in it. I might need money to get to San Antonio. I didn't want to go back but I had no choice.

I ran down the path and scrambled through the gap I had made in the cave entrance. Once inside I began to crawl around on the floor, feeling around for the lost items. Within a few minutes, I had found the wallet. I pawed at the ground seeking the card.

"C'mon, c'mon … where are you?"

And then I felt something. One half of the card. I ran my hand across the surface. It was the half with just the numbers. I needed the half with my name on it too.

"For God's sake, where are you … c'mon. You have to be here somewhere."

I scrabbled around in the grit and dirt, perspiration pouring down my face. The palm of my hand landed on a cigarette butt. It was obvious what it was. I ignored it.

"I don't have time for this … where are you?"

My hand brushed against something else and in my haste, I pushed it aside. I ran my palm back over the same bit of ground again, slowly this time. I had to be patient. Again I felt something next to my hand and this time I clasped it. It wasn't the card. It was crinkly, and crackled lightly when I gripped it. A sweet wrapper. I was about to throw it away when it struck me that it could be of use. A clue. A clue to what, I had no idea but someone had dropped it. That's what they did in detective programmes. Find stuff and keep it. Anything at all. I put the wrapper in my pocket and continued searching for the other half of my credit card. I found another cigarette end. Or it could have been the same one. It was possibly another useful bit of evidence. I picked it up and put it in my pocket along with the sweet wrapper.

It was in the middle of the floor that I finally found the other half of the credit card.

"Yessss."

I stuffed the wallet and the two bits of card into my pocket and headed to the door. Once again, I scrambled through.

On the horizon, the first hint of dawn glowed yellow beneath the rapidly fading night sky.

22

I clambered up the steep path and was halfway to the top when I saw the glint of light, a flicker from within the undergrowth below. I stopped and gazed down at the rocks that fell away towards the sea. There was nothing there. I stepped back a few paces and saw it again, a reddish orange flash. Immediately I knew what it was - the glass screen on my mobile phone glinting in the rising sun. It appeared to be about fifteen to twenty metres below where I was standing. I leant over the handrail to see whether it was possible to climb down. Although the rockface was fairly steep, it seemed manageable at that location, before it again dropped abruptly towards the bay. A number of jagged rocks gave way to several wider, flatter outcrops that were covered in dense, bushy vegetation. I realised that if I was careful and picked my way slowly, I could use the vegetation for grip. I made a mental assessment of precisely where the light was coming from and ducked under the handrail.

I began to inch down the rockface, tentatively feeling for every foothold, gripping at clumps of bushes and ignoring the loose pebbles and grit that rolled away beneath my feet with each step. The sun had now cleared the horizon and turned the water below into a glistening sheet of green and gold. Perspiration began to roll freely down my face as I focused on my descent. I paused to catch my breath and suddenly I felt a moment's doubt. What if I was mistaken? What if it wasn't my phone? What if I had just wasted precious time? I would be a sitting duck if Scalapino showed up right at that point. But I was about halfway down to my target. There was no point in climbing back up having got so far. I dismissed my doubts and carried on.

It took several minutes to reach the spot where I had seen the glint of light. It was the final section of the shallower incline where the slope disappeared down to the beach below. The sight of such a precipitous drop caused me to reel back and fall onto my backside. This was not a place I wanted to be for long. I hurriedly scrabbled around in the shrubbery that I had targeted. And then I saw it.

Suspended between two long, straggly fronds of sun beaten shrub, like some early morning sun seeker in a hammock, my mobile dangled precariously over the precipice. A gentle breeze swayed the end of the plant, rocking the phone back and forth in a rhythmic, bouncing motion.

I took a deep breath, stood up and inched forward, beads of sweat dripping from my brow onto the dusty gravel. As I got closer to the edge, I dropped into a crouch and then onto my hands and knees. Below, white suds of surf sucked at the grey sand and pulled it away from the rocks. The sight of the drop caused my head to spin. I laid flat on my belly, a need to be closer to the ground. I dragged myself forward until my head was over the edge of the rock face and my shoulders in line with the shrub. I stretched out my right arm so that my hand made contact with the plant. The mobile was within gripping distance but my hand was shaking. One clumsy grasp and it was lost. My heart pounded, the effort, the fear and the pressure of the hard ground making my breathing short and shallow. I stretched further, my fingers tantalisingly close. A gust of wind ruffled through my hair and pulled the fronds of the shrub away to my right. I held my breath as the phone swayed and jiggled in its precarious cradle. Warm sweat ran into my eyes. I shook my head to clear my vision and pulled myself closer to the end of the plant. My shoulders were now overhanging the ledge. I stretched again, hands wet with fear, until my fingers finally made contact with one corner of the phone.

A sudden jangling ring shattered the silence, sending a nerve shredding shockwave right through me. Instantly, in some form of fear-inspired reflex, I lurched to my right just as the phone began to topple. My hand clutched at its base, gripping it between thumb and fingers. In an effort to save it slipping away, I swung my arm round and managed to hurl the phone back onto the flatter area of rock behind me. The sudden movement, along with my forward impetus, pulled my body round hard in a left arc, my legs and lower body pitching over the precipice. I was fortunate that my right arm was outstretched and, with a desperate grab, I managed to grasp the main stem of the shrub to stop my fall.

"Holy shit!"

My heart thumped wildly. Tears rolled down my face as a tearing, ripping sound told me the shrub was being uprooted by my weight. I dangled in mid air, slowly slipping downwards, gravel and dirt trickling onto my neck and chest as my free hand clawed at the ground to get a grip. I had slipped down the ledge up to my shoulders before the shrub finally arrested my fall. And then the mobile stopped ringing. Even though I had been desperate to make contact with someone, it had been the wrong time to receive a call.

I dangled for a few seconds, my chest hyperventilating and my face soaked in sweat. Below me, the sea oozed across rocks and sand but I didn't dare look down. Somehow I had to drag myself up onto the ledge. I kicked against the rock face and managed to find a foothold. It relieved the weight on the shrub above and took some of the tension out of my holding arm. I stretched my other arm out across the ground seeking something to grip, digging my fingers into the dirt. To my left I could see a small clump of thick grass. It was enough to gain a hold. I reached out, straining towards it. With a handful of the grass in one hand and the shrub in the other, I began to pull myself upwards.

And then I heard the voices. They had come for me.

High above on the path, I could see three figures. At the front, Scalapino was unmistakeable, muscles bulging through a tight white t-shirt, his bald head glistening in the light. The chatter seemed untroubled, interspersed with laughter. I stayed stock still. At that point going down was not an option. And nor was going up.

In a matter of minutes, they had discovered the broken door. Angry shouts, curses. Even though it was all in Spanish, there was no mistaking that the mood had changed.

I laid my head flat against the ground in an attempt at hiding and began to mutter to myself.

"Don't look down here. Please ... just go away. Don't look this way." And then I remembered the mobile phone. If it rang, I was doomed. I hoped that the caller had left a voice message. If they hadn't, that usually meant a call back. "Not now. Wrong time ... please God."

Scalapino was obviously in a hurry. The broken door had galvanised him into action. I heard the voices again directly above me, this time sharp and decisive. And then they began to fade, until I could hear nothing more.

I clung to my position for another few minutes until I thought it would be safe to try and drag myself up.

Adrenaline rather than strength did it. I managed to get the top half of my body up and over the edge of the rock face and after a moment's breather, I clambered up fully. Relief gave way to nausea and I threw up immediately. But there was no time to feel sorry for myself. I realised I was in immediate danger. I had to get away and find my friends. I picked up my mobile and noticed it had just another one percent of battery life remaining. The missed call was Carlos again. I could call him once I had got back to the roadway at the top of the pathway. I was trapped if I delayed any longer.

I climbed the path and reached the road that the car had stopped on the night before but I had no idea where I was on the island. I knew I had a compass app on my mobile and I checked that. The north facing red arrowhead of the compass needle whirred round and settled. I was facing south and the sea was on my right. That meant I was on the west side of the island, the same side as San Antonio but I still had no idea how far away that was. All I knew was that if I wanted to get back to my friends I had to head south.

My next thought was to get back to my hotel as soon as I could. If I could get in touch with Carlos he could send me a taxi. The problem was I had no idea where to get it sent to. I loaded up Google Maps on my mobile and waited for it to find my location. I watched as it began to zoom in to a location and then, just as it settled on a landmark, fade to a black screen, a small white circle spinning my communication means into oblivion.

"No! Fucking battery." I almost lobbed the phone back into the bushes in sheer frustration.

I followed the coast road for several miles, a journey elongated by my need to duck into the scrubland at the presence of every passing vehicle. I could not risk being spotted. I knew also that the other big risk I ran was going back to the hotel, but I had to contact the lads. Eventually I came to a road lined on either side by rows of trees, their light green fronds contrasting with the yellow soil of scrubland strewn with stones and rocks. There was no pavement, just wide open road. I felt nervous and exposed, my instincts telling me to get out of sight. I continued walking, the dry air and heat causing a thirst that I could not quench, the incessant hum of crickets adding to my tension. I reached a junction. To my right the road passed what appeared to be a gas works plant and then ran out as it reached the sea front. It seemed the safest option. If I followed the sea I would eventually get to the hotel. I turned left and picked my way across the dust covered, rocky surface. I reached a small secluded bay area and realised I was approaching Cala Gració. I continued walking, choosing my foothold carefully on the craggy terrain and took the steep path that descended to the northern side of the beach. I crossed the sand and followed a track that led through the grounds of the Hotel Tanit.

My target was to keep the seafront close on my right side. Once through the hotel grounds I knew the town was not too far ahead and I took the beach pathway again. My shirt stuck to my back and the sun seared into the left side of my face but I was closing in on my destination. As I passed the rows of sea view hotels a beachside trader approached me.

"You want glasses?" he asked, holding out an armful of sunglasses. "Nice Ray-Ban. Suit you," he said, offering me a pair of white frames with mirrored lenses.

I reached out and took the glasses. At worst they could give me some relief for my eyes after walking for two hours in the sun and as a bonus they might work as a disguise. I examined the logo on the side.

"It says Royo Bom," I said.

"Yes, my friend. That's what I say. You like? Only cheap."

"No, you said Ray-Ban. It's a proper brand. I've never heard of Royo Bom."

The trader stared at me for a moment and then smiled.

"Same thing my friend, only it Spanish, you know."

I handed them back and pointed at another pair.

"What about those blue ones?"

"These?" He pulled out another pair. "They very good. They Oakley glasses."

I took them and examined them too.

"It says Oak Lee," I said.

"Yes, that right. Good glasses. Cheap too."

I realised I had no time to worry too much about the brand.

"Okay. I'll take the … err … the Royo Boms. How much?"

"Twenty for you my friend."

"Twenty euros? You're joking. Five."

The trader smiled again.

"Too cheap. I give them you for ten. Ten a deal, okay?"

I realised I only had twenty euros with me but I needed the glasses.

"Ok. Deal."

With the glasses in place I felt a little more secure and made my way back to the Blau Parc. The reception area was dark and cool, its air conditioning running on maximum. I headed for the lift and then thought better of it. Suppose someone was waiting in the corridor, waiting for my return. The thought that someone

177

might be lurking around the hotel suddenly took on a greater significance. If they had been able to discover that I was back on the island then it was a certainty that they knew where I was staying. They could have called at the hotel already. But I was checked in as Jason Jefferies. That may have put them off the trail but I realised that if they followed Cecil back, eventually they would find me. I knew I couldn't stay there. I left the lobby and walked around the corner to the back of the hotel where it adjoined the pathway that ran along the seafront. I climbed onto a ledge and peered over the wall at the pool area. I was in luck. Lying flat out on a sunbed, clutching a bottle of water, was Carlos and he appeared to be fast asleep.

"Hey, Carlos," I called, in a semi-whisper.

There was no reply.

I tried again, this time more loudly.

"Carlos, it's me. Wake up."

He stirred, his head swivelling in the direction of my call.

"Over here," I said.

He stood up and walked towards me.

"Mateo. What are you ... where did you –"

"It's JJ Carlos. I told you."

"Uh? Oh yeah. JJ. But where have you –"

"Never mind that right now mate. I'll explain later. I need you to do something for me. There's a little tapas bar down in the town at the bottom of the West End strip. We passed it, just as you go up into the main bit. I want you to get the others and meet me there in an hour."

"Aye, okay Matt ... JJ. But what's –"

"Don't ask. Just be there in an hour. Oh and tell Ces to bring me some cash. He knows where it is."

He nodded and turned to walk away.

"Hang on Carlos. Let me have some of that water. I'm parched."

I took the bottle from him and glugged down half the contents.

"An hour then."

23

The tapas bar was small, empty and cool, two overhead fans circulating a refreshing breeze. I ordered water and as much tapas as my remaining ten euros would buy and took a corner table. The lads arrived in under an hour, Cecil at their head.

"So what's with the fucking mystery tour geezer? And where'd you get them shades?"

I ignored his last question and proceeded to tell them the story of the previous night's kidnapping. When I had finished, Cecil commented first. "Fucking hell geezer. You are in the shite."

"Thanks Ces," I said, a little deflated at confirmation of what I already knew.

"So what you gonna do then Matt?" Jasper asked.

"It's JJ. How many times have I got to tell you that?"

"Alright Ma ... JJ. Chill mate," Jasper replied, a little taken aback by my poor mood.

"Chill? Frigging chill. How am I supposed to chill when I've got a bald headed psychopath and his gang of henchmen chasing me round the island intent on ... god knows what?"

Cecil stood up.

"Mate, easy. Let's talk it through. This situation calls for a couple of beers first though." He waved a hand at the bar tender and ordered four bottles of Estrella. "Okay, so what d'you want us to do geeze?"

"Well first of all I need you to check me out of the hotel Ces. I can't stay. It won't be too long before they find me there." I turned

179

to Carlos. "And I need you to find me some other accommodation. Something small, out of the way but not too far. You speak the language so see if you can get me a deal. Oh, and I need somebody to pay for it. I've got no cards with me."

"No problem geezer. I'll square it up and you can weigh me in when we get back," Cecil said.

"And what do you want me to do?" Jasper asked.

"Nothing yet, Jas, but I may well need you all if things go pear shaped. In the meantime I can't be seen with any of you. Not unless it's vital that we meet."

"Why not?" Carlos asked.

"Simple. The only reason they know I'm here is because they remembered Cecil from the last trip. Soon as they saw him again they must have got suspicious and followed him."

Cecil shrugged. "I didn't see nobody following me."

"Well you wouldn't would you? You weren't looking and anyway they're not going to make it obvious. The thing is, if I keep a low profile and they see you guys around without me, they may just think they've scared me off."

Jasper raised his beer to take a sip and then paused.

"But they might run into you on your own and then you're in trouble with no backup."

"I told you, I'm going to lay low, stay under cover."

"What in them fucking glasses?" Cecil said. "Where'd you get 'em anyway?"

I fingered the glasses self-consciously.

"I bought them off some bloke along the beach. He was selling stuff. They're Ray-Ban's, the Spanish version."

Cecil laughed loudly. "Spanish Ray-Ban's. Mate, who you trying to blag? They ain't Ray-Ban's. They're a snide pair, ain't they? They ain't legit. What d'you pay for them?"

"Ten euros. I haggled the bloke down. He wanted twenty."

"Haggled? Mate you got mugged off. I would've give him five, tops. Ten euros? That's nearly eight and a half English. For a pair of snide shades? You got well and truly mugged mate."

I pulled the sunglasses off, twirled them around in my hand for a moment and looked at Cecil.

"Fair enough. I kind of knew they weren't the genuine thing but I needed some glasses and the bloke was there selling them. I'd been wandering around all morning and the glare got too much. They were a sort of disguise as well in case I ran into the villains again."

"Let me see 'em," he said, stretching out a hand.

I passed them over and he began to examine the frame.

"Mate, see it says Royo Bom, not Ray-Ban. I told ya."

"I know, I know ... look it doesn't matter does it. I wanted them so I wouldn't be recognised."

"Yeah, you said mate. A disguise? So you wanna look inconspicuous and you go and buy a pair of white, mirrored shades with Royo Bom written all over them?" He put them on and stared towards the doorway.

"So what's wrong with mirrored glasses then?" I asked.

"Nothing's wrong with 'em geezer. But if you wanna keep a low profile they ain't what you should be wearing. It's the mirrors, ain't it? People look at mirrors. They can't help themselves. They gotta look, check themselves out. They don't even know they're doing it half the time."

I wasn't convinced by Cecil's logic and noticed that he had kept the glasses on. He turned towards the others, straightening them on his face with both hands as he did so.

"What d'you think boys? Bit more me, yeah?"

"Cecil's right." Jasper said. "You'd draw attention to yourself in them. You have to get another disguise I reckon."

I picked up my beer for the first time. I hadn't fancied a drink at all but I suddenly needed something to help calm my anxiety.

"Another disguise. Like what? Shave my head? I got a guy out there looking for me who's willing to do that for me already. Apparently he's not called 'Scalp' for nothing." I took a long swig from the bottle and leant back in my seat. "Anyway, listen. I have a plan." I pulled out the cigarette butt and the sweet paper from my pocket and put them on the table. The cigarette end had been stubbed out well before it had been fully smoked. "Oh, and I found these in the cave."

Cecil raised an eyebrow. "And?"

"They're clues aren't they?"

"Clues? What you on about geeze? A fag stub and a sweet paper? Clues to what?"

"I don't know yet ... like, uh … DNA or something. Forensic clues. You could ask Sheryl how it works. She's in that game."

"DNA? Mate, could be anybody's DNA on that fag and it looks like it's been trodden all over the frigging island so I don't reckon there'd be much left of anything on it. And I ain't ringing Sheryl all the way out there in Toronto on the basis of one fag butt. You gotta have more in this plan than that."

I hesitated, doubt creeping in after hearing how easily dismissed my first idea had been.

"Well, there was a second cave and there could be something in there that can help me sort this out. I need to find something that might link to this Felipe bloke and maybe all the way back to the main man they're investigating ... Kurt Kovalevski or Le Roux or whatever his name is."

"So this plan, amigo, how's it gannae work?" Carlos said.

"Simple. I need to get into the other cave. I'm going back out there tonight."

Cecil held up a hand.

"Hold it mate. You ain't going back there on your own. No way. That's asking for trouble. You run into them geezers again and it's game over. Nah, if you're doing that we're coming with ya."

"Yeah, there's four of us," Jasper said. "You already told us there was three of them last night. You have to even the numbers up."

"Aye, the boys are right. You cannae go out there on your own." Carlos turned to look for the bar tender. "Más tapas por favor."

"Okay, okay. If you insist, but we need to be focussed on what we're doing, right."

"Yeah mate, no problem with that. But, how you gonna find that place again?" Cecil asked.

"I can remember the way I came back. I walked every bloody step. It's along the west coast somewhere. "I took a sip from the beer bottle and remembered something else. "I'm going to need my stuff brought over to wherever Carlos finds for me to stay. And I need my phone charger." I turned to Jasper. "And there *is* something you can do, Jas. Hire a car. That okay?"

"Sure mate."

"And once you've done that, we are going to need some tools."

"Tools?"

"Yes. A pair of bolt croppers, a crowbar, a hammer and maybe a screwdriver. Oh, and a roll of Sellotape if you can get one. And a torch."

I watched Jasper's face drop into a puzzled frown.

"We have to break into the cave. So we need tools," I said.

"Sounds like you wanna break into a vault. Where am I gonna get that lot in Ibiza?"

"I don't know Jas. All I know is they didn't build the towns on this island with their bare hands and out of matchsticks and mud, so they must have places to get stuff like we've got back home. You know, like B&Q or something. And I have no idea what we might find in there so I'm just getting prepared for anything." I gestured towards Carlos. "Take Carlos with you. He can do the translation. Once you get the car then you can go looking. Cool?"

"Okay. I'll do my best. Cool."

"Great." I turned to Cecil. "Did you bring any cash Ces?"

"Yeah. You got a couple of hundred euros left."

"Okay, well when we finish up here we better get on the case. We'll meet up at the Golden Buddha around three o'clock and see how you've got on."

I left the tapas bar and immediately felt vulnerable. I had taken Cecil's advice about the glasses and let him keep them. But I was exposed. I was on my own again and I had no base until Carlos sorted out some accommodation. I crossed the street and walked along the seafront. Ahead I spotted a small crowd on the pavement. As I got closer, I realised that they were gathered around a street face-paint artist. She was creating a design on a small boy. I stood and watched for a while as she skilfully transformed his features with deft pen and brush strokes, into a multi-coloured pattern of orange, pink, black, yellow and blue that gradually evolved into the face of a cat.

And that was when I decided.

"How much?" I asked.

"Ten euro," she replied.

"Okay. Deal. Where do you want me?"

"Want you?"

"Yes, so you can work."

"Oh, you want to watch while I paint your son ... or is it a little girl?"

I stared at the crowd.

"Err ... no ... it's ... it's actually for me. A surprise ... for my ... my boy. It's his birthday and ... you know, just a bit of fun."

I heard a giggle in the crowd. The artist looked slightly taken aback.

"Okay. It's usually the children I do but adults are good too. What would you like?"

I pointed at the little boy.

"Same as him please."

"The cat? You like it?"

"Yes, I do. And use as many colours as you want and as much as you want. I need it to be realistic so not even my ... my err ... my wife will recognise me. If it costs a bit more that's fine."

It took twenty-five minutes to transform my face into the image of a cat. A quick check in the mirror and I suddenly felt a lot more at ease. I barely recognised myself. I paid the ten euros and gave the artist a five euro tip.

I had three hours to kill until the rendezvous at the Golden Buddha. I tried not to think about the proposed visit to the caves later that night. I didn't need the stress. I walked along the beach, sat and gazed at the sea and clock watched. With two hours to our meeting time I decided to get something to eat. I found a cosy café just past the marina. It was busy with few tables free but busy was good for me. I needed to be in a crowd. Some of the customers did a double take at my cat face but this was Ibiza and most of them had seen stranger things than a bloke with a painted face.

I found what seemed to be the only quiet table in the building and browsed the menu.

"Do you mind if I sit here?"

I looked up to see a tall pale faced bloke standing by the table indicating the empty seat opposite me. He was cleaning the lenses of a pair of spectacles.

"There aren't any free tables," he said.

"No ... no, go ahead. It's fine."

He sat down opposite me and put on the glasses. I ordered a coke and a cheese and ham toastie.

"Are you a children's entertainer?"

"Entertainer?" The question had taken me by surprise. And then I realised it was my painted face. "Err ... yes, that's it. I mean, yes I am. I do ... err ... kid's shows."

"You're working today then. When's the show? I have a little girl, my daughter, back at my hotel who would –"

"Err, no. Not today. Day off."

"Your day off?"

I was about to answer the question when I spotted him in the doorway. Scalapino. Same white t-shirt I had seen him in earlier, and dark sunglasses. My heart began to thump wildly. He looked across in my direction, a lingering gaze and then looked away. I started to get up, the desire to run overwhelming.

I heard my table companion's voice again.

"You said it's your day off but you're wearing face paint."

"Sorry?" I said, trying to focus.

"Are you performing today?"

"Err ... oh no ... I'm ... I'm just experimenting ... a new look ... for the act. Market research. See what reaction I get."

"Well it's very good. You look exactly like a cat with that make up. I don't suppose I'd recognise you again without it."

His last words hit home. I had intended to disguise myself and perhaps it was working. I sat back down. I had to keep my nerve, ignore my pounding heart and act as normal as it was possible to do

185

in face paint. I shot another glance at Scalapino. He was scanning the restaurant but perhaps he was just looking for somewhere to sit. I decided to engage my table companion in conversation.

"What do you do?" I asked.

"Oh, my job's boring. I hate it with a passion. I'm an accountant."

I looked up to check on Scalapino. He had taken a stool by the bar area.

"Err ... sorry. I didn't catch that. A what?"

"Just a bean counter. My name's Darren by the way. And you are?"

"I'm, uh ... Jason. Most people call me JJ. Sorry, you said a bean counter?" My gaze remained on Scalapino.

"Nice to meet you JJ." Darren held out his hand but I was preoccupied. "Well, anyway ... yes, a big company in the city ... London. Err ... look, am I interrupting you? You seem distracted."

"Distracted? Oh ... no ... it's the ... London you say? Doing?"

"I work the numbers. Somebody has to do it I guess. But it bores me now. I've been doing it too long. I want to be somebody in life, achieve something, you know?"

"Of course ... yeah. Like what?"

"Just to be somebody. To be recognised for something. Some achievement. Maybe it would give me a way out if I was somebody, not just another bloke in a suit."

I had enough worries of my own without having to act as Darren's psychiatrist.

"I suppose, but hey, I mean your job is useful. Nobody'd know how much was in the tin without people like you," I said, gazing over Darren's left shoulder.

Scalapino was chatting to a waitress.

"The tin?" Darren said.

"Yeah ... you know ... the can ... the pot. I'm guessing you need to know how much is in it. Quality control and all that."

"Well that's one way of looking at it. It's all money in one big pot I guess." He turned his head. "Sorry, are you sure you're not waiting for someone? You keep staring over there. I can find somewhere else to sit if I'm taking someone's seat."

186

"No. No, it's fine. I was ... was just looking around."

I didn't want Darren to leave. If he vacated the seat there was a chance I might get Scalapino for company. He had settled on the bar stool and was nursing a drink. It appeared that he intended to stay. The thought of the two of us in such close proximity in the same restaurant, even with my disguise, was getting too much. I lowered my gaze and focussed on Darren.

"Anyway, you were saying ... your job. What goes in first? The beans or the sauce?"

"I'm sorry?"

"I mean, when you've counted the beans do they get put into the sauce or does the sauce get poured over them?" I said, my fingers nervously drumming a beat on the table.

"That's funny. I can see why you're an entertainer," Darren said.

"No, I'm genuinely interested, really. I eat beans ... at home ... for breakfast and well, I've often wondered how many ... how many are in the ... actually in the tin. I mean, you take a forkful and there could be twenty or maybe even forty on the ... on the fork, who knows? So it makes you wonder how many there are in total in the tin ... err ... which, I suppose, is where guys like you come in."

Darren didn't reply but even if he had I wasn't that focussed on what he had to say. It was at that point I noticed that Scalapino's gaze was directed straight at me, a look of curiosity playing on his features. I didn't think it was worth gambling on whether it was the face paint that had attracted his attention or if he was getting suspicious. I decided I had to leave. I leant towards Darren, which had the effect of hiding my features temporarily behind his body.

"Look, nice to meet you Darren, but I have to go. Maybe I'll see you at a show." I paused for a moment whilst I tried to think of a distraction to enable me to leave unnoticed. "Err ... listen. Don't look now but behind you –"

He started to turn around the minute I said it. I stretched out a hand.

"Whoa. I said don't look now. Just listen. There's a bloke at the

187

bar over there, in a white t-shirt and dark glasses. He organises the kid's events. Looks after the tickets and that. If you go and see him, he should be able to get your daughter a front row seat. We're down at the ... err ..." I spotted a notice on the wall. "... the Ocean Beach, round the bay. Tomorrow at one o'clock. Have a word with him and see if he can fix you up. But his English is not that great so be patient. Don't mention me though. I don't want anyone thinking I'm doing favours or I could lose my job. Okay."

He nodded and went to stand up.

"Hang on. Don't just dive in. A bit of subtlety works best. Just say you're on holiday and ask if he knows where you can find any good kids' shows. Talk to him. He used to be a ... a bean counter too. Show an interest. He likes all that. That way he'll probably just offer you tickets without you asking. Good luck."

I waited until he had stood up and had begun to walk towards Scalapino. As he did so, I slipped away from the table. I hurried from the restaurant and took the coastal path in the direction of the Golden Buddha. It wouldn't matter if I was early. I needed to get off the street. I knew I didn't have much time. If Scalapino had recognised me, he wouldn't be distracted for too long by talk of beans and tickets.

24

As I approached the Golden Buddha I took the ramp that led from the main path down to the beach. I would be less conspicuous if I mingled with the crowd for an hour or so, despite my cat face. To my right, a raised wooden decking area was crowded with sunbathers. I pulled off my t-shirt and followed the ramp down onto the sand. At the bottom I turned right so that I was partially hidden by the height of the decking. A furtive glance over my right shoulder back along the path, sent my heart racing. Scalapino was heading in the direction of the beach and was scanning the area. I turned away, head down and picked my way between rows of sunbathers, across the small expanse of beach to the water line. Just as I reached the shore, I spotted two familiar faces.

Alida and Estrid.

My gaze didn't linger for long on their faces. Both were topless, perfectly tanned and stretched out in the smallest of bikini bottoms. I glanced around again. Scalapino was on the paved area in front of the beach ramp. There was no time to stand deliberating about what to do next. The girls would be the perfect cover. If I joined them, I could blend in and just look like any other holidaymaker enjoying the sunshine.

"Hi. How are you? Fancy seeing you here?" I said.

Estrid sat up first, a hand shading her eyes as she focussed.

"Hello," she said, but it was clear she didn't recognise me.

"It's me. Matt ... I mean JJ ... from ...you know, last time. We met in Café Mambo. With Cecil. You remember?" I hoped they did.

Alida rolled onto her side and peered at me.

"JJ? Is it you? But why the face like a pussy?" she asked.

"A pussy?" I was slightly taken a back. And then I remembered my face paint. "Oh, that. Look do you mind if I sit down?" I felt vulnerable standing with Scalapino on the prowl.

Estrid patted the sand beside her.

"Sure. Come and join us. Are you having a nice time?"

I sat down, feeling relieved to be below the height of the decking platform.

"Uh ... yes, yes I am. It's great."

"And the pussy? Is it for the party you are making?" Alida asked.

My mind raced trying to find an explanation. The heat was getting to me. Beads of perspiration rolled down my face.

"Err ... no ... and yes. It's a ... a party game. A group of us try and disguise ourselves and the others have to ... have to find us. And then if they do ... they err ... they get points and win drinks. If they don't find us, then ... well then, we win the drinks."

Alida glanced at Estrid and they both began to laugh.

"Funny games you English men play. Always drinking games, no?"

"I suppose so. Just a bit of fun."

I looked up at the decking and to my horror saw that Scalapino was standing almost above us. Luckily he was facing in the opposite direction. The girls were facing towards the ocean so they hadn't seen him. I had to keep them distracted. If they saw him, they might well say hello and the game would be up.

"Is your friend Cecil here too?" Estrid asked.

"Cecil? Yes, he is but look, I wonder if you could help me ... with the game. I have to hide because I think I saw one of the people that are looking for me and I want to ... to win the drinks."

"Hide? There is nowhere to hide unless you get under the towel," Alida said.

That didn't seem like the best idea. Someone sitting or lying under a towel on a hot beach would stick out like a sore thumb.

"No, I mean hide by ... err, pretending. You know, like, maybe I could pretend, just for a little while, to be with you, like a boyfriend."

They both began to giggle.

"Okay. So which one you want as girlfriend?" Estrid asked.

I hadn't thought of that. I just needed to hide in plain sight. Look like a normal bloke with two girls chilling on a beach.

"I don't know ... err ... both of you are fine."

Estrid's eyes widened in mock horror.

"You want threesome?"

"Threesome ... err ... no ... I mean ... yes. No, I meant ... it doesn't matter who is ... you are both very beautiful. I can't choose which ... "

"Then come and sit between us. You don't have to choose."

Alida shuffled away from Estrid creating a space between them. I stood up and slid into the gap. Just as I did so, I caught sight of Scalapino coming down the ramp onto the beach.

It was a reflex action that made me do it, inspired by fear and the need to hide. In a movement that momentarily took her breath away, I rolled to my right, grabbed Estrid and buried my face in her chest. I heard her gasp and felt her hands on my back. It was Alida that spoke first.

"Not shy any more Matthew I see. My turn next."

I heard the two girls giggling but I stayed stock still, my mind trying to envisage Scalapino walking on by. Estrid began to stroke my hair but my focus was simply on staying still. Perspiration rolled down my face where my cheek lay against her chest. Several minutes must have passed before I dared to look up. I stared straight ahead in the direction I had been laying. No sign of Scalapino. I swivelled around to where Alida sat and looked along the beach. Nothing. I sat bolt upright, feeling embarrassed at grabbing Estrid. I was just about to apologise when I caught sight of yet another familiar face.

Eleanor.

I took a gulp of air, the shock causing my breathing to falter.

"Matthew? What are you doing here? And what's happened to your face?"

I raised a hand to my face and immediately felt the sticky mess that had once been my cat make up. A glance at my hand showed it to be covered in a glutinous mix of orange, pink, black, yellow and blue paint. And then I saw where Eleanor was looking. Estrid's breasts were covered in exactly the same colourful mix, a yellow blob perfectly topping one nipple. I opened my mouth to speak but nothing emerged.

Eleanor did not appear troubled by the same affliction.

"You two timing toe rag. You leave Louise back home in the lurch and come out here to meet up with these two ... two hussies. Typical bloody bloke. And to think that James told me you were going to get engaged to my daughter. Fat chance of that now when I tell her what you're up to. I come out for a quiet walk with my friend and her dog and ... and ... I knew you were trouble when I first met you."

It was then that I spotted the woman with the dog standing a little further back on the decking. Eleanor turned to walk away.

"Mrs ... Eleanor ... listen. I can explain. It's not what you think. It's ... it's ..." I realised that, actually, I couldn't explain. Not without jeopardising Louise's safety. If I said anything about the kidnapping or the reason I had come back out to Ibiza, everything could go horribly wrong.

Eleanor stood for a moment and waited.

"Hmmm. I thought not." She turned on her heel and walked off.

"Who was that?" Estrid asked. "Is she on the game?"

"On the game?" I said, a little surprised at the comment.

"Yes, on the game. She looking for pussy?"

"Pussy? I'm sorry. I ... I don't understand."

"Yes, she found you, the pussy face and now she gets the drinks, right?" Alida chipped in.

"Oh, *that* game. Yes ... yes. That's it. Yes. I lose." Even as I used the word, I realised I was beginning to lose more than just a game.

Estrid interrupted my thought pattern.

"Okay, so now your game is over, we go back to your hotel for the threesome?"

The Golden Buddha was busy, its veranda loungers covered in sunbathers relaxing in the mid-afternoon sun, sipping cold drinks under the watchful gaze of the giant golden Buddha statue that was the centre piece of the patio. I slipped inside the main building, avoiding the curious glances that came my way. It was cooler inside and there were fewer people around. I slumped into a chair and sat for a moment taking deep breaths, trying to restore calm to my body. It was almost impossible. A lack of sleep and the stress of my situation had taken its toll and I was exhausted. I needed to sleep but knew I had to stay alert until I could talk with the lads.

The lads turned up within forty-five minutes of my arrival.

"What's with the fucking warpaint geezer?" Cecil's greeting was direct as usual. "You're more done up than Tonto. Not another one of your disguises is it?"

I ran my hand across my face and looked at my palm.

"Well, yeah. I don't feel safe and with good reason Ces. I've just been followed by Scalapino and then, you'll never guess who I run into. Eleanor."

"Who's Eleanor?" Jasper asked.

"Louise's mum. She caught me on the beach with the two Danish girls. She thinks I'm having a threesome and she's going to call Louise and whatever slim chance I had of getting her back is now a fat chance."

Carlos frowned.

"Mateo, make your –"

"JJ Carlos. JJ. I told you."

"Sorry, lo siento. Aye, you did," Carlos said and scratched his head. "But make your mind up. Which is it? Slim or fat?"

"What?"

"You said a slim chance is now a fat chance?"

I let out a deep sigh. I had more important things on my mind.

"It's a turn of phrase mate. It kind of means the same thing.

193

Slim chance is just a bit of a chance but not much of one, and fat chance is … no chance at all."

"But if a slim chance is a bit of a chance how is it that when there is no chance it gets fatter?"

Cecil intervened.

"Fuck's sake. You two gonna talk bollocks all day? Listen mate, we're meeting here to sort your situation out and you two wanna bang on about the English language." He pointed at Carlos. "This geezer can't even decide whether he wants to talk Spanish or Scottish so you're wasting your time explaining things to him. So let's get down to business. Right."

The three of us nodded in unison.

Cecil continued.

"Right, okay. So first off, this Scalapino geezer can't have recognised you. If he had, he would've grabbed you there and then."

"Yeah, probably never to be seen again."

"Mate, don't get over dramatic. Think about it. It's unlikely they're planning on killing you. Killing people causes inconvenience. I reckon they just want to make sure you're outta the way until after this court thing. You've worried them by turning up back here. They probably guessed you're looking to try and connect them to something. So they get you off the streets and you don't show up for the court appearance, two things happen. One, it makes you look guilty as fuck with the diamond smuggling thing and makes any story you try to tell the police when you do get back home, look like a load of bollocks. And two, their geezer, this Kurt Kova bloke, walks away and your bird's career goes tits up along with any evidence she's got on him."

"But that's even worse," I said.

Cecil laughed. "Trust me geezer, there's nothing worse than getting wasted. Ain't no coming back from that."

"I didn't mean that Ces. I meant I can't afford not to get back before the case and I have to have something to show for it when I do. So I have to keep out of Scalapino's way."

"He's probably just doing the rounds, looking in all the places you might be," Cecil said. "And you, you gotta stop panicking. It draws attention. And talking of which, you also gotta stop doing dumb fuck things like painting your face. It's like them shades mate. You end up looking too fucking obvious."

"I see you've still got them though, Ces," I said.

"Yeah I'm hanging onto them ain't I? But the thing is I ain't trying to hide from nobody so it's cool with me. You don't need to be sticking out like a frigging sore thumb, do ya?"

I suddenly remembered Erin's words about blending in, hiding in plain sight.

Cecil continued. "Anyway, listen, Carlos has sorted you a room –"

"Yeah, Hotel Valencia," Carlos chipped in. "It's about five or six minutes away. Nice and quiet. I got a good deal."

"Yeah, which I'm paying for," Cecil added. "And Jas has got the car and the tools, so we're good to go. Now we just need to know how we're gonna do this."

"Cheers boys. I appreciate it," I said, feeling relieved to have somewhere to hide away. "I need few hours kip to be honest. I'll feel better then."

"We moved your stuff up to the hotel earlier mate," Jasper said. He glanced at the others and then focussed back on me. "So what *is* the plan for tonight then?"

I leant forward and lowered my voice. It wasn't really necessary as there was nobody in earshot, but it made me feel more comfortable.

"There's no big plan. Like I said, we just need to get into that second cave and see if there's anything else in there that might be of use … something that might link to the blokes who kidnapped me, would be a start. We head up there in the early hours, say two o'clock or something. If it's a clear night, that'll help. Did you get a torch?"

"Yeah, I did."

"Good. Okay, so I suggest that once we get there, me and Ces do the break in while you two keep watch. If we find anything of use, we get it back up to the car."

"I'm good with that," Cecil said. "Beer anybody?"

This was no time for an afternoon drinking session.

"Ces, I'm out on my feet. I need to get to this hotel, clean up and sleep. And I need everybody on the ball tonight. So let's leave the beers now, eh?"

There were no protests. They knew how serious the situation was.

Jasper took me to the Hotel Valencia. I checked into my room and within minutes fell into a fitful slumber.

25

At exactly two o'clock in the morning, we headed out along the coast road in the direction I had traipsed along the previous day. By car, it took just fifteen minutes to get to the spot that I recognised. I told Jasper to pull over and I got out of the car.

"I think this is it lads. Looks like it." Ahead on the left, picked out in the glare of a full moon, I spotted a gap in the scrub. "That's it. That's where the path down to the beach starts. Drive up over there. The car won't be seen from the road so easily."

Once the car was parked, I flipped the boot lid, lifted out the bag in which Jasper had placed the tools he had bought and walked to the top of the path. I turned to the boys.

"Jas, you need to stay near the top here. If you see anyone coming, you call one of us and let Carlos know too. Carlos, you come halfway down and wait. Keep an eye on the beach, look out for boats or anything that might look odd to you. I shouldn't think there'll be anything going on at this time in the morning but you never know. If you see anything suspicious, let us know."

Jasper flicked the switch on the torch and shone the beam down the stone and concrete steps.

"Jas, turn that frigging torch off. It'll be seen for miles round here. Give it to Ces. We can get down to the beach by the moonlight. That's for when we get inside."

Jasper handed the torch to Cecil.

"Everybody good?" I said. "We'll be as quick as we can."

I led the way down the steep, winding cliff path followed by

Cecil and Carlos. It was eerily silent, the dark shadows of the rocks creating a ghostly, intimidating aura as we descended. The further we went the more foreboding it became, as if we were heading into a trap. When we had reached the halfway point, I told Carlos to wait. Cecil and I continued on down the remainder of the path.

"Fucking steep ain't it geeze? See why they had to put these steps in."

"I know. Not far now."

We reached the beach at the foot of the cliff face and picked our way across the damp sand towards the two cave storage areas. As we got closer, I could see that the one I had been held in earlier still had the broken door. No attempt had been made to repair it. That could only mean there was nothing in there that needed to be protected, nothing of interest that I might have missed earlier.

"Made a bit of a mess of that door mate," Cecil said.

"Well at least there's no need to go back in." I pointed to the other cave. "We need to get that chain off."

I beckoned to Cecil to give me the torch and I approached the doors. When I was close enough to shield the light with my body, I switched on the torch and shone it through the broken door. There was nothing there that I hadn't already seen. Just the filing cabinet in the corner, one drawer missing, and a drawer that lay buckled and broken on its side. I shone the beam on the other cave door and reached for the chain. I pulled it through the four metal eyebolts so that the padlock slid to one side.

"Okay, let's do it."

Cecil took the bolt croppers from the bag and stepped forward. He placed the end of the tool around one of the eyebolts.

"No, not there Ces. It's too thick. Cut the chain. That way we can hang it back on when we leave."

"What's it matter mate? Let's get it done."

"Wait. If they come back to repair the other door and they see the chain just dangling there, they'll know somebody broke in. If it's not so obvious they may just miss it and it'll buy us time."

"Alright, it's your plan geezer," Cecil replied and moved the bolt croppers to the chain, positioning the open jaws on one of the links. When he was happy that he had a firm grip, he applied leverage to the handles. Nothing happened. Then, as he applied more force, the link snapped cleanly through. Immediately I slid the split end of the chain out of the loop so that it freed up one of the doors. Cecil grabbed the door and pulled it outwards just enough to create a gap that we could get through.

"We're in mate."

I shone the torch into the dark void. The beam played across dank, slime covered stone walls and settled on a tarpaulin that ran across the full width of the cave right at the back. It seemed to be covering something long and curved in shape. I flashed the beam around the remaining area to get my bearings. There was nothing else in there. I focussed the light back on the tarpaulin.

"We need to take a look," I said, nervous about what we might find but spurred on by adrenaline.

Cecil moved quickly to one side of the tarpaulin.

"Grab the other end mate and let's get this thing off."

I did as he said and we yanked the tarpaulin away. It slid to the ground revealing the overturned hull of an old battered boat. I shone the torch along its length and discovered that it was actually only half a boat, the front end, the bow. Its sides were chipped and broken, many of the wooden panels coming away from the frame.

"It's some sort of old fishing boat," I said. "But I'm not sure what it's covered up for. It's rotting away anyway by the looks of it."

"Gimme that torch." Cecil grabbed the torch and moved to one end of the boat. As he shone the beam over it, I could see that it was the end where it had been cut in half. Then he leant forward and aimed the torch under the upturned hull.

"Here mate. In here. Take a look."

I bent down and peered under the boat. The beam from the torch bounced back off what looked like two metal boxes.

"What are they?" I asked.

"How the fuck do I know," Cecil replied. "Boxes, ain't they? We need to move this boat. There ain't enough room to get at 'em from here."

"How're we going to do that? It looks heavy."

I was beginning to feel the anxiety drifting up from my stomach. I patted my pocket to make sure I still had my mobile. Inside the cave with only one way out, I felt very vulnerable.

Cecil stood up and reached for the tool bag. He pulled out the crowbar and leaned over the hull.

"Shine that fucking torch over here geezer. I need to see what I'm doing?"

I played the beam in Cecil's direction and watched as he located a loose plank on the hull. He slipped one end of the crowbar in between the plank and the frame and pushed hard on the bar. The end of the panel began to lift, creaking and straining away from the frame. Once he had loosened one end, he moved the crowbar further along the plank. Again he pushed hard on the bar, levering more of the plank upwards.

"Geezer, grab the end of that wood and push it up."

I took hold of the plank and pushed. Cecil inserted the bar in again and levered. As the plank loosened, I pushed up harder. A splitting, splintering crack suddenly snapped the timber clear off.

"Shit, sorry Ces. I didn't mean to break it."

"S'alright mate. That's what we want. We got a good six foot of timber there. We can use it to lever the boat up, yeah." He picked up the broken plank and slid one end under the hull. "Right, when I push up on this, you pull one of them boxes out and put it under the edge. Okay? Then I'm gonna lower it back onto the box so it props the boat up. Got it?"

"Yeah, got it mate."

I crouched down by Cecil's knees as he shoved up on the timber and got his shoulder under it. The hull of the boat rolled up on its far edge leaving enough space for me to ease underneath.

"Don't drop the fucking thing Ces," I said as I crawled under, sweat streaming down my brow.

Once underneath I could see that there was a row of eight or nine identical black metal boxes with a clasp at the front, each one about twelve inches high and slightly wider. I grabbed the nearest one and shoved it under the edge of the hull.

"Ces, push up some more. I can get another box on top of that one. It'll give us more space to work."

With the hull higher up I placed a second box on top of the first one and called for Cecil to lower the boat. It came to rest on top of the boxes. I then began to pull forward the remaining boxes and shove them out to Cecil. Once they were all out, I crawled from under the boat. Cecil had already begun to lift the box lids.

"What we got," I asked, hoping for some revelation that would make the effort worthwhile.

"Nothing in them two mate."

There were five more boxes out in the open. None of them locked. We opened each one. All empty.

"What're they for? Why shove empty boxes in a cave, hidden under an old boat?" I said, disappointed to have found nothing.

"Looks like storage, don't it. You have boxes to keep stuff in, yeah. And you only hide boxes away in a place like this if the stuff you are keeping ain't legit."

"What like drugs?"

"Yeah, could be ... or could be diamonds mate."

I swallowed hard. Of course.

"Diamonds. That's it then Ces. That's the clue, the evidence we're after."

Cecil chuckled.

"What fucking evidence geezer? We got a loada empty boxes. You hear me? Empty. You don't go to the cops and tell 'em you've solved a major crime 'cos these boxes must mean that Scalp geezer is smuggling diamonds? This don't mean nothing."

Nothing. The word buzzed through my head. I leant back on the hull. It wobbled as my weight came down on one side, causing me to lose my balance. I pulled away, watching as it came back to rest on its temporary prop.

"Hang on a sec. There's these two boxes," I said, pointing at the prop. "They might be empty too but we have to check them. Raise the boat up again and I'll stick another two under there and pull these out."

Cecil levered the hull up and I shoved two more boxes under

the edge. I then grabbed the other two and pulled them free. I was about to open the top one when I felt my mobile buzz.

Jasper.

"What's up mate?"

"A car's pulled in on the far side of the road a bit further down."

"Shit. Who is it?"

"I don't know. Nobody's got out yet but I'm keeping an eye on it. How long you gonna be?"

"Not long. We just need a few minutes. Tell Carlos to get back up and get in the car. If anyone comes this way let me know. If that happens, make yourself scarce for a bit and wait for me to call. Me and Cecil can go down and hide amongst the rocks on the far side of the beach until it's clear."

"Okay, mate. You got anything yet?"

"Not yet, no. Got to go."

I killed the call.

"We have to hurry Ces. Jas has seen a car pull up."

We set to work on the two remaining boxes. And our luck changed.

The top one was empty but the one that had been on the bottom was not. Cecil lifted the lid and found the box contained nine padlocks, each one with a four digit combination dial, and a canvas, army-surplus bag. I lifted the bag out and undid the strap. Inside there was a folded map of the island and a single sheet of white paper. I pulled them out, spread them on the ground and shone the torch. There was nothing remarkable about the map. It was the kind that any tourist could buy in a souvenir shop. We studied it to see if there were any places marked or anything else written on it. There was nothing. The sheet of paper wasn't too enlightening either. Typed across the middle in large letters on three separate rows, was a list of numbers.

3954193626283106/M2613027575125457/3552421036933207/
4032268192318348/392332M01940285118/M3353311828581 75306/
38593011720104176/1910

At the very bottom of the page, there was what appeared to be a short sentence in Spanish.

'Hay sólo un camino, así que siga la luz que brilla.'

"What the fuck's all them numbers mean?" Cecil said.

I scratched my head, just as puzzled.

"It could have something to do with the padlocks. Codes or something."

"Nah, can't be. There's only four digits in the dials."

"Yes, but it could be code for the combinations. Unless ... unless you take each individual number separately and then it could *be* the combinations."

"What d'you mean?"

"Well, take that first one. Could be that 3, 9, 5, 4 is a combination and then the next four numbers, 1, 9, 3, 6 are too and so on. And they just change them frequently."

Cecil picked up one of the padlocks and spun the dial.

"Ces, that's not going to help. You got a whole sheet of numbers and nine padlocks. You've got no chance of picking the right number set for the right padlock. And what's more, we don't have the time to try."

He slung the padlock back into the box. I began to count the numbers on the page.

"What you doing mate?" Cecil asked.

"Counting." I did a quick calculation. "Okay, if you look at it, there's a hundred and twenty numbers there so, if they are the actual four digit codes in combination order, that gives you thirty sets of different four digit combinations."

"Yeah, but mate, there's only nine padlocks. Why would you want thirty combinations?"

"They might be for other padlocks. Or they might reprogramme them from time to time."

Cecil shone the torch on the paper and examined the numbers again.

"But why write 'em all out in them long blocks? And some of

the blocks have got an extra number, so that screws your theory about combinations. And there's a letter in three of 'em."

"I don't know. Maybe they put an extra number in some blocks and then reverse the numbers so the last number in the block becomes the first one next time around. That way they change the combinations so nobody gets too familiar with them. It's only a guess. They could all be in some random code order and then you got ... what ... ten thousand combination possibilities per padlock."

"Do what mate? Ten thousand?"

"Yeah, because each padlock has four dials that go from zero to nine which makes ten possible number options per dial and then if you multiply each –"

"Alright Einstein. Leave it out. Fucking complicated that one. You're right. We ain't got time for all that bollocks. And anyway, you don't know what that letter 'M' is there for."

"But if the boxes are used for diamond smuggling, then security would have to be complicated wouldn't it? And you're right. I've got no idea what the letter could be." I paused whilst the possibilities ran through my mind. "They could even be passwords or even a list of safe combinations ... you know, where they keep the diamonds. Or bank account numbers and sort codes. Could be anything."

Cecil ran a hand through his hair.

"Well you wouldn't exactly call that security would you? Leaving the numbers with the padlocks, or leaving safe combinations and passwords lying around."

"I know, but we don't know where the safes or bank accounts are, so that wouldn't be such a big issue."

"Maybe it's just some geezer's fucking lottery numbers that he forgot he left in there. Whatever it all means, that bit of paper ain't much help. Like you just said, it could be anything. And all that Spanish stuff at the end? What's all that about?"

"I don't know. Carlos will though. We'll ask him."

"Yeah, he will. Anyway, there's fuck all else in here. We better get this lot put back and get outta here." Cecil started to push the boxes back under the boat hull.

"Wait Ces. I'm going to take a picture. That bit of paper has to be something."

I pulled out my mobile and took pictures of the paper, the map, the padlocks and the bag. I had no idea what use they might be, but what we had discovered had to have some meaning. When I had done, I called Jasper.

"What's happening Jas?"

"Nothing mate. The car's still there but I think it's a couple pulled in for a bit of the old slap and tickle. It's been bouncing around like there's an earthquake over there. Apart from that, it's all clear up here."

"Okay, we're on our way."

With everything back in place, we pulled the doors back into position. I looped the chain back through the eyebolts and took the Sellotape from the bag. I tore off several strips and started to tie the two ends of the broken chain together.

"What the fuck you doing with that?" Cecil said.

"Like I said, Ces. I don't want it to look obvious that we've been here."

With the chain held together with several lengths of Sellotape wrapped tightly through the links, I pulled it back through the eyebolts so that the padlock hung in the middle, just as it had been when we arrived.

"Right. We're done."

We made our way back up the path to the car.

26

I awoke in my new hotel room the next morning to the sound of chatter and laughter from the pool. My first floor window overlooked the back of the hotel and the whole poolside area. I checked my watch. Eleven o'clock already. I rolled out of bed and picked up my phone. I had made one decision on my return the night before.

To call Louise.

I realised she may not pick up but I was convinced that Eleanor would have been in touch to say that she had seen me in Ibiza. I had to get my side of the story across. Maybe curiosity would make her answer. I was right.

"Louise. Thanks for answering," I said. "It's me."

"*I know who it is. I told you not to call me. What do you want?*"

Charming, I thought. Giving me attitude. If she knew who it was and didn't want to speak to me, why did she answer?

"I just wanted to tell you what's happening. I'm in Ibiza and –"

"*I know you are. My mum called me.*" An impatient sigh drifted across the line. "*So tell me this. I understand you had your passport confiscated and now you're in Ibiza. How does that work then?*"

"It's complicated Louise. I had to –"

"*It isn't that complicated to me. It looks like it's a straightforward case of breaking the law. First of all you're smuggling diamonds and then you go on the run. So how long exactly have you had ambitions to be an international criminal?*"

"It's not like that Louise. I was –"

"What were you doing with diamonds anyway?"

I wasn't being given much opportunity to talk but the fact Louise had stayed on the line and was asking questions gave me some hope. I wanted to tell her the truth, to trust her. That was the only obvious chance I had of rescuing our relationship. But my head was in turmoil. What if her phone was being tapped? If it was, the police would know my call was made from Ibiza. I had to hold back. And even if the call was not monitored, if I told her what I knew she would surely feel an obligation to talk. There was no reason for her to think that I could solve the situation on my own. She would worry about me too much.

"Look Louise, I'm taking a risk calling you. You're going to have to trust me. There are things –"

"Trust you? What, a bloke who's gallivanting with two tarts out in Ibiza? Don't talk to me about trust, Matthew."

Two tarts? And then I remembered Estrid, Alida and the beach.

"It's not what you think, Louise. Your mum got the wrong end of the stick –"

"Wrong end of the stick? From what my mum told me, it looked like one of them had hold of your stick while you had your head buried in her tits. Don't try and fob me off with some bullshit story Matthew. I hear it all day long from people who are much better at it than you are. You forget I'm a police officer ... was a police officer until you started your life of crime."

I was beginning to wish I had never made the call. This was not how it was meant to go. Exasperation suddenly kicked in.

"Louise, will you just shut up for a minute and listen," I shouted down the line. "Conversations are meant to have two people in them and you won't let me get a word in. Just listen for a minute. If you don't like what you hear when I'm done, just put the phone down. Okay?"

There was silence from the other end but she stayed on the line.

"I'm in Ibiza, yes. I shouldn't be here but I can't explain what I'm doing here right now. That's why I need you to trust me. I'm not gallivanting with tarts ... or anybody for that matter. When I ran into your mum I was actually trying to avoid a situation and

207

she misinterpreted it." I paused for a moment wondering whether I needed to tell her. I decided I had to risk it. "I'm with Cecil –"

"*Cecil?*"

I ignored the scornful fit of laughter.

"And, err ... Jasper and Carlos as well. But, listen, they're helping me with something, that's all. It isn't what it looks like."

"*Nothing seems to be what it looks like then does it? Give me one good reason why I shouldn't report you to the police?*"

"I can't Louise. If you want to, you go ahead. I can't stop you but I'm just asking for some time. I have to be back in court in three weeks. I'm in a mess and I just need time to sort it out. That's all I can say. I'm sorry to be so mysterious. If you can just give me that time ... and some trust."

The line went quiet.

"Louise?"

"*I can't. I'm due in front of a disciplinary hearing on the twentieth. My job, my career is on the line. I'm going to have to tell them everything at that hearing. And that includes any new information. Don't forget they have connected me to you so I have to come clean on everything I know.*"

I glanced at my watch. The 11th of June.

"Okay, I understand. That's just over a week away. That's fine. But please don't say anything to anyone before that. Oh, and did you say anything to Eleanor ... I mean, your mum ... about, you know, the passport thing?"

"*No, I didn't. Why?*"

"No reason, except, I suppose I didn't want her to think I was, you know ... a bad person or anything."

A sense of optimism suddenly enveloped me. Louise hadn't revealed anything about my bogus identity and she also seemed to be agreeing to give me time, although she hadn't exactly said as much.

"*I don't know what she thinks Matthew. Anyway, I have to go. Please don't call me. I can't be involved in whatever you are up to.*"

"Louise. I –"

The line went dead. My wave of optimism was replaced by a crashing sense of doom. No goodbye, no words of comfort, nothing to hang on to. Clinical finality. I sat and stared at the screen. The curling, crushing sensation reared up in my chest. My emotions fighting to get to the surface, seeking an outlet. Onwards, along my throat, into my head, an intense pressure finally emerging in my eyes in a tearful wetness. I gulped, let out a deep breath and gave way to the wave of emotion, the tears trickling down my cheeks. I felt alone, disconnected and trapped.

I stood up and wiped my face with my hands. I had to be positive. If I was to rescue things, I had to complete what I had come to Ibiza to do. I then had to convince Louise that our relationship was worth hanging on to. But now was not the time to dwell on Louise. I needed distraction.

I went to the bathroom and took a long shower. I emerged with a sense of purpose. This had to get done and today was where it had to start in earnest. No more waiting around for something to happen. We had to work with whatever we had found so far. I picked up my mobile from the bed and selected the photos icon. I pulled up the pictures I had taken in the cave. I stopped on the one with the sheet of paper in it and stared at the list of numbers. It was still telling me nothing. The only positive bit of information that I had obtained was the translation of the Spanish words at the end of the page.

According to Carlos, '*Hay sólo un camino, así que siga la luz que brilla*' translated as, '*There is only one way, so follow the light that shines.*' But even in English it still didn't tell us anything.

"Could be about a lighthouse or something," Cecil had remarked as we drove back the night before.

"Maybe it means the name of a boat," Carlos had suggested. "The Shining Light."

"Or some rendezvous point. I mean if you look at the coastline after dark there are loads of lights shining," Jasper had chipped in.

All were feasible since we were surrounded by the ocean and we had found part of an old fishing boat in the cave. Maybe it was some sort of communication signal between boats. But if it was a lighthouse, where was it located and why was there reference to it on the sheet of paper? If it was a boat, it had to be on some sort of register.

I flicked through the other pictures. Padlocks and boxes. The boxes had to be for storage or containers for transferring something from one place to another. Padlocks meant something of value. So my initial thoughts in the cave had to be right. It was clear that Felipe and Scalapino had access to illegal diamonds. I had seen Scalapino at the storage cave after I had escaped. It was perfectly feasible that the boxes were used for a diamond smuggling operation. But Cecil had been right. It wasn't evidence.

I flicked back to the shot of the piece of paper. Maybe the lighthouse was a rendezvous point. But where was the lighthouse? I needed to find out. Maybe I could get some information at the marina. There were plenty of boats there.

The thought of boats brought me to James and to Eleanor. Eleanor knew I was on the island. I needed to speak to her and build bridges again. If I was going to get back with Louise, I needed her on my side. At the same time I could find out if James knew anything about lighthouses.

I tapped out a text to Cecil.

'How's it going Ces? You guys got any ideas on anything yet? Let me know if you have. Going to see James and Eleanor. Let's meet later at tapas bar, 7ish.'

A taxi dropped me at the villa and I walked nervously towards the front door. I wasn't sure what reception I would get from Eleanor but I knew I had to see her. James opened the door. Mofo and Panzer nearly took me back out onto the street in their enthusiasm to welcome me to the villa.

"Panzer, Mofo. Get back here. Now!" James's command was brusque and precise. The two dogs instantly turned and slunk back towards the house. "Matt. I heard you were in town. C'mon in. Nice to see you."

He led me straight out to the poolside, stopping only to grab two beers from the refrigerator. He pulled the tops and handed one of the bottles to me.

"So what can I do for you young fella?"

"Well, actually I came to see Eleanor. Is she in?"

He reached across the table and picked up his cigarettes and lighter.

"No, afraid not. She's gone back to London to be with Louise. Flew out this morning in fact. She was concerned about her. They've been on the phone a bit. Louise said that you two broke up. That right?" He lit a cigarette, took a long draw and blew a plume of smoke into the air.

"Yeah, it is. I'm afraid so."

He pushed the cigarette box towards me.

"I never asked, but you don't smoke at all do you?"

"No, no I don't."

"I should give up myself. I've cut down a lot but it's hard, especially when you're having a beer, you know."

I smiled. I didn't know but I understood.

"So when will Eleanor be back?" I asked.

"God knows Matt. She just said that she'd be spending some time with Louise. Is it urgent? I could give her a call on the mobile."

"No not at all. I just called on the off chance. Just for a chat." I paused for a moment, disappointed that Eleanor was not there but more concerned that whilst she had Louise to herself she could paint the wrong picture of me. I tried to dismiss that thought. "So, James, Cecil tells me you're from Quilty in County Clare. It's where my father was from."

"Is that right? Well, isn't that a coincidence. Have you been out there?" A broad smile lit up his craggy features.

"I have yes."

"Sure it's a fine place. Just a stone's throw from the Atlantic Ocean. I used to go up to Lahinch many a time for the music." James's smile turned into a more serious frown.

"You say your father *was* from Quilty?"

"Yeah ... he died when I was a boy."

211

"Ah, I'm sorry to hear that Matt." He flicked the drooping ash from the end of his cigarette and leant towards me. "So what are you doing back in Ibiza anyway?"

"It's a long story."

"I've got all day son."

I sipped my beer and stared at the distant horizon. A small black blob cut through a series of wispy clouds, a paraglider soaring above the glistening blue waters below, free and unburdened by life's problems, experiencing a carefree moment where no one could touch him. I would have gladly changed places. I turned to face James again.

"There was a bit of a bust up. A lot of things going on. Louise is a bit stressed. She's got a few problems at work. Then there was the engagement thing that didn't go the way I wanted it that night. And then Eleanor saw me with two girls and got the wrong end of the stick. And now Louise thinks I'm out here gallivanting so it's all got to me to be honest."

James shook his head and took a puff on the cigarette.

"Ah, women," he said, "fine creatures but complicated. Us fellas are a lot simpler. But, I'll tell you this Matt. You're not doing yourself any favours being out here if you've had a bust up. At best, it'll look like you're running away and at worst it'll look like you don't care. You need to get back home if you and Louise are going to sort things out. It's no good her sitting there talking to her mother. That'll only make things worse. You weren't exactly flavour of the month with Eleanor, were you? And Eleanor will take her daughter's side, you know that."

"It's not that simple James. In fact it's complicated."

"Nothing's ever *that* complicated son. A lot of the time us fellas bottle it all up and never tell anybody. And then it always seems a lot more complicated than it is. When you tell people your problems it gets it off your chest and sure, doesn't it all seem a lot easier to deal with when you talk."

I liked James. His easy manner and world-weary charm suggested a man who had seen it all, a man of experience. His open face spoke of integrity. Someone you could trust. I felt the urge to confide in him. With his knowledge of the island, perhaps he would be able to help me.

I shuffled in my seat and smiled.

"You're right. Some things shouldn't be bottled up. To be straight with you I only came out here with the boys because ..."

I watched, mesmerised as James stubbed out his cigarette, my words halted in mid flow by the sudden image of a used cigarette being crushed into a butt in the ashtray. A butt that seemed uncannily like the one I had picked up from the cave floor. It too had not been fully smoked.

He sat back in his chair, a quizzical look playing on his features.

"You were saying Matt? You came out with the boys because?"

"Err ... yes, because ... I erm ..." I lifted the beer bottle. "Sorry, my throat ... bit dry." I glugged back half the contents of the bottle and placed it back on the table. "Yes, I came out ... well, it was actually Cecil's idea to come back out. He said I needed cheering up, what with the bust up and that. My head was all over the place so I just agreed. Seemed like a good idea. But, I think you're right. I should get myself back home and sort things out with Louise."

James smiled. "Cecil means well. Is there anything I can help you with? Any advice you need?"

"No, no. It's okay. You made me see that it's not that complicated. I just need to go and sort it out."

And then I remembered the lighthouse issue.

"Anyway, how's business? Boats doing well? Plenty of tourists?"

"Ah sure it's going along fine. Busy time of year. The more flyers we give out the more business we get in. I know one thing. It keeps my printer in beer."

I saw an opportunity.

"Talking of flyers James, we ran into a couple of girls who said they know you. Estrid and Alida. They do flyers for you."

He shrugged. "We have a lot of people doing flyers Matt. They do all sorts of flyers and promotions, all over the place, for a lot of businesses."

"Okay. They're two Scandinavians, blondes."

James hesitated. "What names did you say?"

"Estrid and Alida."

"Oh, sure I know who you mean. Al and her mate. Yeah, now I know. Always remember her as the lads call her Al. The girl with a fella's name. She's been here a few times if I remember. Yeah, nice girls. They do a grand job."

His recognition of the name Al seemed to confirm Cecil's theory. It was a name on the shredded list we had found. Maybe James *was* carrying on with the local girls.

"Do you do any night trips with the boats at all? I wondered as it always fascinated me how the lighthouses work?"

"Lighthouses? Well, they're only out there to warn ships away from rocks. We never take the boats out after dark so it isn't a concern for us."

"Are there many around here?"

James laughed. "You going lighthouse spotting Matt? I've never been asked that before. We have nine of them here in Ibiza, seven of them active. In fact there's one right here in San Antonio although it's not active anymore."

Nine lighthouses. That would make things more complicated.

"Where's the one here then?"

"Ah, it's down there just before you get to the marina, as you walk along from the sunset bars."

"Do they have names? The lighthouses, I mean?"

"Well the one here is called Covas Blancas but it's a museum now. I couldn't tell you all the others. But I'm sure you can find them on a map."

I decided not to question further. I could tell by his face that he was puzzled by my interest.

"Okay, well, listen, thanks for chatting James. I'd better be heading back. Maybe you'd tell Eleanor I called."

"I will son. You want another beer before you go?"

"No, I'm good."

"Where are you staying then? We could maybe catch up before you go."

I hesitated, now unsure of who to trust.

"I was at the Blau Parc but checked out. No need now that I'm going home."

He stood up and held out a hand.

"Well, good to see you Matt. I hope things work out and give my regards to Louise, won't you."

"I will. Thanks." I pointed at the table. "I'll give you a hand to clear up here before I go." I picked up the ashtray.

"Sure don't worry about that Matt. It's hardly been a party now."

"I know but always best to clear up with the woman of the house away or things get on top of you."

James laughed.

"Maybe you're right son. I'm not the only one dishing out the advice today then am I?"

The mobile jangled in my pocket. "Sorry. Got to check. Might be Louise," I said.

"Go ahead. You're sound Matt," James replied. He picked up the empty bottles from the table and headed for the villa, followed by Mofo and Panzer.

I checked the screen.

'Nothing new mate. See u at 7.'

James had disappeared from view. I slipped the used cigarette into my pocket and left the poolside.

27

I found the lads in the tapas bar already when I arrived. Beers were lined up on the table and it looked like the party had started some while earlier. I pulled up a chair next to Carlos and grabbed a spare beer.

"Got something to show you guys," I said. I pulled out two cigarette butts from my pockets and placed them both on the table. "What do you think?"

I was met by puzzled expressions. Cecil broke the silence.

"You got two fag butts there mate, right. This got something to do with finding this fag end in that cave?"

"Exactly Ces. I was at James's place earlier and guess what? The other cigarette end belonged to him. He stubbed it out in front of me." I sat back in my chair. "Now take a closer look. Not only are they the same brand but they've been smoked down to almost the same length. In both cases, it's only about three quarters of the cigarette that's been smoked. That kind of suggests he could have been in the cave. Then when you look at where the caves are and the fact they have boat launch rails and James runs boats, it starts to get a bit more interesting.

Cecil leaned forward to speak.

"Hold it a second. Let me finish," I said. "There's more. James admitted he knew Alida and if you remember Ces, that bit of paper you found in his office had 'Al' on it along with all the other names. He even used the name 'Al.' Called her the girl with a fella's name. And what do we know already? Yup, Alida knows Scalapino."

I picked up my beer and took a swig. Cecil waited until I had put the bottle back down.

"You done now geeze?"

I nodded.

Cecil picked up both cigarette ends.

"Brands the same mate, Fortuna. One of the biggest sellers in Spain. What's that mean d'you think? I tell you what it means. It means that any smoker in the whole population of Ibiza could've dropped one of these."

I stared at Carlos and then at Jasper to see their reaction. Both were non-committal.

"Yeah but I found one of them in the cave. That narrows it right down Ces. With that cave under lock and key there can't be that many people who go in there."

"Don't mean nothing. One of the geezers who's gone in there might have picked it up on the sole of his shoe and it's stuck there. Then when he's in the cave, it's come off on the rough gravel. Same brand James smokes? Co-incidence. You're gonna need more than that to connect up these dots mate."

"Who's James anyway?" Carlos asked.

"It's Louise's mum's bloke," Jasper chipped in.

"I told you Carlos, didn't I? The bloke with the villa where me and Ces stayed when we came out with the girls."

"Och, I cannae remember names Mateo –"

"Too frigging right you can't. It's bloody JJ or Jason but not the M word. Okay?"

"Oh, aye. But you're telling me that your father-in-law would be trying to stitch you up?"

I paused for a moment contemplating what Carlos had said.

"It doesn't make sense, I know. And anyway, he wouldn't exactly be my father-in-law would he? He's not married to Eleanor and he's even less likely to be my father-in-law now I've screwed things up with Louise." I sipped my beer and then contemplated the label for a moment. "Yeah, maybe you're right Carlos. When I think about it, James *was* telling me to go back home and sort things out with Louise."

"Yeah, but he could be bluffing," Jasper said. "Supposing things have changed and now they want you to go back 'cos they know you shouldn't be here and soon as you get back you get arrested. I mean being over here illegally wouldn't do your cred any good with the cops would it?"

I began to pick at the bottle label. Cecil was dismantling my theory and Jasper was keeping it alive. All I wanted was some straightforward evidence.

"Wait a minute. What about the link between James, Alida and Scalapino?

"What link's that geezer?"

"Well, the fact that Alida knows them both?"

"Yeah, I know. You said that. But where's the link?" Cecil asked.

I hesitated, Cecil's repetition of the question causing me to doubt my own conviction.

"Well, the bit of paper for starters. You still have that don't you?"

"Yeah, it's still in my case from last time. But listen mate. This ain't exactly London or New York is it? It's a small town on an island. Scalapino does the doors, that Al bird does flyers. So stands to reason they know one another. She also does flyers for the boats so she knows James. It don't mean that James and Scalapino know one another does it? They might do 'cos it's a small place like I said, but it don't mean they do. Yeah, it might be her name on that paper but, I told you before, it could just as easily be an Alison. As for your man James having boats, so do half the people in this place if you check out the marina and all down the bay. It's built on fishing and tourism mate. "

I sat for a moment in silence, shattered that my detective work was nothing more than an amateur attempt to piece random bits of information together and come up with something that might help me. I was trying to make connections where there were none and I suddenly felt guilty that, in my desperation to find something, I had even considered James, a man who had been nothing other than kind and supportive to me, might be an enemy. I needed another drink.

"Looks like I'm barking up the wrong tree," I said, trying to mask the dejection. "Might as well get a few beers in?"

I gathered up the empty bottles from the table, headed towards the bar and came face to face with Scalapino.

He looked as surprised to see me as I was to see him. He could only just have walked in. I hadn't noticed him before. His gaze turned from surprise to a cold piercing stare of intent. The instant I saw the change I reacted. There was no way past him and I knew I had to stay a step ahead. I let go of the empties. The crash of breaking glass distracted him long enough for me to make an about turn and race between the rows of tables towards a wooden door at the back of the bar. I pushed hard against the door handle but it was locked. It was a store cupboard, not an exit. I turned to see Scalapino lumbering towards me, cutting off any escape. To my right a couple, distracted from their tapas by the commotion, had turned to see what was going on. In the middle of their table, a candle flickered gently in an old wax covered wine bottle. It was the only thing in sight that might double as a weapon. I lunged towards it and snatched it off the table, wielding it like a club at Scalapino. As I grabbed it, a stream of wax poured straight onto a bowl of olives that the couple had as a side dish. The girl let out a high-pitched squeal of surprise. Her bloke leapt from his seat cutting off the gap between Scalapino and me. And he was English.

"What you playing at mate?" he said.

The last thing I needed was an upset customer. As I tried to form a response, I caught sight of Cecil and the boys moving up behind Scalapino. I needed time. I grabbed a handful of the wax covered olives, stuffed them in my mouth and began to chew vigorously. The irate customer's face turned into wide-eyed surprise.

"Err ... they're fine. Delicious. It's a ... a bit of a ... delicacy out here," I said, spitting mouthfuls of olive skin unintentionally in his direction.

"You taking the piss?" was the last thing he said.

Scalapino grabbed him by the neck and flung him onto the floor. In an instant reaction, Cecil leaped onto Scalapino's back, stopping his forward momentum. Scalapino turned, trying to shrug off Cecil but was met by both barrels of a shotgun pointed at his head.

"No fight in my place."

Everything stopped. Cecil backed off. Scalapino stood up straight and glared. The irate customer got to his feet, red faced with embarrassment. I spat the last of the wax covered olives into my hand. All eyes were on the shotgun aimed in our general direction by the bar tender. Nobody moved.

"You no fight here, comprendes? You English. Trouble."

Carlos stepped forward, his hands up as if he was in a cowboy movie. He spoke slowly, in Spanish. Hearing his native tongue seemed to calm the bar tender but he kept the shotgun poised. Carlos lowered one hand and began to point at each of us in turn. A flurry of words were exchanged between the two of them. Scalapino stepped forward to interrupt but the bar tender cocked the gun at him. He stepped back. Carlos continued, more animated with his hand movements as he began to find his flow. When he had finished, the bar tender nodded at Scalapino and waved the shotgun in the direction of the door.

"¡Tu, fuera de aqui!"

"What's he saying Carlos," I asked.

"He's telling him to get out," Carlos replied.

Scalapino spat on the floor and turned to me, a finger pointed at my face.

"Hijo de puta. I come for you."

Cecil intervened, squaring up to Scalapino despite being several inches shorter.

"Geezer, who you talking to? You're a bald headed fuck. If you had hair you'd look a proper prick."

The quizzical look on Scalapino's face galvanised Cecil. It was situation control, power. He decided to emphasis the power in words Scalapino might get. He turned to Carlos.

"Mate, what's the fucking lingo for bald headed prick."

Carlos looked perplexed.

"Leave it Cecil. Nae point."

"There *is* a point Carlos. The geezer's gotta know. He's gotta know he can't go round threatening my mates and calling them names and thinking he's gonna get away with it."

Carlos shrugged, a resigned look crossing his face. He stepped forward and whispered in Cecil's ear. That seemed to be enough for Cecil. He turned back to Scalapino.

"You know what I'm saying?" He pointed a finger in Scalapino's face. "A fucking pelado huevón."

Fire flashed in Scalapino's eyes. His fists clenched in a knuckle-whitening grip. The bar tender saw the signs. He swung the shotgun barrel towards Scalapino.

"No más, hombre." Again he pointed the shotgun towards the door.

Scalapino glared at Cecil and for a moment I thought his anger would get the better of common sense. Cecil stood his ground. Jasper stepped up alongside him. Scalapino continued the face off for another few seconds and then, with a final sneer aimed at Jasper, he turned and left.

With Scalapino out of the way the bar tender lowered the shotgun. I grabbed Carlos by the hand and shook it, relieved to have escaped Scalapino's clutches.

"What was all that about Carlos? What did you say?"

Carlos wiped the perspiration from his brow and sat down.

"This man is the owner of the bar," he said, pointing at the bar tender. "He disnae want anyone fighting in here or any trouble. He said that there are too many mad English holidaymakers in San Antonio already. I told him you'd been thrown out of a club by the big guy and you'd called him a name but that you had apologised. And now, when he saw you here, he wanted to start trouble again."

I wasn't too enamoured about being lumped in with the 'mad English' holiday crowd but it had got me out of a scrape.

"Cheers mate. Let me get you a beer. You deserve it."

"What about me, geeze? I was just about to take that big lump out of the equation," Cecil said.

"Yeah, you too Ces ... cheers. And Jas. I saw you ready too mate. Cool. Beers all round."

Carlos stood up.

"Hold it. First we have to pay for the damage, the broken bottles and then we have to pay for that customer's food." He pointed at the guy who had joined his other half again. "Otherwise, no drinks."

"No problem," I said.

We squared the bill, ordered more beers and went back to our table. As the adrenaline subsided, my anxiety began to return. I turned to Cecil.

"So what was all that about with you and Scalapino? Why did you have to go and antagonise him further?"

Cecil ran a hand through his mop of shaggy hair.

"No offence geezer," he said, looking at Carlos, "but the bloke's as bald as baby's fucking arse. So he ain't got that Irish hair thing going on and –"

"That's because, apparently, he's half Comanche Indian and half Italian," I interrupted.

"He's what?" Jasper said.

"Not the fucking point. It's testosterone, ain't it? No fucking bottle. If the geezer's gonna large it he'll have hair, yeah?" He nodded towards Carlos. "He didn't like that pelado thing, did he? What's that mean then? Prick?"

Carlos smiled.

"Not exactly. It doesn't translate easy. It's something we use in South America. It's an insult … let me see. A lazy bastard whose balls drag along the ground ... a dickhead."

Cecil roared with laughter.

"Even better mate. Nice one. Bald lazy bastard too."

I felt a surge of panic. It was no laughing matter.

"Look, Ces, I'm in the shit here, you know that. I'm not going to second guess a bloke's intention by the amount of hair he's got. You know the deal. I have to sort this out and a bloke's hairstyle isn't in my thinking. As far as I'm concerned he's a villain and whether he's got hair or not, he's after my nuts. The last thing I need is you winding him up further, and now he's going to be on your case too."

222

Cecil narrowed his eyes and brushed his hair back.

"Alright mate, I know what you're saying. It was the heat of the moment, that's all."

"Okay. No worries but we have to be more focussed, clinical. I need to be a step ahead of these guys. I can't be getting into confrontation. I've been here three days now and I haven't got a lot to show for it."

"You're right. That visit to the cave hasn't told you a lot and it won't be long before them guys realise you've been back there," Jasper said. "Maybe we ought to get you out of San An for a while. Maybe find some place in Ibiza Town. You could still try and find out stuff from there. It's only on the other side of the island."

"Maybe Jas. It might be a bit safer. The only problem is it's a bit out of the loop. If something happens here, I'm not on the spot. I might miss it."

"Yeah, but we're still here mate," Cecil said.

"But we're not safe now either," Carlos added. "That big lump will be following us too so he can get to Ma ... JJ."

I swigged my beer, my mind a whirlwind of thoughts. Nothing seemed to be going to plan. One dead end after another. And then one thought jumped out from amongst the conflict.

"Hang on, Jas. What did you say?"

He looked at me, his eyes full of hesitancy.

"Uh ... I just said that maybe you'd be better off in Ibiza Town."

"No. Before that ... about San Antonio."

"Uh ... yeah. Get you out of San An. Why?"

"Oh, nothing. Just a thought." I gulped down the last of my beer and stood up. "I'd better head back. Catch you lot tomorrow. Have a good night."

I reached across the table, picked up the two cigarette ends and stuck them in my pocket.

28

I felt safer staying in my hotel room at night. I lay on my bed deep in thought. At first I couldn't sleep with so much going on in my head but I must have dropped off eventually. I woke up at four in the morning, startled into consciousness by the activity in my brain. I grabbed my mobile and tapped out a text.

'Ces, I need to see you. I've been thinking about something. Meet me for breakfast. There's a café not far from the Blau Parc called Fatso's. Come out of the hotel and go right. Keep straight until you get to the garage on your left. Turn left there and the caf is just along on your right. It's a Brit caf so it's probably the last place Scalp and his mob would expect us to be now we know they are after us. And if you got that bit of paper bring it. See you there at 11.'

It was a straightforward walk for me from the Valencia, round the back streets to Fatso's. Outside in the terrace area many of the tables were already occupied by young post party revellers fuelling up for the day ahead. Bleary eyes scanned menus, perhaps not fully comprehending the choices or still unable to focus their minds on decision making. A steady stream of banter flew across tables, bare chested lads regaling one another with their nightly exploits. The excited laughter of chattering girls, puffing on cigarettes and tapping messages into mobiles, added to the carefree, relaxed atmosphere. I seemed to be the only one with world-weary shoulders.

I went inside and strolled past the long, navy-patterned bar with its silver edging, heading for the back of the room. I took a table by the window. The position afforded me the perfect view of both entrances, the one directly ahead where I had come in and the one halfway along opposite the bar area. It was cooler inside, there were fewer people and it was more discreet. As I sat down my phone buzzed a message. I checked the screen.

'Yeah, gotcha mate. I know Fatso's. Blinding little place. Was down there the other day. Decent bit of grub too. Catch u later.'

At least I knew Cecil was coming but knowing his time keeping, I decided to go ahead and order breakfast. Cecil could sort himself out when he arrived. I ordered a tea and the full English. I had barely eaten the day before and a hearty breakfast had lots of appeal. When it arrived, I tucked in hungrily, my focus switching to the food and little attention on my surroundings. Apart from a table of four girls just ahead of mine, who had come in after me, and the two tables immediately behind me and to my right that were already occupied, I took no further notice of who came and went.

And that was a mistake.

He stopped at the bar just before he got to where my table was situated. I looked up, mid mouthful. His outline was unmistakable, even from behind. Scalapino. The bacon almost stuck in my throat as the shock of seeing him caused an involuntary swallow. My appetite disappeared in a flood of panic. I had to get out but I was rooted to the chair by indecision. If I stood up, I could draw attention to myself. He hadn't seen me but if I stayed where I was, he would do sooner or later. I glanced to my left at the nearest exit. To my dismay, I saw the two villains who had shut me in the cave. They were laughing and staring at a couple of dark haired girls at a table outside. I turned back to the front. To reach the far exit where I had come in, I would have to walk between the two villains and Scalapino. That was not an option.

Scalapino was ordering coffee. It would only be a matter of moments before he turned around. There was no escape. The horror of the previous day's confrontation pulsed through me.

I had no disguise this time, no backup and nowhere to hide. I watched as he picked up a coffee and began to turn around.

Disguise. Hide. The words flashed through my mind in a subconscious command. Instantly I pitched forward, my face aimed at my breakfast. It had to be realistic. I hit it hard, cutlery and tea clattering to the floor as I landed face first on the plate.

The screams and cries from the girls at the next table galvanised the place into action.

"Oh, my God. He's passed out,|" I heard.

"Passed out? He's fucking dead," a female voice said.

I lay there, my face in the beans, trying not to snort up tomato sauce and egg yolk. A pair of hands gripped my shoulders and pulled me upright. I just rolled with it. If I was going to pull this off, I had to make it look authentic. As I was pulled into an upright position, I allowed my head to loll backwards.

"He's breathing." A male voice said. "Somebody call an ambulance. Now." An insistent tone, urgent but no panic.

The same voice whispered in my ear.

"My name's Ben. I'm a first aider back home. I'm going to put you on the floor. Stay cool."

I allowed myself to be moved onto the floor, hopeful that the glutinous mix of beans and sauce stuck to my face would conceal my identity. I kept my eyes tight shut, as much to shut myself off from reality as it was to maintain the illusion of a lack of consciousness.

"He's breathing," Ben said. And then in my ear, "You'll be fine. Can you hear me? What's your name?"

"Err ... Jason ... sorry. Faint ... passed out," I said, grateful to be on the floor and aware that I was surrounded by people. I just hoped that Scalapino was not amongst them.

"Okay Jason, I'm going to put you in the recovery position. Just relax. You taken anything?"

"No ... no. Just faint ..."

"Have you got a medical history? Are you on any medication?"

I knew Ben meant well but I wished he would stop asking questions. I hadn't thought my bogus illness through enough to deal with treatment. In fact I hadn't thought about it at all past keeling over. An ambulance seemed drastic. But I realised Ben's caring approach meant that he was interested in my wellbeing and wouldn't leave me. Scalapino didn't have that same interest and I was sure that if he had noticed who I was, he would have made a move. I decided that I was best off on the floor surrounded by a crowd. And then I remembered Cecil. If he walked in and Scalapino saw him, the game was up.

I tried to sit up but was stopped by Ben.

"Stay there. If you try to get up you may pass out again. Help is on its way."

"But I feel better. I think I can –"

"No. You ought to stay there. You might have an underlying condition that has caused you to black out. You should get checked. Let me take your pulse."

Trust me to find the only sensible Brit in San Antonio. Ben was clearly confusing his first aid qualification with that of a fully qualified medical consultant. But I realised if I got into a debate with him, it would only focus more attention on me. I had to hope that the ambulance would arrive before Cecil. I stayed down on the floor whilst Ben took my wrist and began his pulse check.

"It's quite rapid," he said after a short while.

I'm not bloody surprised I thought. Yours would be rapid too if you were being pursued by a psychopath.

Ben went into reassurance mode, his bedside manner kicking in to full social worker.

"Okay, don't worry Jason. The ambulance will be here soon. They'll take care of you. Do you want me to contact somebody and let them know where you are?"

"No ... no ... it's okay," I said. "I'm fine ... well ... err ... not fine ... but ... I will be."

In the close confines of the cafe, surrounded by people and in the tension of the moment, I had started to perspire heavily.

"You feel very hot Jason. Let me wipe your face, cool you down," Ben said and attempted to turn my face towards him.

I'd had enough. I swivelled my head around, a wild-eyed stare, blazing through sauce covered eyes, directed straight at Ben.

"Fuck off Ben. I'm fine."

Immediately I regretted my reaction. But Ben seemed to roll with it.

"He's hallucinating," he said to nobody in particular. "He's definitely on something."

I gave up, tried to hide my face against the floor and decided I just had to put up with Ben. I had no choice but to wait.

It was almost twenty minutes before the ambulance arrived. Immediately I knew I was in the hands of professionals.

"Hola. You are English?"

I opened one eye and peered through the sauce. A slim young woman, her dark hair tied back in a ponytail, was leaning over me.

"Yes," I answered.

"Okay. Hello. I'm a paramedic. My name is Paloma. What is yours?"

"Uh ... it's ... it's, uh ... Jason."

"Hello Jason. I need to know what has happened. You take something?" Her hand brushed over my face wiping away the debris of my breakfast. In a sudden moment's concern that Scalapino might see who I was, I shrugged her off.

"It's okay. Easy. I will help you. Have you taken drugs ... Mary J, Charlie? No problem, but you must tell me so we can help." Her fingers were on my wrist checking my pulse.

Before I could answer, Ben butted in with his own diagnosis.

"I think he has taken something. His eyes are very wild and he's experiencing mood swings. Maybe Ketamine. He passed out, just fell into his food. Perhaps his muscles were paralysed."

Mood swings. I was on the verge of experiencing a very large mood swing against busybody Ben but I realised I had to maintain control.

"Have you taken Ketamine?" Paloma asked.

"No. I don't even know what it is," I said, alarmed that I was going to be filled with some antidote to something I hadn't taken.

"It's used as an animal tranquilliser," Ben said. "It can make you hallucinate, numbs your body. Maybe that's why you didn't feel anything when you collapsed."

I shot a wild-eyed, butt out nobhead stare at Ben. "Look, I haven't taken any ... any animal tranquillisers or anything else in fact. Why would I take something that's meant for animals?" I turned to Paloma who was my only hope of extricating myself from what was turning into a nightmare. "I just need some air. I need to get out in the fresh air."

"Any medicines?" Paloma asked.

"No, nothing."

"Okay Jason. We put you in a chair and then we take you to hospital. Can you get up?"

There was no way I wanted to get up. Getting up meant facing reality. My lack of response resulted in me being hoisted off the floor and loaded into a wheelchair by two of Paloma's paramedic colleagues. I kept my chin pressed hard against my chest but, from my upright position, I was able to scan the area surreptitiously. Scalapino was at the counter staring at the commotion. I hoped he hadn't recognised me. His two sidekicks were by the door but so were several other customers who had left their tables to watch the spectacle.

Paloma crouched beside me.

"You okay?"

"I feel a little faint ... all these people."

"We leave now for the hospital."

"Hospital? I don't need ... I mean I'll be fine once we're outside."

"We have to take you now. You must be checked. I cannot leave you outside."

The chair began to move towards the door. I kept my head down and stared at my knees as they wheeled me through the crowd. An ambulance was parked on the corner, the word *Ambulancia*, written backwards in red letters across the front. When we reached the pavement, the chair was spun round and I spotted Cecil heading for the cafe. Instinctively I leapt up forgetting my temporary incapacitation. A hand grabbed my arm, restraining me.

"Señor, what you doing?" a male voice asked.

I turned towards the paramedic who was pushing the chair but I needed to alert Cecil not to enter the cafe. Cecil had spotted the ambulance and the crowd. He was yards from the entrance and slowed his pace. I raised my hand and pointed at him.

"That man. He has my medication."

"Medication? You say you have no medication," Paloma said, confusion enveloping her face.

"I ... I forgot. He has it."

I dropped back into the chair as Paloma and one of the paramedics moved towards Cecil. Their colleague dragged the chair back onto a long metal ramp and pulled me into the ambulance. In the distance I could see Paloma and Cecil in animated conversation. Once inside, the paramedic helped me onto a bed, wiped my face and placed an oxygen mask over my mouth and nose. I had just laid back, wondering how I could get out of the ambulance and make an escape, when Cecil entered with Paloma in his wake.

"What the fuck you doing geezer? What's happened?"

I began to explain through the oxygen mask about Scalapino.

"Where is he? What's he done? I'll have the fuck. He's hurt you, yeah?"

"Calm down Ces. No, nothing like that. Listen, I needed to get out of –"

"We go now," Paloma said, as her colleague closed the ambulance door.

"Go? Go where?" Cecil asked.

"Eivissa. Hospital Can Misses."

"Where?"

"Eivissa ... Ibiza Town. It's our hospital. It won't take long."

The ambulance moved off. Cecil turned back to me, his voice dropping to a whisper.

"Mate, we need to get outta here. This Spanish bird's asking about some fucking medication you said I had. I blagged it mate but you can't be pitching up at no hospital."

"I know. But what are we going to do."

Cecil ran his hands through his hair and scanned the ambulance.

"Look mate, we can't do nothing when the ambulance is moving. I'll think of something. Wait until we get there."

We arrived at the hospital within twenty minutes. I breathed in deeply, gulping down the pure oxygen in the hope that it would calm the rising anxiety that had begun to grip my chest. As the ambulance pulled to a halt I leant close to Cecil.

"So what's the plan then?"

Cecil shrugged. "We do a runner, mate. There ain't no plan."

"That's the plan? That's not a plan," I said, my hopes that Cecil had come up with a sensible, civilised way of dealing with the ambulance team who had gone to the trouble of helping me, completely dashed.

"I just said there ain't no plan didn't I? Soon as them doors are open we're outta here geeze. Got it? No fannying about. We leg it," Cecil hissed, his eyes tight with focussed intent.

I took another gulp of oxygen and glanced at Paloma. The doors of the ambulance were pulled open. A stream of sunlight penetrated the interior.

Cecil was on his feet immediately.

"Go mate. Go! Now!"

I swung my legs off the bed and made a dash for the doors just as Cecil leapt onto the tarmac. My head was jolted round hard to the left. At exactly the same time, I felt a sharp sting in my eye. The plastic tube on the oxygen mask had whiplashed away from its cylinder and cracked me in the face. Paloma was too shocked to react.

"Take the fucking mask off nobhead," Cecil shouted as he wheeled around to see where I was.

I flung the mask to one side.

"Sorry Paloma. No medical insurance," I said, trying to avoid eye contact with her.

I leapt from the back of the vehicle just managing to dodge the grasp of the other paramedic who had suddenly found the ability to react to the situation. Cecil was already on the move. I didn't look back. I belted after him, straight down the narrow service road that ran alongside the square, grey hospital block. To my left, several people who had been making their way along the pavement to the entrance, stopped and stared. At the end of the road a dual carriageway lay ahead. Cecil didn't stop to look. He made a beeline for the far side, dodging the traffic and weaving past vehicles that had suddenly come to a skidding halt to avoid him. Head down, I legged it through the path that Cecil had cut, ignoring the blaring horns and venom filled expletives. Once across I stopped to catch my breath.

"We can't hang around here geezer. The hospital staff will be on to the Old Bill already. You don't need no cops on your trail. We gotta keep going, find somewhere less open."

I glanced back towards the hospital.

"Is anyone following us?"

"No idea mate. But we need to move. Dunno what they're like out here about wasting medical services time and I don't intend to find out. They might throw the book at us if they catch us. And you broke their fucking oxygen thing as well."

"It's just a mask Ces," I said, hoping that it was no more than a minor accident.

"Yeah, but you don't wanna be getting in no discussion about it. Let's go."

Ahead, a long, straight avenue ran between two rows of apartment buildings. We had no idea where it led but there was no traffic and it looked quieter than the main road. At its end, a set of floodlights loomed over a sports ground. We turned left and ran along another avenue. On the far corner some builders were making repairs to the tarmac, their noisy machinery adding to my sense of panic. They stopped and stared as we ran past them and down to the next junction, no doubt wondering why two crazy guys were running in the blistering heat.

"Down there," Cecil said.

My shirt was sticking to my back, sweat pouring down my face. I had to stop for a moment.

"Ces, I need a breather. It's so bloody hot." It wasn't so much a fitness issue, more the fact that stress, tension and exertion were not a good mix.

"Mate, we can't stop here. They could be following in a security car or something. We ain't that far from the main town." He pointed ahead. "It'll be safer down there."

I stared in the direction Cecil had pointed. The outline of Ibiza old town, with the magnificent sand coloured Eivissa Castle dominating the horizon, stood out sharply against the cloudless bright blue of the sky. We kept running, the pace slowing as we tired and the heat took its toll. At the next junction we took a left and reached a shopping mall car park. We cut through, crossed another dual carriageway and found ourselves in a busy street full of shops that led towards the town. Surrounded by people and activity it felt safe to slow the pace.

"More like it geezer," Cecil said. "If we get down to the tourist spots we got more cover and maybe we can pick up a taxi."

"I haven't seen a single cab anywhere," I said.

"They'll be where the tourists are mate. Let's head in the direction of that castle. Bound to be something over there."

As we drew closer to the Old Town the streets became narrower, a maze of connecting walkways interlinking rows of boutique shops and cafe bars. We kept on towards the castle. Finally, we came face to face with a long stone ramp that led up to the main entrance of the walled enclosure of the Old Town, the Portal de Ses Taules.

"Mate, I ain't going up that. There won't be no taxis up there. Too narrow ain't it."

I was exhausted. Tired of running. Not only had I started the day trying to get away from Scalapino but now I was running from someone else. I stopped to catch my breath and called out to Cecil.

"Ces. Wait. I've had enough mate. I can't keep running from people all day. There's nobody following us. If there was, we've lost them. I'm gonna need a hospital at this rate. Let's chill for a bit."

Cecil turned and stared at me.

"Chill?"

"Yeah, get a beer somewhere."

Cecil's eyes lit up.

"Mate, now you're talking. Yeah, you're right. We give 'em the slip."

"I'm not sure there was anybody to give the slip to. Maybe we overreacted."

"Nah mate. Trust me. If we'd hung around there they'd be having you in for tests, checking your insurance docs and then wanting ID, all that shit. Next thing you'd be lumbered with a medical bill. Wouldn't have been long before they'd have rumbled your bogus ID. And what for? Just 'cos you're trying to get away from that bald mug."

"Yeah, maybe you're right." I sucked in a gulp of oxygen and suddenly felt calmer. "Right, I've got an idea. Why don't we just call up Jas and get him to come and get us. He's got the car hasn't he?"

Cecil didn't need to reply. His broad grin confirmed his agreement. He pulled his mobile from his pocket and hit the buttons.

29

We sat outside at a bar overlooking the waterfront and waited for Jasper. Nestling under a canopy of palms, the shade afforded some respite from the early afternoon sunshine. Several of the remaining tables were occupied by tourists enjoying lunch. A waiter placed two bottles of Alhambra Especial and a bowl of olives on the blue tablecloth. Cecil pushed his beer to one side and looked me directly in the eyes.

"So, after all that, what exactly did you drag me all the way out here to tell me then?"

"What do you mean?"

"Mate, you sent me a text at four in the morning telling me to meet you at the caf. I get there and you've got half the fucking Ibiza health service out in force and a crowd round you on the street. And you wanna keep a low profile?"

I ignored Cecil's exaggeration. "Did you bring that bit of paper?"

"Bollocks. Sorry mate. I forgot it. What d'you want it for anyway?"

"I want to check the names again. Can you remember any of them, apart from Al?"

Cecil scratched his forehead and sat back.

"I dunno mate. Let's see … Polly, Sue … and the only other one I can remember is Al, like you said. Why? I thought we said they were all that James geezer's birds."

"No, that's what *you* said Ces. They could be and, like I said, he knows Al … but I've been thinking."

Cecil raised his beer and waved the bottle at me.

"Okay. Let's hear it then." He swigged back several mouthfuls and put the beer back on the table, accompanying the movement with a loud belch.

"Well, my dad comes from County Clare and –"

"Yeah I know that but what the fuck's that gotta do with this stuff?"

"Hang on, let me finish. I was going to say, and so, by coincidence, does James. Then yesterday Jas said something about San An - San Antonio."

"So, what's all that supposed to mean, geeze?" Cecil said, his deep frown showing both his impatience and his puzzlement. He reached forward, selected an olive and popped it in his mouth.

"Don't you see? Clare and Ann are women's names but they're also places. So it could be that the names on that list we found in the villa are all names of places, not names of women."

"Yeah? So where the fuck is Polly then? And for that matter Sue?" Cecil replied, waving a hand dismissively in the direction of the ocean and then spitting the olive stone onto the floor.

"I don't know, do I? I'm just speculating. I've not got much to go on and time's running out so I'm just looking at all possibilities."

Cecil sat back and ran his fingers through his hair. Then he turned in the direction of the bar and beckoned to the waiter. The waiter caught the gesture and made a move towards our table. Cecil signalled for two more beers, even though I still had half a bottle left. The waiter acknowledged him with a nod and turned back towards the bar.

"Your problem geezer, is you're thinking too much. You might have a point but keep it simple first before you go getting any wild theories. Why don't we go find Estrid and Al when we get back to San An, and check if they know any of the names on the list. Chances are they might know these other birds' names. It's a small community mate. If they do, then we find them too and start asking some questions. And anyway, the San An bit's a bloke's name, ain't it? Antonio ... means Anthony."

I finished the remainder of my beer and thought about what Cecil had said before answering.

"I suppose so, yeah. But the two girls are going to wonder why we're asking. They've only got to mention something to Scalapino and … well, you know."

"Mate, we got that covered. Remember the party? We just give them that bollocks again about the party we're organising for James. Tell them we're getting a blinding guest list together and we want some hot birds. If they know them then we close that down. If not, then you still got your theory to work on."

The waiter arrived with the beers.

"Muchas gracias señor," Cecil said as he picked up the bottle. He turned back towards me and noticed the concern on my face. "What's that look for mate? Listen, I ain't burning your theory. I'm just saying, keep it simple first. If it turns out these birds all work down here they could be connected with the villains that's chasing you down. You remember that thing a while back? Them two birds in San Antonio they reckon was used as drug mules in Peru or Colombia or somewhere? Supposed to have been shipping coke about and got done? An Irish girl and a Scots girl I think. They worked out here didn't they? Got mixed up with the wrong people and got themselves in the shit. So it happens mate. Just supposing that list of names throws up some who've got themselves involved with this Scalapino and that other geezer … whasisname?"

"Felipe."

"Yeah Felipe. If any of them is involved with them geezers it stands to reason they could be involved in a smuggling operation."

"But if that's the case then James has to be involved. He had the list."

"No, he don't mate. You can still know people and not be involved in whatever else they have going on. I mean, he could just know them 'cos they all do promo work."

"Well you've changed your tune. Weren't long ago you reckoned he was shagging them all."

Cecil laughed.

"I ain't ruling it out mate. You live out here, got a few bob, nice pad and a boat. You hook up with some hot looking birds who are working the season earning fuck all and need to make ends meet … you know the mumble. Some do the sugar daddy thing and some do the old illegal activity swerve, trying to earn a fast buck. Yeah?" He reached over with the beer bottle and clinked it against mine. "Cheers geezer."

"Cheers Ces," I replied. "I suppose you're right. We ought to rule out the obvious first before I get too wrapped up in it all."

Jasper dropped me off at the Valencia. We arranged to meet at Café del Mar for eight o'clock. The time was deliberate. People would be gathering, many of them on the move along the walkway in front of the sunset bars. It would give us a crowd and a crowd meant more cover. It was also a good time to try and find Estrid and Alida before they got into the serious business of dishing out flyers.

We arrived together. There was no way I was going to risk pitching up by myself and waiting for the others. We headed for the seating on the upper tier, two levels up from the bar, and found a table. The open plan design gave us an excellent view of the whole venue, across to Cafe Mambo on the right and over the main bar below. Ahead of us a blue and yellow light stack cast a colourful glow across the wood of the middle floor. To the left, a DJ had begun to ramp up the atmosphere with a mix of funky Del Mar sounds.

Carlos, who had been elected to bar duties, plonked a jug and four glasses on the table in front of us.

"What the fuck's that shit geezer?" Cecil asked, his face screwed into a look of incredulity that would have been more appropriate if he had been asked to drink diesel.

"It's sangria Cecil. You never tried it?" Carlos said.

"It's got fruit floating in it for fuck's sake. If I'd wanted a meal I'd have asked for a knife and fork."

"Och, away wi'ya Cecil. We're in Spain. Can y'no try a wee bit of the local culture for a change man?"

"Listen nobhead. Don't be pulling all that culture bollocks on me. I've done the tapas, yeah, done the Alhambra beer. I'm international geeze. But that's a bird drink ain't it? The minute you go lobbing fucking oranges and lemons and shit, yeah, and lemonade into a drink, it's game over. No proper geezer's gonna drink that." He pointed at the jug as if it was a laboratory experiment that had gone badly wrong.

Jasper intervened.

"Lads, we're here to have a drink and a laugh, right. So nobody's got to drink something they don't fancy. Chill. We got enough aggravation with Matt ... JJ, I mean, without us lot falling out over a frigging drink. So what do you want Ces?"

"Hold on. I'm not here for a laugh," I interrupted. "I'm here because –"

"Yeah, yeah. We know what you're here for geezer but maybe we could all do with a good piss up. It's been nothing but fucking agg since we got here," Cecil said. He pointed at the jug of Sangria. "And if we're gonna have a piss up we can't be drinking pussy drinks like that."

In a show of defiance, Carlos poured himself a glass of the Sangria.

"¡Salud! Suit yourselves."

The events of the past few days had clearly created tension. The last thing I needed was a row within the group. Carlos and Cecil were forever rubbing one another up the wrong way but when it came to the crunch, they were tight. And in my current situation, I needed exactly that - a tight team.

"No worries Ces," I said. "What do you want then?"

"A nice bottle of Duvel would go down well mate."

"What if they don't have it?" I asked.

"They'll have it or something like it. Mate, it's a class bar. None of your nobhead clientele in here," Cecil replied. He stood up and extended his hands out in a wide, sweeping gesture. "Take a look around. See them birds down there? That's what I mean by a class bar. They're dressed up proper. For a start, they got proper shoes on. None of that trainer stuff like the birds back home. What's that about anyway? Birds going out at night in shoes they'd wear to a fucking festival. I wanna go into places where the birds make an effort, you know ... get dressed up, put some quality shoes on. Go in a place like that and it makes you feel good, yeah? There can be no excuse mate. It's gotta be a blinding pair of shoes or else stay home."

"Err ... okay ... uh, I'll get you a beer then," I said. "Bottle of Isleña?"

Cecil nodded.

"I mean check that bird out down there," he said, pointing over the steel balustrade at the lower bar. "Blinding shoes and a nice pair of bangers too."

I turned to follow Cecil's finger and immediately saw a face I recognised.

"Bloody hell, Ces. You know who that is?" I didn't wait for an answer. "Paloma."

"Paloma? Who the fuck's Paloma?"

"From the ambulance. Today. She looks different out of uniform, that's for sure."

"I wouldn't mind seeing her out of uniform," Jasper chipped in. "Got some shape on her."

"You're having a giraffe geeze. That ain't her is it?" Cecil said.

"Well if you took your eyes off her bangers Ces, and looked at her face, you might recognise her," I said. "Anyway, I'm going down there to get your drink and I might have a quick word. I owe her an apology at the very least."

"I'm coming with you Matt," Jasper said.

"Less of the Matt, Jas. It's Jason ... JJ. Don't care which but no M word. Got it?"

"I'm coming too," Cecil said, before Jasper could respond.

"No, Ces. I need you to keep an eye out for the Danish girls. I won't be long."

I made my way down the two short flights of stairs to the bar area, followed by Jasper. Paloma was sitting on a stool checking her mobile.

"Paloma?"

240

She turned her head, a look of recognition flitting across her features.

"Yes?"

"It's me ... Jason."

"Jason? Ah, yes, now I know you. You are the man who ran away."

Up close, her hair now in a loose, free flowing style, she looked slightly older than the fresh faced paramedic that had tended to me earlier. Her makeup, carefully applied to accentuate her dark eyes, gave her a more mature sophisticated look.

"Uh, yes, I am ... and I wanted to apologise. When I saw you here I had to speak to you."

"So why you run away?"

"Err ... well ... I ... I just felt better so I didn't want to waste your time."

She smiled, an eye catching full smile that was both disarming and genuine.

"You don't waste time but you get better too quick. You should still be checked out, you know this?" she said, leaning forward so that the low cut of her sleeveless black dress revealed more of her curves than she had intended.

"Err, yes, I ... of course. I will, when I get home to England. My insurance isn't that good and –"

"You say you have no insurance today."

"Uh ... I did ... I meant ... I have some insurance but not the right type. Anyway, I'm happy to pay for the oxygen."

"You don't have to pay for oxygen," she laughed.

"I meant for the, you know ... for any damage to the oxygen thing ... mask and stuff."

Paloma smiled, rummaged in her handbag and pulled out a packet of cigarettes.

"It's nothing. They repair it easily," she said.

I was about to remark that it seemed odd for someone in the medical profession to smoke when I caught sight of the brand name. Fortuna. The same brand that I had found in the cave. The same brand that James smoked. Perhaps Cecil had a point about it being a popular brand and maybe there was no value in the cigarette stub I had found.

"You smoke?" she asked.

"No, not me."

"And your friend?"

Jasper eased forward.

"No thanks. I'm Jasper by the way." He held out his hand in greeting accompanying the gesture with the Jasper Kane full-on smile. "Nice to meet you Paloma."

Paloma declined Jasper's hand, instead acknowledging his greeting with a smile and a nod of her head.

"So, are you on your own this evening?" Jasper asked.

"No, I wait for my husband. He will be here soon. He have some business to do first. Then we will go for dinner." She extracted a cigarette and placed the pack down on the bar.

Jasper looked crestfallen. A husband complicated matters.

"Well I didn't expect to see you here tonight, Paloma, I must say," I said. "Do you live here?"

"We live a little way out from San Antonio but I work in Eivissa. My husband is a doctor in the same hospital." She lit the cigarette, took a long draw and then blew the smoke high into the air. "Where are you staying?"

I hesitated, my natural caution heightened by the purpose of my trip but Jasper had no such thoughts.

"We're at the Blau Parc. JJ's up at the Valencia. You know them?"

"I've heard of the Blau Parc. Near to the Golden Buddha, I think."

"Yeah, that's the one," Jasper said. "And the Valencia is –"

"Err ... well nice to see you anyway, Paloma. Thank you for your help earlier and sorry again about the, err ... you know ... running away," I said, before Jasper had time to give away too much more information.

Paloma nodded but her focus was over my shoulder. A male voice came from that direction.

"Hola carino."

She stood up. Jasper and I turned to see who had caught her attention. To my utter horror, I came face to face with Felipe. For a split second, he was just as surprised as I was. But he recovered more quickly.

"Matthew. I did not expect to see you so soon, my friend," he said.

A trance like state seemed to grip me, disabling my ability to think coherently. Paloma inadvertently came to my rescue.

"Matthew? No, you make mistake. This is Jason."

"Ah, a mistake," Felipe said, staring directly at me. "You look like a young man I met sometime," he said, a smile playing across his lips but his eyes cold and menacing. He flicked his fingers at a barman who acknowledged him with a brief nod.

"Jason was a patient of mine today," Paloma said. "This is my husband, Doctor Felipe Barrientos."

A flash of annoyance spread over Felipe's features. He shot a disapproving glance at Paloma but quickly regained his composure. Finally, something he didn't want me to know. It gave me an unexpected boost.

"A doctor eh? A very noble profession. Much respected in the community," I said. "You must be held in high esteem on such a small island?"

Felipe ignored the remark but the downward curl of his lower lip told me it had prickled him. He turned to Jasper.

"And you are?"

"The name's Jasper. I'm on holiday with ... with Jason and the boys."

"A holiday. I see," Felipe said, fixing his gaze in my direction again.

"Partly," I said. "In fact, I lost a ring out here that I bought for my fiancée ... a diamond actually, and I came back to find it." The minute I said it I regretted opening my mouth. I could only think that it was due to a burst of over confidence because I had discovered a personal snippet of information about Felipe that I thought I could use against him.

Felipe's eyes flashed defiance.

"I am not sure you will be successful. Out here things can disappear very easily, if it is of expense ... uh ... value." He paused for a moment. "Even people have been known to disappear. You understand?"

"Understand?" I said.

"Yes, sometimes it is best to stop looking when it is ... sin esperanza ... how you say ... without hope?"

"Hopeless," Jasper said helpfully.

The barman placed a tall glass on the bar, a straw emerging between several ice cubes that floated in a dark liquid.

"Si, yes that is it. Hopeless," Felipe said. "Sometimes it is best to leave these things and go home. Start again. You understand?" He reached for his wife's cigarettes.

I didn't answer. I knew it was time to go.

"Nice to meet you Señora Barrientos," I said. "We must leave you to your evening." I turned to Felipe. "You too ... Doctor."

"Maybe we see you before you go home," Paloma said. "How long you stay at the Valencia?"

An ice-cold shiver stopped me in my tracks. I shot a glance at Felipe. He placed the cigarette between his lips, reached into his pocket and pulled out a mobile.

"Buenos noches mi amigo. ¡Hasta luego!" he said, with a nod in my direction.

I knew instantly what he was about to do. Text Scalapino with my hotel location. I didn't think about the consequences. I simply acted out of self-preservation. I reached out and snatched the mobile from his hand. The shock on his face prevented any instant reaction. By the time he had recovered, I was already at the stairs. I legged it up two at a time. As I got to the table where Cecil and Carlos were seated, I glanced over my shoulder. Felipe was on his way up after me. Jasper was gesticulating in several directions and trying to calm both Paloma and the bar staff.

"What was all that chat about geezer?" Cecil said.

"We've got a problem lads," I said and dropped Felipe's mobile into the jug of sangria.

"What the fuck you doing?" Cecil shouted, clearly taken aback.

I didn't have time to explain. Felipe caught me by the shoulder and spun me round.

"My telephone. I want it back now," he said, his eyes ablaze with anger.

Cecil jumped to his feet and in one bound placed himself directly in front of Felipe.

"Who you manhandling fuckwit? Put another hand on my mate here and you'll be sipping more than your drink through a straw."

Felipe backed off.

"Your friend huh? Your friend, he steal my telephone. I come and get it."

"My friend don't nick people's stuff geezer. He must have a reason. So if you want it back, you go get it. It's right there." Cecil pointed at the jug of sangria.

Felipe glanced over Cecil's shoulder and spotted the shadowy outline of his mobile barely visible amongst the fruit that floated in the dark red liquid. His face took on a similar colour.

"Hijos de puta," he said, taking a step towards the table. "¡Os voy a matar a todos!"

Cecil blocked the move. "What's he on about Carlos?"

"He says we are sons of a whore," Carlos replied. "And he's going to kill us all."

Cecil leant forward, his face inches from Felipe's.

"That right geezer? You playing the big man? What's your problem anyway?"

Before Felipe could answer, I intervened.

"This is Doctor Felipe Barrientos," I said, "He's the bloke who –"

"Hang on. Felipe? What ... *that* Felipe?" Cecil said, his stare still firmly fixed on Felipe's face.

"Yup, same bloke. The bloke who's stitching me up with the diamonds. The bloke who nicked my engagement ring. The bloke who's threatening Louise and me and the same bloke that's got his bald headed psycho mate chasing me round the frigging island. Yeah, that Felipe." I picked up the sangria jug and stepped forward so that I was right alongside Felipe.

245

"You want your phone? Okay."

I grabbed Felipe's left forearm and plunged his hand straight into the sangria so that it was completely immersed, the liquid rising up above his wrist, soaking his watch. Although taken by surprise by the movement, he recovered sufficiently to grasp the mobile. I pulled his arm back up sharply so that his hand was clear of the jug.

"Get the phone, Ces," I shouted.

Cecil reacted immediately, snatching the mobile from Felipe's grip. I let go of his hand and stepped back.

"You want the phone back, you give me my ring back," I said. "Until I get that ring, I'm keeping your phone. Come to think of it, it's probably got a lot of contacts on it that the police would be interested in ... doctor."

Felipe spat on the floor.

"Eres un maricón."

"What's that, Carlos?" I asked, never taking my eyes of Felipe.

"He uh ... he says you're a faggot," Carlos answered.

I laughed, enjoying my brief moment of power and control.

"Think what you like doctor but now I have something on you. Your whole career, your marriage, it all goes down the pan ... finishes, ends, if you're connected to criminal activity. You understand *me* now?"

Felipe's top lip curled into a sneer.

"You understand me?" I repeated.

Felipe nodded.

"Good. So to begin with, you call off your goons, Scalapino and his friends. They keep away from me. Then you return my ring by tomorrow night. Here." I beckoned to Carlos. "Hey, Carlos. Can you explain what I just said in Spanish so there's no misunderstanding."

Carlos stepped towards Felipe and began to gabble away in Spanish, punctuating his sentences with elaborate hand movements. Felipe said nothing. His eyes narrowed, dark and brooding, throwing piercing glances in my direction as Carlos spoke. When Carlos had finished, I waved the mobile at Felipe.

"Insurance doctor. Remember that? Yeah, I thought so."

He was about to respond when Jasper appeared behind him.

"What's going on Ma ... err ... Jason? That woman, Paloma was going ballistic. I've managed to calm her down but she was gonna call the cops. So were the staff. I've told them you know each other and it was a bit of a stag do joke but what –"

"Later Jas. Let's clear things up here first," I said.

Cecil poked his finger into Felipe's chest.

"Right, we're done here geezer. You go back down there and tell everybody it's cool, yeah? You don't want us having to talk to the police do ya?"

Felipe nodded, a smirk playing on his lips. He turned towards me.

"Okay, hombre. You want to play a game. Now you have your game." He signalled to Carlos and began a long tirade in Spanish. When he had finished he spat on the floor again and muttered a single word. "Gilipollas." Then he turned on his heel and disappeared down the stairs.

"What's he on about?" I asked Carlos.

"He said you're a wanker," Carlos replied.

"No, all that other stuff."

Carlos picked up his glass of sangria and took a mouthful.

"Mateo, amigo. I dinnae think you should've threatened him. He's angry. He said that you don't know who you're messing with and that you should've done what you were told and not come back here. Their operation will continue and that a little wanker like you won't be allowed to get in the way."

A cold shiver shot along my spine. My moment of power and control evaporated instantly.

"But did he say anything about the phone?"

"No, nothing."

I sat down, puzzled as to what any of the confrontation had achieved. The fact that I had uncovered Felipe's private life, that I knew what he did, had raised the stakes. He was either going to cooperate or react badly. From what Carlos had said, it sounded like the latter. I had the mobile. It was soaked but could be dried out and then it could be evidence. But evidence of what? That he knew Scalapino? But that said nothing at all unless I could link Scalapino to something and even then it didn't mean that Felipe was involved. I had to have something more.

I stood up and checked the bar area. Felipe had gone, Paloma too. And then I remembered something.

"Paloma's got a phone," I said. "He'll be on to Scalapino right now."

Cecil picked up the jug of sangria, and poured a glass.

"No he won't geezer," he said. "His missus ain't gonna have no villain's number in her phone. Nah, he keeps all that stuff he's involved in away from her. I bet she don't even know the bald twat. Never set eyes on him. I mean he weren't exactly big on social graces was he? Not the sort of geezer a Doctor has round to dinner. No mate, trust me. And he ain't gonna have memorised the number either. Who does? People just call up a name and press a button. No need to think about the number." He picked up the glass of sangria and took a long swig. "Ain't bad this stuff, is it?"

Carlos rolled his eyes.

I ignored them both. Cecil had a point but I was nervous. I couldn't gamble on Felipe feeling worried enough to call off his goons. And maybe he couldn't, even if he wanted to. If he was accountable to somebody above him, they wouldn't be worried about his career. Their operation was too important, too big. And they had resources to deal with inconveniences like me. I made a decision.

"Right, guys. Listen. I'm not taking any chances. I'm getting out of San Antonio and going to Ibiza Town. We're on day five and we have bugger all info that adds up to something we can use against Felipe and his mob. We need to rack it up. No partying, nothing. Just focussed." I glanced at Cecil. "Me and Ces can go and clear my stuff from the Valencia and check out. Jas, I need you to find the two Danish girls. You got that sheet of paper Ces?"

Cecil pulled the half-shredded sheet from his pocket. I studied it for a moment, noting the names and dates.

"You know what seems odd, lads? There are eight names on there, seven of which are mentioned twice. But the top one, Caroline, is only mentioned once. And when you look at the dates, most of them are in consecutive months from March to August but Caroline is in January, nearly three months before the next one, Sue, on third of March. Any ideas?"

"Maybe Caroline's not on the scene anymore," Cecil said. "She could've been here last season and spent the winter out here before going back in January or February to wherever she come from."

"I suppose so," I said. "But who are they all?"

I handed the paper to Jasper and explained to him that I needed him to check out all the names with Estrid an Alida. He seemed to warm to the assignment. It involved girls. I asked Carlos to follow Jasper but at a distance and keep an eye out for anything suspicious. I knew that Jasper might well get too involved in his task, especially if he was to find any of the girls on the list, and that his guard might drop. When I had finished I poured myself a sangria, sunk it in one and turned to Carlos.

"And Carlos, tomorrow I need you to do something for me. I need you to find out where the lighthouses are on the island and what they are called."

"Nae problem amigo but what for?" Carlos replied.

"Like we said in the car, I need to know if that Spanish stuff means anything ... what was it?"

"Hay sólo un camino, así que siga la luz que brilla," Carlos said.

"Yeah, the path to the shining light or whatever you translated it to."

Carlos smiled.

"There is only one way so follow the light that shines."

"Yeah, that's it. Check if any of the lighthouses has a name that might tie in with any of that. One of them could be some sort of rendezvous point. And maybe you could do some digging around to see if there's a boat with a name that connects. It could be either."

"Aye, okay. I'll be on it tomorrow."

"Okay, great. And Ces, you need to hang onto that phone. If we can get it dried out there may be something there we can use."

"Yeah mate. I'll stick it in a bowl of rice. They reckon that sorts it."

Carlos laughed.

"What? Are ye'af yer napper? Put it intae a bowl of rice and you'll boil the thing."

"What you on about?" Cecil said. "Not a rice pudding, you nob. A bowl of uncooked rice. Soaks up the water don't it."

I raised a hand to halt the conversation before it developed into a bickering match.

"Lads, we have to go. I'm going to need the car Jas. Where is it?"

Jasper handed me the keys.

"Down the street by the Golden Buddha."

"Cheers Jas."

"You cannae be insured to drive Jasper's car," Carlos said, a worried frown creasing his brow.

"That's the least of my worries right now Carlos. I can't hire one of my own and I need it if I'm going to be over in Ibiza Town. Anyway, let's go. I need to get checked out of my hotel sooner rather than later."

I headed for the stairs and then called out to Jasper and Carlos.

"Keep your mobiles on boys and we'll catch up tomorrow."

30

I woke early and sat up in my bed. I reached over to the small, wooden bedside cabinet, picked up my mobile and checked the screen. No calls, no messages. It was 8.20a.m., too early for the boys to be awake. But I wanted information. Time was moving on and I had an ominous feeling that the risk had increased. I had spent a restless night in a guest house on Passieg de Vara de Rey in the Old Town, my restlessness all brought on by anxiety and nothing to do with my accommodation which was extremely comfortable, quiet and ideal for someone hoping to keep a low profile.

I jumped out of bed and crossed the room to the small balcony area that split one wall from floor to ceiling and opened the wooden shutters. Bright sunlight streamed across the whole area, casting a shadow across the central promenade but picking out the bustle of activity and traffic that meandered along the narrow street immediately below. I stood for a moment embracing its warmth, the early morning heat boosting my sombre mood. The names on the sheet of paper popped into my head. There had to be something more to it than a simple list of girls that were up for a bit of fun with James. If he was having secret liaisons there were easier ways of keeping a little black book. I reached for my mobile again and tapped out a text to Jasper.

'*How did it go Jas? Any news?*'

I stared at the screen for a moment hoping for an instant response. Nothing. I headed for the shower. Ten minutes later, just as I was turning off the water, I heard my mobile ring. I raced from the shower and grabbed the phone from the bed. The display showed 'Jas.'

"Hi Jas. How you doing? I hope I haven't woken you up."

"It's alright Matt ... sorry, JJ. I was awake."

"Matt's okay on the phone. Any news? Did you find out anything?"

"Yeah, but not much. I saw the two Danish birds in a club last night."

"And?"

"I showed them the list but it didn't mean anything to them. They said they knew a couple of girls that could be the same as on the list."

"Okay. Who?"

"Uh ... Pollyanna and ... Kay. Yeah, that was it."

"You sure? You don't sound sure."

"Yeah, I am. Definitely. Just, it was a late night in the end."

I felt a moment's optimism but I wasn't sure why. Jasper had found something but what did it mean? Pollyanna had to be Polly.

"Did they say anything about these two girls? How they know them, where they are."

"Just that they were pretty new on the scene. Pollyanna's from Jersey ... St Helier or somewhere. She just got here last week. The other one, Kay, has been here three weeks. Geordie bird, down from Newcastle. They're both doing the bar promo thing although Kay's trying to get a bit of club dancing work as well."

"So where are they?"

"Just local in San An. Estrid said they'd been helping them out, showing them the ropes."

"And they definitely don't know the other names?"

"That's right mate. 'Fraid not."

"Okay, good work Jas. Thanks."

"No worries Matt. But is it any good to you?"

"Not sure yet to be honest. I need to have a think. Anyway, I have to go. I'll call you guys later."

I killed the call and sat on the bed. Pollyanna and Kay. New girls. Pollyanna was of interest. Not a common name so she could be the same Polly that was on the list. But she had only been in Ibiza a week. Not enough time surely to have become involved with James. As for Kay, there had to be a lot of girls on the island with that name, and the Kay that Jasper had mentioned had only been here three weeks. And then something occurred to me. I punched in Jasper's number again. He answered immediately.

"Jas, sorry mate. I just remembered something. Have you got that bit of paper handy?"

"Yeah, it's here. What's up?"

"I need you to check the dates on it. What's it say for Polly and Kay?"

"Uh, hang on. I'll just get it."

The phone went quiet save for a rustling in the background.

"Okay, got it mate. Let's see, yeah. Polly ... there's two dates. The twenty-eighth of March and tenth of June. Kay's dates are May seventeenth and thirtieth of June."

I thought about what Jasper had told me for a moment. The dates didn't work. If the Danish girls were right, Pollyanna had only been in Ibiza since around 6th June, two days before I came back out, so she couldn't be connected with the first date on the paper next to her name as it was in March. Kay had arrived two weeks earlier, which was 23rd May. So Kay couldn't be connected to the 17th May date as, again, it was too early. But Polly had been around for the second date, 10th June, which had just gone by a few days earlier. And Kay's second date, the 30th June, hadn't happened yet. I scratched my head, wondering if there was any connection at all or if I was going down a blind alley.

"You there Matt?" Jasper's voice snapped me out of my thought pattern.

"Yeah, sorry. I was just, uh…" I stood up and walked towards the balcony. "What about Al, what dates have you got for her?"

"Let's have a look. Yeah, got March the eighteenth and ... and August the fourth."

Alida had arrived in March with Estrid so those dates worked and she had been in Ibiza before. I tried to recall the other names on the list but couldn't.

"What about the others ... I can't remember the names?"

"Let's see ... you got five others, Caroline, Sue, Ann, Jo and Val."

"Okay, so of the ... what is it, eight names, we know three people that they could be - Polly, Kay and Alida ... maybe. But no clue who the others might be."

"Don't look like it, mate."

A blind alley still. I took a deep breath, trying to suppress the frustration I felt. Alida could be one of the names but why nothing that suggested Estrid too? And Alida knew a Polly and a Kay but what was the link, if any? It all meant nothing and neither did the dates. Another question began to materialise in my mind.

"One more thing. What's the next date after today on the list?"

There was a pause before Jasper replied. *"Seventeenth of June. Why?"*

I ignored the question. The seventeenth was just three days away.

"And what name's next to that date?"

"Ann."

Ann. I wasn't sure why I had asked. Jasper's reply hadn't told me anything new.

"Listen, thanks Jas. Thanks for doing all that. I'll talk to you later ... oh, and hang on to that bit of paper."

"Will do mate. By the way, I'm gonna go with Carlos today on his lighthouse and boat check. After what happened last night with that Felipe bloke, it might be better if he's got back up, you know."

"Good. Yeah, you're right. Cheers Jas. I appreciate what you're doing."

"No problem at all mate. We need to get you out of this fix. Anyway, I'm gonna wake up Cecil and get some breakfast. Laters."

With the call over the frustration made it to the surface. I was still no nearer a breakthrough. I flung the mobile onto the bed and watched it bounce once and land, face down, on a pillow. On the street below, there was an increased buzz of activity as tourists emerged from hotels and began to take in the sights. I leant on the ornate metal rail that ran the length of the narrow opening and watched them for a moment, wishing I could be just another visitor, wandering along the promenade, carefree and enjoying the warmth of a glorious Ibiza day. But that was not the case. I had a problem and it had to be solved. And time was running out. Even though I had little to go on in achieving that aim, I had to make use of the day.

I crossed to the bed and picked up my mobile intent on calling Cecil. As I turned the phone over, I noticed that it had randomly opened one of the apps. Maybe the impact of the bounce had caused it. I had no idea.

But what I saw in front of me changed my whole perspective.

31

In the hotel reception I asked if there was an internet café nearby. I was directed to the Chill Café on via Punica, a short walk from the hotel. It was no more than six or seven minutes walk and I found it tucked away at the corner of a junction. I took a seat at a table close to the bar area, facing the doorway, caution now a factor in my thinking. I scanned the area feeling the need to be aware of my environment. Around me, the distressed white wood tables and chairs were filled with customers too engrossed in their laptops to notice who else was sharing their space. A colourful, ornate chandelier–style light fitting hung in the centre of the white-washed ceiling, its purple, pink and green glass beads contrasting vividly against the pale surface.

Once I felt relaxed in my surroundings I ordered a toasted Parma ham and cheese sandwich, a bottle of water and a cup of coffee. Next, I placed my mobile on the tabletop and scrolled though the pictures until I found the ones I had taken in the cave of the metal boxes and the document that contained the numbers and the Spanish phrase. I then logged onto the cafe Wi-Fi and for the next two hours I trawled the internet looking for information. I jotted down what I found until I had formed a list. And then I called Cecil.

"Ces, it's me."

"*How you doing mate. Hotel alright?*"

"Yeah, it's fine. Listen, I think I found something. We need to meet up as soon as you can get here."

"*What you got mate?*"

"I don't want to talk on the phone but I think I have something this time. I need to show you. Oh, and I need you to bring the sheet of paper with the names on it. Jas has it."

"*Alright mate. Can you pick me up?*"

"I'm a bit wary of coming in to San Antonio in daylight after last night."

"*Well, I ain't getting that bus all over the island again. Fucking nightmare getting back yesterday.*

"You don't need to. I'll meet you halfway," I said, and explained my plan.

The car was parked along the kerb outside the hotel. I pulled out and headed for the harbour, took a left turn back towards the town centre and found the long one way street that led out of Ibiza Town. A few moments later, I swung onto the C-731, my destination San Rafael. I had arranged to meet Cecil there as it was roughly halfway between San Antonio and Ibiza Town. Once I had convinced him that I couldn't pick him up and he would have to make his own way, we had agreed to meet at just after midday. The promise of beers on me seemed to swing the deal. I told him I'd find a bar in the town and text him.

It took just over fifteen minutes to reach San Rafael. I pulled the car off the bypass and headed into the town centre. Along the main road I spotted two restaurants almost opposite one another. I cruised past, checking them out but they were both closed. I swung the car round again and headed back. On my right there was another bar, the Centre bar and restaurant. It was open but all of the parking spaces outside were taken. I drove past, turned the car around again and pulled into a parking space almost opposite. I crossed the road, ordered coffee and a beer at the bar and took a seat outside. Then I sent Cecil a text.

'*In San Rafael. Place called the Centre bar restaurant. Sitting out front. You can't miss it. It's got a white awning with the name on it. Once you get off the bus you'll need to walk down from the by-pass. See you soon.*'

257

I got a brief reply.

'In a cab. Be there in five.'

I sipped the coffee and waited for Cecil. When he arrived, he had the expected moan about the journey, grabbed the beer and sat down.

"So what've you dragged me out to the middle of nowhere for? Better be good mate."

"It is good Ces." I pulled two sheets of paper from my pocket, unfolded them and placed them on the table, one on top of the other. "You brought the paper with the girls' names?"

Cecil nodded.

"Get it out then."

He placed the sheet on the table. I lined it up with the papers I had brought and then laid my mobile phone next to them. I tapped the camera icon and selected *'photos.'*

"Sit round this side Ces. You got to see this."

Cecil stood up and took the seat next to mine. He pulled off his sunglasses and stared at the papers.

"Okay, the picture on my phone is the sheet of numbers we found in the cave in the canvas bag. Anyway, when I escaped from the cave the other day, I loaded up the compass app on my phone to check which way I had to go to get back to the hotel."

"Yeah, and?" Cecil said.

"Well, this morning I flung my mobile on the bed and somehow it started up the compass app again. And that's when I spotted a row of coordinates at the bottom. I was too stressed out to notice any numbers after I got out of the cave and then the battery died. Anyway the numbers on the compass were the location coordinates of my hotel in Ibiza Town." I pointed to the top sheet of paper. "Here ... I wrote them down."

38° 54' 33" N 1° 26' 2" E

Cecil stared at the numbers but they didn't seem to mean anything to him. I picked up the mobile and tapped the compass app.

"There you go. Like on here. This is where we are right now."
I pointed to the coordinates on the screen that read 38° 57' 41" N
1° 23' 56" E. "Okay?"

Cecil nodded.

I put the phone down and pointed to the sheet of paper, this
time further down the page.

"So then I wrote the hotel location numbers out again, but
now in the same way the numbers were typed out on the paper
we found in the cave, with no gaps, symbols or letters. See?" I
traced my finger along the written number sequence on the sheet
– 3854331262.

"If you take the numbers in two separate blocks, you get thirty-
eight, fifty-four and thirty-three in the first block. With me?"

Again Cecil nodded.

"Then you have the next three numbers, which in this case are
one, twenty-six and two."

Cecil stared at the sheet and then looked at me, a frown crossing
his brow. I reached for the phone again, closed the compass and
tapped on the camera app.

"Now look at the picture again." I placed my index finger
and thumb on the centre of the screen and zoomed the photo so
that it enlarged one of the number blocks in the picture. "See? If
you divide them up the same way, the first three sets of numbers
are latitude references and the second three are longitude ones.
Normally they'd be punctuated after each number with degrees,
minutes and seconds symbols like on the compass app I just
showed you, but they must have been written out like that to
confuse anyone who saw them."

I sipped my coffee and waited for some comment from Cecil.
He rubbed his chin, his fingers kneading the skin firmly and
studied the numbers. Then he replied.

"Yeah, but mate, if you're right, what you've got is just a block
of six numbers. The numbers in that picture are in blocks of
sixteen or more. Even if you take the numbers in each block and
divide 'em up into sets of six, you still got numbers left over at
the end."

I put my coffee cup back on the table.

"I thought of that Ces. It threw me too at first. I was in an internet cafe earlier and looked up the longitude latitude thing. I tried out the first lot of numbers ... that first line at the top, beginning with thirty-nine, fifty-four, nineteen. I got lucky and came up with a place in Majorca. Then, because they were in blocks with the forward slash symbol separating them, I tried the next sequence of six and came up with another location. It wasn't easy because I didn't know how to pair the numbers up or whether they should just be single numbers. Then I went through each block taking the first six groupings of numbers and each one was a location. Then I thought –"

"Hang on, so what you saying?"

"What I'm saying, is I think I was right yesterday when I said that the girls' names might be places."

"So where are these places then?"

"Check this out," I said, a rush of triumph coursing through my chest. I removed the top sheet of the two bits of paper, revealing the second one underneath.

Cecil stared in silence at the list that appeared in front of him.

San Antonio (Ibiza) - Ann
lat 38° 59'30.5556"N; long 1° 17'20.4972"E

Port de Pollenca (Majorca) - Polly
lat 39° 54'19.0008"N; long 3° 6'26.3808"E

Johannesburg (S. Africa) - Jo
lat -26° 13'0. 1560" S; long 27° 57'51.5700" E

Sousse (Tunisia) - Sue
lat 35° 52'42.1788"N; long 10° 36'9.2844"E

Alghero (Sardinia) - Al
lat 40° 32'26.7468" N; long 8° 19'23.8872" E

Valencia (Spain) - Val
lat 39° 23'32.3592" N; long -0° 19'40.3428" W

Cape Town (S. Africa) - Kay
lat -33° 53'31.5924" S; long 18° 28'58.4724" E

"Fucking hell, mate. You might have something," he said, his eyes still glued to the sheet of paper. "You telling me that these latitude and longitude numbers are these places?"

"That's right. I am. And see how the names tie up with the girl names? Look, Ann for San Antonio and Al isn't Alida at all. It's Alghero in Sardinia. And forget the digits after the full stop. They're just fine tuning."

"Yeah, you're bang on geezer." He picked up the half-shredded sheet that we had found in James's place, studied it for a moment and glanced back at the coordinates I had written out.

"Yeah, but you never said what all the spare numbers were at the end of each block."

I leant forward. "Take a look at the names you have. What other numbers do you have on there?"

Cecil examined the half-shredded sheet again.

"Just dates mate."

"Exactly. That's it. Take Sue on there, right. She's got two dates – third of March and twentieth of July ... third of the third and twentieth of the seventh. Then check out the coordinates I got for Sue." I pointed at the sheet of paper I had brought again. "There, Sousse, beginning thirty-five, fifty-two, forty-two. Now go back to the photo and find that block of numbers and right at the end you'll see three, three, twenty and seven. Third of March and twentieth of July."

Cecil studied the papers and the photograph again. Then he looked up, his gaze fixed on me for a moment before he spoke.

"Mate, that's blinding. You're spot on."

I couldn't help the self-satisfied grin. It was a breakthrough at long last and Cecil had just confirmed it. I finished my coffee and pushed the cup across the table.

"So all they've done is merge the coordinates with the dates to make it more cryptic. I spent almost two hours trying to work out the coordinates but I couldn't understand what the extra numbers meant. But then when the place names started to pan out I began to make the connection to the girls' names. Then it was simple enough to assume that the extra numbers could be the dates. When I tried it, it all fitted. I even tried it on my location. I added today's date to the coordinates for where I was. Look." I indicated a set of numbers halfway down the page that read 3854331262146. "Same numbers as before, only with fourteenth of June added at the end."

Cecil held up my mobile.

"And what about the letter, that 'M' in the numbers on here?"

"Yeah, that confused me too. When I stuck those numbers in it gave me weird readings, like in the middle of the ocean and one in the desert in Egypt. Even though they could have been real locations, they didn't fit with the names. So I did a bit of research and found that if a place is located south of the equator it has a minus latitude number. There's a similar thing going on with longitude too. Anyway, once I knew that, I kind of guessed that the 'M' might mean minus. I asked the guy in the Chill Café what the Spanish was for minus, just to double check, and he said it was 'menos' which can also mean less. Once I stuck a minus sign in front of the numbers that had the 'M' in them, it all started to fit."

"Good work geezer. Bit of a geek in you then. Hadn't noticed that before," Cecil said. He raised the beer bottle and took a long swig. "One thing though, what's the four extra numbers at the end of that one?"

"Which one?"

He pointed at the mobile screen picking out the last block of numbers that read - 38593011720104176/1910.

"There mate. See? Nineteen and ten."

"Ah, that one. That's the location for San Antonio. So you got ten four and seventeen six at the end, which tie in with the dates next to 'Ann' on the list ... tenth of April and seventeenth of

June. The ones after the forward slash, nineteen and ten, must be another date. It's the only one like that so I'm assuming it means there's something happening on the nineteenth of October. If the list hadn't been partly shredded then, my guess is we'd have seen Ann again with more dates next to it."

"Makes sense geezer. But hang on a sec, there's eight names on the list and you've only got seven places that match." He pointed at the name at the top of the sheet. "So where's that then?"

I stared at the name *Caroline* for a moment.

"No idea. There were only seven sets of numbers and when I looked them all up, they gave me the places I've listed."

Cecil necked the remainder of his beer and wiped his mouth.

"Well it could be a place too. How about Carolina?" he said.

"Unlikely mate. It doesn't link with the pattern. Five of these places are all around the Med and two in South Africa. Carolina is in the States. In fact, I looked the name up to see if there were any other places with that name or similar and there's one, in Australia, and that's way out of the loop. But the thing is, Caroline has a date against it so it must be a place like the rest."

"Yeah, maybe. But how are these places linked?"

"Well think about it. The way I see it is that Russian bloke, Kovalevski, is involved in diamond smuggling, importing conflict diamonds from Africa. So the South African link must be key. Then he has to offload them somewhere to ship them back to the UK. So I reckon he uses a number of places as connection points. The dates have to be the days he's importing or shipping or something. And then if you check the map, which I did in the internet cafe, they're all ports with the exception of Johannesburg. Different ports would make sense. Changes the trail all the time. Felipe has to be the go between, coordinating things here in San Antonio. He has the perfect cover too as a doctor, so he'd be the last person you'd expect to be involved in an illegal diamond operation. And that's what all those metal boxes with the padlocks are for. Containers for the diamonds."

Cecil stood up. "Let me get us a beer mate. I reckon you need one after all that detective work."

263

"Coffee, Ces. I'm driving."

He turned and waved a hand dismissively.

"Fuck that shit mate. You should be celebrating. One beer ain't gonna hurt is it?"

"Maybe not," I said, "unless you add in getting stopped for drinking and driving in a car that you don't own with no insurance and a false identity. That could hurt a bit."

"You worry too much mate. One beer and that's it."

He returned to the table within a couple of minutes, two bottles in his hand and reached one to me.

"Cheers geezer," he said. He took a long swig, staring intently at me as he did so. "You know what, I was just thinking. When you mentioned Felipe as the go between and the fact he has the perfect cover as a doc, I had a thought."

"What about?"

"What if Caroline *is* actually a person's name after all, not a place?"

"Okay ... and?"

"Well you know who it is then, don't you?"

"No? Who?"

"Paloma, mate. The doc's missus. Gotta be."

"Paloma? But Ces, you said she was unlikely to know anything about what Felipe's involved in."

He pulled out a seat, span it around so that it was back to front, and sat cross-legged with his arms resting on the back.

"Yeah. So I was wrong. It works two ways. Either he tells her fuck all, or, she's in it with him. And now I think she's in it. The only way he can pull off a double life as a doctor is with somebody's help. Somebody on the inside. She works with him so if she's gotta cover for him in any way, she can. And I'll tell you what. I bet between them they don't earn that much, so the extra bunce coming in from this Kurt geezer don't go amiss either. And once a bird gets used to the lifestyle that sort of money gets you, she ain't giving it up easy, no matter how it comes."

I thought about what Cecil had said. Paloma. I hadn't given her a thought, but it made sense. She smoked the right cigarettes, the

Fortuna brand and she'd quizzed us about where we were staying. If Felipe could lead a double life so could she, and the medical profession was an ideal, respectable guise to hide behind. People would never suspect them. Now we had to prove it.

"Wait a minute. So why, if Caroline is actually Paloma, is there a date next to the name?"

Cecil bit his bottom lip and shrugged.

"Could be anything. Could be a date she had to do something on. Might even be her birthday, I dunno. Could even be a bluff date or –"

"Or, it could be the date the diamonds start being produced, which is why there's such a gap between that and the other dates. And maybe Paloma has some special role or task connected with that."

"And talking of dates look at the list again mate. That date, June seventeenth. Something happening then and it's happening in San Antonio."

I picked up the list and looked at the date next to 'Ann.'

"You're right. What's today?" I checked my watch. "It's the fourteenth so that's … next Tuesday. Maybe a shipment into the caves to be distributed from there?"

"Could be. If you can catch that, get some pictures, it'll be good hard evidence. We gotta go back in two days, on Monday morning, otherwise I'd help you out. We only booked ten days. Thought that'd be enough."

"I just can't be here Ces. Louise has got her disciplinary on the twentieth. That's next Friday. I have to have something before that. Some connections, some evidence of the diamond smuggling. I was hoping to go back on the same flight as you boys."

"Yeah, but that *is* your evidence geezer. Ain't no better evidence than to catch 'em in the act?"

I thought about what Cecil had said but the thought of getting that close to a criminal operation on my own filled me with dread.

"I could call the cops. Get them to set a trap."

"You could mate, but you can't be certain at this point it's gonna happen just like you think. It's still speculation. You got a date, you got a location but that's all you know. Chances are it *is* connected with them caves but if it ain't, then you got the cops sitting around wasting their time. That totally screws your credibility. They ain't gonna come out in force on guesswork."

"So what do I do?"

"Listen, if something's going down on Tuesday it's gonna be the early hours, under cover of dark, yeah. So you take a gamble. You get yourself out there to them caves, lay low, outta sight and keep watch. You see anything, you get photos. Then you call the cops. If it works out, they catch 'em in the act. Then you get outta Dodge. And once you tie up all the other info you got with that, it's done and dusted geeze. Game over. Them scum bags get banged up and you're in the clear."

Cecil made it sound very simple. I knew it wouldn't be and I didn't like the uncertainty of '*if it works out.*'

"Hang on. If something's happening in the early hours like you say, how am I going to take pictures in the dark?"

He paused for a moment as he absorbed the question.

"Mate, they gotta be carrying some light, torches or something. I mean they have to see what they're doing. Get close enough to pick up the images and it's proof that something was going down. It ain't like the cops are gonna want actual mugshots, are they?"

I had no idea what the police might want. All I knew was that Cecil's plan sounded dangerous. I picked up my beer and took a long draught, almost choking on it when a thought flashed through my head.

"Wait a minute. The list ... the list of names. Remember where we found it? James's villa. And the names all fit the places. He *has* to be involved."

A wave of disappointment crept over me. I liked James. I didn't want to think he was involved but the connection could not be ignored.

Cecil nodded. "Yeah, he has mate but we're gonna need more than a bit of paper to prove it." He paused to sip his beer and then placed the bottle down on the table, a decisive glint in his eyes. "We're gonna have to get into the villa geezer, find something else. He has them cabinets in his office. Bit like the ones in the cave when you think about it. There has to be something in 'em that'll connect him to this lot."

The memory of our visit to James's office flicked through my mind like some old, grainy movie. And then something else occurred with far more clarity.

"Sweets ... sweets, Ces."

"Sweets?"

"Yeah, sweets. He had that bowl of sweets in the office. You gave me one of them. And I found a sweet wrapper in the cave. Same as the ones in the office. And then when you add in the cigarette butts ..."

Cecil ran his hands through his hair.

"All circumstantial mate. Nothing there to link him to Felipe or the Russian. We need to get in that office."

"What, a break in?"

"Nah mate. We'd never get past them two fucking wolves he keeps. We need to be a bit subtle. Let's get him out for a beer, get him pissed off his face and then let *him* get us in the villa."

"But how can we guarantee he'll get as pissed as that Ces? Like you said, he's got the Irish gene so he can probably hold his liquor."

"No problem mate. We help it along a bit. There's plenty of geezers out here selling stuff that'd take an elephant out of the equation. Trust me. We spike his booze up a bit and maybe even do the dogs too. So, I reckon you should text him or give him a ring and invite him out tonight." He spotted my hesitancy. "Just tell him it's your last night and you thought it'd be nice for us lads to have a drink with him, especially since his missus ain't around."

I didn't like the thought of drugging up anyone, let alone James but I realised I had no choice. I tapped out a text and waited for a reply.

"Right Ces. Done. Finish your drink. I want to hook up with Jas and Carlos and see how the lighthouse and boat check is going. It could still be important."

I picked up all the papers, folded them together and placed them in my pocket. We downed our drinks and stepped into the warm sunlight. Across the street, I saw two figures emerge from the Bar Cruce Sant Rafel restaurant. Immediately I recognised them. Felipe and Scalapino.

But they had spotted us too.

32

Surprises sometimes take a while to sink in. Unpleasant surprises can take longer whilst the brain tries to make sense of precisely what it doesn't want to see. The figures across the street, a matter of metres away, were definitely an unpleasant surprise.

I reached for the car door, intending to drive off but I froze, my gaze focussed on the figures heading across the road, my brain trying to deal with the unpleasant information. I could not comprehend the fact that Felipe could be in the same town as me. Cecil seemed not to have seen them as he was on the passenger side of the car, by the pavement. By the time I had recovered my composure and opened the car door, Felipe was halfway along the pavement and calling out to me.

"Matthew, wait. I have your ring."

I shot a glance at Cecil who had turned in the direction of the voice.

"He was supposed to meet me with the ring tonight," I said under my breath. "What d'you think?"

"Let's see," Cecil answered. He walked round the car to the driver's door and stood next to me. Felipe had stepped into the road and stopped, Scalapino at his shoulder.

"But what's he doing here? He can't have followed us, surely? Maybe it's where he lives. Paloma said they live outside San Antonio."

"Maybe … and it's Saturday so he might have a day off. Bit of a coincidence he's here but I bet he ain't got no ring with him.

Why would he have it if he was supposed to be coming down to del Mar tonight?"

"You don't have the mobile with you, do you?"

"Nah mate. It's at the hotel. I tucked it away in the ceiling cavity in the bathroom. And even if I did have it, we need to hang on to it now. But he ain't gonna know I ain't got it on me. Let's blag it, see what he's got."

It wasn't a strategy I fancied but there was the possibility Felipe might have the engagement ring with him and I had to find out.

Cecil puffed out his chest and stood square on to Felipe, who had begun to walk slowly towards me.

"You have my telephone, amigo?" Felipe asked.

"Let's see the ring first," Cecil replied.

Felipe glanced away for a second and laughed.

"You want to play like that, hombre? You want to be difficult?"

"It ain't gotta be difficult geezer, but the thing is, I don't trust you or your bald-headed psycho lackey, so I wanna see the ring first before you get your phone. And I wanna see it up close so I know you ain't trying to pull some move on us with a shite bit of cheap junk. Yeah? You getting my drift?"

I wasn't convinced that Felipe followed all of Cecil's South London style outburst, but it seemed that he had got the gist. He nodded to Scalapino who walked towards the car. I watched as he reached into his pocket, a moment of apprehension engulfing me. And I was right. In a quick, jerky movement he pulled out a snub nosed pistol and pointed it at Cecil, inches from his chest. Cecil didn't react. I did.

"Whoa," I shouted, my hand held out in a halt indication. "No need for that. I'm sure we can sort this out without any violence."

Felipe ignored me.

"The telephone, hombre." Felipe held out a hand, his fingers moving rapidly back and forth in a beckoning motion.

"Easy geezer. It's in the car." He nodded at me. "Keys, mate. Gimme the keys."

I fumbled in my pocket for the keys and handed them to Cecil. He clicked the unlock button on the fob and reached for the door handle. He released the catch and gripped the top of the door. Scalapino took a step forward. As he did, Cecil flung the door outwards in a sudden violent movement so that it caught him mid forearm, sending the gun spinning from his grasp. It hit the tarmac, swirling across the ground before coming to rest in centre of the road a few feet away. Scalapino gripped his arm in a reflex action to the pain. With Scalapino momentarily off guard, Cecil aimed a kick catching him straight between the legs. He doubled up and fell to the ground clutching his groin, his face contorted in agony. Felipe moved towards Cecil.

"Don't fucking try it nobhead or you'll be rubbing your bollocks too," Cecil hissed, his fists raised in a fighter's stance.

A screech of tyres along the road caused me to look up. From the car park of the Bar Cruce restaurant, a large black Mercedes had pulled out and was heading our way.

Felipe had back up.

Cecil saw it too. He pushed me hard in the back.

"Get in the fucking car geezer. We're outta here."

I fell forward into the driving seat, quickly righted myself and started the engine. Cecil came around the car and dived into the front seat.

"Go geezer. Go for fuck's sake."

I hit the pedal and accelerated away from the kerb. The Mercedes lurched across the road attempting to cut off our escape. The two vehicles missed a collision by millimetres. As I sped away I caught sight of Felipe in the rear view mirror, tugging Scalapino to his feet. The Mercedes reversed up alongside them and the driver jumped out. He stopped in the middle of the road, bent down and picked something up, presumably the gun. Cecil had watched what was happening over his shoulder.

"They're gonna come after us geezer. Floor it."

I yanked the steering wheel hard to the right, took a sliding right turn opposite the San Creu restaurant that I had passed earlier and kicked down on the gas. The car lurched back as it picked up the sudden acceleration. The road ahead became a blur of tarmac and hedgerow. But it was too open and too straight. They would catch us easily in the Mercedes. Up ahead I spotted a turning leading onto a narrower, twisting road that cut through tree lined fields. I pulled the steering wheel to the right again and took the turn in a screech of burning rubber and blue smoke.

"Where the fuck you going, geezer?"

"I'm just trying to lose them, Ces. We're too visible on that main road."

"Lose them? You've just left fucking great skid marks all over that bend. You might as well send up a fucking flare."

I ignored Cecil and focussed on the road ahead. It was far more remote, its edges lined by lengths of stone walling, low lying shrubs, vegetation and trees. My gaze darted nervously to the rear view mirror but there was no one behind.

"Might have given them the slip," I said, looking across at Cecil.

"Geezer, keep your eyes on the road, there's a fucking car coming."

The road wasn't wide enough for the two cars to get by. I had to slow right down and pull in tight to one side so we could pass each other. It cost me time and speed. I glanced back in the mirror and saw it. The unmistakeable shape of the Mercedes coming up fast, a cloud of dust in its wake.

"Shit, they're behind us," I shouted.

Cecil turned and looked behind. "Hit the gas geezer. They're catching us."

I stamped on the accelerator. The car bounced forward as we picked up speed but the Mercedes was getting closer. A T-junction lay ahead. The last thing we needed was a stop.

"Which way Ces? Right or left?" I yelled out.

"How the fuck should I know. I've no fucking idea where we are."

The car sped towards the junction.

"Right or left? Which?" Sweat poured down my face.

"Hang a right. It makes no fucking odds."

I swerved the car to the right and took the corner without checking to see if anything was coming. I was just relying on it being a quiet, remote country road with very few vehicles. Luckily, the route was virtually just a single track, a tree lined strip winding its way through the open countryside. Behind us the Mercedes was closing fast. Our only hope was that the tight bends would slow down such a big car. I floored it again, keeping a tight grip on the steering wheel as the car took the bends at speed. The winding road bought us a slight advantage. The Mercedes would disappear momentarily from view as we rounded the bends. But it was only a matter of time before they caught up.

And then we hit another junction. This time the main carriageway, signposted 'Sant Antoni' to the right and 'Santa Eularia' to the left. I approached it far too fast. The view to the right was good but to the left it was concealed by a row of trees. I stamped on the brake to slow down, aware that the Mercedes was closing.

"What the fuck you slowing down for geezer?" Cecil shouted.

"The junction Ces. It's blind on my side and there's a stop sign."

"We ain't stopping geeze. Trust me. They got a gun in that car behind. You just gotta go for it."

I knew Cecil was right. With my stomach churning, I closed my eyes for a split second, hit the gas and screeched through the right turn onto the carriageway. The blare of a horn told me just how close we had been to an accident. A petrol tanker loomed right up behind us, the driver gesticulating from his cab window. I hit the accelerator to get a safe distance ahead, grateful that the tanker would have slowed Felipe and his mob exiting the junction. And then I realised if I kept just in front of the tanker it would make it more difficult for Felipe to overtake and if he did, he was unlikely to try anything with a witness so close.

I kept ahead of the tanker for just over a mile until we reached the outskirts of San Rafael again. Up ahead was another T-junction and, just before it, a sharp bend that doubled back on itself. I had no idea which way the tanker might go at the junction and I knew I could not use it as cover for much longer. With all my instincts urging me to get out of sight, I swung the car into a hard left turn. The sudden change of direction threw the back end round in a sliding, skidding swerve. I yanked the steering back to the right to counteract the slide.

"Where the fuck you going now?" Cecil shouted.

"I'm trying to lose them. It's a narrower road. We need to get out of sight and I don't seem to be shaking them off. We can't outrun them in this." As I said it, I checked the mirror and caught sight of the Mercedes tearing past the turning. It had bought us some time but I knew they'd realise where we had gone once they reached the junction, a mere fifty metres further on.

The road rose in a shallow incline in between rows of whitewashed houses. I sped along, faster than I should have done in what was a residential area. But I needed to get ahead of Felipe and hide out somewhere. At the top of the hill, the tall bell tower of a white-washed church loomed over another T-junction. Again a right or left decision had to be made. I took a right.

Wrong choice.

The road came to a dead end in the shape of a rounded off block paved court yard that acted as a parking area for the church. On the opposite side, a long stone wall bordered a line of residential properties and led to a narrow dirt track that ran alongside them.

"Bollocks." The expletive slipped out in frustration. I glanced through the open window in the direction of the church entrance to ensure I hadn't offended a passing priest or nun.

Cecil had no such concerns.

"Turn the fucking thing round geezer and let's get outta here. We get caught up here we're trapped."

I slammed the gears into reverse and spun the back of the car round towards a low white wall that enclosed the parking area. Then I shifted into first gear and pressed the accelerator. The engine spluttered for a moment then cut out.

"What the fuck?" Cecil shouted out.

I turned the ignition key. The engine turned and stuttered into a half-hearted attempt at starting. I tried again and this time it just kept turning over but wouldn't fire. And then I noticed the gauge.

"Petrol. We're out of frigging petrol," I said, a fit of despair rapidly creeping up on me.

274

"What? No fucking juice? What's going on? Who's s'posed to be filling it up all this time?" Cecil said, as if it was incredible that cars should just pack up.

"I didn't think to ... Jasper's been driving it. I just didn't look at the gauge."

"Well, we ain't go time to be hanging about here. C'mon. Leave it. Let's go."

The full extent of the church was apparent once we stepped out into the blistering heat of the day. A number of curved arches formed the portico of a large building that dominated the hillside and overlooked an expanse of open country that dropped down to a lush valley beneath. A light breeze blowing up from the valley was the only relief from the heat.

In a mindless panic I ran towards the church.

"Where you going? You ain't got time to be sight-seeing geezer," Cecil shouted. "We need to find a way outta here."

Ignoring him, I went through the entrance arch, opened the door and entered a haven of calm. Two rows of wooden pews led towards an altar that was overshadowed by a magnificent sculpted golden backdrop filled with saintly images. In the cool, shadowy silence I felt tranquil, protected, free of panic. It seemed like the ideal hiding place.

Cecil had other ideas. His voice shattered the moment.

"Geezer, what you doing? We ain't seeking sanctuary. We gotta get outta here. Them villains ain't got no respect for religion so don't be thinking you're safe in a frigging church."

I turned to see Cecil's face poking round the door. The urgency in his voice immediately destroyed any ideas that I had about remaining in the church.

I followed him outside and scanned the area. There was no point in heading back the way we had just come. We would undoubtedly run into Felipe and his henchmen. In the other direction, at the top of the dirt track, a white, wooden sign, half concealed by overhanging shrubs, indicated 'Sant Antoni.' The car park itself was almost empty save for a single dust covered Citroen parked against the wall and what looked like an antique motor bike with a

275

sidecar attached, near the church entrance. Cecil tried the car door. It was locked. Next he approached the motor bike and examined it.

"It's got the keys in it mate," he called out. "Somebody's very trusting round here. C'mon, what you waiting for. This'll get us outta Dodge."

I stared at Cecil not quite believing that he intended to take the bike.

"What is it? I've never seen a bike like that before? It looks like one of those bikes they had in the war. The ones you see in films with Germans riding round in them in Nazi uniform."

It was definitely old but in reasonable condition, its black bodywork polished so that the thin white piping that edged the wheel guards and the sidecar stood out. The sidecar itself was shaped like a 1940's pram, its wheel topped by the same style wheel guard that the bike had but with a lamp on top.

Cecil stared at it for a moment.

"It's a Neval Dnepr, whatever the fuck that is," he said, pointing at a sign on the front of the sidecar. "It looks well old."

"Well whatever it is I can't ride a motorbike," I said.

"You don't have to geezer. You're in the side car," Cecil replied and straddled the bike.

I was about to comment when, from the corner of my eye, I caught sight of the front of the Mercedes emerging from the junction side road that we had come out of just a few minutes earlier. I legged it towards the bike.

"They're here Ces," I said and jumped into the side car.

Cecil turned the key and fired up the motor. It started first time. He swung the bike round and revved the throttle.

"Can you ride this thing?" I asked, feeling suddenly vulnerable in Cecil's hands.

"Not really mate. Rode a scooter once. Can't be much difference. Always a first time." He pointed the bike towards the dirt track, revved the engine and jerked forward. The Mercedes pulled to a halt alongside the church.

The first shot rang out like a crack of lightning, bounced off the stone wall and grazed the paint on the sidecar.

"Shit, they're shooting at us," I shouted, trying to make myself heard over the roar of the motorbike engine.

"Yeah, I know. Keep your head down and hold on."

The next shot split the dirt and gravel on the makeshift roadway and ricocheted into a tree, splintering a branch. Cecil hit full throttle and sped into the safety of the winding dirt track, a cloud of dust and grit splurting from beneath the wheels.

"I don't reckon they'll get that big Merc down here mate," he shouted.

The track wound down between a number of stone walled farm buildings and then flattened out into a meandering dirt road, a strip of grass running through its centre. The sidecar bounced and shook as the bike powered over the dips and ruts. I felt certain that at any second, I would be ejected straight into the hedgerow. I gripped the edges as hard as I could and held on as we bounced along at a speed that was far too fast for the terrain.

It took less than a minute to reach the end of the track where it came out onto a main road. We took a left down to the roundabout and then joined the slip road to San Antonio.

"Looks like we lost 'em, geezer," Cecil shouted out, his hair catching the wind as he throttled up the bike.

33

I sat in the sidecar, the wind rushing past my face as Cecil shot along the C-731, and took stock of things. I was in a stolen motorbike, I had a false passport, a diamond rap to answer, and I'd entered the country illegally. I was dead meat if Scalapino caught up with me and I would be locked up forever if the authorities got me first. And I had also lost my girlfriend. How has it come to this, Matthew Malarkey, I asked myself. At forty-one, I should be settled, doing nice things with the woman in my life, enjoying relaxing days with my friends, perhaps even thinking about starting a family. But life was not working that way. I thought about Erin's comment – '... *you play the cards you are dealt. You make the best connections with the hand you have and then bluff like Doc Holiday on three shots of firewater.*' It seemed that every hand I had been dealt had turned into a losing one. I needed a break.

A dull thud and a simultaneous metallic crack shook me out of my self-pity. I spun round to my left, in the direction of the sound. Looming up behind us was the black Merc. Cecil hadn't heard anything with the noise of the bike engine. He was focussed straight ahead, his eyes streaming as the wind blew straight into his face. I leant towards him and poked him hard in the side.

"They've found us. The Merc's on our tail and they're shooting at us again," I screamed. "You've got to get us off the road."

Cecil shot a look over his left shoulder. The Mercedes had pulled across into the right hand lane and was right behind us.

They were closing the gap fast. He yanked the bike hard to the left so that we were tight to the central reservation, an attempt at avoiding the pursuing vehicle, but it veered across in his wake, now close enough to run us off the road. The sudden change of direction caused the sidecar's wheel to leave the road.

"Ces, for God's sake man you're gonna turn us over."

He didn't hear or chose not to respond. My sidecar, on the left hand drive motorbike, was now fully exposed, an easy target. Another sharp crack. This time the bullet glanced off the tarmac and cut through the spokes of the sidecar wheel. Cecil flung the bike around sharply to the right and just as forcefully back again to the left. I knew what he was trying to do - stop the Merc getting alongside and make us a hard to hit target, but we were just as likely to get killed by his reckless driving as we were by one of Scalapino's bullets.

Another violent swerve threw the sidecar off its wheel again. The whole machine was being thrown about like a waltzer ride at a fair. The wheel crashed back down onto the road accompanied by a loud creaking and grinding noise from under my seat, the frantic direction changes straining the framework that joined bike and sidecar together. Yet another sudden, snaking swerve bounced the bike across the tarmac and threw me hard against the door, my feet swinging across the floor in the opposite direction. I gripped the edges of my seat and started to pray. My thoughts flashed back to the brief moments I had spent in the church. I'd never been particularly spiritual but, as the bike careered across the carriageway at speed, it felt like a good time to get religion. And then I realised there was something solid at the front end of the sidecar.

I stretched down between my feet and managed to feel the rounded tip of the object. The bike veered across the road, throwing me off balance again. In my peripheral vision, I caught a glimpse of the Mercedes swinging in behind the bike, its nose just missing our rear end by inches. Cecil was doing his best to avoid the menacing Merc, his face contorted by tension and concentration. Again I stretched down into the front of the sidecar, this time managing to grab the top of the solid object. I pulled it out. It was about twelve inches high and covered in a single sheet of soft tissue wrapping paper. I tore the paper away and to my utter surprise realised I was holding a statue, a solid stone sculpture of a holy man wearing a blue cloak over a long white robe. He had one hand clasped to his chest and the other held a wooden staff in an upright position. Stuck on one side, two strips of Sellotape keeping it in position, was a label that said, '*St. Christopher, patron saint of travellers.*' What it was doing in the motorbike sidecar was beyond me but since we had found the bike outside the church in San Rafael, I presumed it had to belong to either the priest or one of his parishioners. It really didn't matter who it belonged to. If ever two travellers needed a patron saint it was right at that moment.

Cecil pulled the bike into another wild turn so that it veered across the two lanes of the carriageway from left to right. The Mercedes went with it, a looping action that kept the car almost tied to our rear. Up ahead a bus stop was positioned on the right side of the road, a lay-by in front of it for buses to pull in. On the other side of the bus stop, a pedestrian bridge spanned the carriageway, a long concrete walkway rising gradually to its topmost part. Cecil yanked the bike around so it was running straight again. The Mercedes took advantage of the head on position and in a burst of acceleration, rammed the back of the sidecar. The impact thudded through me and almost pushed us round in a three hundred and sixty degree turn. Only Cecil's quick reflexes prevented the spin as he dragged the bike back to the right to correct the swerve. We were sitting ducks. The car slewed across the carriageway in pursuit. Sooner or later, they would get us.

In a moment of desperation and a total desire to fight back, I took action. Grabbing the statue from my lap, and with one brief apologetic look at its reverential, bearded face, I lobbed it high over my shoulder in the direction of the oncoming Mercedes. The holy man spun in an arc through the air coming down head first, like a targeted missile, right onto the windscreen of the chasing vehicle. The impact split the screen, sending a swirling spider's web pattern right across the driver's side, completely blotting out his view of the road. The car lurched forward, a sudden rush of acceleration as the shock of the impact caused the driver to lose control. Its front end slammed into the back of the sidecar sending a massive shockwave straight through the frame. Instantly sidecar and bike parted company, the metal structure splitting, wrenching the frame apart and tearing off the whole of the left side with the force of impact. The sudden separation of the two parts sent the bike careering off to the left and the sidecar veering sharply to the right, heading directly for the bus stop lay-by.

Instinct kicked in.

With only one wheel on the sidecar, I realised it would only be a matter of seconds before it lost balance and tipped over. At the speed it was travelling, that could only result in disaster and serious injury. I shifted my weight right over the single wheel, leaning over the edge like a wind surfer balancing his board. In the background, I heard the crash of crumpling metal as the Mercedes spun round on the carriageway, hit the concrete central reservation barrier and then flipped over onto its side. At the same time, the sidecar mounted the raised pavement on a direct collision course with the bus shelter. I shifted my weight again back to the centre so that it swerved past it, and then immediately back over the wheel so that it didn't collide with the metal crash barrier that separated the lay-by from the road. The movement, more by luck than judgement, put me on a direct line with the pedestrian bridge walkway. The sidecar hurtled up the walkway between two steel handrails, its base bouncing off the concrete in a shower of sparks and a terrifying grinding racket from underneath.

I clung on desperately, leaning as far out to the right as I could to try and keep the weight over the wheel. But it was too dangerous to keep that position, the railings on the right side perilously close to my head. Fearful that I could also be thrown out through the huge gap where the left side had once been, I kept my weight hard over to the right, tucked my head and shoulders into a forward stoop and prayed to Saint Christopher. My pleas seemed to be

281

heard. On the steep incline my stricken transportation started to lose momentum until just a few metres from the top, where the bridge turned at right angles to cross the carriageway, it flopped over onto one side.

I crawled out of the seat, unhurt and grateful not to have come to any harm. The sidecar lay there wrecked, its single wheel spinning out its final revolutions. And then I remembered Cecil. In the fight to stay in some sort of control of my bit of our shattered vehicle, I had lost track of him. I ran the few metres to the top of the bridge and scanned the road as far as I could see. No sign of him. That had to mean he hadn't crashed. Below me, steam and smoke billowed from the stricken Mercedes. I could just make out some movement as the occupants struggled to open doors that had now become heavy trapdoors as it lay on its side.

And then I heard the sound of an engine.

I turned to my right and spotted a cloud of dust and the unmistakeable sight of a motorbike ploughing across the dirt, weaving its way along the rocky scrubland that lined the side of the road. It pulled up underneath the bridge, one panel of the broken sidecar still attached.

"You alright geeze? What you doing up there?"

"I'm fine. I didn't come up here to sightsee did I?" I called out. "The sidecar's wrecked though."

"I wouldn't worry about that mate. Get yourself down here and let's get outta here. The emergency services will be on their way any minute to sort out them villains and we don't wanna be around when they get here."

I legged it down the footbridge to where Cecil had stopped.

"Good work with the Merc mate. I see you lob something at it. What was it?"

"Let's just say it was Divine Intervention for now Ces. I'll tell you later when I've calmed down. You're right, we need to get going."

"Jump on the back then, geeze. We'll cut across these fields, find some dirt track that'll get us away from here fast and then we gotta lose this bike."

I straddled the bike behind Cecil as he revved up the engine.

"Hang on tight mate. Once we drop the bike, we'll get a taxi some place, head back to yours and get cleaned up. We got a night out with James to take care of."

34

We dumped the motorbike in a country lane not far from San Rafael and took the bus back to my hotel in Ibiza Town. Carlos had telephoned but had nothing to report on lighthouses or boats with names that had anything to do with shining lights. With his ability to speak fluent Spanish, he had made a number of enquiries but could come up with nothing that fitted the Spanish wording on the sheet of numbers. It looked like a dead end.

Once we had reached my room, I stashed the papers with the names and places information on, in the drawer next to my bed and stretched out while Cecil went for a shower.

On the journey back to town we had put a plan in place for dealing with James. He had replied to my text and agreed to meet at Savannah, along the Sunset Strip. But we knew that if we were right and James was connected to the diamond operation, we could be heading into a trap. It was a risk we had to take. The plan was simple, probably far too simple given that we were dealing with hardened, professional criminals. Carlos and Jasper would be at the bar too but would keep a low profile and stay on the lookout for any trouble. The minute anything looked like going wrong they were to create mayhem by starting a brawl that would get the security staff involved and give us a fighting chance of making an exit. It wasn't sophisticated but it was all we had. If Scalapino and his thugs showed up, it would be another indicator that James was involved.

Cecil stepped out of the shower, towelling his hair with one hand and scratching his balls with the other.

"You know what we forgot mate?" he said. "The fucking drugs."

I hesitated, unsure that it was something I could do.

"Do we need to? I was thinking that maybe –"

Cecil cut me short.

"Oi, geezer. Don't be doing all that frigging thinking. If we're gonna have a plan we gotta stick to it. Don't go wimping out of it now. The geezers you're dealing with don't have no second thoughts about doing what they need to do to get the job done. And that includes killing people. That's what gives 'em an advantage over mugs who get a guilty conscience about doing stuff." He sat on the bed and flicked his hair back off his face. "It's like a title fight ain't it? You show a bit of weakness and you get stamped on mate. And anyway, nobody's asking you to kill anybody are they? All we gotta do is get James off his tits, loosen his tongue a bit and then get in his villa. And we need to find out if he knows Paloma, yeah?"

I was stung by the mug remark and the suggestion that I might be showing weakness.

"Okay, so what do we do about it? About the drugs?"

"Gimme that phone mate. I'll get it sorted. Got no battery left in mine."

I was just about to hand my mobile to Cecil when it rang. I checked the screen. Erin Farrell.

"Erin? You okay?"

"*Yeah, I'm fine. How are you getting on?*"

"So so ... getting there. Is there a problem?"

"*Maybe. When are you coming back?*"

"Uh ... well, I had no fixed date but soon. Why, what's the problem?"

There was a pause on the line.

"*It's JJ. He's booked a holiday. He needs his passport.*"

My heart sank.

"A holiday? Why? I mean .... where? I thought you said he wouldn't be travelling anywhere with a broken arm so he wouldn't need a passport?"

"I did, but he's changed his mind. He wants to go to the South of France for a few days. He said a bit of sun would help his recovery. I tried to talk him out of it but he wants me to pick up the passport as I still have his locker key."

"The South of France? When?"

"Tuesday."

"Tuesday? That's ... shit ... that's three days' time."

"I know. That's why I've called you. He's booked on a flight out at five in the afternoon."

"Five? Five o'clock? That's even worse. That means I have to be back by Tuesday lunchtime." I paced across the room to the balcony and stared out at the street. Normality below me, but mayhem around me. "Can't you ... can't you do anything Erin?"

"Like what? It's his passport and he thinks it's safely tucked up in his locker. He doesn't know it's already on a holiday of its own."

I ignored the mockery in Erin's tone.

"I dunno. Tell him ... tell him he won't get much of a tan with his arm in plaster or something."

"Oh sure, that'll stop him going alright. Listen Matthew, he's organised the flight through work. He's even got a friend booked on the same flight. Luckily he has a record of his passport info for the booking or we'd be right in the mire. There's nothing I can do. I need to get that passport to him and I need it by Tuesday afternoon at the latest. I'm sorry."

I turned back to face the room and caught Cecil's enquiring look. I shook my head, waved my hand in a dismissive gesture and returned to the call. I knew I couldn't let Erin down. She had stuck her neck out for me.

"Okay, Erin. I'll be there with the passport. Don't worry."

"Thanks a million, Matthew. I did say it was a gamble."

I ended the call and threw the mobile to Cecil.

"What's all that about geezer?" he asked.

"The dodgy passport. I have to give it back by Tuesday afternoon. And Tuesday's the seventeenth. I need to be at the caves then to see if I can get pictures of whatever might be going on there. I'm screwed Ces."

"Hold it geezer. Yeah, Tuesday is the seventeenth but if anything's going down it'll be in the early hours, like I said before. They ain't gonna be doing nothing before midnight so my guess is that it's gotta be happening between midnight and dawn when there ain't so many people about. It's all families and that up that way. They ain't partying all night ... bit of dinner, kids asleep and then it's a bit of the old holiday mumble swerve with the missus and everybody's fast a kip by two."

I stared vacantly at Cecil, not quite following his logic.

"What I'm saying is, if these villains are up to something on Tuesday it ain't gonna be before midnight when there's people about. So it'll be after midnight on Monday, which is the early hours of Tuesday morning, ain't it. Yeah? You gotta get the passport back Tuesday afternoon. Plenty of time, so stop panicking."

I sat down on the bed.

"Plenty of time? It's cutting it all a bit fine. I've got tomorrow, Monday and Tuesday morning. Two and half days to clear my name, save Louise's career and rescue our relationship. Nothing too serious then, eh?" I flung my arms in the air, despondency replacing the positivity I'd felt about making the earlier breakthrough with the names and numbers. "I need a drink."

Cecil stood up, the towel now wrapped around him, and stared at the mobile.

"Right, listen geezer. I'm gonna call Jas. Then we get a couple of beers somewhere here and then taxi it back to San An. I'll get changed and then we head out to meet James. Okay. You stay calm. You need a cool head. You made some progress here so let's not fuck it up by panicking. I told ya, me and the boys gotta go Monday anyway. So, let's get it done."

I nodded. There were few other options open to me.

"Ces, while you got Jas on we need him to sort the hire car. Ask him if he can get the hire extended until I go home. I could do with some transport. Oh, and see if he can get out to San Rafael and pick it up. I can drop it at the airport on Tuesday."

"Done geeze," Cecil replied. He pushed the telephone icon on the screen and called up my list of contacts. Under *recent calls,* he found Jasper. There was a brief exchange of greeting and then Cecil got to the point.

"You know the streets mate. I need you to score some gear for me."

Cecil listened intently to the response and then continued.

"What I need is, something that'll immobilise a grown man and is strong enough to take a couple of wild dogs outta the equation for a few hours as well, yeah."

There was another pause. Cecil nodded as he listened.

"Yeah, all them geezers doing the snide glasses and dick noses to mug tourists ... mate, they'll get you anything you want. A pair of shades and a side order of Charlie, sixty euros a touch. You'll get 'em down to half what they're asking. They ain't making no wedge selling dodgy bins and plastic noses shaped like cocks, trust me. That's all just a cover for their proper mumble, ain't it? Just do a deal with 'em."

I had heard enough. I knew it had to be done but I didn't want to contemplate the details. I headed for the shower.

35

We hooked up with Jasper and Carlos at Savannah at 9.00p.m., half an hour before we were due to meet James. The sun had closed down another day and the buzz around the sunset bars had settled into an early evening chill out. We took a table at the canopied seafront terrace and ordered drinks.

"No probs with the old Special K then Jas?" Cecil said.

"Easy enough," Jasper replied. "The two Danish birds pointed me in the right direction."

"Special K?" I said.

"Yeah, the ket. Ketamine."

"Hang on, Jas. You involved them? They know James."

"Chill ... JJ. I told them it was for me. Said I was going clubbing later. They're still asking when that party's gonna happen though."

I sipped my drink and decided that, with time running out, I had to focus on what we had to get done.

"D'you get the steaks?" Cecil asked, nodding towards Carlos.

"Aye, two big juicy ones," Carlos replied, holding up a shopping bag.

"The steaks?" I said.

"Yeah mate. To take the dogs out of it. Seen it done in films. They lace a couple of steaks with some knockout powder and no more worries about getting your leg chewed off."

"Knockout powder? What the ketamine? I didn't know that's what you meant Ces. You could kill them."

"What d'you think I meant then? How else did you think we'd neutralise two dogs the size of fucking grizzlies?"

"I don't know. I thought you meant something ... something more recreational."

"What, like get 'em to smoke a couple of fat spliffs by the pool until they was so chilled out they wouldn't give a toss who walked through their territory? Mate, get real. This ain't no fucking game." Cecil turned back towards Carlos. "You dosed 'em up?"

"I did, aye. Both steaks, exactly like it said on the internet. Should be good for a few hours at least."

"Good man Carlos. Now once James gets here, give it half an hour or so, make sure there's no mumble here and then get yourself up to his villa. It's an in and out job. Lob the steaks over the gate and then get back down the town. The dogs'll be on them like a bitch in heat."

"Nae problem Cecil. I got it under control," Carlos said.

"Right, one more thing boys. Apart from getting in the villa, we gotta make some connections. Yeah? James, that Felipe prick, the bald fuck and Paloma. So after Carlos has gone on dog feeding duties, Jas, you come over to us like you just seen us here and give it the old chat. Something about running into a blinding looking Spanish bird called Paloma and she worked at the hospital. See if we get any reaction from the Irish geezer. Tumble?"

"Yeah, got it dude. Funny enough I used to do a bit of acting back in the day."

"Yeah, nativity play at school's what Matt here tells me geezer," Cecil said, slapping Jasper hard across the shoulders.

I kicked Cecil's leg under the table.

"It's Jason, Ces ... or JJ," I said.

"Alright geezer. Keep your hair on. Anybody'd think MI fucking five was on your case."

Normally I didn't have to worry about Cecil as he rarely used my name but I was tense, on edge, scared that something would go wrong.

Cecil beckoned to a waitress who was flitting between tables, a tray of empties balanced in one hand, her eyes scanning the clientele to ensure she didn't miss a request.

"Cuatro botellas de cerveza, por favor," he said, holding up four fingers.

"Four beers coming up boys. I'm from Manchester," she said with a wink that seemed to be specifically directed at Jasper.

"You're learning the lingo then, pal," Carlos said, a grin playing on his face.

"The essentials geezer. Enough to survive, know what I'm saying?" With his order acknowledged, Cecil sat back in his seat. "We good then lads?"

Carlos and Jasper nodded their agreement. I didn't feel good at all but it was far too late to come up with an alternative. It was a situation I hadn't asked for. Another crap hand of cards flung down on the green baize of my life. I just had to pick them up and play them, make the best of the hand, just like Erin had said.

The waitress returned with our drinks. Cecil threw twenty euros on the table and grabbed a bottle.

A sudden wave of emotion crept over me, probably driven by the doom and gloom that seemed permanently poised to rip through my sub-conscious. I picked up one of the beer bottles and held it aloft.

"Cheers boys. I want you to know that ... well, whatever happens, whatever shit goes down tonight, I appreciate what you've done and ... and what you're still doing. You didn't have to but you've been there ... and ... you know ... I just want to say thanks. You are, all of you, blinding mates."

The reaction was instinctive. Four friends, bonded by that friendship but now glued together by shared experiences. Four bottles of beer clanked together in our midst, a small token action but a huge symbolic gesture of togetherness.

Carlos's Latin blood responded instantly.

"Hey, Mateo, amigo. Los hermanos, brothers ... family ... we stick together. One of us has trouble, we all have trouble."

Inevitably Cecil restored reality.

"Carlos, chill man. Yeah, we're mates but right now we ain't got no time for all that man hugging shit. The Irish fella's gonna be here in the next fifteen, yeah. So we gotta get on the programme." He pointed at Carlos and Jasper. "You two better get in position. We're on our game now."

Jasper nodded, a brief smile playing on his face. He slapped Carlos on the back and stood up.

"Hang on boys. I want to get a photo," I said. I beckoned to the waitress and asked her if she could take a picture of us as a group. I handed her my mobile. "Wait a sec. It'll need the flash." I took the phone back, scrolled to '*On*' in the flash options and gave it back to the waitress.

The four of us lined up in front of the table, beers in hand and posed for the camera. When the picture had been taken Cecil and I sat back down. Jasper nodded to Carlos.

"C'mon Carlos. Bring your beer." Then he reached into his pocket and pulled out some keys. He threw them across the table to me. "The car mate. All sorted. Fuelled it up and it's down by the Buddha along the beach road, about a couple of hundred metres. The bloke said we can leave it at the airport. But, remember mate, he doesn't know it's got another driver on it so go easy."

"Great thanks Jas. I will. I'll square you up when I get home."

Jasper and Carlos left the table, crossed the walkway that separated the canopied seating area and went into the main part of the building. I watched as they stationed themselves by the bar so that they had a perfect view of where Cecil and I were seated.

Once we were by ourselves, Cecil leant across the table towards me.

"Mate, I know you're wound up but it'll be cool. Just act normal, like you're on an ordinary night out, no fuck ups. You're in a trendy bar, nice drinks, good staff and service. Just relax like it's a normal night. You with me?"

I nodded but inside I could feel the tension building.

"To be honest Ces, I'm frigging worried about drugging James. You giving him the same stuff as the dogs? I mean, supposing he had a bad reaction and it ended up killing him. I'd be up for murder as well as all the other things I've got hanging over my head. What exactly does it do anyway?"

"Easy mate. We ain't gonna give him the same amount. Just enough to get him chilled out. It relaxes the muscles so he'll think he's more pissed than he is and then if he starts hallucinating, that'll do the job. He'll wanna go home so we take him back there. We give the dogs a higher dose so they get disorientated and then, with the muscle effect, they won't be going anywhere. Jas'll just drop a bit of powder in his booze and we wait for it to kick in. Trust me mate, it's gotta be done if we're gonna get an opportunity to search his gaff."

I wasn't that confident about the plan but there was no turning back.

James walked in at 9.30p.m., an air of confidence about him that can only be presented by someone who is at ease with life. He offered me his hand.

"Good to see you young fella," he said as he shook my hand, his gaze direct and focussed. He turned to Cecil.

"And good to see you again Cecil. I hope you're taking care of Matthew here. Not leading him astray now," he said with a playful wink.

Cecil laughed and shook James's hand.

"Nah, mate. Just a few quiet ones here and there. Enjoying the sun mostly."

James grinned and pulled out a chair. He beckoned the waitress over and ordered three Jack Daniels and cokes. As we waited for the drinks, I asked the question that had been playing on my mind.

"How's Louise. Have you heard anything?"

James glanced at Cecil and then back at me.

"She's okay. I heard from Eleanor but she hasn't said a lot really. She's staying with Louise for the minute. I told her you're going back. Tomorrow then is it?"

"Tuesday. I'll be booking a morning flight," I said. Instantly I regretted giving the information. James was implicated in the diamond operation and I should have been more wary about what

I said. But it was difficult for me. I liked him and his easy-going manner made it hard for me to see him as anything other than a nice man. I tried to move on. "Err ... the boys go back first, early hours of Monday, so this was the last real opportunity to get a drink with you." I tried to look nonchalant. "Anyway, when's Eleanor coming back?"

"I don't know yet. Sure she'll probably be back after you go home. Depends what Louise wants to do ... you know, you two and her job and all. Eleanor worries about her. You going to try and make a go of it?"

The waitress appeared with the drinks.

"Of course I'll try," I said.

Four JD's later Jasper made his move.

"Lads. I didn't think you'd still be here," he said in an exaggerated manner, attempting to feign surprise at seeing us. "I'm supposed to be meeting up with Carlos. You haven't seen him have you?"

Although Jasper's overacting seemed a little strange, at least we now knew that Carlos had gone off to do the deed with the steaks.

I did the introductions and ordered a drink for Jasper. Cecil wasted no time and immediately began to lead him.

"So where you been tonight then mate? Chatting the birds up again?"

"Uh ... oh yeah. I was ... actually, I met a nice one tonight. Spanish she was. Her name was ... erm ... Paloma." The fleeting look he threw in James's direction as he said the name was a bit too contrived but James seemed not to read anything into it.

"Oh yeah," Cecil said, taking up the theme, "nice. She live out here? What's she do."

"She said she worked at the hospital, over in Ibiza Town. Nice girl," Jasper replied. "Paramedic or something."

I studied James's face as Jasper spoke. There appeared to be no reaction to any of the exchanges. He casually pulled out a cigarette and lit it, blowing smoke high into the night air.

Cecil focussed on Jasper again.

"A paramedic. Good job. What d'you say her name was?"

"Paloma."

"Yeah, Paloma. You gonna keep in touch?"

"Uh ... well, you know... I'd like to," Jasper said, a confused look on his face, unsure about where he was supposed to go with the conversation. Cecil knew where it was going.

"What d'you think James? I reckon that the Spanish birds are more clued up than the tourists. I reckon they'd see right through a geezer like Jas with all his chat up lines."

James laughed. "That's true enough. He'll have to work hard with that one."

Cecil was straight on it. "Why, d'you know her then?"

"Not at all," James replied with a shake of his head. "Sure I've been here long enough to know a lot of the Spanish residents but I don't know any Palomas, I have to say. I meant, generally. The locals see you boys out here year after year and they know your style ... booze and women. The Spanish girls don't fall for all that guff."

Cecil's eyes narrowed. He realised there was nowhere else he could take that part of the conversation. He picked up his glass, drained the contents and elbowed Jas.

"Your round ain't it mate. Four more I reckon."

Jasper stood up to go to the bar. James told him not to worry as they did table service but he insisted on going to the bar himself. I knew then that he was about to spike James's drink.

"I'll come with you," I said, my anxiety level spiralling so much that I felt unable to sit at the table with James, knowing that Jasper could potentially poison him. It would also enable me to see that Jasper didn't get over enthusiastic with the drug.

Jasper ordered four Jack Daniels and Cokes. The barman placed the four drinks on the bar, each with a different coloured straw emerging between the ice cubes. When the barman had turned away, Jasper made his move. He pulled a small sachet from his pocket and tipped the white powdered contents straight into one of the glasses. He gave it a quick stir with the straw so that it dissolved instantly and then picked up two of the glasses. He indicated the other two with a nod of his head.

"Job done. Give that one to James, the one with the yellow straw."

"Why me?" I asked, my nervousness making me wonder whether I could even carry the drinks.

"Because you're sitting next to him and I've got these two now. Chill, it'll be cool," Jasper replied, and began to walk off back to our table.

I wasn't happy. It made no difference which one of us did it but I would have felt more comfortable had Jasper carried the spiked drink. I looked around and noticed three girls heading to the bar. They couldn't have seen anything. I checked right and left but the bar area was clear. I picked up the two remaining drinks and turned sharply, intent on getting back to the table and getting rid of the dodgy drink as quick as possible.

My turn was too sharp. My left arm caught one of the girls as I wheeled around, slopping Jack Daniels and Coke from one of the glasses all over her leg and foot. She squealed in surprise and jumped back.

"I'm so sorry." I said. "I was just ... here, let me get you a napkin."

I placed the two glasses on the bar and grabbed a handful of serviettes from a dispenser.

The girl took them from me and began to wipe the liquid from her leg.

"I'm really sorry. I wasn't looking. You okay? Your dress okay?"

She smiled. "It's fine. It's only my leg. Don't worry. I expect a lot more will get spilt before we finish tonight. What's your name?"

"It's Matth ... I mean ... Jason. Sorry, I have to go. I'm with ... with ... some people."

"Okay. Might see you later then, Jason," she said with a flirty wink.

I turned back to the bar to retrieve the drinks. They were there but now both glasses had yellow straws in them. I stood staring at them for a moment, incomprehension disabling any further movement. The barman saw my surprise.

"S'okay mate. I topped it up for you. Accidents happen eh?"

Topped it up. Great. But which one had I spilt? And then I found the ability to speak.

"Erm ... thanks ... but which one? I mean, which one had the ... was it, that I spilt?"

"Dunno now mate. Does it matter?"

My mind raced. The one with the yellow straw had been in my right hand so when I turned I had spilt the drink in my left. I tried to recall it. It was the one with the green straw. I had to have put them back on the bar in the same arrangement. So if the barman topped it up, he had to have taken the one on my left, his right, and then he would have put it back down again in the same place. But how could I be sure?

"No, but is the one you topped up on the left or the right," I asked. "My left, I mean."

"No idea mate. They're both JD's and coke yeah?"

"Yes, but which one had the green straw?"

"You superstitious or something? I told you. I was just doing you a favour. Customer service, you know. You spilt your drink. Bit of an accident so I topped it up. That's all."

"But why did you change the straw?"

"I just did. It's just a straw. You want a green straw. No problem." He pulled out the yellow straw from the glass on the left and replaced it with a green one. "Okay now?"

There was nothing else I could do. I didn't want a scene. I had to assume that the one on the right was the spiked drink. I picked up both glasses, returned to the table and placed the two drinks in the middle.

"You alright mate?" Jasper asked. "You look pale." He grabbed the glass with the yellow straw and stuck it in front of James. "Sorry about the delay James. Matt fannying about. Cheers."

James raised his glass, returned the greeting and took a sip.

I had no choice. I did the same.

36

I woke up in a darkened room. My eyes would not focus. I blinked several times and tried to sit up. My body seemed reluctant to cooperate. I was on a sofa. I laid back down. In the centre of the white ceiling above me, a large brass coloured fan whirred slowly, sending a cool stream of air downward across my prone body. I heard the sound of a door opening and then a voice that sounded remote but vaguely familiar.

"Morning young fella. Get this down you. It'll sharpen you up."

I struggled to turn my head. My eyes began to focus.

James.

He was walking towards me, a cup in one hand and a small glass in the other.

"So how are you feeling this morning Matt?"

"Groggy. Where am I?"

"You're in my place. You were a bit of a state last night. I was going to stick you in a taxi but Cecil said they'd probably not take you in that condition and his hotel wouldn't let anyone in if they couldn't stand up, so I took you back here."

I pulled myself into a sitting position and rubbed my head which throbbed as if it had been hit by a baseball bat.

"Couldn't stand up?"

"That's right. You were having trouble getting one foot in front of the other at one point. There's no way we could've left you on your own."

I felt too rough to be embarrassed. "Where's Cecil then?" I asked.

"He went back but he's coming out later to fetch you."

I took the cup from James, the potent aroma of coffee sending a wave of nausea through me. He saw my reaction and offered me the glass.

"Here, get this down you."

"What is it?"

"Underberg. It'll either kill you or cure you. I swear by it if I've hit the sauce a bit too hard. Go on, get it down you."

I took the glass, sniffed the contents and instantly recoiled.

"Don't be feckin smelling it. Jasus, man. Knock it back. You drunk enough poison last night so I don't know why you're turning your nose up at this."

"What's in it? It stinks."

"It's full of herbs and a drop of alcohol. I wouldn't be worrying about what's in it."

"Alcohol? I don't need any more alcohol."

"Matt, listen to me. Drink it up. It's not meant to be a shot. It's for medicinal, digestive purposes." He went over to the window and pulled open the shutters, sending a stream of sunlight across the room. "Go on now. Drink it and stop being a feckin wimp."

The word 'wimp' did it. I necked the contents of the glass, my face involuntarily screwing up in distaste at the intense bitterness. But it stayed down. I stretched out and placed the glass on small wooden side table that stood next to the sofa.

"You'll feel right as rain in five minutes. I wish I could get the dogs to take one each too."

I suddenly remembered something about the dogs and steaks but I wasn't sure what. And then my senses hit full alert.

"The dogs. What's happened? They're not dead are they?"

"Dead? Why would they be feckin dead?"

"Uh ... I meant ... err... deadly ... dangerous. Deadly dangerous, I mean, they look quite fierce don't they."

James's brow furrowed as he tried to make sense of what I was saying.

"Ah, they're both pussycats and behaving like it. When we got back last night Panzer was sound asleep on one of the sun loungers and Mofo was on the feckin blow up airbed in the middle of the pool sparko. God only knows what's going on with them two."

I sat bolt upright, a mishmash of memories flashing through my mind.

"Err … perhaps they've got the … uh, holiday spirit. Where are they now?"

"They're mooching about outside. They seem to be off their food too. I'm going to take them out for a long walk, see if I can sharpen the pair of them up a bit. They must have a bug or something."

"Yeah … a bug. Probably." I scratched my head, hoping that some clarity would be restored to my thought processes. "So what happened last night? Last thing I remember was having a few drinks in that bar, Savannah."

James sat down in an armchair opposite.

"To be honest with you Matt. I don't know. One minute you were right as rain then you seemed to lose the plot. We ended up down the West End … what a place that is. The girls down there got next to nothing on. They'd be arrested back in my day. Mind you, I wasn't objecting."

"But where did we go? I don't remember any of that?"

"We hit a few bars … Joe Spoons, Delilah's, Bar Amsterdam, Gallery Bar, Murphy's, Capone's … you name it. Cecil had them all on his list. That boy can drink. And then we ran into that wee Scottish fella, Carlos –"

"He's half South American," I said.

"Anyway, it seemed to me you were the only one that the booze hit that hard. You were gabbling on, some nonsense about throwing a party for me and stuff about jewellery. Lot of other shit too about shining lights. I don't know whether you were seeing them or trying to tell me about them, but you got more and more incoherent and to be honest I started to ignore it in the end. If I didn't know better, I'd say somebody loaded your drink with something. Once you started staggering I knew it was game over."

I reached for the coffee, the mention of loaded drink blasting through my skull until it settled on the previously blurred memory of the plan to drug James and search his villa. And then I recalled the yellow straws. Clearly things had not gone as planned.

"You feeling any better?" James asked.

Surprisingly I did. The Underberg had performed some sort of magic.

"Yeah, I am actually. I'm really sorry about last night James. It's been a long week. Maybe the late nights caught up with me."

"Think nothing of it young fella. It happens." James stood up. "You drink your coffee now. I better get these two dogs of mine out and about. You stay here and wait for Cecil. Help yourself to anything you need. There's water in the fridge if you want it. Have a swim too. It might liven you up. I'll be a few hours or so. If you're away before I get back, have a good trip home. Oh, and sort it out with Louise." He shook my hand and smiled. "Take it easy now."

With James gone I pulled out my mobile and sent a text to Cecil. He replied saying he was on his way. I finished the coffee and took a walk outside to the pool. The sun shimmered across its surface, the water sparkling like the polished facet of a cut diamond. My thoughts returned to the unfinished business of the night before and I decided I had to take advantage of the opportunity that James absence from the villa afforded me.

I went back inside and made my way to the hallway. I stopped by the office door and tried the handle. It turned easily. The door was unlocked. I eased it open and stepped inside. With the shutters closed the room was in semi-darkness. I decide to leave them closed and flicked the light switch. The office was exactly as I remembered it from my first visit. I crossed to the desk and tried the drawers. They were locked. On one side of the desk, next to the glass bowl of sweets, sat the small metal container with two sets of keys in it that I had seen before. The filing tray was still empty as it had been last time. James seemed to be surprisingly lax on security. Perhaps the fact that he had two large dogs made him confident that his premises would not be breached.

I sat in the leather chair and tried one set of keys in the desk. The drawer slid out. It was filled with office paraphernalia - a hole punch, pens, post-it-notes, a geometry set, a staple machine and a box of staples. I tried the drawer below. It was full of empty A4 wallets for filing. Another drawer had boxes of rewritable CDs. The final desk drawer contained a laptop. I pulled it out and switched it on but it required a password. There was no way I could get into it. I placed it back in the drawer and locked the desk. Next I picked up the other set of keys and went to the filing cabinets. A knock on the front door stopped me in my tracks. I left the office and went out to find Cecil standing outside. There was no greeting.

"Don't tell me geezer. I know what you've done. You've mixed up the fucking drinks ain't ya? Mate, you were in full wobbly man mode, talking bollocks. I had to slap you a couple of times to shut you up. I swear mate, I thought you was gonna tell James the whole mumble. What the fuck happened?"

"I don't know Ces. There was some mix up with the straws I think. Look, it doesn't matter now. We're in the villa. That's what we wanted. James is out for a couple of hours. We need to get the search done and get out."

Cecil followed me inside and we went into the office. I opened the two filing cabinets. One of them had nothing in it but boat records in all three drawers. Cecil pulled them out and scanned through them. There were papers for four boats, each of them with names linked to James's Irish roots – *Man of Quilty, Tromoro Lady, Ennis Seafarer and Lahinch*. The papers were nothing more than repair history, maintenance logs and receipts for work carried out, all in in one drawer. In another drawer the files contained schedules and routes for the tours. I took a close look, hoping to see something that might tie in with any information I had but there seemed to be nothing at all. The main routes were all the tourist spots – Cala Bassa beach, Cala Conta beach and Formentera island, the furthest destination. The rest were confined to the San Antonio Bay area for snorkelling and general leisure trips. The third drawer had several pages of fuel logs with receipts attached and dates noted in a column, none of which meant a lot to me. I took pictures of several of the pages for the sake of having the information.

The second filing cabinet was identical with three drawers too. One of them was empty and another full of records for crew payments and personnel documents. None of it revealed anything. Then I opened the bottom drawer to find it sub-divided into files, each of them labelled with the details of what it contained. I scanned through some of the labels to see if anything jumped out – ACCOUNTANT, BANK, CAR, INSURANCE, IT, LEGAL, LICENCES, MARKETING, MEDICAL, PROPERTY, TELEPHONE, VET.

"Doesn't seem to be much here, Ces," I said. "All looks normal."

"What was you expecting to find then geezer? A fucking file marked diamonds. You gotta look through them."

"I did. Nothing there."

"A proper look geezer, not just a flick through."

I pulled out each file one by one and began to examine the contents more closely. The bank file contained statements for six different accounts. James and Eleanor had one each, one joint one and three connected to the business. One of the business accounts had a seriously healthy balance.

"Check this," I said. "One of these business accounts has over a hundred and seventy-five thousand euros in it. That's not bad for a small tourist boat operation."

"What about the personal accounts?"

"I flicked through the documents. Looks fairly normal. A few thousand euros in each one."

Cecil scratched his chin.

"That's a lot of dough in that business account but if you was involved in an illegal diamond operation you might expect to see a lot more than that," he said. "Check the accountant file. He might have another account tucked away that his accountant siphons money into."

I looked through the file marked 'ACCOUNTANT' but there was

nothing there to suggest anything out of the ordinary. I decided to photograph the business account statement that showed the large balance. Next I pulled out the file marked 'CAR.' It contained a map of Ibiza and a map of the world. Nothing else.

"What's in that then, mate?"

"Not a lot," I said. "Just some maps. I suppose it's normal to have maps if you have a car but a bit odd that there's nothing directly to do with your car in a car file. You'd expect to see some records wouldn't you? Like service stuff or something. It's a pretty new car but even Range Rovers need a service."

I opened up both maps, checking to see if there were any markings on them, any places highlighted. The map of Ibiza had nothing on it. I unfolded the world map. Again nothing. I scrutinised the places that I had identified from the longitude and latitude list but there were no markings at those locations. I pulled out my mobile and photographed both maps.

"What you taking a picture for geezer, if there's nothing on it?" Cecil enquired.

"I don't know, Ces. Just so I can remember I suppose."

I put the file back and worked my way through the remainder. There was nothing that could be considered the slightest clue to James being involved in anything illegal. After an hour we had drawn a blank.

"We better get out of here Ces. There's nothing here mate."

Cecil did one more sweep around the office, including a check on the paper shredder, but found nothing of interest. He grabbed a sweet from the bowl on the desk and unwrapped it.

"You checked the other rooms?"

I hadn't. We spent another twenty minutes checking the rest of the villa but once again we found nothing that would suggest that James had any involvement with Felipe, Scalapino, Paloma or anything to do with diamonds.

I headed towards the kitchen. "I need a glass of water. I'm parched."

Cecil followed me to the kitchen. In the fridge I found the water that James had mentioned. I opened one of the cupboards to get a glass. Pinned on the inside of the door was a calendar. I stared at it for a moment noticing that several dates in June were ringed.

"You seen this, Ces?" I said, pointing to the calendar. "I wonder if it means anything."

He took a closer look.

"The seventeenth is ringed mate. That's the date on the list for San Antonio, weren't it?"

"Yeah, it was. Maybe that's it. That ties James in, doesn't it?"

"Ties him in to what? It ain't the only date ringed is it? There's other dates in June marked up too." He flipped the pages of the calendar. "Yeah, there's quite a few other ones marked over the other months. Take a couple of pictures and we can check to see if they match any of the dates we got. But it could just be an ordinary calendar. People do that don't they, mark dates on calendars. It could be coincidence that the seventeenth is ringed."

"What about after June? Anything marked up there?"

Cecil thumbed through the pages but there was nothing else marked.

"Maybe he just marks it up month by month when it gets to the month in question," I said.

I poured the water and drank down the whole glass in one go. I looked at the calendar again, disappointed that every single link I thought I had made seemed to have an answer. Once again I came to the conclusion that perhaps I was wrong about James.

"I don't get it. We found that typed up list in James's shredder which ties in nicely with the list of numbers we discovered in the cave, yet there isn't a single thing here to link him to diamonds. And, I'll tell you what. He seemed quite chilled about leaving me here in his place on my own and with you coming up today too. And he even brought me back here last night. Either he is super confident or he has it all locked down so tightly he knows we'd never find anything."

"Maybe mate. And, I'm thinking. You got Scalapino and his pond-life mates chasing you round the fucking island and if James is connected with them, there's no reason why he couldn't just set you up so they could find you. It would be fairly easy."

I stared at Cecil for a moment, absorbing what he had said.

"You mean like right now?"

37

We legged it out of the villa onto Carretera Cap Negret, the road that ran along the front of James's property. It was deserted. We started to walk in an easterly direction and after five minutes or so, reached a roundabout at a busy intersection where we were able to pick up a taxi. It dropped Cecil close to the Blau Parc and then took me on to Ibiza Town. Once back in the safety of my hotel I took a long shower and tried to weigh up what I had so far.

There was nothing new in James's villa that proved conclusive. We had overreacted to the possibility of Scalapino showing up there. He had been in a car accident along with Felipe so it was highly likely that both of them would have been detained in hospital overnight. Perhaps that meant they would be out of my hair until I was able to go home. I smiled at the irony of Felipe ending up in his own hospital. And then the thought of going home kicked in properly. I had a lot of loose ends for my trouble and no way of linking them to anything of substance. And now there was limited time to do anything.

I took out my mobile and looked at the pictures I had taken. The stuff in the cave – metal boxes with their padlocks; the paper with the list of numbers on it; the map of Ibiza, and the canvas bag. Then I had the pictures I had taken earlier in the villa – the boat routes, the fuel bills, the bank statement, more maps and the calendar we had found in the kitchen. I flicked back to the calendar pictures and stared at the dates. Then I remembered I had the original list with the names and dates on it, folded up with my latitude and longitude notes. I took the papers from the bedside drawer, unfolded the one with the dates on it and began to see if there was any common ground with the calendar pictures. Apart from 17th June, I found two others – 16th January and 10th April. James's calendar had numerous other entries but those three dates were the only ones common to the list dates.

I unfolded the latitude and longitude list. The April and June dates were relevant to 'Ann' or San Antonio but the January date fitted with Caroline. If Caroline was Paloma that could be a link. But how? I had no way of knowing if it was coincidence or something concrete. Unless ... unless there was something on Felipe's mobile that tied in too. I called Cecil.

"Ces. You need to take Felipe's mobile back home with you tomorrow. The minute you get there, you have to find someone who can get into it and get information from it. In particular, I need to know if there is anything listed for sixteenth of January."

"*Alright geezer. Will do. But what you found?*"

"Nothing much, but the calendar in James's kitchen and the list of places have a date in common that is key. Sixteenth of January. It could link to Paloma. It's the date next to Caroline."

"*Gotcha mate. No worries. Anyway, you coming back this way? It's our last day mate and we thought we'd have few liveners before we head out to the airport. Fucking two o'clock in the morning flight. That's a killer.*"

"Course I will. Oh and talking of flights Ces, I need you to book me one for Tuesday morning. I've got no credit cards have I? I need to be back Tuesday afternoon with this frigging passport so it's got to be a morning flight at the latest."

I read out my passport information to Cecil and he said he'd get it done. We arranged to meet at the tapas bar at four thirty and then move on to the Golden Buddha.

The four of us met up as arranged and cracked a few beers. I felt a brief sense of relief at the prospect of going home, mixed with the disappointment of not having something more solid to aide my case. I had decided that I would take what I had to Diana and hope that she could use some of it to connect in to what she already knew about Kurt Kovalevski.

The banter kicked into gear quite quickly about my lost night out the previous night. I had to endure it. There was no choice when you end up drugging yourself accidently. I tried to roll with it.

"I remember you mentioning Paloma," I said to Jasper. "And then at the bar, colliding with some girl and spilling one of the drinks. That's where it started to go wrong."

"But all the same geezer, you gotta be some sort of nobhead, ain't ya, to take yourself out of the game when you was supposed to be doing James. Mind you, it seems Carlos here did a good job on the dogs."

"Aye, well if you want something done properly boys, I'm your man."

"Anyway, thanks for all your efforts boys," I said. "If I can get some evidence tonight it'll be a result otherwise I just I hope that what I've got so far will be enough to help Louise."

"Let's hope so geezer, otherwise you gotta be loading up on the Duty Free perfumes and gifts if you're gonna straighten that one out," Cecil said with a grin.

"Not a bad idea," Jasper chipped in.

I turned to Jasper.

"What's not a bad idea Jas?"

"You know a little gift or something for Louise." He stretched out an arm. "Maybe you should get one of these bracelets for her. A little pressie goes down well with the ladies."

"What, instead of the diamond ring I had intended to give her, you mean? Oh yeah, that'll go a long way to fixing things. As far as Louise is concerned, I've been swanning around Ibiza with my mates all week and then I just pitch up and give her a cheap bit of crap. Yeah right. She'll be well impressed."

I shook my head trying to figure out what logic was running through Jasper's mind. He was used to sweet talking the girls but my situation required a lot more than sweet talk and a present. I needed a whole United Nations peace keeping force. I rolled my eyes at him and sipped my beer.

"Chill mate. It's a bit of fun," he said, reacting to my disdain. "Get her name engraved, shows a bit of thought. Check it out. We go past the bloke who's selling the stuff on the way back to the Buddha."

We finished up in the tapas bar, crossed the road and made our way along the palmed line pavement to the market stalls. The street was lively with early evening, pre-dinner sightseers, promenading between the stalls, soaking up the relaxed atmosphere before the crazy club crowd hit the scene.

We found the stall Jasper had mentioned and browsed the wares. In addition to bracelets, an array of cheap earrings, necklaces, leather wristbands and beads were on display. The vendor spotted Jasper's bracelet and figured another sale could be made. He held out an identical bracelet towards me.

"You like?" He said. "Only fifteen euro."

"Fifteen?" Jasper said. "I paid ten for mine."

"Okay. Ten," the vendor said.

I looked at the bracelet but shook my head.

"No problem, it's five for you my friend. Deal?"

"No thanks," I said and turned away.

Jasper grabbed my arm.

"At least check out your name mate. We've all done it."

The vendor heard what Jasper had said and wasn't going to let a potential sale slip away easily. He picked up a book that was positioned on a table behind the stall.

"What's your name my friend?"

"It's ... it's ... Matthew," I said, checking that nobody else had overheard me.

"Ah, Matthew. Good name. From the bible," the vendor said as he flicked through the pages of the book. He stopped at a particular page and then turned the book around towards me, indicating a line halfway down a list of alphabetical names. "Here. You look."

I leant forward to get a closer look. Next to the name Matthew, were the words, 'Gift from God.' I couldn't help but smile. I turned to the lads.

"There you go boys. Spot on eh?"

"Leave it out geezer," Cecil said. "It's all a con, ain't it."

"You want, my friend?" the vendor asked, holding out a bracelet towards me.

The positive result amused me. I decided to ask him about another name.

"Have you got the name Louise in your book, please?"

Again the vendor checked the book. He found Louise and pointed it out exactly as he had done with Matthew. '*Renowned Warrior*,' was the meaning next to the name.

"See, mate. Bit of fun. Told you didn't I? Why don't you get one each for the two of you? Only ten euros. You're getting a better deal than I did," Jasper said.

I nodded to the vendor and he set about engraving two bracelets. As he carried out his work, the boys engaged in a bit of banter about what the names of a variety of people they knew might turn out to be.

"I wonder what that Scalapino's name means," Carlos said,

Cecil laughed and held both hands out as if the answer was obvious.

"That's an easy one geezer. Bald twat, probably."

"Or Felipe," Jasper said.

"Let's ask the bloke then," I said.

The vendor responded to my question but didn't refer to his book this time, probably because it was a Spanish name. Felipe meant someone who loves horses.

"Check out Paloma too," Carlos said.

Again the vendor seemed to know the meaning of the name without reference to his book.

"Paloma mean dove," he said. He smiled and handed over the two bracelets that he had engraved for me.

"What about Caroline? What's its meaning," I asked.

A quick browse through his book and the vendor came back with, '*Song of happiness.*'

"C'mon boys. Let's get going. Enough of this shit. We got a few beers with our names on them waiting for us in the Buddha," Cecil said impatiently and began to walk off.

Jasper patted me on the back as we started to follow Cecil.

"There you go mate. A couple of his and hers bracelets. All helps oil the wheels."

I had to chuckle at Jasper's optimism. It would take more than a couple of cheap bracelets to repair the bond with Louise.

"I suppose so Jas, but things aren't that simple right now with Louise. And on top of that she's had her mum with her for a few days and she isn't exactly my biggest fan."

Jasper stopped in his tracks. I turned round to see what he was doing.

"Maybe you should get one for her mum too. Keep her sweet."

"You *are* joking Jas? The handbag I bought her cost two hundred and fifty quid and that didn't seem to thaw her out that much. She's got expensive taste. A five euro bracelet isn't going to do anything other than confirm her opinion that I'm the wrong bloke for her daughter."

"You bought her a handbag?"

"Yeah ... it's a long story. I set fire to her last one and ... listen, never mind. Let's just go and get a few beers like Ces said. It's your last day."

"Set fire to it? That's funny mate," Jasper said, a broad grin cracking his face.

"Well, let's just say she didn't see the funny side of it at the time. Anyway, c'mon. Let's go."

Jasper ignored me and turned back towards the vendor's stall, calling out over his shoulder as he did so.

"It's Eleanor, isn't it?"

I walked towards him, resigned to the fact that he wasn't letting the bracelet thing go.

"Yeah, it is."

I heard Cecil shout, "Oi, you two nobheads coming? Me and Carlos here are dying of thirst."

I waved a hand indicating that they should carry on and we would catch them up. Jasper was speaking to the vendor.

"Check out Eleanor, por favour."

The vendor frowned. "Helen?"

312

"No, Eleanor. Begins with an E."

The vendor nodded and picked up his book. He flicked through a few of the pages and then turned the book towards us pointing to a line midway down the page.

"Si?"

I focussed on his finger and found the name Eleanor. In an instant my day was shattered by total shock and disbelief. Next to the name were two words.

'Shining Light.'

38

I was alone in Ibiza. The boys were on their way home. Each of them knew what Jasper and I had uncovered, but all were sworn to secrecy. The shock of what my discovery might mean had begun to sink in. I lay on my bed, my mind a flood of mixed emotions. If Eleanor was the mysterious '*Luz que brilla,*' the light that shines that the Spanish sentence referred to, the implications were horrendous. Louise's mother mixed up in a criminal organisation. And I would be the one to reveal it. It would surely kill off any hope of reconciliation with Louise. But if I didn't reveal what I knew, I was back to square one.

Cecil had given me my ticket and fifty euros to get me through my final day. He had promised to find out what he could from Felipe's mobile. With any luck I could make the connections between each of the players, once he had been able to access its data.

But now I couldn't sleep. I rolled off the bed and opened the cabinet drawer. I pulled out the papers and spread them on the bed. I felt the need to go through the information I had been able to find up to that point. I ran through what I knew so far and tried to put it into some sort of coherent context.

Diamonds were being smuggled from Africa and ending up in the UK. The raid on the warehouses that Diana had told me about had pointed to that. Kurt Kovalevski was a suspect. San Antonio was being used as a pick up point. It had to be because of the storage caves although perhaps there were storage caves in other places. I stared at the list of ports that I had compiled from the girls' names and the latitude and longitude details. They were all based around the Mediterranean – Valencia, Puerto Pollenca, Sousse and Alghero with San Antonio fairly central to them all. And then there was Cape Town and Johannesburg.

I tried to take a step back and look at it logically. The operation started in Africa somewhere. I remembered that Diana had told me that but I couldn't recall where. Smuggling diamonds held a lot of risk so perhaps a number of routes were required in order to minimise suspicion and evade capture. They had to travel as part of bigger consignments of legitimate goods. Perhaps Johannesburg was a drop off point for cargo that was then moved on elsewhere. I pulled up the picture of the world map and zoomed in on the map of Africa. But the detail blurred to unreadable the more I zoomed in. I decided to load Google maps for a better view.

Cape Town was on the south-west coast of South Africa, a thriving port and an ideal shipping location, although a long way round to the Mediterranean. Maybe the cargo route was to Johannesburg and then on to Cape Town. From there, ships heading up the west coast of Africa to the Mediterranean could be used to carry the illicit diamonds to whatever ports they were going to. I scrolled up through the map, past the numerous countries that made up the great continent of Africa – Angola, Congo, Cameroon, Nigeria, Algeria and came to Sousse on Tunisia's Mediterranean coast. It would make more sense to take cargo by road to that location rather than sail around the coastline of most of Western and North Africa. But that depended where it started out. It could be a route chosen to avoid detection.

I stood up and paced across the room to the balcony. I threw open the shutter and stared at the street below. It was almost four in the morning but there was still activity on the streets. A young couple holding hands and giggling as they made their way back from a night out; an elderly man walking his dog; a four-wheel drive car trying to squeeze into a small parking space on the far side of the road. I watched for a moment, mildly amused at the many manoeuvres the driver had to make to get into the space, but without success. And for some reason I thought of James's car and wondered again why there had been limited information in the car folder in his filing cabinet. And in that moment, something struck me.

I raced back to the bed and scrolled back down through Google maps. There it was, right next to Cameroon – the Central African Republic. CAR. The very place Diana had mentioned as the source of conflict diamonds. I had scrolled right past it but it must have registered. The one place name on the list I had been unable to identify. The place name that matched Caroline, 16th January.

I sat on the bed and thought things through again. So Paloma wasn't Caroline. Paloma could well be oblivious to the whole of Felipe's extra-curricular activities, just as Cecil had originally thought.

I tried to get back into logical mode. Diamonds were being smuggled out of the Central African Republic and either being driven south down to Johannesburg for transport on to Cape Town and then shipment round to the Med, or driven north to Tunisia and ending up in Sousse for eventual movement on to the UK. San Antonio was the hub for storing the illegal diamonds until the time was right to move them on across Europe. Or something like that. I could not be sure. If I was right and San Antonio was a holding location, that was where Eleanor came in. And maybe James was totally innocent. His demeanour and relaxed manner with me seemed to suggest that.

I had several pieces of a jigsaw now but I still felt that it needed something to pull it together. If Eleanor was the '*shining light*' then James's boats had to be involved. But they were simply pleasure boats. They probably didn't have the range to go to the ports I had identified. Valencia alone was a four and a half hour sea crossing one way. The only possible explanation that worked was that his boats were being used to meet up with other vessels at key rendezvous points within easy range of Ibiza, to offload the illegal cargo and take it to a storage area that was inaccessible to bigger boats. Once the main cargo ships had docked at the ports and had been unloaded, or the road transport had arrived in Tunisia, the diamonds were loaded onto smaller boats that rendezvoused with James's craft. And all organised by Eleanor. That had to be it, but I needed to prove it.

And the proof was likely to be in the early hours of Tuesday morning, the next rendezvous date.

39

The following day, Monday, I got up early and headed straight to the Chill Café on via Punica. I sent an email to Diana telling her that I needed to see her on Tuesday afternoon and that I had some important information. I then spent an hour looking around for somewhere I could buy a pair of binoculars. I found a cheap pair in a shop on the Avenue Isidor Macabich, ten minutes away from my hotel. I returned to the hotel and decided to call Louise. She answered after three rings.

"Louise. It's me. I know you said not to call but I wanted to speak with you."

"*Hello Matthew. You still living it up in Ibiza then?*"

"Yes … I mean no, I'm not living it up. I'm still here but … how are you?"

"*You rang to see how I was? Is that it? My job is on the line and in a few days I will lose it and you rang to see how I am? How do you think I am Matthew?*"

"I'm sure you are not too –"

"*Dead right I'm not too good but I'm glad you are having a fab time in Ibiza.*"

"I'm not having a fab time … I just wanted to … is your mum still with you? James said she went to see you."

"*Yes, she is. And she tells me that you're coming home tomorrow. Well, if that's right make sure you keep well away from here. You understand?*"

I sensed that there was no point in continuing the discussion. I had no idea why I had rung other than that I had entertained the fleeting idea of trying to break the news to her about her mum. But there was no good way to do that. Louise's attitude to me seemed to have hardened. I could only assume Eleanor had succeeded in turning her against me.

"I understand. I'm sorry," I said and ended the call.

Next, I telephoned the Can Misses hospital and asked for Doctor Felipe Barrientos.

"*I am sorry but he is off sick right now,*" the operator said after trying his extension.

That was good news but I needed to know how sick. It was my last full day in Ibiza and I wanted to know if I should be on the lookout for him or Scalapino. James must have told Eleanor that I was going back home and if Eleanor knew, then Felipe would know too. I called the hospital again, this time asking for patient information. I immediately met with a barrier.

"*We cannot give you patient information on the telephone, Señor,*" I was told.

"But I'm a friend from England and I was due to come and see Doctor Barrientos ... Felipe ... and now somebody told me he was in an accident. All I want to do is find out if he's okay. He's not answering his telephone. I'm not asking anything personal. I'm just worried."

The receptionist must have felt sorry for me. She asked me to hold on and then came back to me a minute later.

"*Doctor Barrientos was discharged this morning. That is all I can tell you Señor.*"

I ended the call. That was bad news. If Felipe was out, he would be looking for me and if he knew I was going back home he would intensify the search. I needed to lay low for the day.

I took a bus to San Antonio and located Jasper's hire car exactly where he said he had left it. Then I drove out of town and headed for Cala Bassa beach, a twenty minute drive around the bay. I parked up and took the slatted timber walkway that ran through the tangle of gnarled and twisted juniper trees at the back of the beach. To one side, several roped off areas containing rows of luxurious sun loungers and canopied bars and restaurants, were strategically positioned in the shade.

After a short stroll, I found a set of stone steps that led onto the beach. I kicked off my deck shoes and stepped onto the sand. It felt good, the grains slipping gently away from beneath my feet as I picked my way between the umbrellas and sun loungers. It created a sense of carefree freedom, something I had not known for a while. I decided to enjoy it. Half a day of anonymity in the sun. The whoosh of the rolling water reinforced that feeling, the waves depositing their foamy contents onto the sand, sucking up the glistening grains and dragging them into the depths of the ocean. Across the bay the distant outline of San Antonio lay splashed, like a streak of white paint, across the green backdrop of the surrounding hills.

I stripped off my shirt and picked my way between rows of sunbathers, heading towards a rocky outcrop on the far side of the bay. To my right, a bar throbbed with the boom of heavy bass music kicking out of large black speakers, the smiling clientele enjoying cold drinks and a party atmosphere away from the intense gaze of the sun. Further along, on the approach to the bar, a sand sculptor was busy putting the finishing touches to some extravagant creation. I crossed the sand and took a small detour to admire his work, the magnificent, highly detailed design of a galloping horse in full flight. The artist, a sun hat pulled down tightly on his head, was so engrossed with the complex flourishes of the tail, that he didn't bother to look up. I searched in my pocket for a coin, dropped two euros into a box that he had placed on a table nearby and carried on towards the seafront.

I was stopped in my tracks by a shout.

"JJ. JJ. Hello."

I heard the calls but didn't react at first. The second call made me react.

"JJ. Matt."

Who was calling me Matt?

I turned to see a hand waving enthusiastically in the air and a beaming smile directed right at me.

Estrid. In nothing more than white bikini bottoms, her hair bunched on top of her head. So much for an afternoon of anonymity. But the possibility of an afternoon spent in the company of an attractive, topless blonde certainly had appeal. It was the kind of thing Cecil meant when he said, '*keep the dream alive.*' And he was right. The following day I would be back in London having to face the harsh realities of criminal charges. I crossed the sand towards her.

"Hi Estrid. What are you doing here?"

"I was going to ask you that. I'm just enjoying the sun."

"Oh, yeah ... me too. It's my last day so I'm making the most of it."

"Your last day? That's a shame. You going home?"

"Yes. Got a morning flight tomorrow. All good things come to an end."

Estrid frowned. "So what about the party?"

"The party?"

"Yes, for James."

I hesitated, unsure as to whether I should be truthful or not. She seemed like a really nice, straightforward girl. Almost an innocent abroad. I felt guilty but on the other hand I didn't want her to think badly of me for lying. I fudged it.

"Well it's ... uh, still being organised. A few things to sort out yet. The way things are going it could be next year before he gets a birthday party. And he does have another birthday then too." I laughed, hoping that my excuse would do for now. "Anyway, where's your friend today?"

"Alida? She's got stuff to do. She's out tonight and had some things to get ready." She indicated an adjacent sunbed. "Hey, sit down. Relax. Enjoy your last day."

I pulled the sun lounger across the sand and sat on one side of it so that I was facing her. We talked for a bit. I broached the subject of Scalapino but she said she hadn't seen him and that he hadn't been working the night before. I hoped that meant that he was in some way incapacitated from the car accident and that he wouldn't be bothering me again. The thought of freedom from

Scalapino's endless pursuit gave me a boost. I leant back on the sun lounger savouring the warmth of the sun that was now blazing down from a cloudless sky. It didn't take long for its intensity to make me restless.

"I'm going for a swim Estrid. I need to cool off. Coming in?"

"I've been in twice already," she replied. "I'm going to sunbathe a while longer." She pointed to a blue blow up sunbed. "Why don't you take the inflatable with you and chill for a while."

I spent the best part of an hour floating aimlessly along on the gently moving tide, the sun still blisteringly hot, but able to roll off the inflatable for a cooling swim when it got too much. All around me holiday makers were enjoying the afternoon, splashing in the surf, playing ball games and generally just loving their brief escape from the confines of their everyday routine. As I lay on the inflatable gazing at the huge expanse of clear blue sky above, rocked gently by the undulating current, I felt totally alone. Alone in my own small space on the ocean. No one could touch me out here. I was a tiny blob on the surface, insignificant. No one knew where I was. I had a moment's freedom from everything that had engulfed me over the past few weeks. But I knew it couldn't last.

I paddled back towards the beach and made my way over to Estrid who was sitting on the edge of her sun lounger applying sunscreen to her arms.

"How was that then?" she asked.

"Bit cold at first, but great once you are in."

She giggled. "Everybody says that." She handed me the bottle of sunscreen. "Can you do my back, please?"

"Err ... sure."

I sat down on the sun lounger, squirted a dollop of the cream into my hand and began to apply it to Estrid's tanned back.

"Mmm, that's nice," she said, her head bent forward so I had access to her neck. "Don't forget the sides."

I squeezed the sunscreen bottle and deposited another splurge of the white liquid into my hand. I applied it along the small of Estrid's back just above her bikini bottoms, then eased my hand up and along her side until I reached the soft flesh just below her shoulder. I did the same on her other side, smoothing the slippery liquid in with slow, gentle strokes. I swallowed hard, my mouth dry.

My thoughts flashed back to my earlier conversation with Louise. '*You still living it up in Ibiza then?*' she'd said. I smoothed my hand down along Estrid's right side in one long slow stroke. A tiny murmur of pleasure escaped from her lips. I suddenly felt guilty. But why? I wasn't doing anything wrong. I was just putting sunscreen onto somebody. But would Louise see it like that if she were here? To her it would look like I was stroking a very fit looking, young, tanned, Scandinavian blonde. That *would* look like living it up in Ibiza. But why was I worried about Louise if I wasn't doing anything wrong? And Louise had effectively dumped me. I had to admit to myself I fancied Estrid and the intimate situation I found myself in with her had suddenly focused me on that. And because of that realisation, the guilt had kicked in. I was trying to rescue my relationship but here I was, secretly enjoying hands-on contact with another girl that I fancied. And there was no escaping the fact that I was enjoying it.

Lost in thought my hand inadvertently brushed the curve of Estrid's breast. She raised her head and glanced over her shoulder.

"That's nice JJ. Really nice. You have good hands."

Encouraged by her reaction, I let my hand slip gently forward, moving it onto her breast, my oil covered palm sliding over her firm nipple. She leant back towards me, her head thrown back so that it rested against mine. My mind raced with conflicting thoughts again. Yes, I was enjoying it. But what was I doing? This was not what I came to Ibiza for. I tried to move my hand away but Estrid clasped her own over it.

"It's okay."

I allowed my hand to linger for a moment. And then I pulled away.

"I'm sorry. I ... err ... I'm ... shall we ... shall we get a drink?" I said, the tension of the moment getting to me.

Estrid smiled, her eyes playful, soaking up my unease.

"Okay. If you want. Are you getting a little hot?"

I took a deep breath and focussed on resealing the cap on the sunscreen bottle.

"Uh ... I'm ... I'm a bit thirsty. It is hot," I said, as I handed the bottle to Estrid.

She stood up and turned to face me. In the circumstances a full on view of her body that close up was not helpful. She pulled the clasp from her hair and shook it out in a blonde, cascading wave. Her smile told me she knew the effect she was having.

I focussed my thoughts on the drinks.

"What would you like? Err ... to drink, I mean?"

"I'll come with you," she replied and reached out for her beach bag. "But first, let me take your picture. If you are going home I would like to have it." She opened the bag and took out a camera. "Ok, smile."

She fired off three consecutive shots and then stared at the back of the camera.

"Great. They're cool. Take a look."

I took the camera and stared at the screen.

"Yeah, very good. Nice camera. Let me take some of you. Maybe you could email them to me."

She nodded and flashed a show-stopping smile that I took as my cue to hit the camera button. I checked my handiwork and was pleased with the results. Estrid was model material. I showed them to her.

"Nice. You take a good picture." She placed the bag over her shoulder. "Let's go get that drink then."

Boosted by Estrid's positive comment about my photography skills, I followed, firing off shots with the camera. I ran alongside her and shot some more angles. As my enthusiasm grew, I raced ahead of her and, feigning professional expertise, I walked backwards, shooting several more action frames as she strolled towards me. She played to the camera, encouraging me.

Carried away in the moment and mesmerised by Estrid's playful poses, I didn't see it. I felt it. The cold, clammy grip on my ankles as I stumbled backwards. My fall was cushioned by the mounds of rounded dune-like sand that formed the magnificent sculpture of the galloping horse. My backside crushed the ornate tail and bulbous rear end of the charging beast that had been patiently moulded into a work of art by the beach sculptor. As I landed, I heard the yell of an alarmed adult and the simultaneous scream of a child, completely taken aback by my unexpected intervention. In surprise, and embarrassment at my ungainly tumble in front of Estrid, I leapt up, my right foot coming down right in the middle of the sculpture. I swivelled round, at first unaware that the mounds of sand were in fact a sculpture. It was only when I spotted the reddening face of the artist himself that I realised what had happened. He flung off his sun hat and started to rush towards me. And then he stopped, a look of recognition on his face. At almost exactly the same time as he halted, I recognised him too. Ben. Ben, the do-gooder first aider that I had run into in Fatso's. Ben, who had tried to diagnose my pretend illness.

"You," he said. "The druggie."

"Druggie?" I said, kicking off a clump of wet, soggy sand that had clung to my right foot. Unfortunately, the flight of the clump of sand was interrupted by the ice cream cornet of a little girl standing next to a tall, bespectacled, pale faced man who seemed to have a black eye. She screamed, a scream exactly like the one I had just heard.

I stood aghast for a moment. A tear had appeared in the corner of the little girl's eye and her face began to crumple as she stared at her sand speckled ice cream. Estrid saw the tear as well and immediately went to comfort her. The man next to her just stared at me, open mouthed. And then I recognised him too. Darren, the bean counter accountant. The man that had mistaken me for a children's entertainer and whom I had used as a decoy when I was trying to elude Scalapino. It crossed my mind that his black eye could be the response he received from Scalapino, after I had sent him to ask about children's shows. He hadn't recognised me without the cat face makeup. Just as well, as Ben seemed intent on making the most of the fact he had met me before.

"Yes, you're the guy who was on ketamine. They took you to hospital."

"No, I wasn't. Look, I'm sorry about the –"

"Yes, you were. I'm Ben. I remember you. You're out of control ... all those drugs."

I glanced at Estrid who had managed to calm the little girl and was now taking an interest in my conversation with Ben.

"Hang on. Yes, I did go to hospital but that was for ... for ... a ... something else ... a ... an allergy. Yes, an allergy. I don't use drugs and I don't even know what ketamine's for," I said, trying to forget my experience at James's villa.

Ben was his helpful self.

"Yes, you do. The paramedic told you. It's an animal tranquilliser."

I glanced at the Ben's obliterated horse sculpture and tried to ignore the fact that this particular animal had been well and truly tranquillised.

"Look, gentlemen," I said, "this is not getting us anywhere. This was an accident. I'm really sorry that I stood all over your sculpture Ben, but I'm sure you can rebuild it." I looked at Darren. "And I'm really sorry that I ruined your daughter's ice cream." I took some money from my wallet. "Here's twenty euros for the sculpture Ben, for any money you've lost. And, Darren, take this five euros and get your little girl another ice cream."

Darren's open-mouthed gawping expression turned to puzzlement.

"How do you know my name?"

I realised my error.

"I'm ... err ... I'm ...because ..."

"He's psychic," Estrid said. "We're from Denmark and we deal with the paranormal. We see things, strange things. Can read minds."

"Uh ... yes, that's right," I said. I placed my fingers on either side of my head and bowed slightly. "Yes, I can see something. You work with ... with money. An accountant perhaps? Yes, in a big building ... England. But wait. I'm getting something. You don't like it. No, you feel trapped." I looked up. Darren had his mouth open again, a glazed look in his eyes. I carried on, suddenly enjoying the fact that I had turned the situation around. "And ... there's a ... a woman. A woman in your office ... a secretary maybe. You would like to –"

"Erm, you know, I think I had better go," Darren said. He grabbed the little girl's hand. "My daughter's tired. I'll get her another ice cream like you say. Thank you." He reached out and took the five euros.

I threw the twenty euros into Ben's hat, turned, and walked towards the bar. Estrid followed and we found a table close to the bar. I ordered two bottles of cold beer. She opened her beach bag, took out her bikini top and a floaty, white sarong and put them on.

"Hey, thanks for that Estrid. You know, the paranormal thing."

"It's no problem. I could see you were uncomfortable. But how did you know these things about that man?" she asked.

I smiled.

"Just a guess. He had glasses, he was very pale and so I just guessed he could be an accountant." I didn't want to tell her that I had met him before. It seemed too complicated. It was easier to dismiss it.

"But you got his name right too?"

"Another guess. I was going to go through the alphabet but somehow got fixed on 'D' and just got lucky. Maybe I am psychic," I laughed, hoping that what I had said was plausible.

"And the woman in his office?"

"Yet another guess. He doesn't get out of the office much. You saw how pale he was. So I figured he was bored and anyone who's bored in an office fantasises about their colleagues."

Estrid laughed. "You *are* funny JJ. I like you. You make me laugh."

"That's nice. Thank you." I clinked my beer bottle against hers. "Cheers."

She leant forward, her hand on my upper thigh and kissed me on the cheek.

"Why don't we go back to my place? I'm not working until nine o'clock and it is your last night."

I was tempted. So very tempted. My week had been nothing

but turmoil and stress. But I couldn't forget the reason I was back out in Ibiza. The reason for all that turmoil and stress. The woman I loved was in serious difficulties through no fault of her own. I couldn't let her down ... in any way.

"I can't Estrid. Not this time. I have something important I have to do tonight. I know you won't understand right now but it really is very important. We *will* keep in touch though, please."

She gave me her mobile number and scribbled out her email address on a napkin. I put it in my pocket - and questioned my decision making.

40

I packed my things for my return home and placed the bag in the boot of the car. I tried to get some sleep knowing that it could be a long night ahead. But it was impossible. My mind was too active, my body filled with nervous energy and apprehension. I took a walk around the streets, hoping the activity would get rid of my restlessness but to no avail. After half an hour of wandering around I found myself down by the port. Across the street a crowd of people were milling around a busy bar area. I walked over and was encouraged to take a seat at the Zoo Bar by eager marketing staff offering two for one drinks and a shot. I settled for a beer. The crowd was lively but I couldn't get into the atmosphere. I was too anxious about what the night might have in store. I left after the first beer, walked further down the pedestrianised avenue and found another bar, the Tango Bar. Again I was offered a similar two for one deal. This time I took both beers but declined the shot. I needed to keep focussed.

I finished the first beer and finally accepted that I was not in the right frame of mind for socialising. There was nothing that could distract me. I returned to my room, aware that the only thing that could relieve my troubled state of mind was to face up to what I had to do and get it underway.

With the flight scheduled for a 10.30 departure the following morning, I decided to settle my hotel bill so that I could make a fast exit after breakfast. It was another debt I owed Cecil. Once I had done that, I made my way out to the car, fired up the engine and headed across to the west side of the island.

I reached the point where the path led to the caves at around 11.00p.m. I drove on past until I found a secluded spot in the trees about one hundred metres further along the main road. Satisfied that the car was well concealed, I rummaged about in the boot and found the tool bag that Jasper had bought to store the tools for our cave break-in. I pulled out the torch, grabbed the binoculars, closed the boot and walked the short distance back to the cliff path, my nerves tingling with anxiety at every step. When I reached the top, I paused by the handrail and scanned the area. The night was still, a warm, gentle breeze flicking the tops of the foliage that lined the cliff face. A full moon meant that there was no need for the torch after all. I made my way down along the path until I had reached halfway. At that point, I ducked under the wooden rail and tentatively picked my way through the scrub until I found the place where I had hidden from Scalapino before. I dug myself in between two large clumps of bushes and waited. From my vantage point, I had a perfect view of the cave doors and the bay below. And then I noticed that the one I had broken through had been repaired, a sure sign that it would be needed.

It was 2.15a.m. before I heard the first sign of activity, a car engine humming in the distance and then silence. Almost three hour hours curled up in the same position had left me stiff and I was feeling the onset of cramp. I stretched out my legs in an attempt to get my circulation moving. Then I moved into a kneeling position and peered through the shrubbery. At first I could see nothing and then I spotted four silhouettes moving steadily along the path, their shadowy images picked out against the lighter rock face behind. I pulled out the binoculars and raised them to my eyes, attempting to train the focus on the moving figures. The lens panned across the landscape, a blur of shadows and dark hues. A black shape flashed across my view and then was lost as I scanned hurriedly along the path. I panned back, adjusting the focus and picked out the four moving shapes, this time steadying the binoculars so that I managed to settle on them. They were moving in single file, three men in a line, two of whom I recognised from my last encounter at the caves, and a smaller figure bringing up the rear. All of them dressed in black. But there was no sign of Scalapino. Perhaps his injuries in the car chase had incapacitated him.

I lowered the binoculars and looked out across the ocean to check for activity. There was nothing to see except the ghostly shimmer of bright moonlight rolling across its rippled surface. Again I trained the binoculars on the moving figures, this time focussing on them individually. The lead two were definitely familiar but the other male figure was not. I concentrated on the smaller figure at the back. The outline of the smaller frame appeared to be that of a woman, the tighter clothing accentuating her shape. She had a black baseball cap pulled down so that the peak hid most of the top of her face but a blond tuft of hair protruding from the back made me take notice. I focussed on the lower half of her face. In a nano-second, my brain compiled the bits of information and created a picture.

Alida.

I almost dropped the binoculars in shock. I had spent the afternoon with her friend, Estrid, on the beach. I had asked about Alida. Estrid's reply flashed into my mind ... 'She's out tonight and had some things to get ready ...' and in that moment I realised Alida was involved. Involved in Felipe's operation. My mind raced through the connections. Scalapino knew Alida. Alida knew James and James was with Eleanor. So James could not be ruled out.

I was soon to have proof that even if I couldn't be sure if James was involved, his boats were.

The low hum of an engine from behind me caused me to turn and stare across the bay. From the western side of the tree lined cliff face, a familiar shaped boat cruised slowly into view. I watched as it steered a course into the bay and then stopped some one hundred metres out from the shoreline. I focussed the binoculars and scanned along the hull until I was able to pick out the name.

'Tromoro Lady.' One of James's vessels.

Ahead and below my line of sight, I saw the doors of the cave on the far side being opened. One of the figures shone a beam of light onto the door and I watched the chain drop away as the padlock was released. A single flash of torchlight was then directed back towards the boat.

With the doors open, beams of torchlight were played across the interior. Then the four figures disappeared from view into the rear of the cave. After a few moments they emerged again carrying the metal boxes that Cecil and I had discovered on our visit. Each box was placed in a line to one side of the cave entrance. At the same time, a yellow inflatable was lowered into the water from the boat. Similar shaped metal boxes were then transferred from the boat to the dinghy between crew members. Once they had finished, two crew jumped into the dinghy and rowed towards the shore. When they reached the concrete slipway, they dragged the dinghy free of the water and began to unload the boxes. At the same time, the empty boxes were brought down to the dingy from the cave by the four members of Felipe's gang.

I had to get a picture but I needed to move closer.

Slowly, staying close to the ground, I shuffled through the scrub nearer to the beach area. The land fell away gradually across the horizontal line of the rockface, but I was careful to take my time so that I didn't lose my footing.

I managed to get within fifty or sixty metres of the caves before I decided that I was close enough. I could see clearly into the opening and I was still more than twenty metres above the beach. I crouched down low amongst the shrubs and peered through the binoculars again. The two guys I had recognised were the same ones who had been with Scalapino at Fatso's Cafe. The third one was the driver of the Mercedes that had pursued Cecil and me from San Rafael two days earlier. Close up it was apparent that three of the fingers on his right hand were strapped together, a small splint between them. I hoped that Scalapino's injuries were more severe. The girl was definitely Alida.

I reached into a pocket for my mobile so that I could capture the activity on camera. As I pulled it out, the car keys came with it and dropped to the ground.

"Bollocks," I said under my breath as I palmed the ground to retrieve them.

They should have been somewhere next to me but it was sod's law they had hit a rock and bounced. I scrabbled around in the gravel but I couldn't find them. I thought about using the torch but I realised I could not risk revealing my position.

There was another burst of activity below me as Felipe's team started to take the metal boxes from the slipway into the cave, one of them shining a torch beam into the opening, presumably so they could stack their booty.

I had to capture that as evidence. I raised the phone above the shrubbery and positioned it landscape style. I checked the display and waited until I had several of the figures carrying boxes towards the cave doors in the frame. With the perfect shot on the screen, I clicked the camera button. Instantly, in a series of clicks, a flash illuminated the scene like the sudden ignition of a firework.

"Oh fuck."

The curse flew from my lips as the shock of what I had done caused an involuntary muscle spasm to trigger my finger again on the button. Yet another flash split the darkness revealing my presence to whoever cared to look.

I dropped to my knees to try and conceal my presence but it was too late. The cries and shouts from the beach told me I had been spotted. I cursed again, ruing the fact that I had left the camera flash in the on position after the picture in Savannah. But there was no time for regret. I had to get away - and quickly.

I scrabbled around in the dirt once more, looking for the car keys. Nothing. They had to be there but I ran the risk of not being able to find them at all if I wandered too far in my search. I needed the torch. It didn't matter about lights anymore. The shouts were getting closer. I flicked the torch switch and frantically scoured the ground. The beam picked up the silvery glint of metal. I pounced on it immediately, grabbed the keys and began to scramble up the rock strewn bank. I got to the path roughly twenty metres ahead of my pursuers, two of the dark clothed guys who had been with Alida. I ducked under the wooden rail and ran at full pelt along the concrete, bounding up the stepped sections in frantic, lung bursting leaps. At the curve, just a short distance from the top, I spotted a boulder in amongst the shrubs. It was about the size of a football and I knew if I could get it onto the path, it could be an ankle breaker for anyone hurrying around the curve in the dark. I grabbed it with both hands and rolled it onto the gravel. It cost me vital seconds. I could hear the pounding of fast approaching footsteps closing on me. In a final sinew tearing burst, I raced up the last steep section to the top of the path. As I made it on to the flat just before the road, a piercing yelp of pain cut through the night. I didn't stop to find out what had happened. I kept on running, hoping that my impromptu trap had done the job.

I legged it across the scrub. To my left I spotted the dark outline of a four by four vehicle tucked away in the trees a few metres from the road. It had to be the transport the gang had arrived in. For all I knew there could be a driver waiting for his accomplices. I kept running, full tilt. I reached the car, my chest heaving with the exertion, my body gasping for air. I flung open the door and dived into the driving seat. Drops of sweat dripped onto my arm as I fumbled with the ignition. I shot a glance into the mirror. Looming up close, just yards from the back of the car, was my remaining pursuer. In my haste to get the car started, I dropped the keys on the floor. I made a grab for them with one hand and at the same time hit the door lock. I was just in time. My pursuer was right outside. He grabbed the door handle and yanked it hard. It didn't budge. He took a couple of steps back, jumped forward and drop kicked the door. The car rocked violently.

"C'mon, c'mon," I screamed at the car as I shakily inserted the keys. One turn of the key and I had ignition. I slammed the gear lever into first and hit the accelerator hard. The car lurched into a left sided swerve, the tyres spinning, screaming for grip in a cloud of dust and smoke. The lack of forward thrust panicked me. My pursuer again launched himself at the car in an uncontrolled fury just as I realised the handbrake was still on. I yanked it free. The car shot forward, knocking my attacker to the ground and screeched its way onto the tarmac. I kept my foot hard on the gas without a backward glance.

41

I drove aimlessly out of adrenaline fuelled fear for a full five minutes paying no attention to anything other than the need to put some distance between me and the gang of villains. I hadn't thought about the possibility of being discovered nor what I would do in such circumstances. The plan had been to get photographic proof of the smuggling operation, tie it up with the information I already had and then reveal all to Diana in our meeting on Tuesday once I got back to London. The fact that I had been discovered changed things. It wouldn't take the villains long to work out that it was me who had been spying on them.

I pulled over to the side of the road and checked my mobile. The compass said I was heading north. I needed to get across to the other side of the island. I couldn't risk turning back so I followed several minor side roads until eventually I came to the PMV-812. The road took a winding route through densely wooded countryside but at least I was going in the right direction. With a clear open road ahead, I took a decision – to go straight to the airport. I could sleep in the car for a few hours before I handed it back and then get cleaned up and changed in the airport terminal. My head was telling me that I needed to be off the island. There was no point in going back to the hotel. I had paid my bill. There was no need to risk discovery.

I pointed the car in the direction of the airport and some clarity of thought began to form in my mind. I had just witnessed part of an operation that could lead to the break-up of the diamond smuggling ring. I had managed to take a couple of pictures. I had evidence that would support the rest of the information I had been able to gather. And then the doubts set in. How good was that evidence? How did I know for certain that there were illegal conflict diamonds in the boxes? I had to tell someone before the gang had a chance to cover their tracks.

I pulled into the side of the road and reached for my mobile. I dialled a number. A bleary voice answered after five rings.

"*Hello, Diana Twist.*"

"Diana. It's Matthew. Matthew Malarkey. I'm really sorry to –"

"*Matthew? It's three-thirty in the morning.*"

I checked my watch. London was an hour behind.

"I know. I'm really sorry but it's urgent. Look, don't ask but I'm in Ibiza and –"

"*Ibiza? But you have no passport. How did you –*"

"I'll explain when I see you. I don't have time right now. Just listen. I need you to do something and it has to be done straight away."

As concisely as I could, I gave Diana a rundown of what I had discovered. I left out everything else, about Eleanor, James and Felipe and the information I had gathered. I told her that it was critical to alert the appropriate authorities on the island to the fact that a diamond smuggling operation was underway and get them to intercept the gang. I gave her the precise location and asked her to leave my name out of it.

When I had finished the call, I felt a sense of relief. There was no point in me speaking to the police. I could not be involved at that stage. I knew I could trust Diana to handle the situation correctly and her legal status would give her more credibility. I also knew that I wanted the information that went to the authorities at that point, kept to a bare minimum. They would begin their own investigation immediately but I would be back in the UK before they had anything at all to work with. And I wanted to handle the Eleanor connection myself.

And then, for some reason I began to worry about Alida. How had she become mixed up with the operation? Instinct told me she was just a pawn, an innocent that had got involved in something that turned out to be bigger than she had expected. A girl who needed money to survive a long, tough holiday season trying to make ends meet. The once-a-year tourist saw the glamour of the lifestyle – sun, sea, fun, parties – and many of them, based on nothing more than their two week trip, when they had plenty of spending money and a carefree outlook, thought that this was how it would be all the time. One big fun party. But then reality would kick in. Surviving in any tourist resort was just another job. The daily grind of making sure you had food and somewhere to sleep. If the opportunity came to make more money, then it was something to grab on to. Alida had spent two seasons before this one on the island so probably knew about the hardship.

And then I wondered if Estrid was involved. There was only one way to find out. I called her number.

"Hi Estrid. It's JJ. What are you up to?"

"Hi JJ. Nice surprise to hear you. I'm in the West End Strip. Just finishing and going home soon. You want to meet?"

I felt some reassurance that she was doing what she came out to do.

"Err ... no. I can't. I'm not around that way. Have you heard from Alida?"

"No, why?"

"Oh nothing ... It's okay but I need you to do something. Just call or text her. Tell her that she needs to get home as soon as possible. Tell her that some of the friends she is with are in trouble with the police and she needs to get home. But don't say that I –"

"Trouble? What trouble? Is she okay?"

"Yes, she's fine. Just do it. She'll understand. Trust me ... please. But don't tell her I called. That's very important. Good luck."

I hung up without waiting for Estrid's reaction. There was no time for further discussion.

I arrived at the airport at 5.00a.m. and drove straight into the car park. I managed to get an hour's fitful sleep on the back seat of the car and then realised that there was no more point in trying to

337

force myself to sleep for longer. It wasn't happening. I unloaded my bag from the boot and left the bag of tools that Jasper had bought where they were. Somebody could use them. They were not the sort of thing I could take on a plane, even if I wanted to. I dropped the hire car keys at the reception desk and made my way into the airport terminal. My first point of call was the nearest restaurant. I had almost four hours to kill before my flight and I needed coffee and food. With no sleep, I was banking on plenty of caffeine to keep me alert.

I sent a text to Cecil.

'Hi Ces. On my way back. Got the pix. All ok. Can you get Felipe's mobile over to Diana Twist at Twist, Swivell and Spinn. Will explain later. She'll need it. Tell her it's from me. Cheers.'

I closed the 'Messages' app and clicked on the 'Photos' icon. I scrolled through the pictures until I found the ones from the bay. They were not exactly award-winning shots but they had captured the scene and the images of people moving around the cave entrance and, more importantly, handling the boxes. On their own, they would mean nothing but placed with the other information I had, they were a useful bit of evidence.

Right after breakfast I found the washrooms. I freshened up as best I could and changed into the cabin crew uniform. At least I looked smarter and with a day's stubble, had a passing resemblance to the passport picture. There was nothing I could do about the eyebrows. The moment of truth would come at the check-in desk.

Two hours before the flight I made my way to check-in desk six. I took a deep breath to calm my nerves and handed over my ticket and passport. I needn't have worried. Apart from a casual reference to the fact that I could use the crew channel, to which I replied that I wasn't working yet, my only moment of concern was the double take the member of airline staff did at my passport photo. I resolved to sort out the eyebrow thing somehow, before I got to Gatwick.

With forty-five minutes to go before departure, I headed for the designated gate, gate 13. I tried to ignore the nagging thought that the gate number was some sort of portent of further ill starred misfortune. But the closer I got to the aircraft the more I began to relax. I took a seat and focused on an English newspaper that I'd bought in the terminal. As I browsed the pages, the text started to become a blur, each paragraph blending into one complete block of incomprehensible newsprint. My eyelids drooped, heavy with the need to sleep.

It was a child's voice that shook me into full alert mode.

"Hello."

I focused as quickly as I could. A little girl in a red t-shirt and white shorts stood directly in front of me. Under one arm she was clutching a small dark brown teddy bear.

"You are the nice man who buyed me ice cream," she said.

And then I remembered who she was and I was glad she had said 'nice.'

I smiled at her but I was uneasy about the attention. That attention racked up a few more notches when her father appeared. Darren.

"Rachael. Come here. Don't annoy the man. He's trying to read."

I glanced in his direction and immediately he recognised me.

"I know you, don't I? Yes, you're the chap from the beach."

"Err ... yes. Sorry about the other day. I hope everything is alright."

He took his daughter by the hand.

"I thought I recognised that voice too. I couldn't think where and then I remembered meeting that children's entertainer. That was you, wasn't it?"

"Err ... well ... I –"

"Yes it was you." He looked at my uniform. "And you claimed you were a Danish psychic yesterday. And now you're a pilot. Who exactly are you?"

The conversation was the last thing I needed. Fellow passengers began to take a quizzical interest. I had no idea how to respond. Tiredness and stress had dulled my cognitive flexibility. But I had to say something.

"I'm … err … kind of all three ... a ... erm ... psychic pilot who entertains kids. But, as of yesterday, I've quit the entertainment business. No money in it. Kids don't find it funny anymore. They'd sooner play on their iPhones. And I'm giving up the psychic thing too ... not that you can ever quit being psychic. I could go back to it. Who knows what the future holds. You can never tell. Well ... unless you *are* psychic, which means you ... err ... can of course, but I ... I will still be a pilot. But the entertainment thing is all ... all history."

Darren stared hard at me for a moment before he spoke.

"Well I sincerely hope you are not piloting this flight because if you are, we are not flying on it."

"No, no ... I'm not. I'm not working until later and then I'm with Scandinavian Airlines, flying to ... uh … Scandinavia. We go there a lot because ... it's Scandinavia. But, anyway, no, I'm just ordinary Joe Public on this one. Just trying to get home, you know. Like everybody else." I gestured at the rest of the room where groups of passengers were filling up the vacant seating areas. "So, no need to miss the flight because of me. It'll be fine. No problems. A nice easy flight back home. Relax and enjoy it. I'll probably just doze off and sleep the whole way."

That seemed to satisfy Darren. I certainly didn't need him pointing me out as a potential problem and I had no inclination to explain my uniform either. If he thought I was a pilot that was his issue. He dragged his daughter away.

As she walked away, she turned, waved her teddy bear and said, "Bye."

42

I stepped from the air bridge onto the aircraft and felt an instant sense of relief. The last leg of the journey back. Just the passage through Gatwick at the other end to contend with and I was home and dry. I was shattered from lack of sleep and was looking forward to getting some shuteye once I was in my seat.

Ahead of me, the queue to board had slowed as an attentive flight attendant checked the passengers' boarding passes and indicated the approximate location of their seats. When my turn came, I showed mine to the blonde attendant. She hesitated for a moment, her attention on my uniform. I said nothing.

"Half way along on the left Sir," she said.

I thanked her and moved into the cabin. As I reached my seat, I heard my name.

"Matthew."

I turned abruptly and came face to face with Erin.

"Well well. Same flight again. We must stop meeting like this," she said, a broad smile showing off her perfectly white teeth.

I was pleased to see her and then I remembered my ID issue.

"Erin. I'm still Jason. Remember?"

Her hand shot up in front of her mouth.

"Oops. My mistake. But what are you doing wearing the uniform? You don't need it now. You'll only attract attention. Soon as we get airborne you go and change. Fold it up and bring it back to your seat. I'll take care of it."

"Okay," I said, as I placed my bag in the overhead locker.

"And no doubt you've got JJ's passport. I'll need that back the minute you are clear the other side. I'm meeting him as soon as we get back. He knows I'm on an inbound flight. Then I'll give you a lift home. Oh, and I still have your debit card in the car."

"Thanks Erin. I appreciate what you've done."

"It's no problem. Now, take your seat and I'll bring you a drink once we're in the air. G and T?"

I nodded, slid into my seat and fastened my safety belt. I didn't take much notice of the remaining passengers. I was tired and not interested in interacting. I just needed some peace and quiet and some anonymity.

Perhaps it was fate or the randomness of numbers, seat numbers in this case, that decided I was not going to have that luxury. As I settled in to my seat, I spotted Darren making his way down the aisle. He was checking seat numbers as he approached, his daughter trailing behind him. I averted my gaze and prayed that he would be somewhere at the back of the aircraft. What were the chances of him being in the neighbouring seats? As it turned out the chances were extremely good. He stopped next to me and gawped twice at the seat number display on the ceiling.

"You again. Looks like we're together." He nodded in the direction of the two seats to my right. "We're in the window and middle seat."

"Okay, no problem," I said, trying to keep the discussion to a minimum. I stepped into the aisle to let him and his daughter into the seats.

"Hello. Ted says hello too," the little girl said, her smile full of the excitement only a child can have amidst groups of jostling adults.

"Hello Rachael," I said.

"Ted is sitting by the window so he can see the fluffy clouds," she replied and pressed the bear's face up against the window.

I sat back down in my seat, fastened my seatbelt again and wished I had nothing more to worry about other than the fluffy clouds.

The flight took off on time. As soon as we were airborne, Darren slipped into a quiet doze, his head lolling to one side but his sub-conscious mind fighting the movement and trying to correct it. Once the safety belt signs had been switched off I jumped up, grabbed my bag and went to the lavatory. I locked the door and changed into jeans, a T-shirt and a light jacket, which I carried over my arm. Then I folded the uniform neatly, and took it back to my seat. Erin came by a few minutes later with a small bottle of Bombay gin and a can of tonic.

"There you go mister. Relax now. I'm going to be busy for a while but if you need anything just press the attendant button. One of us will sort you out." She winked and picked up the uniform. "I'll take this," she said and made her way to the front of the aircraft.

I poured the gin and tonic, took a sip, savouring the strong tangy taste and sat back in my seat. All I needed was a smooth flight and a problem free entry through passport control and I could focus on clearing my name and rescuing things with Louise. Having Erin on the flight gave me renewed confidence that things would be fine. She knew my story and I felt less isolated.

The thought of passport control suddenly focussed me on my dodgy identity. I pulled the passport from my jacket pocket, opened it and stared at Jason Jefferies. I had the stubble look to pull off that part of the image but I was concerned again about the eyebrows. The earlier experience at the check-in when the staff member had done a double-take at the picture, had created doubt in my mind. The eyebrows definitely needed work but I had nothing with me that could fix them. I remembered how Erin had applied the theatrical make up for me before the flight out. Perhaps she would have an answer.

I pressed the attendant button. Within a minute the blonde flight attendant was at my seat.

"Can I help you Sir?" she asked.

"Oh … I wanted to see the … the other lady. The one with the dark hair. Her name's Erin … I think."

"She's busy in business class at the moment Sir. Is there anything I can do?"

343

I hesitated. I could have waited a bit longer for Erin but I had just called for a flight attendant and I didn't want her to think that I was a time waster. Nor did I want to draw too much attention to myself by having her speak to her colleagues and label me a fusspot who wanted a specific person. I decided I would ask.

"Err ... yes. This might sound like a strange request –"

"Don't worry Sir. I've heard them all before. How can I help?"

"Err ... well, I wondered if you were wearing any ... err ... any –"

"Don't go there Sir. I've heard that one many times. Save your breath. It's not that original."

"No? You mean –"

"Yes, I mean a few drinks on these holiday flights and some blokes just come right out with it."

"Really? Blokes? I wouldn't have thought it was that common."

"Trust me Sir, it is. Now is there anything else I can help you with?"

"No, I just wanted to know if you had any –"

She rolled her eyes and leant towards me.

"Yes, I do, white for your information. What *is* this obsession you blokes have with girls in uniform?"

I was taken aback by her answer.

"White? Not black? I just wanted to –"

My sentence was cut abruptly as the aircraft dropped in a sudden, stomach churning dip and then bounced around like a car rumbling across speed bumps. The first dip was so sudden that I instinctively reached out and grabbed the flight attendant's arm. She pitched forward towards me, almost landing in my lap as the bumps and my grab caused her to lose balance. The 'fasten seat belts' light came on accompanied by the 'bong' of the cabin PA system. The flight attendant quickly regained her composure.

"I know what you wanted to know Sir. Now behave yourself or I'll have to report this to the Captain." She turned to leave.

"Sorry? What's the Captain got to do with it?" I said. "I was just wondering if you had any ... any eye liner ... you know, mascara.

I couldn't tell if you were wearing it. I'm not too good at that sort of thing."

She started to laugh, then leaned in close.

"Mascara. Why didn't you say? You can't tell? You blokes, you think the perfectly made up look is the norm. No wonder when we take it off you get confused. Why do you want to know?"

"Uh ... I need to borrow some."

"Borrow some?"

"Yes, my ... my mother is meeting me at the airport and I ... I want to look my best."

She smiled, a knowing smile.

"Your mother? Oh okay, right. I see." She winked as if we now had a shared secret. "Hey, it's none of my business but why didn't you just say you wanted to do your eyes?"

"I was trying to. Oh, and about the white thing. I want the black variety."

She shot me a quizzical look.

"Give me five minutes and then pop up to the galley area and I'll do it for you."

"Okay, thanks," I said. I would rather have had Erin do it for me but I thought that it might be best to get it done when the offer was there, just in case something occurred later on that would mean Erin wouldn't have time. In any case I was so exhausted I just wanted to get it out of the way.

I waited about ten minutes and then I made my way to the galley. The flight attendant was waiting for me.

"Take a seat Sir. My name's Susie. What's yours?"

"It's ... Jason."

"Nice to meet you Jason. Okay, I've found some nice mascara and liner in my make-up bag so we'll make you look nice for your ... mother."

Susie got to work outlining my eyes and then with small, flicking brush strokes, began to apply a dark mixture to my eyelashes. I began to feel slightly concerned as she worked.

"Err ... sorry, Susie. Last time I had it done it was just my eyebrows. Are you sure this is right?"

"Don't be silly Jason. Of course it is. It all has to match or you won't look right. Trust me. You'll learn after a while. Perhaps we should catch up once we're back home and I can give you a make-up lesson. I used to do make-up in a store before I joined the airline." She stopped what she was doing for a moment and leant in close to my ear. "I like a man in make-up actually. It turns me on."

I turned abruptly towards her.

"Make-up? Are you definitely sure this is right? I really just want my eyebrows done … a bit darker that's all."

"Be still Jason. You don't want to look weird. Let me do it properly."

With a flourish, she pulled out a long thin pen that looked like a marker and began to trace along my eyebrows. After a few minutes, she stood back admiring her work.

"There you go. All done. Okay. Now I have to get on. Let me have your number when we land."

I stood up and began to make my way back to my seat, trying to avoid eye contact with the passengers. But there was one I couldn't avoid. He was too obvious, so obvious that I wondered why I hadn't seen him before. It was the neck brace that caught my attention, a solid piece of hinged, moulded plastic complete with padding, tucked up hard underneath the chin and high up against the back of the head, encasing the whole neck. And then I noticed the dark Homburg hat and the wrap around shades. The whole image, that of a gangster. I faltered in my step for a second. Despite the hat and glasses, I was certain it was him.

Scalapino.

I hurried back to my seat and sat down, my breathing coming in heaving fits. How could Scalapino have boarded the plane without me seeing him? I hadn't noticed him in the departure lounge. But I had been trying to keep a low profile myself so was not paying too much attention to anyone else. He must have boarded after me as he was nearer the front of the aircraft. It can't have been coincidence that he was on my flight to London. There was no doubt he was following me. But I couldn't figure out how he could have known which flight I would be on. He would have known which day I was flying back as James had told Eleanor, I knew that much. But I was travelling as Jason Jefferies. And then I remembered that Jasper had referred to me as Jason in front of Felipe when we had encountered him and Paloma at Café del Mar. And Alida knew I was using Jason too. With the right financial persuasion they could have obtained passenger manifest information from someone on the inside and been able to pinpoint my flight.

I took a huge gulp of the remaining gin and tonic and finished it off. I needed another one. I was about to press the flight attendant button again when Erin appeared by my seat.

"Matthew, you eejit. What're you doing? Susie just told me that you had her doing your eyes up. Look at the feckin state of you. You'll have half the airport looking at you when you arrive for god's sake."

I ignored Erin's use of my real name. I had more to be concerned with.

"Never mind that, Erin. There's a fella on here who's after me and he's intent on doing me serious harm. You have to tell the Captain. He needs to alert the authorities."

"What? Who? What are you on about? You need to get that eye make-up off and quick."

I ran my fingers across both eyes trying to remove the make-up.

"Not like that. Jeez, you've smudged the stuff. You look like a bloody panda."

"Forget that Erin. I'm serious. That bloke is intent on killing me. The bloke with the neck brace. Up there on the left side."

Erin turned to look along the aisle.

"Where?"

"The bloke with the hat." I pointed along the aisle. "There. You have to get him off the plane."

"I can't get him off the bloody plane. We're above France."

"Well, inform the Captain then. It's urgent."

Erin bit her bottom lip and glanced along the cabin aisle again.

"What do I tell him? He'll need an explanation. We have to be sure he's done something. What has he done?"

I gave Erin a quick rundown of my history with Scalapino. When I'd finished she said she'd have a word with the Captain and went off in the direction of the cockpit.

My agitated state must have disturbed Darren. He snorted a couple of times as he came out of his slumber. He turned to check on Rachael who had fallen asleep with Ted as a pillow. Then he turned in my direction and lurched back in shock.

"Bloody hell man. What's happened to you? Your eyes. You gave me a fright. What's going –?"

"It's okay Darren. It's …" I struggled for an explanation, my focus further along the aisle on the back of Scalapino's head. "I've been asked to do a performance, a kid's party, when I get off the flight. Just one more. You know how it is. Couldn't turn it down … an old friend. So, just getting ready."

"A party? I thought you'd given that up. And what are you supposed to be anyway?"

"I'm a … a … a skunk," I said, trying to recall what Erin had said I looked like and then remembering it was a panda.

"A skunk? You're going to entertain children dressed as a skunk?"

"Well, yes," I said, glancing down the aisle again. "Some odd kids about eh? I'm … I'm Simon Skunk. You heard of him?"

"No. Can't say I have but you'd frighten most kids to death with those eyes. I'm glad Rachael's asleep."

Erin arrived back to rescue me from my awkward discussion with Darren.

"The Captain's agreed to see you."

"The Captain?" Darren said, his brow knitted in curiosity.

"Err … yes," I said, as I undid my seatbelt. "It's his daughter that I'm doing the party for. Just some last minute details."

Erin leaned in close and whispered.

"He can't go radioing in to get someone arrested without some more detail so you'll have to come to the flight deck."

"What did you tell him?" I asked.

"I just said that it had been reported to me by a passenger that he'd been stalked on Ibiza and threatened and that now the person involved was on the flight and that it was the passenger's concern that there could be an incident and that he feared for his safety. Any threat to the aircraft is taken seriously. He needs to see you. Follow me."

I got up from my seat and followed Erin to the flight deck.

43

As we walked towards the front of the aircraft, my thoughts turned to Louise. What was she doing right now? How was she spending her day now that she was suspended from work? Probably with her mother. If Louise would agree to meet with me when I returned, how would I break the news to her that Eleanor was leading a double life? That she was leading a life that was contrary to all that her daughter had stood for in her professional capacity. The life of a criminal. There was no other way to describe it. And I had to break that news. My thoughts turned to Diana. Had she been able to alert the authorities? What was the outcome? If so, maybe I was close to breaking the smuggling operation.

But, I had another problem. Scalapino, sitting just a few rows ahead. He would surely not try to apprehend me on the aircraft. There was no point in that. His plan had to be to follow me back to London and then make a move. As I neared his seat, I glanced in his direction. His head was down, a magazine in his hand. Just another passenger whiling away the hours of the flight.

Erin beckoned to Susie and pointed ahead. Susie parted the grey curtain that separated the two cabin areas and followed Erin towards the flight deck door. When we reached the door, Erin told me to wait. Susie took up a position to one side of the door. Erin tapped in some numbers on a key pad and waited. Within a few seconds, I heard a mechanical click and Erin reached for the door handle. She pulled it open and beckoned me forward. I entered the flight deck followed by Erin. Erin stepped through and Susie moved into position to guard the door as Erin reached back to pull it closed.

But she was too late.

None of us had seen him leave his seat. I had probably blocked Susie's view as I waited for the door to open. She was no match for the hulking Scalapino. In a swiftly executed movement, he leapt forward, shoved Susie aside and grabbed the door in a powerful iron-fisted grip, preventing Erin from pulling it shut. He yanked it fully open, grabbed Erin by her blouse and dragged her out through the door, flinging her with such force that she fell face first onto the floor. Stunned by the speed and surprise of the attack, the pilot and co-pilot sat rooted to their seats in open-mouthed disbelief. By the time my reflexes kicked in Scalapino was in the cockpit. In desperation I threw myself at him but a powerful right hand swipe caught me square on the side of the head, shoving me back into the co-pilot. Scalapino pulled the door shut and came after me.

"You can't come in here," the Captain yelled, finally rising from his seat on the left of the cabin.

Scalapino said nothing, his maniacal gaze fixed on me as he threw his full body weight towards me.

The Captain, seizing the opportunity to catch Scalapino off balance, rained a series of blows onto his back. But they had no effect other than to irritate him. He tossed his Homburg hat to one side, revealing a bandaged head to accompany his neck brace, and turned his wrath on the Captain. A single crushing knockout blow smashed into the Captain's jaw sending two of his teeth flying into the instrument display behind him. The effect was instant oblivion. His body crumpled and fell to the floor.

With the Captain taken care of, Scalapino focussed his gaze on me. I had managed to pull myself back onto my feet and was square onto him. The co-pilot rose from his seat and tried to reason with him. But he was beyond reason. His sole intention was to get to me.

I saw the first punch coming, a huge arcing swing that was intended to remove my head with sheer power. The split second advantage that my anticipation had given me fired my reflexes and I ducked the deadly blow. The co-pilot hadn't seen Scalapino's intention. He took the full force of the punch on the right side of his face. I heard the crack as his jaw dislocated. Blood shot from his mouth, spurting across the side window as his eyes lost their focus. He reeled across the flight deck from the force and was out cold before he hit the ground.

The enormity of what had just happened suddenly hit me, completely squashing any fear I had of Scalapino.

"You fucking idiot. You've just killed the pilots," I said. "We're … twenty… thirty … thousands of feet up and nobody's flying this frigging plane and we're locked in here and –"

He didn't let me finish. I half expected it. I saw the pent up rage in his eyes. A rage that had obliterated all rational thinking. A deep guttural snarl was the only signal of his next move, a raging stomp towards me, his arms outstretched like Frankenstein's monster. Instinctively I stepped to one side to avoid his advance but in the confined space, I had nowhere to go. My legs hit the pilot's seat and I stumbled backwards onto it. Scalapino took full advantage of my prone position, diving onto me and grasping my throat in a fierce, suffocating grip. The intense pressure on my windpipe caused me to choke and splutter. My head felt like it would explode as his grip tightened. I flailed about trying to get hold of something to give me some leverage to right myself, or something to use as a weapon, the pulse in my neck pounding as my brain fought for oxygen.

Again I clutched at thin air, desperation taking hold as my eyes began to blur. My left hand suddenly gripped something. A hard, lever-like object. I squeezed tight, trying to pick it up so that I could use it to defend myself. It wouldn't budge. I squeezed again, this time feeling a button click. A pulsing alarm sound echoed through the cockpit but as I fought for oxygen, I was only vaguely aware of it. I yanked the lever again. The aircraft lurched hard to the right, tilting over at a sharp angle. I heard the muffled screams from behind the door as the sudden change of direction kicked in. The abrupt movement momentarily threw Scalapino off balance causing his grip to slacken for a moment. I took full advantage, dragging myself into a semi-seated position. Again I reached out with my hand, this time finding a cold metallic object. At the top it had a nozzle and a tube. A fire extinguisher. I pulled hard, yanking it away from its housing and in the same movement, swung it fiercely through the air landing a sickening blow on Scalapino's already damaged head. The existing wound didn't stand a chance. Blood seeped through the bandage, like the contents of a pot of spilt paint, as he lost consciousness and slumped heavily to one side at my feet.

I fell back into the seat, my heart pounding, my lungs still gasping for air. As my head cleared, I became aware of the alarm sound again. And then I noticed the tilt of the aircraft and panic set in. I swung round in the seat to see what I had grabbed. To the left side of the seat a short control stick, like a game console control, emerged through a rubber housing that was fixed to a panel by the side window. I pushed it to the left. The aircraft tilted back to horizontal. But the alarm, a siren of some sort, continued to pulse. On the display in front of me, a warning light flashed red. Instinctively I pushed the button. The alarm cut out but almost immediately, a buzzer started to go off adding to my confusion. At the same time there was a loud thump on the door. I jumped up, tripping across the three bodies on the floor. I tried the door but it wouldn't open. Then I heard the muffled shouts.

"Captain. Can you hear me? Captain."

Erin.

I shouted at the door.

"Erin …it's me. Matthew. The pilots are dead. The plane's out of control. How do I get out? ... Erin?"

"Matthew? Matthew. Calm down and listen. Can you hear a buzzer?"

"Yes."

"Okay. It's the door release buzzer. There's a switch on the panel that operates the door. Just press that and let me in."

I fumbled about and found the switch. I released it and Erin came through the door.

"Oh my God," she shouted as she spotted the three stricken bodies.

"I think they're all dead," I said. "And there's nobody flying the plane. You have to take over."

The aircraft had remained in the horizontal position but seemed to be losing height.

"I can't fly a feckin plane. I'm cabin crew. It should be on auto." Erin dropped to her knees next to the Captain's prone body. "He's breathing."

There was a commotion behind us.

"You can't come in here Sir." Susie stuck her head around the door. "The passengers are panicking. We need to tell them something. Now."

The door was pushed open. Darren's face appeared.

"What the hell's going on?" He spotted the two felled pilots and almost joined them as the blood drained from his face. "Oh my God ... we're all going to die."

"Calm down, Sir. Get back to your seat. It's under control," Susie said, her voice remarkably measured in the circumstances.

"But who's flying the plane and why are we losing height?" Darren shrieked, hysteria only one wrong answer away. The last thing we needed was Darren sending the passengers into a fear induced frenzy.

"I am. I'm flying it," I said. "I'm a pilot ... remember?"

Darren's mouth opened but nothing came out.

"Sir, you need to go back to your seat, fasten your belt and stay calm," Susie said, leading him back out through the door.

Erin called after her.

"Susie, get me the first aid kit and some towels." She looked up at me. "Matthew get in the pilot's seat."

"Me? I was ... I was just trying to calm that idiot down. I can't fly a plane. You've got to revive the Captain."

"I'm trying to. He's out cold and so's the co-pilot and I think his jaw's broken. Look at the size of it."

"The plane Erin. We need a bloody pilot ... one of them," I shouted, pointing at the prone pilots.

"Just get in the seat Matthew and get on to ATC."

"ATC?"

"Air traffic control. Can you not hear the radio?"

I hadn't heard anything above the din in the cockpit. Erin saw my hesitation.

"Pick up the headset and talk to them. They'll see we're off course. They'll talk you through it. Get you back on autopilot."

"Me?"

"Yes, you. Somebody has to do it. Now go on."

"How do you get it on autopilot?"

"I don't know. I told you. Get onto ATC."

"If we're not on autopilot we're going to crash."

"For God's sake Matthew. We're not. Just get the feckin controls. Get in the seat. Get in the seat. Go on. Now." Erin's eyes blazed fear but her training enabled her to keep her composure. "Somebody has to take control. It's not that hard. It flies its feckin self ... they're always saying that. Just talk to ATC."

Susie turned up with a first aid kit, towels and a bowl of water.

"Great. I'll see if I can get one of these two conscious," Erin said. "Susie, make a passenger announcement. Just say that one of the crew has suffered an illness but everything is under control. Tell them we hit some turbulence or something. Anything. We don't want panic."

I heard desperation in Erin's voice. She was trying to take control of a critical situation and she had enough on her plate without me being a problem. Flies itself, she'd said. There was no choice. Surveying the passengers to see if they had a pilot amongst them would definitely cause panic. And I also felt responsible. Seeing Scalapino crushed on the floor brought me a sense of calm, relief that I knew where he was and that he was totally incapacitated. My relief lasted about thirty-five seconds.

Erin stood up, her face fixed in a determined, no nonsense expression.

"Matthew. Stop feckin daydreaming and get in the seat for god's sake. That's the last time I'm saying it."

I gulped down a mouthful of air and slid into the pilot's seat.

44

The transition from total chaos to relative calm in the cockpit brought a rush of awareness of my surroundings. But I felt no calm at all. There was a voice trying to make contact over the radio but I couldn't make sense of it.

And now I was in the pilot's seat.

Confronted by a spaceship-like array of instruments and brightly lit panels in front of me, next to me and overhead, my brain could only comprehend one thing - how comfortable the seat felt. The incredible array of lights, switches and knobs were just a dimension too far. My mind had never had to take in so much information in one go. And each individual light told me that it had some vital function. Some vital role in operating the aircraft. Keeping it airborne. It was brain overload, a sudden awareness of total incompetency. And my brain's way of coping with my new reality was to focus on how comfortable my seat was.

"FST 45XT, this is French ATC. Are you receiving me?"

"Matthew, for god's sake man answer."

I turned and looked at Erin, my blank expression conveying my ignorance.

"The headset. There," she said, her brow furrowed in concentration. "Press that black trigger button on the stick. There," she said again, pointing at the sidestick.

I crammed the headset on and squeezed the button that Erin had indicated.

"Err ... hello. Hello? Err ... we are ... err ... receiving."

"FST 45XT, fly heading 340 degrees and speed Mach 0.78."

The instruction caused immediate brain freeze.

"Err ... sorry ... I ... I don't ..."

Erin grabbed the headset.

"We have the Captain ..." She tapped me on the shoulder. "Press the button again. They can't hear me."

I reached for the sidestick and inadvertently pulled it back and towards me. The aircraft pitched upwards and sideways at the same time.

"Shit. What's happening?"

"Don't pull the feckin stick like that Matthew. Straighten it out."

I eased the sidestick back to the left and the aircraft levelled out. Another gentle movement forward of the sidestick and the nose of the aircraft came back down.

"Press the comms button again," Erin said.

I stared at the sidestick.

"The comms button? What ... this red one?"

"No. The one you pressed before. The black one at the front of the stick."

I did as Erin said.

"This is FST 45XT. We have our Captain and First Officer incapacitated, and we have a civilian in charge of the aircraft. No other flight personnel available but we are under control. Please give precise instructions."

There was a pause and then a calm authoritative voice came through the speaker.

"Okay. This is French ATC. What is your name FST 45XT?"

Erin handed the headset back.

"Why don't you fly it, Erin," I said. "You seem to know what you're doing."

"I've no idea. I'd be useless. I've just seen the pilots squeeze that trigger button and talk into the headset. That's all. And I've got a crew to organise back there. Now get on with it."

"Are you receiving FST 45XT? What is your name?"

My name. I hesitated. I had no idea what to say. My whole

cover was about to be blown. But it was an emergency. And then I had an idea.

"It's ... it's Darren."

Erin rolled her eyes and mouthed something. I waved her away.

"*Merci. Darren, I am Stéphane. I will give you some instructions and later I will hand you over to London control. But first, you must engage autopilot. Which seat are you in? Left side or right?*"

"I'm in the left one."

"*Okay, the pilot's side. On the control panel in front of you, you will see two buttons marked AP1 and AP2, just to the right. Press one of them to engage autopilot.*"

I stared at the control panel, an intense row of knobs, switches, buttons and lights. At first they were just a blur of controls. But I knew I had to focus and stay calm. My eyes alighted on the AP buttons.

"Got it. Which one? Which do I press?"

"*It doesn't matter,*" Stéphane responded.

I pressed the button.

"Done it."

Stéphane came back on the speaker.

"*Good. We need to keep in communication. When you speak to us Darren, hold the black trigger button on the front of your sidestick. That's the communications button. Not the red one on top. That disengages autopilot. Okay.*"

Black, red. Buttons. Triggers. I had to keep a grip.

"Okay."

"*Have you flown an aircraft before Darren?*"

"Err ... no, never. I've played a flight simulator thing on my iPad. I don't know if it's the same ... or anything."

Stéphane ignored my comment.

"*Okay. I am going to give you some instructions to programme the autopilot.*"

"Okay."

"*At the top of your FCU there is a –*"

"Sorry ... FCU?"

"*Flight Control Unit. The panel you just used for the AP button.*"

At the top, just below your window, there is a panel with rows of knobs on it. Can you see?"

"Knobs?"

"Yes, knobs. You have speed, heading and altitude. I am going to give you some settings for each one. Okay?"

"Yes ... yes. Okay." Stéphane's tone was measured, cool, in control. I suddenly felt that I didn't need to fly the plane. He would. I began to relax and stretched out my legs. My right foot came down on a large angled surface. The aircraft began to turn right." Immediately the alarm went off again.

"Stéphane? Stéphane? Monsieur ... the plane, it's turning again and the alarm's on. What do I do?"

"Is your foot on the rudder Darren?"

I looked down at the floor in front of me.

"The rudder. Err, yes it is."

"Then take it off and press the AP1 or AP2 button again to engage autopilot. You have disengaged it. The pedal does that too."

I was operating on adrenaline but there was too much information to deal with. It seemed that many of the controls did the same thing. I pressed the AP1 button and then squeezed the communications button again. Just as I was about to speak to Stéphane, a low, throaty groan caused me to turn around. Scalapino was stirring, his fingers clawing at the floor, some basic Neanderthal survival instinct dragging him back to consciousness. That could not happen.

"Hit the fucker ... he's moving," I shouted at Erin.

"Sorry ... Darren? I do not understand your last communication."

Erin didn't need a second command. She grabbed the fire extinguisher from the floor and struck Scalapino firmly on the base of his skull. He hit the floor in a total stupor.

"FST 45XT? Darren? Are you receiving?"

"Err ... yes ... yes ... loud and clear."

"Your last communication. I did not understand it?"

"Oh ... no, forget it. It was ... sorry about that."

"Okay. I want you to bring the aircraft back, heading north-

west and then you should programme the following settings on the FCU. Climb flight level three eight zero. Fly heading three four zero degrees and speed Mach zero decimal seven eight. I will take you through each instruction."

Stéphane carefully took me through each stage of his directions. I did exactly as I was told. I turned the knobs as instructed. I had no idea what Mach zero seven eight was. The display showed I had made the correct inputs with the controls.

"Err ... Stéphane. What speed is that," I asked.

"It's four hundred and sixty knots."

It still didn't mean anything and I felt some perverse need to understand what I was dealing with.

"Do you know what that is in miles an hour?" I asked.

"It's approximately five hundred and thirty miles an hour," Stéphane replied.

Five hundred and thirty miles an hour. Drops of perspiration began to break out on my forehead. I wished I hadn't asked. I was in charge of a missile that was travelling at a speed that was incomprehensible to my everyday life.

"Darren? Are you receiving? Is everything okay?"

"Yes ... yes. Thank you. All seems okay."

"Good. Well done Darren. Maintain the selected heading for now. I will come back to you shortly."

I sat back in the seat, Stéphane's positive comment creating a moment's respite from the tension in my body. I turned to see what was going on behind me. Erin was bathing the co-pilots face.

"How're they doing?" I asked.

"It's not good. The co-pilot may have concussion as well as a broken jaw. He's semi-conscious and rambling on about what he wants to do to Susie ... feckin perv. He's in no state to fly a plane. I've stopped the Captain's bleeding but he doesn't look good either. He's been sick twice. You may have to land this thing."

Land. The words hit my subconscious almost as hard as the fire extinguisher had hit Scalapino. Stéphane was in control. But I had to get the aircraft onto the ground with a hundred and fifty people on board.

"It'll be fine Matthew. They'll get you down safely," Erin said, her smile reassuring but her eyes not showing the same conviction. "And why did you say you're name was Darren to ATC?"

The mention of Darren's name reminded me of my plan. And in that moment, maybe because my own fate was out of my hands, maybe because I knew there were only two outcomes in the situation, failure or success, I suddenly felt super charged. I had nothing to lose.

"I'll tell you later. Can you get someone to bring him up here? He's the guy who came in earlier."

"We can't have passengers on the flight deck Matthew. It's not –"

"Just do it Erin. This is not a normal situation. And while you're about it can you get somebody to tie him up." I pointed at Scalapino. "I don't want him coming to and running amok."

I released the flight deck door and Erin went out. Moments later, she returned with Darren.

"What's going on?" he asked, surprise and apprehension clearly displayed in his tense, knotted brow.

"Darren, sit down there." I pointed to the co-pilot's seat. "Now listen carefully. I need a favour. You remember how you told me that time we were in the cafe that you hated your job?"

"I do, yes."

"Good. And you said you wanted to be recognised for something, some achievement."

Darren shuffled in the seat.

"Yes. I remember that."

"Well, now's your chance. Your chance to stop being just another bloke in a suit. A way out, like you're looking for."

"How? What do I have to do?"

"Okay, listen carefully. I'm going to take this aircraft back to London so we're all cool. Everything will be fine. But the thing is I'm off duty and ... well, I really don't want it to be known that I've been in control here. It's not a problem but I don't want all the attention once we land. I want to get home to ... err ... Scandinavia as quickly as I can. ATC ... that's air traffic control for you non-pilots ... they know that the Captain has been incapacitated and that a passenger is flying the aircraft. So that passenger can be you. And once we arrive –"

"But I can't fly a plane, can I. How am I supposed –?"

"Hang on. I just said I'd fly it. But when we land I'm going back out to the cabin and then it looks like you've brought it back safely. It's your way out. You'll be a celebrity. These chances don't come along often so grab it."

He looked confused.

"But why don't you just tell them you're a pilot and everything is under control? It is an emergency situation, isn't it?"

"I just told you. I *could* do that but I need to get ... back, get home like I said." I stared directly into his eyes. "I'm actually doing you a favour here and maybe it'll make up for all that inconvenience on the island. Think about it. You'd be a hero. It's life changing."

Darren's expression showed me he was tempted. I played on it.

"And you'd be doing me a favour too. I don't normally fly this type of plane. I'm normally on a ... on a ... erm, jumbo ... transatlantic seven four ... err ... plane. And all the debrief stuff is a pain at the best of times let alone after an emergency situation. What d'you say?"

Darren hesitated. The moment was interrupted by air traffic control.

"*FST 45XT ... Darren. This is Stéphane. Are you receiving?*"

Darren shot a glance across at me. I winked back and pressed the communication button.

"Receiving."

"*Okay, you are now two hundred miles from your destination. Contact London control on one three one decimal seven five. I have made clear the situation.*"

Stéphane then went through a series of instructions and eventually I had contact with London control.

"*FST 45XT ... Darren. This is London control. My name is Martin. I have been briefed on your situation. Descend flight level one five zero.*"

362

Martin took me through a series of directions that I followed on the flight control unit.

"*Okay, Darren, I'm going to position you onto ILS, the Instrument Landing System. This will position the aircraft for landing. We will turn right, heading zero eight zero degrees, descend three thousand feet ... three zero, zero, zero, QNH 1021, speed two one zero knots. Select flaps one.*"

Martin again talked me through each stage.

"Err ... I can't see a flaps button," I said.

I sensed the concern from Darren in the adjacent seat.

"It's okay ... different aircraft, that's all," I whispered.

"*It's in the centre console between the seats, marked flaps. It's a lever. Pull it back to position one.*"

"Got it."

The aircraft slowed.

"*FST 45XT, Darren, you are cleared. ILS runway two six L, speed one six zero. Press the button marked APPR on the right side of FCU.*"

The aircraft bounced slightly as it descended, the green meadows of England now clearly visible. An unexpected wave of panic gripped me. I was minutes from touchdown. The speed and size of the aircraft had suddenly become intensely realistic as we approached the ground. There was no going back. I had to keep a grip.

Martin's voice interrupted my thoughts.

"*FST 45XT, press the APPR button now on the FCU. Then select flaps two.*"

I pressed the button and pulled the lever into position two and immediately noticed how clammy my hands were.

"*FST 45XT, Darren you are now on a direct heading for the runway. The localiser will guide you on auto but there are some things you need to do. So listen carefully.*"

Martin took me through another series of instructions designed to slow the aircraft to the right speed. At four miles from the runway, he issued another instruction.

"*FST 45XT, you need to lower the landing gear now. Move the lever from up to down on the panel in front of you. Then select flaps three. And then flaps full.*"

Ahead, the long grey strip of tarmac seemed a small target. I pulled the lever all the way down as instructed. A low rumble from beneath told me that something had happened. I grabbed the sidestick, intent upon speaking to ATC. In my haste, I hit the red button and disconnected the autopilot. The alarm immediately kicked in. Every sinew in my body seemed to tighten up. The sensation of speed was unbearable. And my nerve finally cracked. On the FCU the light flashed red. Instinctively I pressed the button again, disabling the alarm. But my hand was still on the sidestick control pushing it left.

"*FST 45XT you are out of line and you are too high on approach. You will have to make a manual landing now. Come back to the right, a small movement on your sidestick and ease it forward. You need two red and two white lights on your landing approach.*"

I eased the sidestick gently to the right and searched the display for the lights.

"What lights? Where?"

"*Look ahead at the runway. The precision approach path indicator lights will guide you.*"

It was all too much information. I glanced across at Darren. His fingers gripped the armrest as if he was trying to squeeze juice out of an orange.

"Darren. For fuck's sake, I need your help here. What lights is he talking about?"

Darren suddenly found the power of speech.

"Out there. You have four white lights," he said, pointing through the cockpit window.

I stared ahead through the window at the runway that was looming up fast. The aircraft seemed to be in line again and I could see four continuous strips of horizontal white lights either side of the runway. Martin had said two white and two red.

"*FST 45XT. You are too high on your approach. Ease the sidestick forward.*"

I eased the sidestick forward gently

"That's it. Two red and two white," Darren shouted.

I took a deep breath and held the stick in position. The runway rushed towards us, the centre white line that cut through the grey tarmac, speeding below the aircraft. My mind shot back to the statue of St Christopher, the patron saint of travellers that I had lobbed out of the motorbike in Ibiza. I hoped that now was not his time for retribution.

As the ground loomed closer the sensation of speed seemed to increase. The aircraft wobbled from side to side as it rode the air currents. I had a sudden total sense of helplessness, the inevitable coming together of aircraft and ground just seconds away.

"FST 45XT, close thrust levers ..."

I missed the command completely, lost to a sense of imminent disaster. At the very last second, in a reflex action driven by fear of the impending contact, I pulled the nose of the aircraft up and pushed my feet hard against the floor, bracing myself for impact.

We hit the tarmac too fast. The left side wheels struck the ground with a thump that sent a shock wave through me. Another thump quickly followed, accompanied by a screeching skid as the right side wheels then made contact and the aircraft bounced once before coming back down.

"FST 45XT, select reverse thrust. Reverse thrust levers now."

Darren reacted first, grabbed the centre lever and pulled it back fully. Immediately a hard deceleration shot through the plane.

"FST 45XT ... brake now."

In response to the urgency of the command, I stamped on the large pedals next to my feet. The aircraft slewed across the runway in an abrupt swerve to the right. I pulled off the left side rudder and it swerved back across to the left. My inability to find a balance between the two pedals threw the aircraft into a zigzag path along the runway.

"There are toe brakes at the top of the rudders. Use your toe brakes."

I found the brakes more by accident than intent and pressed down. Gradually the aircraft slowed until it reached a speed manageable to a novice."

"Well done Darren. Nice landing. To the left of your sidestick there is a small flat wheel ... a tiller. It will move the nose wheel and help you keep straight. Continue braking."

I fumbled around and found the tiller. Gradually the aircraft straightened out and then came to a halt as I applied the brakes.

I slumped back in my seat, my shirt drenched with perspiration, my hands shaking with relief. I glanced across at Darren. He seemed equally relieved but his inane grin told me that he had come to terms with being a hero. Outside mayhem had broken out, the siren screams and flashing lights of emergency vehicles filling the air as they rushed towards the aircraft.

I dragged myself out of the pilot's seat on legs that did well to support me in the circumstances. I nodded at Darren.

"Thanks Darren. You did well. You're on your own now mate. I'm out of here."

45

We were detained until early afternoon whilst the authorities went through the incident and checked the passenger list. The two injured pilots were taken off the aircraft first and rushed to hospital. Scalapino was taken away by another medical team. I had initially hidden in the crew lavatory until most of the passengers had disembarked and then I sidled off at the back, with the final few passengers, and boarded a bus that took us to the terminal. We were escorted to a holding area and our passports checked. My moment of truth, the moment I had been dreading. I needed to clear immigration and get to my meeting with Diana.

"Your name Sir," the customs officer said, as he checked my passport.

"It's Jason Jeffries."

He raised his eyes from the passport and looked directly at me.

"Sorry, Sir?"

"Jason Jeffries," I said again, this time trying to say it with more conviction.

"And how are you spelling that Sir?"

"Sorry?"

"How do you spell your name ... your surname?"

I thought it an odd question but given the extraordinary circumstances of our arrival at Gatwick, I put it down to just another security check.

"It's ... J-E-F-F-R-I-E-S," I replied, spelling out the letters as precisely as I could.

The customs officer glanced again at the passport.

"Sorry Sir. Could you just spell that again?"

I swallowed hard, an anxious gulp. I hoped he was just hard of hearing.

"Uh … J-E-double F… " I hesitated. "R-I-E-S."

He looked up from the passport. "Really? That's not what it says here."

A warm flush rushed to my face.

"Well, it should do. I'm Jason Jeffries."

"Well, your passport says Jefferies, Sir, with an extra E in the middle. That's Jeff -ER-ies in my book. But you said Jeffries. And you spelt it wrong too. You missed the middle E out. Most people can spell their own name." His eyes narrowed as he focussed on my face. "Unless of course they're not who they say they are."

I had no response. Nothing left to argue with. Exhaustion, tension, stress and the sheer burden of trying to solve the smuggling accusation over the previous few weeks, finally hit me. I had failed at the final hurdle. The game was up. I had just needed to get from the airport to Diana's office and I had a chance. Scalapino had screwed it all up for me.

"I'm afraid I'm going to have to detain you for questioning Sir."

"Detain me? But I'm the bloke who rescued the frigging aircraft. You can't detain me. I just landed it and saved a plane load of passengers."

"Nice try Sir, but I'm afraid we know exactly who saved that aircraft. Proper hero that fella. And you couldn't make it up. The bloke's an accountant. Just shows you, doesn't it? Don't judge people eh? Talking of judges, come this way."

"No hang on, it was ..." I stopped mid sentence. I realised I could not steal Darren's thunder. I'd been rumbled. Arguing the toss wouldn't get me anywhere and, after what I had been through, I needed calm and normality. I needed someone who could bring a sense of logic to the chaos around me."

Diana Twist.

"I want my lawyer."

It took Diana no more than an hour to get me out of the airport. In her presence, I made a statement. The police confirmed that I was on bail and that I had a court date to answer other charges. I explained that the real Jason Jefferies had no knowledge of the fact I had his passport. I said that I had simply found it and that the temptation had been too much for me given that my own had been confiscated. I certainly did not want to implicate Erin.

From the airport, Diana took me back to her office. There she explained to me exactly what had happened so far. The Spanish police had followed up her call the night before and had discovered a cache of illegal diamonds in the caves. But by the time they had arrived, there was nobody there. No boat and none of Felipe's gang. Cecil had dropped off Felipe's mobile phone, as I had asked him to, and it was being examined by police IT forensic experts.

I gave Diana the partially shredded list of code names from James's office along with the details of the co-ordinates I had been able to work out. I showed her the pictures that I had taken in the cave and the ones of the cargo being unloaded on the beach. She downloaded them to her computer. I handed over the cigarette butt and the sweet paper as part of my evidence gathering.

And then I revealed the crucial piece of information that I knew I was going to have to deal with on a personal level too. Eleanor's involvement.

When I had finished Diana sat back in her chair.

"You took a massive risk going back out there. And with a false passport. I'll deal with that in court however. For now, there's plenty here to make connections and when we get the data from the mobile telephone perhaps we'll have enough to tie it all together. Certainly the diamond discovery is vital. But we need to be able to make some solid connections to the people behind the operation. It may be that the Spanish police will have to raid your future mother in law's residence."

"I don't think that's happening," I said.

"Of course it will. As soon as we alert the police here, they'll see to it that the Spanish authorities do whatever it takes. This is an international crime ring we're talking about."

"No, I meant the mother in law thing." I took a deep breath and shuffled in my seat. "Look Diana … I need a favour … a few hours. I need to talk to Louise before you get her mother involved. I owe her that."

Diana shrugged. "Of course Matthew. But time is of the essence here. And Louise needs to understand that her mother *will* be arrested. But if she cooperates with the police, they may be able to work out a deal."

"A deal?"

"Yes. A lighter prison sentence. It depends on her involvement of course but if you can get Louise to persuade Eleanor to turn herself in, it can only help."

I grimaced. "I'll look forward to that conversation then. Oh, one other thing. You said you were going to get in touch with the Border Force staff who stopped me with the package and see if you could discover why I was picked out. Any luck with that?"

"Yes, I did indeed." Diana eased a sheet of paper from beneath a pink folder. "Let's see. Acting suspiciously in the Customs Hall when collecting your luggage. Apparently you knocked a pregnant woman onto a conveyor belt and spilt a load of confectionary over the floor. A member of the public reported seeing someone behaving in an agitated manner and became concerned. Is that right?"

I thought back to our arrival in the customs hall after the first trip. I remembered the ruddy faced bloke taking my suitcase. I remembered banging into the pregnant woman. And suddenly the whole weirdness of that experience sank in.

"That's it. Has to be. I'll bet the so-called member of the public was the one who tried to take my bag. Part of Felipe's set up. Must have been. He deliberately drew attention to me ... for the cameras. He made a right show of trying to take my bag. Yeah. And the woman. She must've been involved too. She was standing too close. I bet she wasn't even pregnant. And the bloke didn't seem too bothered about a pregnant woman falling onto the carousel."

"Well whatever they did, it focussed the Border Force staff and that's why they stopped you."

I left Diana's office feeling both foolish and concerned. I sent Cecil a text to tell him I was back safely and that I would be in touch.

It was with massive apprehension that I called Louise. Her last words to me were still engraved in my sub-conscious. '... *make sure you keep well away from here, you understand.*' The thing is, I did understand. I understood exactly why she felt that way. But I made the call. It had to be done. I told her that I had some things I needed to sort out and that I had to see her. She wasn't keen but once I had told her that I had some information that may help her disciplinary, she relented. We agreed to meet in a coffee shop in Kingston.

Her stony, all business expression as she walked in told me that this would not be an easy conversation.

"Nice tan Matthew. Glad you enjoyed Ibiza," was her greeting.

"Louise, take a seat. Just give me time to talk ... please."

She pulled out a seat at the table and sat down.

"Do you ... a coffee, maybe?"

"I didn't come here for coffee. Just get to the point."

"Okay, okay. Look, Louise, what I'm going to tell you isn't easy and ... well, you are not going to like it."

"Matthew. I have a disciplinary in three days time, where they will probably throw the book at me and end my career. That's what I'm not going to like. So whatever pathetic story you've got for your cock up this time, it's not going to register on my like or not like radar. So stop wasting my day and get on with it."

"Okay." I took a deep breath. "You've been set up. You've been set up by the very people that you've been investigating and they got to you through me. And what's happening to you on Friday is exactly what they wanted."

I paused for a moment, checking her reaction. It was controlled but I saw the curiosity in her eyes.

"Set up? By who?" Her voice was flat, trying to contain that curiosity.

I spread my hands in an open gesture.

"Look, do you think for one minute I would suddenly decide

371

to smuggle diamonds into the country? Of course I wouldn't. I was set up by connections of this Kurt Kovalevski bloke that you've been investigating. They threatened me when we were out in Ibiza the first time and said if I didn't take a package back for them, that you would be in danger too. They said that all I had to do was deliver the package and that you'd be fine. But they made sure I was stopped by customs when we got back."

Louise looked up, but said nothing.

"Don't you see? They made sure I was caught with illegal diamonds knowing it wouldn't be long before I was connected to you. Once that happened, they knew you'd be taken off the case and your evidence thrown out ... and then you'd be dismissed from the police service in disgrace. That's what they wanted. These are not your two-bit scumbags that mug old ladies. These are people who do things properly. So your disciplinary is going exactly how they planned it."

Louise puffed out her cheeks and stared across the room.

"So why didn't you say something? If this is right I could have got it investigated."

"I told you. They threatened you. Threatened your life. They told me that you had to stop your investigation or there'd be trouble. Then they saw to it that I was involved too. I couldn't tell you. My story would not have been believable once I was caught with the diamonds and there was still the threat."

"And why is it any more believable now?"

"Because I have information. That's why I went back to Ibiza. I had to get some sort of proof ... to find out who was behind it and link it back to Kurt Kovalevski. But they came after me then. With you suspended they had to eliminate me as a risk."

Louise leant forward across the table, a spark of interest in her eyes, the first indication that I had seen since she came in that she might accept my story.

"So who *is* behind it then? What information do you have?"

"That's the tough bit Louise. The bit you are not going to like." I stood up. "I need to get a coffee or something first. I didn't sleep all last night. I'm struggling here. Do you want one?"

She nodded.

I walked up to the counter, ordered two cappuccinos and wondered why the attendant was staring so intently at me. I waited for the coffee to be served and tried to form some words in my head that would enable me to tell Louise exactly what I had discovered. There were none that made what I had to say more palatable.

"No chocolate Sir?" the attendant said.

"Err ... sorry? Err ... yes ... I mean no. Just in the one." And then I recognised the green apron and smiled. "Sorry about last time ... you know, the spillage. I was distracted. But then that's what aprons are for, I guess."

I picked up the drinks and turned to walk back to the table. And almost immediately, I stopped in my tracks.

Standing next to Louise, was Eleanor.

46

I was so taken aback that I froze on the spot. I glanced at the two coffees I was carrying and in a moment of sheer confusion, I thought that I should go back to the counter and get Eleanor one.

She saw my hesitation and beckoned me to the table.

"Hello Matthew. You look surprised to see me."

I glanced at Louise. She looked just as surprised.

"Sit down. Don't stand there gawping," Eleanor said. She pulled out a seat next to her daughter. "Louise didn't know I was coming. She told me she was going to meet with you and I guessed why. So I followed her here. I thought it might be better coming from me."

Louise turned and looked at her mother.

"What's going on mum? What might be better?" She turned back towards me. "Matthew?"

"It's okay darling. Matthew had something to tell you but I think I should be the one who tells you."

Louise frowned, her expression one of total bewilderment.

Eleanor continued.

"I understand you know now Matthew. I heard about what's happened. I have to say I'm relieved."

I nodded. Louise went to say something but Eleanor stopped her.

"When I was in South Africa all those years ago, after I split up with your father, I met a man called Kurt Le Roux. I was new to the property business back then and struggled at first. I needed a place to live and he lent me a lot of money to buy a property. It was a lot more than I needed but he persuaded me that I should invest. The properties I was selling in the Western Cape were high end, much sought after, very exclusive. I had my head turned I suppose and he gave me the money to buy a place that I really couldn't afford. I was a woman on my own, new to the country and I couldn't get a loan. I wasn't in great shape after the divorce and, well, it seemed like somebody was willing to help me. The problem was that he also kept adding a high rate of interest to the loan so no matter how hard I worked, it was almost impossible to clear. It was like having a mortgage over twenty years but paying the interest only. I realised quite quickly that he was a crook. And I also found out that his real name was Kurt Kovalevski."

Louise gasped, the shock of hearing the name of the man she had been investigating almost too much for her to take in. She opened her mouth to speak but Eleanor hushed her.

"When the company moved me to Ibiza I thought there was a chance to break away. I still owed him a lot of money but I had more earning potential so I thought I'd cope. Soon after I got to Ibiza I met James. I never told him anything about the debt. I was too ashamed I suppose. James had his boats but he'd hit a rough patch. Business wasn't that good, so he had his own money problems. There seemed little sense in burdening him with mine too. When Kurt found out that I'd left the property business and was helping to run a boat company, he saw an opportunity. He told me that if I helped him out from time to time, letting him use a boat to ferry goods about locally, he'd let me off that months payment and that he'd reduce the debt by the same amount. I had no choice really. I didn't ask any questions. I knew better than that. I just made the boat available when he needed it. I knew that whatever he was doing was illegal but I thought that if I didn't find out I couldn't be held responsible. I thought it might be cannabis or something ... for the holiday resorts."

"I can't believe this ... it can't be –"

"Louise, please. Let your mum finish. It's true," I said. "It's what I wanted to tell you. I'm sorry."

"Don't be sorry Matthew. It's not your fault," Eleanor said, a tear trickling onto her cheek.

"But when did you find out about the diamonds?" I asked.

Eleanor wiped away the tear with the back of her hand.

"I didn't know anything at first, like I said. It was only when Kurt started using the boats more frequently that I found out. I confronted him. I told him that I couldn't keep letting boats out to him. There were maintenance costs, fuel ... not to mention the risk to James's business. And then he just told me what he was doing. But he also said that he'd start paying me a regular retainer for the use of the boats and that he would double it by taking the equivalent amount off my debt. He said that he would only ever need the boats at night so it wouldn't affect the business. But he told me that if I didn't do it, he'd ruin the business for me and James and I'd still owe him all that money. So I had no choice really. What else could I do?"

The single tear turned to a flood. Louise clasped her mother close, a tight, comforting embrace.

"I'm so sorry darling. I ... I tried to warn you. I wanted you out ... away from danger ... the job ... it was too ..." Eleanor's convulsive sobs rendered everything else incomprehensible. Years of holding onto a secret, suddenly released in a single outpouring. At that moment, I understood her hurt. But I was confused at the same time. Why had I been targeted so ruthlessly by Felipe and Scalapino? It wasn't the right moment to ask.

Eleanor's sobs abated. She sat up and wiped her eyes, eyes that were red and puffy from the outburst. She sniffled several times and then began to speak again.

"So I cooperated. I let him have the boats he needed whenever he asked and he paid me. The more trade he did the more money I received. It helped us rebuild the business. We were able to replace the two boats that James had needed to sell and get back on our feet. James didn't know anything of course. He still doesn't. He just thought that business had turned around. I ran all the admin side so it was easy for me." Eleanor looked up at me. "James likes you, Matthew. He said you were a nice guy. He said you'd be good for Louise."

"I like him too Eleanor. He's a straight talking bloke. No airs and graces. He reminds me a bit of my father in a way." I was relieved to hear that James was not involved. But it was time to ask some questions. "Eleanor, you know that these guys threatened me out there. They threatened Louise too and I just don't understand that."

Eleanor bowed her head and stared at the table for a moment. When she returned my gaze, the tears had begun to trickle again.

"Felipe Barrientos runs the operation down there for Kurt. He can be ruthless. Once the guys in the UK found out that Louise was involved in their operation and that she was my daughter, they put so much pressure on me." Eleanor turned to Louise. "They threatened ... threatened to ... I pleaded with them to leave you alone darling. Felipe was told to pressurise me. He was adamant that you had to be stopped. I promised him I would make it happen without him having to resort to ... other means. When James invited you both out I saw an opportunity. I told Felipe that you were coming here but I made him swear that you would be safe. I told him that if any harm came to you darling, I would blow the whole operation to the authorities and I didn't care what they did to me. They needed me. I ran the Ibiza distribution outlets as well. Their operation was too finely tuned to do without my boats and tourist boats were an ideal cover. I knew too much for them to take a risk with me. So Felipe came up with the plan to set Matthew up and discredit you darling. It was the best option. I had to go along with it."

"But Felipe and his mad, psycho henchman didn't stop there did they? They pursued me and would have killed me." I said.

"That's because you went back. If you had left it alone they would have left you alone."

"What, and I get done for smuggling too and end up mixed up with a criminal organisation? All I knew was that Louise's career was in danger and that I was being wrongly accused of something I hadn't done. And then Louise dumped me. What was I supposed to do?"

"I don't know Matthew. It was out of my control."

"But you could have warned me. I mean, like, that day you saw me on the beach."

"No, I couldn't. I had to go along with things. I had so much pressure. They were asking me where you were hiding. They thought I must know because of Louise and because you knew James. They told me that they would come for James too if I

377

didn't give them information. I did say to James that he should try and convince you to go back home."

"But why didn't you just go to the police mum? That would have sorted it out," Louise said.

Eleanor wiped her eyes.

"It's easy for you. You *are* the police. You believe they will protect people. But it's not that simple. These people don't fear the law. I had years of it ... years of threats, years of blackmail ... that's what it was ... and I could have lost my daughter and the man I love too. What choice did I have?"

I'd heard enough. She was right. I couldn't see what choices she had in the circumstances.

"So why are you here Eleanor? Why are you telling us all this now?" I asked.

She let out a deep sigh as if it was the last breath she wanted to take.

"Because I can fix it now. I can make it up to Louise. I can end years of turmoil, years of exploitation. You have made a breakthrough Matthew and there's Louise's investigations too. I'll make a signed statement to the police and that way we'll have enough to see an end to Kurt Kovalevski's empire once and for all."

I looked at Louise. I knew her dilemma. It was her mother she was dealing with. No matter how she viewed the situation professionally, she could hardly hand her to the police herself.

"Eleanor, listen. I have a lawyer, Diana Twist, who's been working on this. She has a lot of evidence. By tomorrow, she'll have the data from Felipe's mobile and I'm willing to bet that you'll be part of that. Why don't you come with me tomorrow to see Diana and make a full statement in her office." I looked at Louise. "I am sure the National Crime Agency will look upon any cooperation that takes down this syndicate with leniency."

Louise nodded.

Eleanor wiped away a tear.

"Okay. I will. Thank you Matthew. And I'm so sorry." She reached across the table, her hand gently brushing mine. "James is right. You *are* one of the nice guys."

47

Things moved quickly over the next two days. They had to. Louise's disciplinary date was pending and we needed something in place to give her the best possible chance of convincing the panel that she was on the right side. Eleanor was as good as her word and turned up at Diana's office. She made a statement and named names, most notably Kurt Kovalevski and Felipe Barrientos. She didn't know Johnny Scalapino personally although she knew of him. His name was included in her statement. I asked if she knew of anyone called Alida. She didn't. Alida must have been just another naïve young girl looking for a fun filled summer who got sucked into the big machine by the promise of easy money. I was glad I had warned Estrid and hoped that she had acted upon it.

By mid afternoon on Thursday the data from Felipe's mobile had been delivered to Diana. Names, text messages, the call log and GPS details, all provided incriminating evidence. Data linking Eleanor to Felipe confirmed facts contained in her statement. Eleanor offered up her own telephone records to show her links to Kovalevski. In addition she said she could supply fuel records that would indicate that the boats had to be working far more than their normal recorded tourist workload. An irrevocable case was coming together.

With new evidence compiled in the case against Kovalevski, Louise attended her disciplinary hearing with optimism. The panel took the view that she may well have been the victim of a conspiracy but adjourned the hearing until after my court case, as the outcome of that was pivotal to her defence. That court appearance was to follow exactly two weeks later. As the days slipped by I became more and more anxious about how it would turn out. I had not helped matters by breaking my bail conditions and I prayed that the court would not hold that against me.

I needn't have worried. In Diana's skilled hands the case was a formality. I was severely reprimanded for skipping bail but my investigative accomplishment, uncovering evidence against Kovalevski, was recognized by the court, although in a somewhat muted manner. Diana explained that they do not like to encourage civilians to take the law into their own hands, even if the outcome is a positive one. I was warned about future conduct and walked away a free man, my reputation restored.

With the court case over, my name cleared and Louise effectively exonerated of any wrongdoing, it was time for a celebration. And there was only one bar to celebrate in. MacFadden's. Cecil wasted no time at all in rounding up the troops. Carlos called ahead to make sure that Hanka and Janka had the Champagne on ice, ready for the impromptu party.

And it was a party. Weeks of frustration and uncertainty for both Louise and me were over. It was time to throw caution to the wind and enjoy a few hours of carefree downtime. With Eleanor's deal in the bag, Kurt Kovalevski's empire would come crashing down in the next few weeks. He wouldn't see a party for many years to come. I was relieved, not just for my sake but for Louise too. Her hard work investigating his criminal empire looked like being a success after all.

I decided to call a toast. I hoisted myself onto a chair and called for some hush. Even the regulars enjoying a lunchtime drink in the bar paid attention.

"Ladies and gentlemen, friends. Some quiet … please." I tapped the side of my glass with a knife that I'd picked up from one of the tables. "Guys, your attention … just for a moment." The clink of steel against the glass seemed to focus the party goers.

"I just want to say a few things. I know everybody's in party mood and good spirits ... and trust me, after the few weeks I've had, I'm right there with you. But for a moment I just want to be serious. I need to say thank you to a few people. To Diana, who once again, has used her knowledge and skills and maybe even her good looks ..." I threw a subtle wink in her direction, "... no, seriously ... her undoubted expertise, to plead my case successfully, in front of the people who matter. That's the law, in case anybody's wondering. Thank you Diana."

"To Erin, who backed me up when I was desperate. She doesn't always play by the book but, you know what ... sometimes that's what it takes to get things done. And for her bravery too when things got very difficult out there." I raised my glass and saluted both women. "And I also want to thank the lads, my friends ... Jasper, Carlos and Cecil, who stuck by me and supported me when the proverbial hit the fan, as they always have done. Thank you guys. I appreciate it ... but no more adventures ... please." A ripple of amusement rolled round the room.

"And finally, to Louise. You, have had to endure a tough time. I'm glad that's over and I'm sorry that I couldn't have been as up front with you as I wanted. But I know you understand that now. Things happen in life sometimes, and they can cause rifts and splits with the people we care about. But where we have a bond, where we have a connection, as you and I have Louise ... and as you and your mum do too, those relationships will survive the toughest things."

I saw Louise wipe away a small tear from her cheek. I raised my glass in her direction. She smiled, and that was enough.

"Okay, that's it. Time to party."

I stepped down from the chair to a big hug from Louise. All seemed right in the world again.

And then Cecil called for silence.

"Hang on folks. Before you all go getting too pissed, I got a little announcement of my own to make."

I took a deep breath. Whenever Cecil held court, it was a good idea to be on the alert.

"So first of all, let's raise a glass to a successful end to this whole stupid mumble. My mate Matt here's got himself in one or two scrapes over the years but he flew close to the wire on this one … literally this time. Anyway, he went out there to Ibiza on a mission and he got the job done. But what most of you don't know is, it weren't his only Ibiza mission."

I took a mouthful of Champagne and wondered what Cecil was going to say. And then he beckoned Louise forward. She hesitated for a moment and then stepped towards him, her expression a mix of curiosity and bemusement.

Cecil didn't disappoint. As soon as Louise was in touching distance, he grabbed her hand, dropped to one knee and pulled out a small square box from his jacket pocket.

"Louise Penny … will you marry this geezer here behind me?"

Louise looked too stunned to answer. If Cecil had not continued to grip her hand, I was certain she would have fallen over. I was totally staggered. He'd not said anything to me at all.

"So, what's it gonna be darling?" Cecil asked, his gaze fixed on Louise who remained too astounded to respond.

Her speechless state did not seem to deter him. He let go of Louise's hand and opened the box to reveal a sparkling diamond ring. It was an exact replica of the one that Felipe had stolen from me in Ibiza. In fact, it had to be the one. How he had recovered it I had no idea, but it was the wrong time to ask.

The bizarre proposal suddenly registered with Louise. The utter shock that had spread across her face as Cecil produced the ring was banished in an instant by a broad, beaming smile.

"I will. Of course I'll marry that … that geezer, Cecil."

As Cecil got to his feet Louise rushed towards me, flung her arms around me and wrapped me in a warm, loving embrace.

"It took you long enough to ask," she said, her voice cracking with emotion.

I laughed. "I still haven't asked, have I? But I do … I am ... I'm asking now."

"Well you heard my answer Mister Malarkey. It's a yes, a big yes." Louise squeezed me tightly again. "Did you know that Cecil was going to do this?"

"No. Not a clue. Honest. For a minute I thought he was proposing to you himself. And, I have to say, it's the first time I've ever heard the answer before I've asked the question."

Louise released me from her grip, her face turning serious for a moment.

"So how did Cecil know you'd want this then?"

"I was going to ask you before we went out to Ibiza. He knew that."

"Why didn't –"

"Aha ... hang on. It's a long story. We've got plenty of time. Let's mingle a bit. Everyone's going to want to see that ring ... in fact I do too."

I ignored Louise's enquiring look.

"I want to see you wearing it, instead of seeing it in the box I mean."

I led her to the bar and topped up her glass. She took a sip and then put the glass down.

"Be right back. I'm going outside to call Sheryl and tell her my news."

"Hang on a sec. I've got another bit of jewellery for you." I reached into my jacket pocket and pulled out a white paper bag. I opened it and took out the two engraved bracelets I had bought in San Antonio. I handed both to Louise.

"What are they?" Louise said, staring at the engraving.

"Oh, they are incredibly expensive ancient lucky charms. One each. For you, the Renowned Warrior and me, a Gift from God."

Louise smiled and slapped my shoulder.

"You wish. Wait there Gift from God. I'm going to make that call to Sheryl."

Erin and Diana approached.

"Congratulations Matthew," Diana said. "I'm pleased it all worked out for you."

"Thank you Diana. I see you two are getting along fine then. You'll make a great pair. Erin's always getting into scrapes and you specialise in getting people out of them."

Erin laughed and kissed me on the cheek.

"Congratulations Matthew. Looks like we've both missed out on the handsome Matthew Malarkey then."

I couldn't help the blush and to hide my embarrassment I changed the subject.

"Did JJ get away for his holiday?"

"He did," Erin said, "a day late but it's sorted."

My mobile buzzed, interrupting any further chat. Estrid on WhatsApp.

'Hi Matthew. Just to say I'm thinking of coming over to England at Christmas. Maybe we could get together. Let me know. And Alida says, hi.'

I hit the off button. I would deal with that another time.

It was almost an hour later before Cecil and I got to talk alone. Carlos had popped another bottle and I was leaning on the bar, tie askew, shirt sleeves rolled up, feeling content with the world. Jasper was nearby, attempting to chat up Diana. I was straining to pick up snippets of his lines when Cecil approached.

"You alright geeze?"

"Yeah … yeah, I'm good mate."

"That Erin's got some spirit ain't she. Just giving her the old chat. Yeah, I remember all that from Vegas."

"She'd be a handful Ces," I said.

"Mate, nothing I couldn't take down. So what's the mumble with her? She seeing anybody, anything going on?"

"I don't know, to be honest."

"Geezer, I wasn't asking for her full medical history. Just more than I don't know."

I laughed. If Cecil wanted to know something he'd find a way without me. I nodded towards Jasper.

"Looks like you're not the only one trying your luck."

Cecil raised an eyebrow.

"He's got no chance mate. She's out of his league. What's he on about anyway?"

I winked at Cecil and we shuffled closer to Jasper to catch his conversation.

"Yeah, San An's pretty cool. You ought to try it." His voice had the hint of a Champagne drawl. "I could show you the sights, maybe soak up a few rays on the beach, you know."

I shot a glance in Diana's direction to see her reaction. The hint of a smile played across her red lips. She flicked her hair back with a gentle movement of her head.

"I'm more St Tropez than Ibiza darling. And in any case, as a Northern European blonde who gets sunburn in moonlight, beach holidays seem slightly overrated. Covering oneself from head to foot with factor ninety, just to be able to sit outside without risking hospitalisation, can be rather tedious."

She reached for her Champagne glass, her elegant fingers sliding along the stem, and I caught the surreptitious wink over Jasper's shoulder.

"Good luck with that then Jas," I whispered to myself as I turned towards the bar. I pulled a bottle of Champagne from the ice bucket and topped up Cecil's glass, followed by my own.

"So, you going to tell me or not?" I said, as I lowered the bottle back into the melting ice.

"Tell ya what?"

"Don't give me that Ces. How you got the ring back."

He ran a hand through his hair and grinned.

"I didn't get it back, did I?"

"What d'you mean?"

"It's not the same one and you owe me a bag."

"A bag?"

"Bag of sand, mate. A grand ... for the ring."

"What you bought it?" I hadn't given cost a thought. In all the excitement, I assumed that Cecil had got the first ring back. That had cost me two grand and now he was talking another grand.

Cecil noticed my astonishment.

"Geezer, what's up with ya? These things ain't gonna get done for nothing are they? You'll get the insurance on the ring that got nicked, pay me the bag and then you're a grand ahead, yeah?"

In the confusion of the past few weeks, I hadn't thought about insurance either.

"But where did you get it? The ring. It's identical to the first one but it's cost you a thousand quid less. How come?"

Cecil laughed and took a long swig of Champagne.

"I'm observant ain't I? I remembered what it looked like and you'd told me what it was made of … and it's a diamond. Ain't that difficult."

"Yes, but how did you get it so cheap, is what I'm asking?"

He took my elbow and pulled me to one side.

"Mate, this is between you and me right. You keep schtum, okay?"

"Okay." My mind buzzed with the possibilities.

"You remember when we got pulled at customs and you split open the package and everything spilled over the floor?"

I remembered the moment all too vividly. Cecil racing to help me clear it up. The customs officer shouting at him to stop.

"Yeah, I do. Why?"

"Well mate, I managed to grab one of them stones that fell out the package and as I stood up, I slipped it into my hair. Another good reason to have a thick head of Irish hair." He laughed and raised his champagne glass.

"What? You did what?" I stood for a moment, mouth open in astonishment. And then a thought hit me. "Hang on Ces. That's ill –"

"Mate, don't go all self-righteous on me now. Don't be giving me that illegal bollocks. The deal's done. I took the stone to a jeweller who was happy enough to ask no questions for the right price. He's lasered it, polished it up, set it in a platinum band and nobody knows any different."

I was speechless. Cecil was not.

"Look at it this way geezer. You was the victim of a crime right? Them villains took the ring that you'd paid your hard earned for and you ain't got it back. So a little mumble like this is payback."

"But I get the insurance ..."

"Call that compensation for all the aggravation you had. And mate, don't go saying nothing to Louise, will ya? She's still a cop, even if she *is* gonna be your missus. And there's some things birds don't need to know. Yeah?"

I stood for a moment contemplating what Cecil had said. Compensation. I hadn't got the original ring back. He was right, and without it, I would have had to wait to propose to Louise. And now the engagement ring had only cost me half as much as the original.

"What can I say Ces? I mean ... just, thanks mate."

"No problem geezer. No proposal means no stag night and we can't have that can we? Maybe a little mumble to Dublin? Party like demi-gods? What d'ya think?"

I looked at him and couldn't help but smile. Always helping his friends and always an angle. But I'd had my fill of wild adventures. I raised my glass in a salute.

"That's not happening Cecil."

Spanish to English Translation

Spanish	English
buenas noches.	good night.
cuatro botellas de cerveza, por favor	four bottles of beer, please
él no toma azúcar en el café	he doesn't take sugar in coffee
él piensa que somos estúpidos	he thinks that we are stupid
eres un maricón	you are a faggot
espero que duermas bien	I hope you sleep well
estoy bien	I'm fine
estúpido	stupid
¡fuera de aqui!	(you, get) out of here
gilipollas	wanker, dickhead
¡hasta luego!	see you later
Hay sólo un camino, así que siga la luz que brilla	There is only one way, so follow the light that shines
hijo de puta	son of a bitch
hola	hello
hola carino	hello love/honey

lo siento	sorry (apology)
los grillos	the crickets
los hermanos	brothers
los idiotas	idiots
los servicios	the toilets/washrooms
mañana	tomorrow
más tapas por favor	more tapas please
menos	less/fewer/minus
mi nombre es	my name is
muchas gracias señor	thank you very much sir
No más, hombre	no more man
novia	girlfriend
os voy a matar a todos	I am going to kill all of you
pelado gilipollas	bald dickhead/wanker
revisarle los bolsillos	check the pockets
salir del coche	get out of the car
¡salud!	cheers
sin esperanza	without hope
tu comprendes	understand

About the Author

Patrick Shanahan is the author of three novels in the Pursuit Series of books, each of them featuring his main creation Matthew Malarkey. Patrick was born in South West London and now lives in the Surrey area. As an independent author, Patrick writes from his home office and is currently producing a script for Cupid's Pursuit (the first book in the series).

Also by Patrick Shanahan

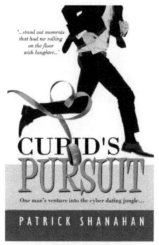

Cupid's Pursuit

Vegas Pursuit (Fleeing Sin City)

www.pursuitseries.com